The House on Willow Street

By the same author:

Woman to Woman
She's the One
Never Too Late
Someone Like You
What She Wants
Just Between Us
Best of Friends
Always and Forever
Past Secrets
Lessons in Heartbreak
Once in a Lifetime
Homecoming

Christmas Magic (short stories)

CATHY KELLY

The House on Willow Street

HarperCollins*Publishers*

HarperCollins*Publishers*
77–85 Fulham Palace Road,
Hammersmith, London W6 8JB

www.harpercollins.co.uk

Published by HarperCollins*Publishers* 2012
1

A catalogue record for this book
is available from the British Library

ISBN: 978-0-00-737361-1

Set in Sabon by Palimpsest Book Production Limited
Falkirk, Stirlingshire

Printed and bound in Great Britain by
Clays Ltd, St Ives plc

MIX
Paper from
responsible sources
FSC C007454

Find out more about HarperCollins and the environment at
www.harpercollins.co.uk/green

To my darling husband, John, and our wonderful sons, Dylan and Murray. And the Puplets of Loveliness, Dinky, Licky, Scamp, who were there for all of it.

Prologue

Danae Rahill had long since learned that a postmistress's job in a small town had a lot more to it than the ability to speedily process pensions or organize money transfers.

She'd run Avalon Post Office for fifteen years and she saw everything. It was impossible not to. Without wishing to, the extremely private Danae found herself the holder of many of the town's secrets.

She saw money sent to the Misses McGinty's brother in London, who'd gone there fifty years ago to make his fortune and was now living in a hostel.

'The building work has dried up, you know,' said one of the little Miss McGintys, her tiny papery hands finishing writing the address she knew by heart.

Danae was aware the hostel was one where Irish men went when the drinking got out of control and they needed a bed to sleep in.

'It must be terrible for such a good man not to have a job any more,' she said kindly.

Danae saw widower Mr Dineen post endless parcels and letters to his children around the world, but never heard of him getting on a plane to visit any of them.

She saw registered letters to solicitors, tear-stained funeral

1

cards, wedding invitations and, on two occasions, sad, hastily written notes informing guests that the wedding was cancelled. She saw savings accounts fall to nothing with job losses and saw lonely people for whom collecting their pension was a rare chance to speak to another human being.

People felt safe confiding in Danae because it was well known that she would never discuss their personal details with anyone else. And she wasn't married. There was no Mr Rahill to tell stories to at night in the cottage at the top of Willow Street. Danae was never seen in coffee shops gossiping with a gaggle of friends. She was, everyone in Avalon agreed, discreet.

She might gently enquire as to whether some plan or ambition had worked out or not, but equally she could tell without asking when the person wanted that last conversation forgotten entirely.

Danae was kindness personified.

And yet a few of the more perceptive residents of Avalon felt that there was some mystery surrounding their postmistress because, while she knew so much of the details of their lives, they knew almost nothing about *her*, even though she'd lived in their town for some eighteen years.

'She's always so interested and yet . . .' Mrs Ryan, in charge of the church cleaning schedule and an avid reader of Scandinavian crime novels, tried to find the right words for it, '. . . she's still a bit . . . distant.'

'That's it exactly,' agreed Mrs Moloney, who loved a good gossip but could never glean so much as a scrap of information from Danae. The postmistress was so tight-lipped that the KGB couldn't have got any secrets out of her.

For a start, there was her name: Danae. Completely strange. Not a proper saint's name or anything.

Dan-ay, she said it.

'Greek or some such,' sniffed Mrs Ryan, who was an Agnes and proud of it.

'I don't even know when her husband died,' said Mrs Moloney.

'If there ever *was* a husband,' said Mrs Lombardy.

Mrs Lombardy was widowed and not a day passed without her talking about her beloved Roberto, who grew nicer and kinder the longer he was dead. In her opinion, it was a widow's job to keep the memory of her husband alive. Once, she'd idly enquired after Danae's husband, because she was a Mrs after all, even if she did live alone in that small cottage at the far end of Willow Street with nothing but a dog and a few mad chickens for company.

'He is no longer with us,' Danae had said, and Mrs Lombardy had seen the shutters coming down on Danae's face.

'Ah sure, he might have run off with someone else,' Mrs Ryan said. 'The poor pet.'

Of course, she looked different too.

The three women felt that the long, tortoiseshell hair ought to be neatly tied up, or that the postmistress should maintain a more dignified exterior, instead of wearing long, trailing clothes that looked second-hand. And as for the jewellery, *well*.

'I always say that you can't go wrong with a nice string of pearls,' said Mrs Byrne, in charge of the church flowers. Many years of repeating this mantra had ensured that her husband, known all over town as *Poor Bernard*, had given her pearls as an anniversary gift.

'As for those mad big necklaces, giant lumps of things on bits of leather, amber and whatnot . . .' said Mrs Lombardy. 'What's wrong with a nice crucifix, that's what I want to know?'

Danae was being discussed over Friday-morning coffee in the Avalon Hotel and Spa, and the hotel owner, one Belle Kennedy, who was very light on her feet for such a large and imposing lady, was listening intently to the conversation.

Belle had ears like a bat.

'Comes in handy when you have a lot of staff,' she told Danae later that day, having dashed into the post office to

3

pick up a couple of books of stamps because the hotel franking machine had gone on the blink yet again and *someone* hadn't got it fixed as they'd promised.

'I swear on my life, I'm going to kill that girl in the back office,' Belle said grimly. 'She hasn't done a tap of work since she got engaged. Not getting the franking machine sorted is the tip of the iceberg. She reads bridal magazines under her desk when she thinks no one's around. As if it really matters what colour the blinking roses on the tables at the reception are.'

Like Danae, Belle was in her early fifties. She had been married twice and was long beyond girlish delight over bridal arrangements. It was a wonder the hotel did such good business in wedding receptions, because Belle viewed all matrimony as a risky venture destined for failure. The only issue, Belle said, was *when* it would fail.

'The Witches of Eastwick were talking about you in the hotel coffee shop this morning,' she told her friend. 'They reckon you're hiding more than pre-paid envelopes behind that glass barrier.'

'Nobody's interested in me,' said Danae cheerily. 'You've a great imagination, Belle. It's probably you they were talking about, Madam Entrepreneur.'

Danae's day was busy, it being a normal September morning in Avalon's post office.

Raphael, who ran the Avalon Deli, told Danae he was worried about his wife, Marie-France, because she had an awful cough and refused to go to the doctor.

'"I do not need a doctor, I am not sick,"' she keeps saying,' he reported tiredly.

Danae carefully weighed the package going to the Pontis' only son, who was living in Paris.

If she was the sort of person who gave advice, she might suggest that Raphael mention his mother's cough to their son. Marie-France would abseil down the side of the house on a spider's thread if her son asked her to. A few words in that direction would do more good than constantly telling Marie-France to go to the doctor – something that might be construed as nagging instead of love and worry.

But Danae didn't give advice, didn't push her nose in where it didn't belong.

Father Liam came in and told her the parish was going broke because people weren't attending Mass and putting their few coins in the basket any more.

'They're deserting the church when they need us now more than ever,' he said, wild-eyed.

Danae sensed that Father Liam was tired of work, tired of everyone expecting him to understand their woes when he had woes of his own. In a normal job, Father Liam would be long retired so he could take his blood pressure daily and keep away from stress.

Worse, said Father Liam, the new curate, Father Olumbuko, who was strong and full of beans, wasn't even Irish.

'He's from Nigeria!' shrieked Father Liam, as if this explained everything. 'He doesn't know how we do things round here.'

Danae reckoned it would do Avalon no harm to learn how things were done in Nigeria but kept this thought to herself.

Danae nipped into the back to put the kettle on and, from there, heard the buzzer that signalled a person opening the post office door.

'No rush, Danae,' said a clear, friendly voice.

It was Tess Power. Tess ran the local antique shop, Something Old, a tempting establishment that Danae had trained herself not to enter lest she was overwhelmed with the desire to buy something ludicrous that she hadn't known she wanted until she saw it in Tess's beautiful shop. For it *was* beautiful: like a miniature version of an exquisite mansion, with brocade chairs, rosewood dressing tables, silver knick-knacks and antique velvet cloaks artfully used to display jewellery.

People were known to have gone into Something Old to buy a small birthday gift and come out hours later, having just *had* to have a diamanté brooch in the shape of a flamingo, a set of bone-handled teaspoons and a creaky chair for beside the telephone.

'Tess Power could sell ice to the Eskimos,' was Belle's estimation of her.

It was from Belle that Danae had discovered that Tess was one of the Powers who'd once owned Avalon House, the huge and now deserted mansion overlooking the town that had been founded by their ancestors, the de Paors, back in feudal times.

The family had run out of money a long time ago, and the house had been sold shortly before Tess's father died. There was a sister, too.

'Wild,' was Belle's one-word summation of Suki Power.

Suki had run off and married into a famous American political dynasty, the Richardsons.

'Quite like the Kennedys,' said Belle, 'but better-looking.'

After spending three years smiling like the ideal politician's wife, Suki had divorced her husband and gone on to write a bestseller about feminism.

To Danae, student of humankind, she sounded interesting, perhaps even as interesting as Tess, who was quietly beautiful and seemed to hide her beauty for some unfathomable reason.

'Hello, Tess, how are you?' asked Danae, emerging from the back room with her tea.

'Fine, thank you.' said Tess. She was standing by the notice-board, clad in an elderly grey wool sweater and old but pressed jeans. Danae had only ever seen her wear variations on this theme.

Tess had to be early forties, given that she had a teenage son, but she somehow looked younger, despite not wearing even a hint of make-up on her lovely, fine-boned face. Her fair hair was cut short and curled haphazardly, as if the most maintenance it ever got was a hand run through it in

6

exasperation in the morning. Despite all that, hers was a face observant people looked at twice, admiring the fine planes of her cheekbones and the elegant swan-like neck highlighted by the short hair clustered around her skull.

'I wanted to ask if I could stick a notice about my shop on your board, that's all.'

'Of course,' said Danae with a smile.

Normally, she liked to check notices to ensure there was nothing that might shock the more delicate members of the community, but she was pretty sure that anything Tess would stick on the board would be exemplary. The vetting system had been in place since some joker had stuck up a card looking for ladies to join Avalon's first burlesque dance club:

Experienced bosom-tassel twirlers required!

Most of the ladies of Avalon had all roared with laughter, although poor Father Liam allegedly needed a squirt of his inhaler when he heard.

'How's business?' Danae asked.

Tess grimaced. 'Not good. That's why I've typed up the notices. I'm sticking them all over the place and heading into Arklow later to put some up there too. It's to remind people that the antique shop is here, to encourage them to bring things in or else to come in and shop. The summer season used to be enough to keep me going, but not any more.' She looked Danae in the eye.

Danae kept a professional smile on her face. Although she didn't know her well, she sensed that Tess was not the sort of person who'd want sympathy or false assurances that everything would turn out fine in the end, or that the antique shop would stay open when other businesses were going under because of the recession.

Instead, she said: 'Chin up, that's all we can do.'

'That's my motto exactly,' Tess said, breaking into a smile.

7

Her large grey eyes sparkled, the full lips curved up and, for a moment, Danae was reminded of a famous oil portrait of an aristocratic eighteenth-century beauty, with fair curls like Tess's clustered round a lovely, lively face. Someone who looked like Tess Power ought to have plenty of men interested in her, yet the most recent local gossip had it that her husband had left her and their two children.

Still, appearances could be deceptive. Danae Rahill knew that better than most.

When she'd shut the post office for the day, Danae headed home. She loved her adopted town. It was very different from the city where she'd grown up. After her father died, she and her mother had lived in a cramped three-room flat on the fourth floor of an old tenement building. They'd shared the bathroom with everyone else on that floor. Poverty had been the uniting factor in the tenements. People put washing and bags of coal on their balconies instead of window boxes.

Everyone should have been close, but they weren't – not to Danae's family, at least. Danae's mother created a barrier between them and their neighbours.

'We're better than the likes of them,' Sybil would say every day, after some fresh embarrassment, such as having to queue for the toilet because the Mister Rourke from number seven had a gyppy stomach thanks to a feed of pints on payday. 'Tell them nothing, Danae. We don't want other people knowing our business.'

As she grew older, Danae found other reasons to keep her own counsel.

When she'd first moved to Avalon, Danae had spent every spare moment exploring the pretty town, tracing its history in the varying architectural styles. Originally it had been a village consisting of a few grace-and-favour cottages for workers from the De Paor estate. These tiny brick homes arranged in undulating lines on the hillside were currently much in vogue with city dwellers who wanted a seaside hideaway. There were few other buildings that dated back to that period, one exception being the Avalon Hotel and Spa, which Belle ran. The rest of the town was a hotchpotch of American-style wooden houses built by a 1930s developer near the seafront, with a couple of modern housing estates and pretty, small-windowed Irish cottages scattered here and there.

Danae's cottage was on the sparsely populated southern side of Avalon, right at the top end of Willow Street, a long, steep road that wound up the hill. The only neighbouring buildings were the ruins of a medieval abbey, which sat to her right, and Avalon House, which loomed behind her. Huge granite gateposts with battered iron gates marked the entrance to the once tree-lined avenue. Many of the trees were gone now, damaged like the great house itself, which had sat empty these last ten years.

Below Willow Street lay the sweep of Avalon Bay with its horseshoe-shaped sandy beach, which had been drawing seaside-loving holidaymakers to the area for many years.

Avalon was a resort town with a population of about five thousand at most during the winter, swelling to at least three times that figure in summer. Two caravan parks on the dunes were home to many of the visitors; those with money went to The Dunes, a beautifully kept site where a hundred, mainly privately-owned mobile homes, sat in splendour amid pretty little gardens. Further up the beach lay Cabana-Land, host to as many caravans as the owner could squeeze in and scene of much partying, despite signs warning 'no barbecues on the beach'.

The steep hillside where Danae lived was a very different landscape to the rest of the town. Here, wild rhododendrons grew in drifts and the Avalon woods began, a vast hardwood forest planted many centuries before by Tess Power's ancestors. Danae's cottage was surrounded by a lush garden hidden from the sea winds by a crescent of trees, among them ash and elders, with one oak she was sure wouldn't last the winter.

She liked to rest her fingers on the cracked bark, feeling the lifeblood of this ancient giant throb into her.

Ferns that wouldn't grow anywhere else in Avalon thrived in the sylvan sanctuary of her garden, while the winter roses bloomed with glorious blossoms. Her daffodils and crocuses came up weeks before anyone else's, and the tiny sea orchids that only grew on the spiky grass on the sea dunes ran riot, forming wild clumps everywhere in the shelter of Danae's domain.

When she got out of the car and opened the gate to the garden, Lady, a dog with the silvery grey fur and luminous pale blue eyes of a timber wolf, ran towards her, followed by the hens, clucking loudly as if to tell her their news. Danae hugged Lady first, then patted the hens' sleek feathers, careful to pet all eight or else there would be jealousy.

Cora, the latest battery hen she'd rescued, was wildly jealous of the others. Having received two weeks' daily nurturing from Danae, Cora had clearly decided that Danae was her saviour and favouritest person ever. She was still quite bald from her two years as a battery hen, but her personality shone through her strange haircut.

The funniest of the hens was Mara. Named after Danae's niece, Mara was a sheeny Rhode Island Red who had been rescued by the local ISPCA. She was a flibbertigibbet of a creature, all fluffy bloomers and ruffled wing feathers at the slightest noise. Occasionally she would opt to remain in the henhouse at feeding time, waiting to be coaxed out like a reluctant diva, while in high winds she would climb atop the henhouse and stand there clucking like a female Heathcliff, impervious to the weather.

'She's completely mad,' Mara pointed out when her chicken namesake introduced herself by landing on top of Mara's lime-green Fiat Uno and sitting there in delighted splendour like the Queen of the Nile, wings stretched out. 'Is that why she's called after me?'

'No!' Danae laughed. 'She's beautiful and she nestled against me instantly the first time I met her. That's what did it for me. Plus,' Danae went on, 'she's a redhead and her flame shines brightly.'

Mara, who was eccentrically unique and had fiercely red hair that rippled around her face like glossy lava, grinned.

'As excuses go, that's perfect,' she'd said.

Mara hadn't been to visit for far too long, Danae realized as she petted the hens. There had been talk in her brother's family of an engagement between Mara and a man at work, which was anticipated 'any day now', according to Morris, Danae's younger brother.

The wind had begun to howl through the forest and there were swollen, dark clouds overhead. There would be no stars visible tonight. Danae loved staring up at the night sky, seeing the Great and Little Bears, the rippling Orion's Belt and, her favourite, Cassiopeia. The spikily drawn big W was the first constellation she'd ever identified all those years ago, when she used to sit on the fire escape in the hostel and stare out, unseeing, at the darkness above.

One night, someone had handed her a tissue to dry her eyes and had started gently pointing out the stars until Danae's tears had stopped falling and she found herself looking *at* something instead of staring at nothingness, seeing only her own pain. That night had been a watershed for Danae. It had been the first time she'd emerged from the pain to look at the world and to hear another human being taking the time to be kind to her. That night had marked the first time in years she'd allowed anybody to comfort her.

Years later, the stars still had the power to touch her deeply. It was impossible to look up at the heavens without feeling that you were a mere fragment of the great universe, and that one day, the problems that beset you would mean nothing. Few tears could survive that realization.

She spent the evening inside by the fire, with some knitting on her lap and Lady asleep at her feet. Outside, the wind howled ferociously and rain beat down on the roof with a fierce tattoo. At five minutes to midnight, Danae opened the back door and stared out at the storm that was battering the trees in her garden. From indoors, the howling wind and torrential rain had sounded as if they were going to lift every slate from the roof and hurl the very house itself into the sea. But once she'd stepped outside, into the eye of the storm, the torrent felt instantly calmer. It was only when she was standing on the wet grass, feeling the whip of the wind on her cheeks that she felt safe.

A storm this elemental demanded respect. A respect that could only be shown by standing in the midst of it, not cowering beneath man-made roof or hiding behind stone walls.

The noise was different outside the house: rain landed more softly on grass and danced lightly on bronzed leaves. Without windows to wail against, the wind lashed the circle of ancient trees in Danae's garden. But the trees fought back, unbending. Their leaves whipped, their branches flexed, but the trunks stood immovable.

Danae walked stiffly across the small lawn to the largest, oldest tree, her beloved oak with its barrel trunk. Under the shelter of the giant oak, Danae leaned back and felt Lady's cold nose reach questing into her hand.

Lady wasn't afraid of storms. Her gleaming eyes shone up at her mistress with utter devotion.

Danae wasn't afraid of storms, either. It was the same with the dark. People who'd never felt the pure darkness of life itself were scared when night fell. People who understood the darkness knew that lack of light wasn't the problem.

Lightning rent the sky and even Lady quivered at the sight.

Something was happening, Danae decided. That was what such wild September storms signified: newcomers and a change. A change for Avalon.

Danae was no longer scared of change. Life was all change. Endlessly, unrelentingly. And all she wanted was peace, but it never came.

Autumn

Chapter One

Early mornings in Avalon were among Tess Power's favourite times of the day. On a weekend, nine-year-old Kitty would sleepily climb into her bed and snuggle up to her mother. And sometimes – only sometimes, because he often forgot – Zach would bring her a cup of tea in bed. This would never happen on a weekday like today, when Zach remained buried under his duvet until she hauled him out to go to school.

'Teenagers need extra sleep, Ma,' he'd plead. 'It's official: I read it on the Internet. Ten minutes more . . .'

Anything to do with her two beloved children made her happy – unless it was detention for Zach or an argument with Kitty over eating any foodstuff which could be classed as a vegetable: 'I hate broccoli and tomatoes and all greens, so there!'

That aside, Zach and Kitty's existence made Tess giddy with happiness. But there was something special about weekday mornings like this one, when she would slip out while the children were still sleeping and take Silkie, the family's fawn-coloured whippet, for a walk in the woods beside the home where she'd grown up.

Up here with the wind whistling around them it felt as if

Tess and Silkie were the only creatures in the world. As they approached the abbey ruins, Silkie suddenly turned and ran with easy greyhound grace over fallen leaves and twigs in the direction of the great house. Tess hesitated a moment before following. Even though she came up here almost every day for a bit of early morning meditation while gazing out to sea, she rarely went too close to Avalon House.

It was nearly two decades since she had left her old home, had watched it sold to strangers, knowing how desolate her father would have been if he'd lived to see it. And despite that lapse of time the pain had not lost its edge, so she tended to steer clear of the house, rarely venturing into the grounds, let alone inside.

Silkie, thrilled with this rare adventure, had found a path through the undergrowth. Tess didn't know what was drawing her towards Avalon House, but she followed, picking her way gently through the brambles and briars that had taken over the beautiful gardens her father had worked so hard to maintain. He had loved that garden, and it was strange that neither Tess nor Suki, her older sister, had shown even the slightest interest in gardening. Back then, they'd looked on gardening as a grown-up's pastime. Now, Tess found that the smell of freshly dug earth took her back to the lovingly tended gardens of the house at the end of Willow Street and awakened an overwhelming sense of loss.

Stop being so melodramatic, she told herself briskly, lots of people have to move from the house they were born in!

Yes, that was the attitude. Show some Power backbone.

She marched on, determined to have a good walk. She was perfectly able to approach the house and look at it and check how far into disrepair it was falling. The American telecoms millionaire who'd bought it ten years ago had lost all his money and now there was no chance that he and his wife would come here to restore the house to its former glory.

Avalon House was not the most beautiful piece of

architecture, but it was certainly majestic, and its hotchpotch of styles reflected the fluctuating fortunes of the de Paors. There was a Victorian great hall, a Norman tower that nobody was ever allowed in because it was a danger zone, and a crumbling Georgian wing. The entire place was shabby and decaying when Tess and Suki were children. They'd lived in the most modern part of the house, which dated back just over a century; despite the vast space, the only inhabitable parts of the old building were the kitchen, the library with its panelling and huge fireplace, and the back stairs that led to the bedrooms.

The De Paor fortune had long since vanished, leaving no cash for fires or modern heating. As a child, Tess had been conditioned to turn the lights off and to put as many blankets as she could on the bed to keep out the icy breeze that wound up from the coast to the house on the hill. Kids from the village school used to tease her about her big home, but once they'd actually *been* there, they were less likely to do so.

However, none of her schoolfriends had Greek goddesses, albeit crumbling and dressed with lichen, in their gardens. Nor did they have an eighteenth-century family silver teapot (one of the last items to be sold) or huge oil paintings of dusty, aristocratic ancestors staring down at them from the gallery. Her father had held on to the paintings till the end, convinced they were worth something.

Now Tess knew better. None of the portraits had been by important painters, and no one had been interested in paying a vast sum for someone else's ancestors.

Yet the house and the name *had* meant something in Avalon, and people had instinctively placed Tess in the category of elite. It didn't matter that her clothes were threadbare or that she had jam sandwiches for lunch, she was a De Paor, although the name had been anglicized to Power many years before. She lived in a big house. Her father wore elegant, if somewhat tatty, riding clothes to the village shop and spoke in clipped British tones.

Only one person in her younger life had ever seemed impervious to the patina of glamour about her name and her home: Cashel Reilly.

Tess didn't do regrets. Didn't believe in them. What was the point? The past was full of hard lessons to be learned stoically, not memories to be sobbed over. But it was a different story with Cashel Reilly.

How ironic to be dwelling on memories of Cashel and heartbreak when she'd come here this morning to have a serious think about Kevin, herself and the separation.

Nine months earlier, when the cracks in their marriage became too wide to pretend they weren't there, she and Kevin had both agreed that counselling should help. One of her husband's better qualities was the way he was open to ideas other men wouldn't dream of countenancing. There had never been any danger of him dismissing her suggestion that they see a marriage counsellor.

'We love each other,' Kevin said the day she'd suggested it, 'but . . .'

That 'but' contained so much.

But we never spend any time with each other any more. *But* we never make love. *But* we lead separate lives and are happy to do so.

The counsellor had been wonderful. Kind and compassionate and not hell-bent on keeping them together no matter what. As the weeks went by – weeks of date nights and long conversations without argumentative statements starting '*You always* . . . !' – Tess began to face the truth she'd wanted not to see.

Their marriage was over. Living with Kevin was like living with a brother, and had felt so for years.

There was no fierce passion. If she was entirely honest, there never had been. Kevin was the man she'd fallen for on the rebound. She'd been twenty-three then, still a romantic, vulnerable. Now, at the age of forty-one, she no longer dreamed of a knight on a white horse racing to save her. Nobody saved you, Tess had discovered; you had to do that yourself. Yet some part of her longed for the sort of love that had been missing from her relationship with Kevin right from the start. You couldn't rekindle a love that had never existed. It was a sobering thought. Reaching that decision meant breaking up their family, hurting Kitty and Zach.

All the while, Tess felt guilty because she wondered whether she had done the wrong thing by marrying him in the first place. But their marriage had given her Zach; now a tall and strong seventeen-year-old, with a mop of dark hair like his father. And Kitty, nine years old, was the spitting image of her aunt Suki at the same age, with that widow's peak and the pale blonde Power hair streaming down her back in a silky curtain. These days, Suki's lustrous mane owed more to the hairdresser's bottle with its many shades in the platinum spectrum. Tess's own hair resembled their mother's, a muted strawberry blonde that gave her pale lashes which she couldn't be bothered to dye, despite Suki's urging.

Kitty, Suki and Tess shared the delicate Power bone structure, the heart-shaped face that ended in a dainty pointed chin and the large grey eyes.

Many times over the years, Kevin had told her she was beautiful, as if he couldn't believe his luck in finding this aristocratic flower with her tiny frame, hand-span waist and long legs. She couldn't quite believe him, though. She'd only believed one man who'd told her she was beautiful.

With six months of counselling behind them, Tess and Kevin had agreed on a trial separation, in case they were wrong, in case being apart would make them realize what they had after all.

'This isn't for ever,' Kevin told Zach, who'd sat mutinously, head bent down and dark curls covering his eyes.

'Bullshit,' Zach muttered, loud enough for both adults to hear. 'I think it's stupid.' He'd sounded more like his little sister than a seventeen-year-old. 'You want a divorce and you're trying to pretend to us that you don't.'

'I'll only be down the road in Granny's house, in the flat at the back. She hasn't rented it out for the summer yet, so it's mine. Ours,' Kevin corrected himself. 'You'll see as much of me as you see of me here.'

Kitty had gone and curled up on Kevin's lap so she resembled a small creature, nuzzling against him.

Tess had been on the verge of insisting that they forget it, abandon the whole painful business of separation, when Kitty had fixed her with a firm gaze and said: 'Can we get a kitten, then?'

In the three months since Kevin had moved out, Tess had found that single motherhood was more difficult than she'd expected. Kevin had always been fairly hopeless when it came to housework, but now that he was gone, she'd realized how much another adult added to the family, even if the other adult appeared to do little apart from arriving home expecting dinner and tousling Kitty's hair affectionately as she got her mother to sign her homework notebook. He used to put out the bins, deal with anything electrical and was the one who went round the house at night, locking doors and checking that the windows were shut. Now that she had full responsibility for these tasks herself, Tess realized the value of Kevin being there, always kind, always good-humoured, another person with whom to sit in front of the television at night. Someone in the bed beside her. Someone to talk to about her day.

In the first week of his being gone, she'd felt the relief at their having finally acted on the fact that they'd never really been right for each other and the children had been the glue holding them together. Only separation would tell them the truth.

And then the questions had come: had she been stupid? Perhaps they should have continued with marriage counselling, not decided so quickly that separation was a good plan.

Was it such a good plan, she wondered. Had been wondering for some time.

Silkie came and lay down on her feet, a signal that she was getting bored.

'Time to go, pet,' Tess said, with a quick glance at her watch. 'Nearly a quarter past seven, let's go home and haul them out of bed.'

Tess had brought Zach and Kitty up here a few times; not on her walks with Silkie, though. Instead, they'd gone through the huge, rusty iron front gates, which local kids had long ago wrenched open, and up the beautiful avenue lined with trees. She'd wanted her children to see their birthright.

'This is where your aunt Suki and I used to live with your darling granddad.'

Granddad was a bit of an unknown to both her children as he'd died before they were born. The only grandparent they knew was Helen, Kevin's mother. Granny Helen liked to play Monopoly, got very upset when she lost, and could be counted upon to give fabulous presents at Christmas.

Zach had been twelve the first time Tess took him to Avalon House. He'd looked at it in awe, pleading to go inside and see the rooms.

'It's huge!' he'd said, eyes wide with amazement. 'Nothing like our house, Ma.'

'I know,' said Tess cheerfully. It was hard trying to be cheerful as it hit her that, after generations of owning, Avalon House was no longer theirs. It wasn't the size, the fact that it dwarfed their own tiny house ten times over, that made her mourn the loss. It was the sense that this had been home. This was where she'd been so happy as a child until . . . until it had all gone wrong.

21

Kitty had been much younger when she first took an interest in the house.

'It's a palace, Mum,' she'd said delightedly when they arrived. 'It's as if Cinderella could arrive here in her pumpkin coach with horses and silvery plumes coming out of their hair.'

Tess had laughed at her beautiful eight-year-old daughter's fabulous imagination; in Kitty's world even a crumbling old moss-covered ruin of a house could be sprinkled with fairy dust and transformed into a palace.

'Why don't we live here?' Kitty wanted to know.

Tess was used to straightforward questions. Children were so gloriously honest.

'The house was in my father's – your grandfather's – family for a long, long time, but the family fortune was nearly gone when your grandfather inherited it. When I was born there was only a teeny-weeny bit of money left. Big houses cost a lot because the roof is always leaking, so your granddad knew we would have to sell. He and I were going to move to a small cottage in the village – the one we live in now – but he got very sick and died, so I had to sell Avalon House and move all by myself.'

'Oh, Mum,' said Kitty, throwing her arms around her mother's waist. 'You must have been so sad.'

Tess's eyes had teared up. 'Well, I was a bit sad, darling, but Zach came along and then you, so how could I possibly be sad when I had my two beautiful angels?'

'Yes,' said Kitty, instantly cheered up. 'Can I see your bedroom, Mum? What was it like? Was it very princessy?'

Tess thought of all this now as she made her way round the back of the house, following on Silkie's trail through the brambles. The old knot garden, created by her great-great-grandmother, was nothing more than a big mound of thistles. The walls surrounding the orchard were in a state of collapse. Tess could understand why nobody wanted to buy Avalon

House; beautiful as it was, perched high on the hill overlooking Avalon and the sea, it would cost an absolute fortune to make it habitable again. Soon it would go the way of the Abbey and be reduced to a pile of stones, and the past would be buried with it.

Tess pulled up sharply. Told herself there was no point thinking about the old days. The future was what mattered.

'Come on, Silkie,' she said briskly, then she turned and headed away from the house. Soon, the beautiful sweep of Avalon Bay opened out in front of her and picking up speed she strode down the drive. There was a lot to do today. She didn't have time to get lost in the past.

Zach's bedroom smelled of teenager: socks, some new, desperately cheap aftershave he adored, and the musky man/boy scent so different from the little boy smell she used to adore.

'Time to get up, love,' she said, giving his shoulder a shake and putting a cup of tea on his bedside locker.

A grunt from under the covers told her he was alive and sort of awake.

'I'll be back in ten minutes with the cold cloth if you're not up,' she warned. She'd used the cold cloth on her sister too. Years ago, the threat of a cold, wet flannel shoved under the covers had been the only way to get Suki out of bed of a morning.

Kitty was easier to wake. Tess kissed her gently on the cheek and made Kitty's favourite cuddly toy, Moo, dance on the pillow for a minute, whispering 'Time for breakfast!' in Moo's bovine voice.

By eight, both of her children were at the table, Kitty chatting happily and Zach bent over his cereal sleepily.

Silkie, happy after her walk and breakfast, lay under the kitchen table, hoping for crumbs.

The next hurdle for Tess was making Kitty's lunch while simultaneously eating her own breakfast and checking that whatever she'd taken out of the freezer the night before was on the way to defrosting for dinner.

'Why don't we fall off the Earth if it's round and it's in space?' Kitty wanted to know.

Tess considered this. 'It's gravity,' she said. 'There's a magnetic pull . . .'

She stalled, wondering how to explain it all and trying to dredge the facts from her mind. Kitty asked a lot of questions. At least the heaven and angel phase was over, but she feared that 'Where do babies come from?' wouldn't be far away.

'Can you explain why we don't all fall off the Earth, Zach, love?' she begged her son.

He looked up from his bowl. 'Gravity, Newton, Laws of Physics. Don't ask me, I dropped physics last year.'

'What's physics?' said Kitty. 'Is it a person who can see the future? Julia says her mum's always going to physics. She says they might win the lottery, but only on a Wednesday night. Do we do the lottery, Mum?'

'No,' said Tess. 'But we should,' she added, thinking of their bank balance.

'We could do it on Wednesday,' Kitty said, 'with my pocket money.'

'You've spent all your pocket money,' teased Zach.

'Have not.'

'Yes you have.'

'I have money in my Princess Jasmine tin,' Kitty replied haughtily. 'Loads of money. More than you.'

'She probably does,' remarked Tess, putting a plate with two poached eggs in front of her son. Zach's appetite had gone crazy in the past year and he hoovered up food. Since breakfast was considered the most vital meal of the day, she was trying to get him to eat protein each morning, even though he said eggs made him 'want to puke'.

'No puking,' Tess instructed. 'You've got games today.'

When she'd dropped Kitty off at school and deposited Zach

at the bus stop, she came home and spent half an hour tidying the house before she left for work. She loved her children's rooms in the morning when they were safely in school. Even Zach's teenage den, with its lurking, smelly sports socks balled up under the bed.

On all but the most rushed days, she felt a little Zen enter her soul when she went into the rooms of the two people she loved best.

The added peace came from the fact that her darlings weren't actually there, so she could safely adore them and the idea of them – without being asked for something or told she was unfair, that all the other kids had such and such, that really, *if she could only lend him some pocket money, an advance . . . ?*

Kitty had been right at breakfast: she probably did have more money than Zach. He was forever lending fivers to other people or spending on silly things.

Kitty's bedroom was still a shrine to dolls, soft toys with huge eyes and Sylvanian creatures with complicated houses and endless teeny accessories that were forever getting lost.

'Mum, I can't find the cakes for the cake shop!' was a constant refrain in the house and Tess had spent ages on her hands and knees with Kitty, looking under the furniture for minuscule slices of plastic cake, with her daughter's lovely little face anxious at the thought of Mrs Squirrel not being able to run her cake shop.

This morning, Tess did a bit of sorting out in the Sylvanian village, then moved on to close the half-opened drawers and tie back the curtains before tidying the dressing table There was growing evidence of the emergence of Kitty's tweenage years with silvery bracelets and girlish perfumes in glittery flacons clustered on the table. Moo, Kitty's cuddly cow, loved to greyness, had a place of honour on her pink gingham heart cushion and it was Tess's favourite job to make the bed and enthrone Moo on the cushion, ready for that night.

It didn't matter that on the way to school Kitty could loudly sing along in the car to questionably explicit pop songs that made Tess wince: as soon as it was time for bed, Kitty morphed back into a nine-year-old who liked to snuggle under her pink-and-yellow-striped duvet, hold Moo close and wait for her bedtime story with the clear-eyed innocence of a child.

Once it was all tidy, Tess gave the room one last fond glance and moved on to Zach's room. Zach's domain was painted a lovely turquoise colour, but these days, none of the walls were visible because of posters of bands, footballers and Formula One drivers.

The rule was that Zach had to put clean sheets on his bed once a week and run the vacuum cleaner over the carpet. Since Tess had found the Great Cup Mould Experiments under the bed, he had to rinse out any mugs on a daily basis – and he was actually very good about doing it.

Seventeen-year-olds didn't like their mothers tidying up their bedrooms. It was all part of the process of growing up. Like the part that said mothers had to let go. Tess knew that. Had known it from the first day Zach stopped holding her hand as they walked into the village school.

'Ma – let *go of my hand*!'

He'd been seven and a bit at the time. Tall for his age, dark shaggy hair already ruffled despite being brushed into submission minutes earlier at home.

Tess had let go of his hand and smiled down at her dark-eyed son, even though she felt like crying. *He was growing up. So fast.*

'Am I embarrassing you?' she asked with the same smile that always shone through in her voice when she spoke to her son.

Because she adored him so much, she was determined that she would not be a clingy mother, not make him the vessel for all her hopes and dreams.

26

'Yes!' he'd replied, shrugging his schoolbag higher over his shoulder as a sign of his macho-ness.

Tess had watched him march into the classroom without giving her a second glance.

Ten years on, he still hugged her. Not every day, not the way he had as a small child. But he was an affectionate boy, and now that he towered over her, he'd lean down and give her a hug.

He called her 'Ma'.

'See ya, Ma,' he'd say cheerily as he was about to leave the house for school.

He reminded her of his grandfather, her own beloved father. Zach had the same silver-grey eyes with lashes so black it looked as if he wore eyeliner. He had her father's patrician features too, and his gentleness. For all that he played prop forward on the school rugby team, Zach Power was a gentle giant. All the girls in Avalon loved him. The ones he'd been to primary school with gazed at him with a combination of fondness and attraction. Tess could see that too: he also had the charisma of his father, the indefinable characteristic that would make women look at him always.

For the past two months he'd hauled the bins to the gate on Thursday night for the Friday-morning collection, trying to fill Kevin's shoes. Every time he did it, Tess battled the twin emotions of pride and sadness.

Huge pride at him behaving like the man of the house, and sadness that it was necessary.

From the hallway below, Silkie yelped, eager for her next trip out – she knew her daily itinerary as well as Tess did.

Tess grabbed Zach's laundry basket and went slowly downstairs. Silkie was standing at the bottom of the stairs, looking forlorn.

'I'll put the washing on and we'll go.'

Tess walked to work every day, come rain or shine. She

27

and Silkie would set out from the house on Rathmore Terrace, through the garden Tess was always planning to spend many hours on but never did, and out the white wooden gate.

Instantly, Silkie would pull on the extendable lead, sticking her nose into the gatepost in case some passing dog had marked it.

'Come on,' Tess said most mornings. 'No loitering.'

Every second house was home to one of Silkie's friends, so there were delighted squeaks at the house of Horace, a Great Dane who lumbered over to greet her and then lumbered back to the porch to rest his giant bones; a bit of rough-housing with Rusty, a shiny black collie who loved games and had to be told not to follow them; a few tender doggy kisses with Bernie and Ben, twin cockapoos who could rip any neighbourhood dustbin apart in minutes and caused chaos when they were in their owners' holiday home.

By the time she and Tess had come to the end of their street and turned down the hill on to the lane that led to Main, Silkie would be panting with happy dogginess.

Their next stop was St Ethelred's, the oldest Presbyterian church in the country, where tour buses paused for tourists to take pictures of the twelfth-century building, the moss-flecked tombs and small crooked headstones. The graveyard was watched over by three towering oaks that were at least, according to the local tree man, two hundred years old. At this hour of the morning, the great wooden door under the arched porch was locked. The rector would be along at ten to open up, with Mrs Farquarhar-White following him in to bustle around and polish things.

On warm, sunny mornings, Tess would take the time to stroll into the grounds with Silkie, drinking in the serenity that inhabited this sacred space. Today, however, a breeze that felt as if it had come straight from Siberia ruffled Tess's short fair hair as she stood at the church gate, so instead of going in she waited for Silkie to snuffle amongst the dog roses for any rabbits who'd dared to visit, then the two of them set off down the lane again.

Cars passed her by, some of the drivers waving or smiling hello, others too caught up in their morning routine to do anything.

Tess was happiest when the tourist season began to wind down and locals got their town back. With the school holiday over, the caravan parks had mostly emptied out and Avalon was beginning to fall back into the relaxed and gentle routine that would continue through autumn and into winter.

Not that she objected to the summer visitors – they kept the town going, and provided a bit of excitement for local teenagers. Cabana-Land – which used to be called The Park when she was young – had always had a reputation as party central. She remembered how, back in the early eighties, she'd longed to stay out late at The Park like her elder sister. Suki never paid any attention to the curfew imposed by their father. On summer nights she would shimmy down the drainpipe wearing her spray-on stone-washed jeans, with her sandals in her hand, hissing, 'Don't tell him or I'll *kill* you!' at a worried Tess as she peered down at her from their bedroom window.

There was a seven-year age gap between the two sisters and in those days, Suki and Tess had been complete opposites. Suki hated homework, was breezily unconcerned when she got into trouble at school, and by the time she reached her teens she had mastered the art of swaying her hips so that men couldn't take their eyes off her as she walked through Avalon. She was taller than Tess, with the same blonde hair and the widow's peak, inherited from their long-dead mother, and full lips that she made use of with a carefully practised pout.

Tess, on the other hand, was never late with her homework, fretted over whether she'd get top marks on her history test, and was never in trouble either at home or school. She was the pale version of her sister, chiaroscuro in action, with strawberry blonde hair, and a fragility that made her perfect for ballet classes – if only they could have afforded them.

The biggest difference between the sisters was that Tess loved living in Avalon, while Suki couldn't wait to escape. She longed to live somewhere exotic, having failed to realize what Tess had grasped even as a child: that for the visitors who came from far-flung places, Avalon *was* exotic. City dwellers were charmed by the crooked main street with its scattering of gift and coffee shops and a single butcher's. People from other countries thought that the high cross in the central town square with its working water pump and stone horse trough was adorable. They beamed with delight when grizzled old farmers like Joe McCreddin stomped out of the post office in his farming clothes and threadbare cloth cap with his trousers held up with baler twine, as if he'd been sent from central casting just for their amusement.

And they all loved Something Old, the antique and curio shop Tess had run for seventeen years.

Tess knew that her business had survived this long because she understood her clientele. She knew the pain of selling treasured heirlooms because money was in short supply.

'My family owned a big old house which was once full of the most glorious antiques,' she'd say, 'and we never had a ha'penny. By the time I was ten, my father had sold just about everything of value, including old books, furniture and silver dating back two hundred years.'

Zach helped too. Tess took him along on all her calls to buy antiques, right from when he was a baby, strapped in his car seat, big round eyes staring out of a chubby face. People liked having a baby arrive: it made the painful process of parting with heirlooms a little easier to bear.

She and Zach would be invited in for tea, cake would be produced, then stiff old gentlemen would unstiffen and reveal how they hated having to sell the sideboard or the vase their

30

great-granddad had brought back from India, but there was no other option.

Her success also owed much to her innate kindness and sense of fairness.

'You'll never make a fortune selling a Ming vase on after buying it for twenty quid,' said one lady, who was delighted to find that her set of old china was actually a full and unchipped early Wedgwood, worth at least five times what she'd thought.

'Money earned in that way doesn't bring you luck or happiness,' said Tess. She simply wouldn't have been able to sleep at night if she'd conned anybody out of a precious piece.

As always, Tess felt a glow of pride in her town as she turned on to Main. Few of the visitors who stopped to admire the quaint shopfronts and exteriors were aware of the transformation that had taken place in the town ten years earlier, and the effort that had been put in by local businesses in order to achieve it. They had been forced to up their game by the construction of a bypass that stopped cars passing through the town on their way to Wexford. Belle, who at that time was the lady mayor as well as the owner of the Avalon Hotel and Spa, had started the ball rolling by calling a town meeting.

'The caravan parks and the beach aren't enough,' she warned. 'We need to revamp this town, brand it, put it on the map or we'll all go out of business.'

Dessie Lynch, proprietor of Dessie's Bar and Lounge (*Come for breakfast and stay all day!*), disagreed. 'The pub's doing grand,' he blustered. 'I'm making a fortune.'

'People drinking in misery,' said Belle with a fierce glare. 'When all the locals have destroyed their livers and are sitting at home on Antabuse tablets, you'll be out of business too.'

Galvanized by their strong-willed mayoress, local traders had set about tidying up the town; shopfronts were painted and a unifying theme was agreed upon – Avalon was to be restored to look like the Victorian village it had once been. The chip shop reluctantly gave up its red neon sign and now did twice the business selling old-fashioned fish and chips wrapped in newspaper. The council was squeezed until they came up with the money to clean the high cross and the stone horse troughs that surrounded it. The water pumps were repaired and repainted, and a team of locals volunteered to hack away the brambles that had grown up around the ruined abbey and graveyard high above the town to turn them into a tourist attraction too. There hadn't been enough money to pay for research into the abbey's history so they could print up booklets and make an accurate sign, but illustrated pamphlets had been printed for St Ethelred's.

The result was an increase in the town's business and a second term of office for Belle.

Drawing level with Dillon's Mini-Market, Tess tied Silkie's lead to the railings beside the flower stand. Immediately the whippet adopted the resigned expression she always used on these occasions: *Abandoned Dog in Pain* would be the title if anyone were to paint her. Tess knew that dogs couldn't actually make their eyes bigger just by trying, but Silkie did a very good impression of it: two dark pools of misery taking over her narrow, fawn-coloured face.

Inside, Tess grabbed a newspaper and a small carton of milk. She nodded hello to a few of the other shoppers, then went to the counter where Seanie Dillon held court.

'Grand morning, isn't it, Tess?' he said.

Seanie had a word for everyone, yet understood when someone was in a rush to open up their shop. He could wax lyrical on the village for interested tourists, telling them about that time the snow fell so heavily that several people got stuck inside the shop overnight and they all had a party with the roasted chicken, bread baked on the premises and an emergency cocktail made out of wine, cranberry juice and some out-of-date maraschino cherries.

'Lovely day,' Tess replied. 'A soft day, as my father liked to call it.'

'Ah, your father, there was a great man,' sighed Seanie.

Tess took her change and wondered why she'd mentioned her father. She'd dreamed of him the night before; the same dream she always had of him, on the terrace of the old house with his binoculars trained on the woods behind, watching out for birds.

'I'd swear I saw a falcon earlier,' he'd say excitedly. He was fascinated by all birds but particularly birds of prey, which was surprising, given that he was the gentlest, least feral person she'd ever met.

Above all, he was interested in everything – politics, art, other people. He'd have loved Something Old, even if he'd have hated to see his daughter working so hard and still not making enough money from the business. He would have liked Kevin too and if he'd only been alive he would have never let her consider something as crazed as a trial separation.

Milk purchased, Silkie and Tess walked across the square and the last few yards up Church Street to her shop. She nodded hello to Mrs Byrne and Mrs Lombardy, who were out doing their morning shop, an event which always looked like a patrol of the area to Tess, as their eyes beadily took in everything and everyone. A bit of paint flaking off a flowerpot in the square, and they'd be up to report it to Belle in the hotel.

So far as Tess was concerned, the only negative to living in such a small community was that it was hard to have secrets. Since she and Kevin had separated, Tess had told the true story to a few people she trusted, hoping that this would stop any rumour-mongering. But who knew? That was the question. Would Mrs Byrne or Mrs Lombardy have spotted what was going on by now? They mustn't have, Tess decided. Else they'd have stopped her to console her – and look for a smidge more information.

She smiled at the thought. She was happy in Avalon. Not for her the itchy feet of the traveller. Not like Suki, that was for sure.

Something Old occupied the bottom half of a former bakery. Upstairs was a beautician's salon, and the scent of lovely relaxing aromatherapy treatments often drifted downstairs. Tess's premises consisted of two large rooms with a bow window at the front, and then a smaller storage room at the back, along with a kitchenette, toilet and a lean-to where she kept old, unsellable stuff that she couldn't bear to part with.

As soon as they were inside, Silkie made for her dog bed behind the counter. After her two walks, she would sleep there all morning quite contentedly. Tess carried on into the kitchenette where she boiled the kettle for her second cup of coffee.

Tess loved her shop. Not everyone understood its appeal. To some, it might have looked like the maddest collection of old things set out on display. But to connoisseurs of antiques and those who purred with happiness when they found four strange little apostle spoons tied up with ribbon or a delicate single cup and saucer of such thin china that the light shone through, Something Old was a treasure trove.

It was all too easy to while away the morning half-listening to the radio as she opened a box of items bought in a job lot at an auction. Tess had found some gems that way; pieces that nobody had realized were precious in the mad dash of the executor's sale. Some just needed a bit of work to restore them to their former glory. Like the silver trinkets that were dull nothings until she'd burnished them to a glossy sheen, or the filigree pieces of jewellery tossed unnoticed in the bottom of a box, which could be delicately polished up with toothpaste and a cotton bud, to reveal the beauty of marcasite or the glitter of jet.

She had two boxes to open today, mixed bags from a recent auction, and as she went to collect them, she realized that the light on the answerphone was winking red at her.

Sometimes people rang asking if they could bring something in so she'd value it, or saying they had antiques to sell and perhaps she'd like to see them.

The answer machine voice told her the message had been left at nine the previous night. '*Hello, my name is Carmen, I'm working with Redmond Suarez on a biography of the Richardson family in the United States, and I'm trying to contact a Therese Power or . . .*' the voice faltered. '*Therese de Paor. Sorry, I don't know how to pronounce it. We're looking for connections of Ms Suki Richardson. If you can help, please call this number and we'll ring you right back. Thank you.*'

Tess stood motionless for a moment. Every instinct in her body screamed that there was something very, very worrying about this message.

If Suki knew of anybody working on a book about the Richardsons, the wealthy political family into which Suki had once married, then she'd have told Tess. The Richardsons were powerful people and if someone wanted to talk to anyone connected with the family, a note on their fabulous creamy stock paper would have arrived, possibly even a phone call from Antoinette herself – not that Tess had had any contact with the Richardsons since Suki's divorce. But she was quite sure that, if someone was digging into the past, they'd have been in touch, loftily asking her not to cooperate. That was the way they did things, with a decree along the lines of a royal one.

But there had been nothing. No correspondence from the Richardsons, no mention of this from Suki herself.

No, there was something strange going on.

Chapter Two

Suki Richardson stood in the wings at Kirkenfeld Academy and wondered why she'd agreed to trek all this way into the middle of nowhere in a howling gale.

As in so many of the colleges where she was asked to speak, the radiators were ancient and stone cold. Suki knew from years of delivering speeches in draughty halls that an extra layer made all the difference, so tonight, under her purple suit, she wore a black thermal vest.

'Where does your idea for a lecture begin?' an earnest young girl had asked earlier, probably hoping to steal a march on the second-year students by putting a direct question to Suki, author of the feminist tract on their Women's Studies course. 'Is it an idea previously addressed in your books, or something new?'

Suki had smiled at her, toying with the idea of telling the truth: *It begins with the phone call telling me the fee for showing up. That and the latest bill.'*

'It's an idea I'd like to explore further,' she'd told the student in a husky voice thickened by years of smoking. She couldn't tell the truth: that her days of making money from TV and book sales were over; that since Jethro she'd been broke; that the bank kept sending hostile letters to the house.

Life had come full circle: she was poor. Same as she'd been all those years ago, growing up in the de Paor mausoleum in Avalon, always the kid in the shabby clothes with the jam sandwiches for school lunch.

Suki shivered. She hated being poor.

The woman at the lectern coughed into the microphone and began:

'Our next speaker needs no introduction . . .'

Under her carefully applied layers of Clinique, Suki allowed herself a small smile. Why did people kick off with that – and then, inevitably, follow it with an introduction?

Nevertheless, she enjoyed listening to the introductions. Hearing her accomplishments listed out loud made her seem less of a failure. The litany of things she'd achieved made it sound as though she'd done something with her life.

'. . . at twenty-four, she married Kyle Richardson IV, future United States ambassador to Italy . . .'

Poor old Kyle; he'd had no idea what he was letting himself in for. His father had, she recalled. Kyle Richardson III had soon realized that Kyle IV had bitten off more than he could chew, but by then the engagement was in the Washington papers and they'd been to dinner in Katharine Graham's house, so it was a done deal. The Richardsons were fierce Republicans, flinty political warriors and very rich. There had been many women sniffing round Kyle IV, or Junior, as his father liked to call him. Junior would inherit a whole pile of money, the company – highest-grossing combat arms manufacturer in the US, what else? – and possibly his father's senate seat. It was the way things were done.

'. . . the enfant terrible of politics published her debut polemic, *Women and Their Wars* when she was twenty-nine . . .'

The reviews had been fabulous. Being beautiful helped. As her publisher at the time, Eric Gold, had pointed out: 'Beautiful women who write feminist tracts get way more publicity than plain ones. People assume that unattractive women turn feminist because they're bitter about their lack of femininity. They're intrigued when someone as gorgeous as you speaks out for the sisterhood.'

Nobody could accuse Suki Richardson, with her full cherry-red lips, blonde hair and a figure straight out of the upper rack of the magazine store of being bitter about her femininity.

'. . . she was one of the most respected feminists of her generation . . .'

What did *that* mean – *was* and *of her generation*? That lumped her in with a whole load of greying, hairy-armpitted members of the sisterhood who'd written one book before sloping off into obscurity.

She'd expected more, given that *Women and Their Wars* was on the Women's Studies foundation course here at Kirkenfeld College.

Realizing that the head of the faculty was looking at her, Suki forced herself to smile again. That damned book had been published years ago; she had written three more since then, yet *Women and Their Wars* was all anyone ever talked about. That and her marriage to Kyle Richardson, her years with Jethro, and the fact that she was beautiful.

How ironic that, for all her feminist credentials, she seemed doomed to be defined by the very things she railed against: her men and her looks.

Of course it didn't help that the next two books she'd written had bombed spectacularly. She'd done a coast-to-coast tour for her last book and still nobody had bought it, despite her enduring countless visits to radio stations where she was questioned endlessly about the Richardsons and what they were *really like*.

At least people still wanted to hear what she had to say, particularly when she got on to her pet subject about women and children: '*What is this rubbish about biological clocks? Younger women should have children, not older ones. If there's one thing I hate it's hearing about some movie star who reaches fifty, then realizes she hasn't had kids yet and plays IVF roulette until she gets one. Kids need young mothers who can roll on the floor with them and play. Not older ones . . .'*

But it seemed as if Suki Richardson's diatribes had lost their appeal. Once upon a time, audiences used to tune in hoping that she would tear into some television host who dared question her or fellow panellists who didn't share her views. Producers used to think she was TV dynamite. But not these days. She'd become invisible since the years with Jethro. Add to that the fact that her books were out of print, apart from *Women and Their Wars*, which was only available in selected college bookstores, and it all added up to one equation: penury.

It cost a lot to live the way she'd got used to living before she'd left Jethro: she had acquired a taste for designer clothes and the best restaurants. And Dr Frederik cost a bloody fortune; invisible, top-of-the-range cosmetic surgery did not come cheap. Not that a tweak and a mini droplet of Botox here and there didn't fit in with feminism, but her public might think otherwise. God forbid that Suki Richardson should be outed as having resorted to Sculptra to keep her face looking young. Not after she'd publicly declared that *'women should stop trying to stop the years! Wrinkles are the proof that we have lived!'*

Unfortunately she had acquired a little too much proof of having lived. At forty-eight, she seemed to have more than her fair share of lines. Who knew that smoking created all those lines around the mouth?

And she'd probably have a whole new set of frown lines after the phone call from Eric Gold.

Eric had always been straight with her. She wished they were still friends, because he was one of the few people she could rely on to tell her the truth, even when it hurt.

'I got a letter requesting an interview from this guy who's writing a book about the Richardsons.'

'Ye-s,' said Suki.

She'd been enjoying a nice afternoon relaxing in her cosy house in Falmouth, lying on the couch watching TV.

'He's particularly interested in you. Says you're *mysterious*. His words, not mine.'

Suki had stood up to get the phone: now, she groped for a chair to sit on.

'You still there?'

'I'm still here, Eric.'

'Yeah, well, I told him he'd have to get clearance from you first if he wanted me to talk to you. After all, I was your publisher, the book's still in print so we do business together.'

Once, Eric might have said *I'm your friend*, but not any more. Not that it mattered right now; there was no time to think about old friendships destroyed with someone out there talking about putting her in a biography.

Or autobiography, perhaps?

'Is he writing it with Kyle?' she asked hopefully.

That would be fine. Tricky, but fine. Kyle wouldn't want to rock any boats, so he'd stick to the official story of their divorce: *We were just two very different people who got married too young. We have the greatest affection for each other even after all these years.*

There were plenty of nice photos of their marriage to illustrate a coffee-table book. They'd made a photogenic couple. Suki had moved her wardrobe up a notch, trying to fit in with the waspy Richardson clan – in vain, as it happened. Nobody could have impressed Junior's mother, Antoinette the Ice Queen.

'No.' Eric's mellow voice interrupted her fantasy. 'It's a Redmond Suarez book.'

Suki nearly dropped the phone but she managed to steady herself. Suarez was the sort of unofficial biographer to make a subject's blood run cold. His work was always unauthorized – nobody would authorize the things he wrote. He invariably managed to dig out *everything*, every little secret a person had hoped would remain hidden. If he was trawling through the Richardson family, then they would all be shaking in their shoes. And so was she.

'Oh God,' she said.

'Oy vey,' agreed Eric. 'Not good news for anyone involved, I take it.'

'Well, you know . . .' she said helplessly.

'Yeah, I know. He says he's researching now and will be writing next year with a view to publication in the fall.'

'Nearly a year of research,' breathed Suki.

Imagine what he could find out in a year! Suki hated research. That was one of the obstacles getting in the way of the new book. *That* and the fact that everything was riding on it.

'I'll get my assistant to scan the letter and email it to you,' Eric said. 'I won't be cooperating, but you can bet your bottom dollar that other people will, Suki.'

'I'm sure,' she said dully. 'Thanks for the call. How is . . . ?' Too late, she realized she'd forgotten the name of his wife.

'Keren,' he said drily. 'She's great. Ciao.'

Suki winced as she placed the receiver on the cradle. Eric was one of those she'd burned during the Jethro years. It had all seemed so much fun at the time: living the high life on the touring scene, never returning phone calls, being too stoned to care about old friends. In turn, the old friends had moved on with their lives.

It was only after Suki had hung up that she realized he hadn't asked her how she was or if she was happy. At least *she'd* made the effort, even if she couldn't remember his damned wife's name.

Her sister, Tess could stay friends forever. Tess had maintained contact with her old classmates from school, she'd go to dinner with them and have civilized conversations about life. Suki wouldn't recognize any of *her* old classmates in a

41

police line-up. It was crash and burn with old acquaintances where she was concerned. Always had been.

Suddenly, she became aware of the sound of clapping. Her introduction was over. It was time to stand up and do her thing, become the Suki who fought the feminist fight, not the Suki who was scared to the pit of her stomach.

Suki opted out of dinner with the faculty when someone suggested a vegan restaurant in town that served organic, low-alcohol wine. Give her strength! Screw vegans and all who sailed in them. She wanted pasta with a cream sauce or steak Diane, thank you very much.

Plus, she'd bet her fee that they'd order one glass of crappy organic wine each. Nobody drank any more. Two drinks and they were offering rehab advice, and she'd had enough of that to last her a lifetime.

Back in the horrible little hotel room the faculty had booked for her she took off her ball-busting purple trouser suit with satin lapels and hung it in the wardrobe. Her speech outfit scared the hell out of men; maybe because purple was such a *sexual* colour.

'I hate that goddamn purple pant suit,' Mick had said as she was leaving the house earlier that day to catch the train to Kirkenfeld.

He was leaning against the doorjamb of their bedroom, still in the T-shirt he'd worn in bed. He'd done what he did most days and just pulled his jeans and boots on. Even so shabbily dressed, he was incredibly attractive: part-Irish, part-Italian, part something else, with intense blue eyes and jet black hair. His band hadn't landed a gig in over a month, so he spent a lot of time sitting on the porch, smoking weed and messing around on her laptop.

'New song ideas, honey,' he said when she tried to ask what he was doing.

She didn't believe him.

42

They were so broke, yet she couldn't ask him to get a regular job. It wouldn't be fair. He wasn't that sort of person.

'Music is a calling, babe,' he'd say. 'I don't turn up at nine like regular guys. I need the muse.'

No, it was no good depending on Mick, Suki thought as she changed into her brown sweatpants. She was going to have to sort out their lack of money by herself.

First, however, she needed a drink. She closed the wardrobe and went to check out the mini bar. It was entirely empty.

Please phone if you'd like the mini bar filled, said a plaintive little note on the top shelf. Damn straight she wanted it filled up. A stiff drink might help her unwind.

She ordered a double vodka tonic from room service. She'd have dinner downstairs with wine, and then, hopefully, she'd sleep. Provided she could get that damned Suarez book out of her mind.

Suddenly, even a boring night with the vegans sounded better than another evening of worrying herself sick.

Throwing open her suitcase – Suki never unpacked; what was the point for one night? – she began rifling through her stuff in search of the loose gold cashmere knit sweater she'd planned to wear tomorrow on the way home. That and her brown sweatpants would see her all right in this dump.

A petite young waitress delivered her drink.

'Thanks,' Suki said at the door, and scrawled her name and a big tip in the gratuity space, before taking her vodka and tonic off the girl's tray. She always tipped well, no matter how broke she was. She'd done enough waitressing to appreciate the need. The faculty could afford a tip on her non-organic drink.

She added half the tonic and had it finished in five minutes. As the large dose of Stolichnaya, her favourite, hit her she finally began to feel buoyed up. The speech had gone well, they'd liked her. She still had it – why didn't anyone realize that any more?

As she walked in to the sedate restaurant in the hotel, heads turned. They always did. Suki had been ultra blonde since she started using her pocket money to buy hair dye to lighten her natural fair colour. Now, at forty-eight her hair was a shoulder-length, swirling collage of honey golds. Her skin, too, was gold from the remnants of a summer tan and daily walks along the beach. The cheekbones and full lips that had been a siren-call to Avalon's men all those years ago were holding up well. If anyone looked closely, they'd see the slight hooding of her eyes, but she didn't want anyone to look closely. Her gold sweater hung sexily from one smooth, tanned shoulder. Suki's clothes always appeared to be holding on to her body for a fragment of time, as if they might come off at any moment.

'You're sex incarnate, honey,' Jethro had said in surprise the first night he met her, in the green room of the television chat show where they were both appearing.

'You too,' thought Suki, but she hadn't said it. After all, she'd been invited on the show so she could skewer his rock band's treatment of women in their videos.

And after she'd finished ripping him apart on screen, unable to stop herself staring at him hungrily all the while, he'd pulled her into his dressing room. It had been the best sex of Suki's life, the best. Afterwards, there were always drugs, but that first time, it had been her and Jethro, pure and clean.

Mick was hideously jealous of her two years with Jethro, even though it had been over four years since she'd seen him.

The jealousy was understandable, Suki knew. Michelangelo O'Neill played in a small-town rock band who'd never made it, while Jethro *was* TradeWind, one of the most famous bands of the seventies and eighties. TradeWind performed in stadiums and Madison Square Gardens, and MTV had practically played them on a loop during their big years.

Mick and the Survivors had lost their residency in the Clambake Bar because the recession was biting, no matter what the folks in Washington said.

The effects of the vodka were telling her she needed another drink and something carb-laden for dinner.

'Table for one,' she said to the girl behind the desk, ignoring the man on duty. For all her outward sexuality, Suki Richardson had spent a lot of her life being wary of men.

At her table, she put on her glasses, took out a novel, a notepad and her pen – men were less likely to bother women when they had a pen and notebook – and set about trying to think her way out of trouble.

Through pasta starter, a steak so bloody that a good vet could have brought it back to life, and the hideous yet delicious concoction that was chocolate and banana caramel pie, she did her best to plan an escape clause.

She could throw herself on the mercy of Suarez: *Don't write about me, I was so young, I didn't know what I was doing. I can tell you everything else about the Richardsons . . .*

No, unlikely to work. She'd read his Jackie Kennedy book, his Nancy Reagan book and the Bush series. He'd have too many insiders telling him everything there was to know about Suki Power. And if she spilled on the Richardsons, they'd find out and her name would be mud.

Meet him and tell him the truth . . . ? Well, some of it. God forbid that she should tell the whole truth. Only Tess knew . . .

Tess. In that instant, Suki realized that all the damage limitation in the world wouldn't fix it if Suarez got to Tess.

Not that her sister would say anything. Loyal to the end, that was Tess. No, Tess wouldn't talk. But she was an innocent. If someone like Suarez turned up in Avalon, he'd ferret out the truth all right.

Suki's lovely dinner began to churn inside her. There was nothing for it: she'd have to go home. Back to Avalon.

Not yet, though.

She didn't have the money, and Mick was so down about the band having nowhere to play that she couldn't go off and

45

leave him, much as she wanted to escape sometimes. His sadness sapped her energy, made the house feel full of misery and apathy.

No, she'd phone Tess and talk to her. Tess would understand. They might be like chalk and cheese, but they were on the same wavelength.

She'd talk to her sister, figure out what this damn Suarez guy knew, and then take it from there. She couldn't cope with her life going into freefall again. She simply couldn't.

Chapter Three

S he shouldn't have come. *Why* had she come?

In the ballroom of a small, pretty castle outside Kildare, Mara Wilson stood behind a pillar and wondered if it wasn't too late to sneak off. To pretend a migraine. Sudden onset of shellfish poisoning. A suppurating leg sore that could be fatal . . .

'Mara, sweetheart! You came!'

Jack's mother grabbed her in a hug and Mara knew the moment to escape the love of her life's wedding was lost.

Resplendent in mother-of-the-groom cerise pink with what looked like half a flamingo's plumage pinned on to her head, Jack's mother, Sissy, was half crying, half laughing as she heaped affection on Mara.

'It's been so long since we saw you and we miss you. Oh, remember the fun we had, that Christmas. You're fabulous to come today, one in a million – that's what I told Jack: Mara is one in a million.'

Unfortunately, Mara thought, smiling back grittily, Jack Taylor had decided that he didn't want to marry one in a million. He'd chosen someone else. Tawhnee, of the long, long legs, long black hair and olive skin that looked fabulous in virginal white. Mara had stayed discreetly at the back of the church for the ceremony, on the inner pew so she wouldn't be in the bridal couple's eyeline when they made their triumphant walk down the aisle. But even from inside, with a woman in a cartwheel of a hat outside her, she'd still been able to see her rival and the man Mara had loved.

Jack looked like . . . well, Jack. Handsome, louche, a man's man with a naughty smile on his face and his fair hair chopped to show off the clean jaw. And Tawhnee resembled a model from a bridal catalogue. Gleaming café au lait skin, courtesy of her Brazilian mother, long black hair and a smile on her beautiful face. She was the perfect bride and as Mara stared at her she finally realized it was over: Jack had married Tawhnee. Tall, elegant Tawhnee, as opposed to short, curvy Mara. He'd never be with Mara again. It was all too late.

When Tawhnee had arrived in Kearney Property Partners straight out of college, she'd been assigned to Mara.

'I can't hand her over to any of the men,' Jack had confided to Mara at breakfast one day when she'd stayed over at his place and they were having coffee and toast before rushing to the office.

'Why not?' Mara had demanded.

'She's too good looking. And young, very young,' Jack had added quickly when Mara had poked him with one of her bare feet. 'She's just a kid, right? Twenty-three or -four. I need a woman to take care of her. I need lovely you to do it.'

'Lovely me?' Mara got off her seat and slid on to Jack's lap.

He liked her body on his, her curves nestled against his hardness.

They'd woken at six and made lazy, sleepy love. She felt adored and sensual, like a cat bathed in the sun after a hot day. Jack didn't invite her to stay over often and never midweek, so it was a real treat.

'Yes, lovely you,' Jack said, and kissed her on the lips.

'I'll take care of her,' Mara said, visualizing an innocent young graduate who'd gaze up to her new mentor. In fact, Mara had had to look up to Tawhnee, who was at least five nine in her bare feet. She was an object of sin in a dress and during the five days Mara mentored her, not a single man – from client to colleague – could set eyes on Tawhnee without their jaw dropping open.

'It's sex appeal, that's what it is. Raw bloody sex appeal,' Mara told Cici, her flatmate.

'So? You're not the Hunchback of Notre Dame yourself,' snapped back Cici. 'She's nothing but a kid.'

'You are not getting the picture,' Mara said. 'This girl is Playboy fabulous. I have no idea why she wants to work for us. She could earn a fortune if she headed to a go-go bar.'

'She might want to make money from her mind,' Cici pointed out loftily. 'You're labelling her. I was reading a thing on the Web about how beautiful women aren't taken seriously and other women are jealous of them.' Cici loved the Internet and had to be hauled away from her laptop late at night to get some zeds.

'True. I'm being a cow,' Mara said, sighing. 'I'll try harder.'

She didn't have to. Tawhnee was suddenly and mysteriously whisked away to work with Jack.

He was director of operations. It was unusual for such a lowly trainee to be working with Jack, but as he said himself: 'She needs to get to grips with this side of the business. What film should we go to see tonight? You pick. We've gone to loads of films I've picked. It's your choice.'

In retrospect, she'd been very trusting. All the '*let's go and see a film*' and '*shall we have dinner out*' had kept her fears at bay. Her boyfriend was being ultra-attentive, therefore there was no way he could be lusting after Tawhnee, even if every other man in the office was.

Like, *hello!*

And then it was too late.

49

Mara was under her desk, trying to find her favourite purple pen when two of the guys came into the office after an auction.

'Lucky bastard,' said one. 'I wouldn't mind doing the tango with Tawhnee.'

'Yeah, Jack's always had a way with the girls. I thought Mara had settled him down, but a leopard—'

'—doesn't change his spots,' agreed the other one.

'And she's hot. An über babe.'

'Mara's lovely and she's great fun but not—'

'Yeah, not in Tawhnee's league. *Who is*, right? Don't get me wrong, Mara's cute and she can look sexy, it has to be said, but she wears all those mad old clothes and she is short. Basically, compared to Tawhnee, she's . . .'

'Yeah, ordinary. While, Tawhnee, phew! She's so hot, she's on fire.'

'Yeah, spot on. Tawhnee's a Ferrari, isn't she, and Mara . . . Well, she's not, is she?'

Under the desk, Mara wanted to dig a hole so deep that she came out in another country. Another planet, even. She stayed where she was for a few moments, like an animal frozen in pain. It was hard to know what hurt most. The realization that Jack was indeed cheating on her with Tawhnee, or the knowledge that the men she worked with and lunched with and joked with saw her simply as an ordinary but occasionally sexy girl who liked 'mad old clothes'. All those times she'd thought she'd pulled it off and camouflaged herself successfully into something different – something chic, elegant, stylish – with her fabulous vintage outfits, she'd been wrong.

Talent, kindness, laughing at their bad jokes . . . none of it meant anything compared to being tall, slim and hot. She was ordinary beside the Ferrari that was Tawhnee.

She waited till the phone rang to crawl out the other side where a handy filing cabinet hid her, and ran from the room to find Jack.

He was in his office alone, eyes focusing on his mobile,

texting. At the door, Mara stared at him and wondered if she'd been nothing more than a diverting, wait-till-the-Ferrari-comes-along girl for him too.

He'd said he loved her, loved her shape, her petiteness; he'd called her his pocket Venus, and said he hated skinny women who nibbled on celery.

'You grab life with both hands,' he'd murmured when they were lying in bed after the first time they made love.

'And I eat it!' said Mara triumphantly, wriggling on top of him to nuzzle his neck. She'd never met anyone who shared her sensuality until she'd found him. They were so well matched in many ways, but none so much as when they were in bed.

For the first time in her life, Mara Wilson had met a man who loved her as she was – with the wild, red curls, an even wilder dress sense and an hourglass body, albeit a short one. Jack adored her 1950s clothes fetish. He told her she looked fantastic in fitted angora sweaters and tight skirts worn with red lippie, Betty Boop high shoes and eyeliner applied with a sexy little flick.

And all the while he probably thought she was ordinary too. She was his ordinary fling while he waited for something better to come along.

'Yes?' he said now, without looking up from his phone.

Mara said nothing and Jack finally flicked a gaze at the door. 'Oh, hi, it's you.'

Swiftly, he pressed a couple of buttons, deleting or getting out of whatever text he'd been writing, Mara realized. He smiled guiltily at her and that's when she knew for sure. It took one look at his face to know the truth.

'Is it true?' she asked. 'About you and Tawhnee?'

'I'm sorry,' he said feebly.

'Sorry? Is that the best you can do, Jack?' she asked quietly. She wouldn't shout. Not here. She would leave with dignity.

'I wanted to tell you for ages,' he insisted.

'Why didn't you?'

He shrugged.

Mara felt curiously numb. This must be shock, she thought.

'I've got a headache. I'm going home now.'

'Of course,' Jack said. 'Take tomorrow too. Er, headaches can really get you down . . .'

She left and grabbed her things from her desk. The guys were chatting.

'Hi, Mara, what's up?' said the one who'd called her ordinary.

She looked at him through the haze of numbness, then stumbled from the room.

Cici had volunteered to go with Mara to the wedding.

'Thanks, but no thanks. I'll look totally sad if I come with you. No offence, but coming with a female friend is like wearing a badge that says *I'm a loser who couldn't get a date.* Brad Pitt is about the only man I could bring and not look like a sad cow.'

'OK then, but promise me you'll dance like there's nobody watching,' Cici added.

'Isn't that the advice from a fridge magnet?' Mara demanded.

'Fridge magnets can be very clever,' her friend replied. '*A clean kitchen is the sign of a boring person*, and all that.'

'True.'

There was a pause.

'I always danced like there was nobody watching,' Mara said mournfully. 'Jack loved that about me. He said I was a free spirit. Although not as free as Tawhnee.'

'She was obviously free with everything, from her favours to her skirt lengths,' Cici said caustically.

Mara smiled. That was the thing about a good girlfriend: she'd fight your corner like a caged lioness. If you were injured, she was injured too and she remembered all the hurts and would never forgive anyone for inflicting them on you.

'She has great legs,' Mara admitted.

'All people of twenty-four have great legs. It's only when you get to thirty that your knees sag and the cellulite hits.'

Cici was thirty-five to Mara's thirty-three and considered herself an expert on ageing issues. Mara could remember being mildly uninterested when Cici had complained about cellulite spreading over her thighs like an invasion of sponges. Then one day, it had happened to her and she'd understood. Was that to be her fate for ever – understanding when it was too late?

The wedding band were murdering 'I Only Have Eyes for You' when Jack appeared beside her, urbane in his dinner jacket.

'Mara, you look wonderful.'

Mara had maxed out her credit card on a designer number from an expensive shop that catered for petite women. She'd been going to wear one of her vintage specials, but she hadn't the heart for it: she'd show Jack and everyone else that she could do 'normal' clothes too. So at great expense, she'd bought a bosom-defying turquoise prom dress worn with very high, open-toed shoes. She'd curled her hair with rollers and clipped it up on one side with a turquoise-and-pink flower brooch. Her lips were MAC's iconic scarlet Ruby Woo, her seamed stockings were in a straight line, and she knew she looked as good as she could. Not mainstream, no, but good. Not *ordinary*, she hoped.

'Would you like to dance?'

Dance with Jack?

It must be a dream. A very strange dream, she decided. Soon, a big white rabbit would appear, along with a deranged woman screeching 'Off with their heads!' and possibly Johnny Depp wearing contact lenses and a lot of make-up.

Still, even if it was a dream, she'd go along. Nobody could think she was a bad loser if they saw her dancing with her former lover.

'Of course,' she said, beaming at him.

Smile all the time, had been Cici's other advice. *If you stop smiling, even for a minute, they'll all be sure you're going to cry, so smile like you are having the time of your life.*

Amazingly, Jack seemed to be buying the fake grin and grinned right back at her.

Mara steeled herself for a speedy and guilty whisk round the dance floor. Tawhnee was sure to be watching, narrow-eyed. She might be young and beautiful, but she wasn't stupid.

However, instead of the expected quick dance, Jack held Mara very close.

Mara's ability to smile despite the pain inside cut off suddenly.

'Don't do that,' she snapped at him.

'Do what?'

He was still smiling, seemingly perfectly happy.

Jack loved a party and what he loved even more was one of *his* parties. His wedding party would therefore be the ultimate in all-about-himness.

'Smile at me like that.'

'Like what?'

'Like you weren't my boyfriend for two years and didn't dump me for Tawhnee, like that.'

'Oh.'

Even Jack's skin wasn't thick enough for that to bounce off.

They twirled some more, stony-faced now. Jack loosened his grip. Mara knew she should say nothing, but she couldn't. Her mouth refused to obey. Instead of hissing *You bastard!* which had been on the tip of her tongue for some time, she demanded: 'Why did you invite me?'

'Why did you come?' he countered.

'Because if I didn't come, everyone in work would think I was bitter and enraged.'

'But—'

If Jack had been about to say 'obviously you *are* bitter and enraged . . .' some part of his brain kicked in and told him not to.

'I wanted us to be friends,' he said forlornly.

Friends! After two years of thinking he was the love of her life, now he wanted to be friends.

Suddenly, Mara no longer cared what it all looked like.

She pulled herself away.

'Goodbye, Jack,' she snapped, and stormed off in the direction of the French windows.

It was a cold evening, but because much of the castle's beauty lay in its outdoors, lights lit up the patios where bay trees in pots were draped with giant cream bows.

If she could only hold the tears and the anger in until she was alone, Mara told herself, she'd be fine.

The fairy lights sprinkled around in the trees gave the place a storybook feel. It was such a pretty venue: the old castle with its turrets and its coat of arms, the huge hall ablaze with candles, the giant heaters outside on the verandah surrounded by mini-lanterns. It was the perfect setting for an autumn wedding.

She shivered as she crossed the stone flags to stand under a heater.

This could have been me, thought Mara with a pang of sorrow. I could have been the bride surrounded by my family, wearing old lace, rushing upstairs to the four-poster bed of the bridal suite to make legal love to my husband for the first time.

Instead, she was facing a taxi ride to a B&B in the local village, because the family had snaffled all the castle bedrooms. Her room in the B&B was tiny and freezing, situated under the eaves, and the bed was a small, creaky double – she'd sat on it earlier and the crank of springs was so loud it had made her bounce up again with fright. If she'd lost her mind and taken another guest back for a wild night of casual frolicking, the B&B owners would undoubtedly bang on the door to get them to keep the noise down because of the bed springs.

'I thought you'd be happy,' said a slightly plaintive voice.

She wheeled around in shock. Jack stood beside her.

Mara closed her eyes to the lovely view and wondered if Jack had always been this emotionally unevolved? What kind of man would assume that she'd be happy to be at his wedding to the woman for whom he'd dumped her? But perhaps Jack *could* assume that.

She hadn't had tantrums when he'd left. She'd taken it like a grown-up. Dignity was the preserve of the ordinary girl, she'd decided.

'Why isn't it me here tonight?' she asked now as, from inside, she could hear the wedding band strike up another tune.

'Ah, Mara, now's not the time for this—' Jack began.

He had his tormented face on. Mara knew his every expression. The sallow handsome face could take on so many different looks, and she'd seen them all.

'Now is exactly the time,' she said quietly. 'Tell me – what does she have that I haven't?'

The instant the question was out, she regretted it. The answer could have been eight years, bought breasts and much longer legs.

Jack reached into the jacket of his suit and took out a single cigarette. He was supposed to have given up. Tawhnee was very anti-smoking. Nothing had convinced Mara that she'd lost him as much as Jack's agreeing not to smoke any more. If Tawhnee could do that, she could do anything.

'It's only the one,' he muttered, cradling his fingers around a match to light the cigarette, then inhaling like a drowning man reaching the surface.

'You're a great girl, Mara . . .' he said.

'Why do I think there's a *but* coming?' she said with a hint of bitterness.

'You know me so well,' he said, laughing softly.

'Not well enough, apparently.'

'I didn't mean to fall in love with Tawhnee,' Jack said, after he'd smoked at least half of the cigarette.

'It just happened,' Mara said. 'That is such a cliché, Jack.'

'That's me: Mr Cliché,' he joked.

'Very funny. So what's the BUT. The but that I don't have.'

She wanted him to say it. *Because you were never The One, Mara. Because I was continually looking over your shoulder and then Tawhnee came along . . .* She wanted him to tell the truth instead of the lies he clearly had been spouting when they were together.

'There's no "but". You're perfect,' Jack said.

'If I'm perfect, why didn't you stay with me?'

'I don't know. She came to work for us, she's stunning – not that you're not stunning too,' Jack said hastily.

'You told me you liked the way I looked, and then you go and fall in love with a woman who is the complete opposite of me,' she said. Except for the boobs, she thought grimly. In addition to her supermodel sleekness and legs up to the armpits, Tawhnee had gravity-defying boobs. The office women were convinced that Tawhnee had had a boob job. The office men didn't care.

Jack said nothing.

Mara wasn't to be deflected. 'I want to know why,' she said. 'That's all. Why you've married Tawhnee when, despite two years with me, you never even so much as asked me what I thought about marriage? It's because I wasn't *the one*, isn't it? I was simply the one you could play around with while you waited for her to show up.'

It wasn't as if Mara had been pinning her hopes on a wedding, but the longer she went out with Jack, the more she began to think that such an event might happen one day. She was sure that he loved her as much as she loved him. That Jack Taylor, a man who could have any woman he wanted, had really chosen a petite red-head who'd thought she was ordinary for years until she'd met him, and he'd told her she was special. She'd begun to believe all the things he'd said.

That she was the sexiest woman he'd ever met. And the funniest. And the most beautiful . . . Except he'd never asked *her* to marry him.

Four months after she'd found out he was cheating on her, he'd announced his engagement to Tawhnee. Today, a mere two months later, they were married.

'You didn't talk about marriage either,' he bleated. 'I didn't think you were the kind of woman who's into all that sort of thing'.

'What gave you that idea?'

Jack had one last card. 'Tawhnee said she wanted to get married. She said it on our first date.'

'Really?' said Mara, sigh and word wrapped into one.

Was that what it would have taken? If Mara had told Jack she was the marrying kind of girl, instead of the let's-go-to-bed-and-have-fun sort of girl, would it have been her today in the long white dress?

'Give me that cigarette.'

She plucked it from his fingers and took a long drag. She wasn't actually a smoker, not really. When they'd been together, she'd had a few when they were out partying. Liking the idea of taking a cigarette from his mouth. It was such an intimate thing to do. But tonight, she wanted to do something self-destructive, and letting nicotine hit her was the only thing to hand. She'd promised herself she would not drink too much: to turn into the drunken ex at a wedding would be too humiliating.

She coughed and felt her guts loosen.

'Yeuch.' She stubbed the cigarette out on the balustrade.

'I hadn't finished with that!' wailed Jack.

Mara patted his cheek. 'That's precisely what I said to Tawhnee, but hey, that's life.'

Mara left him standing there. She collected her handbag from her chair, and smiled at the people at her table. They were colleagues from work and most of them had been so sweet to her.

'Jack's a fool,' Pat from accounts said for about the fifth time that evening.

'I'd go out with you tomorrow,' slurred Henry, who sold higher class properties because he'd been to all the right schools and looked immaculate in navy pinstripe.

His wife, a frosted blonde who was equally posh and very kind, slapped him gently. 'Don't be silly, Henry. What about me?'

'You could come too,' Henry said happily.

'I'm going to head off,' Mara interrupted, before Henry could get on to the subject of threesomes.

'Good plan,' said Veronica, who worked with Mara and had her junior doctor fiancé in tow. He was asleep in his chair and someone had put a garland of flowers on his head. 'You've done your bit.' She got up to hug Mara. 'We all think you're so brave for coming,' she whispered. 'At least you've got two weeks before they're back from honeymoon. Apparently, Tawhnee will carry on working with Jack for the next year, so you've got some breathing space to get your head around it all.'

Mara inhaled sharply. 'Nobody told me that.'

Tawhnee was supposed to leave, that's what Jack had told her in the early, painful days of finding out. Tawhnee would be leaving at Christmas.

'Easier not to know, isn't it?' Veronica said.

No, thought Mara suddenly, *it isn't*.

Her whole career at Kearney Property Partners was changing and nobody had thought to tell her. She was the silly, cuckolded girl who'd been so in love with Jack Taylor that she'd forgotten about herself. She'd handed him her heart and her job on a plate.

'Thanks for telling me,' she said to Veronica.

'You're so brave,' Veronica said again. 'Please, please, find yourself a total stud within the next two weeks so you can drag him into the office for lunch on their first day back from honeymoon. Ideally, you should be practically having sex with the stud on the reception desk when they come in.'

Mara laughed, thinking of movies where desperate women hired escorts for weddings and office parties so they wouldn't be seen as hopeless cases. Perhaps she should have rented a hunk for tonight. Someone to look as if he couldn't wait to rip her dress off with his teeth – even if he was being paid for it. But then that would be fake and, suddenly, Mara was in no mood for fake.

Like she was in no mood to go back into the office and pretend. She looked at all the smiling faces round the table, all wishing her well, and knew she wouldn't be able to carry on working there for much longer.

'See you all next week,' she said brightly and whisked her jacket – vintage fake leopard print – off the chair.

Outside, she asked Reception to call her a taxi, and then hid in a big armchair near the door, hoping nobody from the wedding party would spot her escaping.

She rang Cici, who was out with some friends.

Mara whispered what Veronica had told her. 'Even Veronica's getting married,' wailed Mara down the phone. 'The whole world is at it. Was a law brought in making marriage compulsory and nobody told me about it?'

'Don't be daft. You don't want to get married, not really.'

'I do.'

'You don't. Jack's a prat. Geddit? Jack's a prat. He'd make you miserable. What if the two of you had got married and he'd met Tawhnee afterwards? What then, tell me?'

'He'd still have run off with her,' Mara said, feeling like the voice of doom in her own Greek chorus. 'Does loving a shallow man make me shallow too?'

'No, simply a typical woman,' advised Cici, wise after several bottles of Miller. 'You'll feel better tomorrow and we'll think of a plan to have fun, right?'

'Right.'

The taxi driver told her she was a sensible girl to be going home early.

'The town's full of mad young women running around in this cold with no coats on. Young girls today, I don't understand them. Nice to see a sensible one like yourself.'

In the back seat, Mara made assenting noises out of politeness. She wasn't in the least bit sensible, she merely looked it and always had. Even at school, silliness was assumed to be an attribute of the tall, mascara'd minxes who wore their uniform skirts rolled up and had liaisons behind the bike shed. Everyone thought that small, quiet girls who did their homework had to be sensible, nice girls, even if they had wild red hair and a penchant for spending their pocket money on mad clothes.

In the B&B, the landlady was astonished to see a wedding guest home before eleven.

'I'm working very hard and I'm exhausted,' Mara said, because she didn't want another person to tell her she was a rock of sense in a crazy world.

Then she went to her room, locked the door and allowed the tears to fall. Sensible and dumped – what more could a woman ask for?

Chapter Four

October ripped through Avalon with unprecedented storms that made the sea lash the rocks at the edge of the Valley of the Diamonds, the prettiest cove on Avalon Bay. From Danae's house, she could see the frothing of rough waves crashing into the shore. The last of the visitors had left Avalon and it was back to its off-season population of six thousand souls.

On Willow Street, another of the ancient willows had sheared from its roots overnight, like a piece of sculpture broken by a hurricane. Danae wished someone from the council would move it, put it out of its pain. She didn't know why, but she felt these beautiful trees could feel pain like humans could. The magnolias in her garden appeared to have curled in on themselves, no bud ready to unfurl, and there was no scent of honey in the air at night from the honeysuckle, only the icy chill of winter approaching.

Danae's walks with Lady were shorter affairs, as neither of them could cope with being out for long in such wild winds. She wrapped a scarf around her mouth when she walked because it felt as if the wind was trying to steal her breath.

'You don't like it much either, do you, darling?' she said

to Lady late one afternoon as they faced into the wind climbing the hill towards Avalon House. Above them, the FOR SALE sign swayed perilously in the wind, dirty and battered from hanging there so long.

Lady's favourite walk was over the stile into the woods that belonged to Avalon House, where she could cavort over fallen logs searching for rabbits and squirrels. A few months ago, the woods had been wild with the remains of sea aster and bell heathers, with the delicate purple heads of selfheal clustering here and there amid the leaves. But now, the flowers were gone and a wildness had taken over the place.

Lady loped on, knowing the way to go, past a couple of sycamores twisted towards the ground from decades of high winds. To the right were the ruins of the old abbey, nothing now but half a gable wall of ancient brick. Small stones sticking up around its grassy meadows were crude gravestones dating back to the time when people left a simple marker at a burial site instead of a grand headstone.

Danae found these little stone markers so touching: some dated from the Famine years and she could picture the hunger-ravaged mourners burying their loved ones, wanting to know where the grave was so they could return to pray there, if they lived that long.

On the other side of the abbey was a holy well where locals had been leaving prayers and offerings long before Christianity had claimed the well for St Edel.

Lady turned as they reached the abbey ruins and ran with easy grace over leaves and fallen twigs in the direction of the back of the great house, following the trail of another dog, Danae thought.

Even though there was nothing to stop her because some of the windows were glassless and open to the world, Danae had never been inside the house itself. She felt it would be disrespectful to the place somehow. Although she knew there were many who dismissed such things as hocus pocus, Danae was sensitive to atmosphere, She could tell that this house had known kindness and goodness in its day. And now there was a sense of sadness that no family lived here any more, the silence broken only by the wind in the trees instead of the sound of dogs barking or children laughing.

Calling Lady to her side, Danae turned to make her way back to Willow Street and home. Despite the wild beauty of the woods, she was suddenly anxious to leave this melancholy place. Or perhaps it wasn't the place that was the problem but the time of year.

It had been in October that Danae got married and the month would forever remind her of a second-hand wedding dress and how hopeful she'd been as a young bride. Thirty years ago, she had known so little when she stood at the altar. Marriage back then was immersed in the ceremony of the Catholic church, with a dusting of glamour from the movies, where girls like the young Grace Kelly glowed on screen at her one true love. Marriage was till death do you part, your place was by your husband's side. Good wives knew that.

Once the ring was on the bride's finger, happiness was guaranteed – wasn't it?

With the benefit of hindsight, Danae marvelled at her innocence. She should have known better: after all, she'd spent all those years living with her mother while a selection of 'uncles' trailed in and out of their lives, some kind, some not. And yet Danae had hoped that *he* was out there, her special one true love.

She'd been convinced that Antonio was the one, and had entered into marriage never doubting for a moment that they would be together for ever. How foolish could you get!

Young women today were made of stronger stuff and they knew more.

Or did they?

Her brother, Morris had phoned earlier and told her the

latest news about Mara. The poor girl was devastated by Jack's betrayal and there was nothing they could do to help her.

Danae had done what any big sister should do: she had listened and tried to offer comfort.

Morris was ready to go down to Galway and give Jack a piece of his mind or even a few slaps – fighting words indeed from Morris, a man who'd never slapped anyone in his life. 'She pretends she's fine, only she's not,' he said mournfully. 'Girls today always try to pretend they're strong for some reason, but Mara is such a softie, even though she lets on she's as tough as old boots. Just a total softie.'

His voice trailed off then, but Danae resisted the urge to leap in with offers of help. She knew that if Morris wanted her to do something, he'd ask, though it was very rare that he did ask anything of her. She tried so very hard not to interfere in case she brought her own bad luck to Morris and his wife and children.

Yet she was so drawn to them. That warm and loving little family seemed to her to epitomize love at its best, and she had to try hard to keep some distance, otherwise she'd have been there all the time, haunting them, like a cold person trying to warm their hands at a fire. It made more sense to live on her own in Avalon with her beloved animals. She was the woman on the fishing boat, the Jonah: it was better that she stayed away and kept her bad luck with her.

'Elsie is in bits about it, of course,' Morris went on. 'She blames the girl Jack ran off with. Don't suppose it matters much who you blame, it's too late now. I wish you'd talk to her, Danae,' he added. 'Mara listens to you. She's not going to listen to her dad. Elsie simply cries when she's on the phone. To think I had that young pup here in our house . . .'

'I'll phone,' she'd promised, without a moment's hesitation.

As soon as she got home after her walk, Danae made herself

a cup of tea, sat in front of the log fire and dialled Mara's number.

Her niece sounded in remarkably good form on the phone, although Danae suspected she was making a huge effort to sound upbeat.

It was undoubtedly habit: she was so used to blithely saying 'I'm fine' when anybody asked her how she was feeling that she probably almost believed it herself. There had been a time when Danae had done exactly the same thing. It was surprisingly easy to convince people that your life was wonderful when it was the exact opposite.

'I'm going to be on a career break soon,' Mara said blithely. 'I gave in my notice earlier this week. Apart from a few waitressing shifts, there's not much for me here, but it's nice to have some time off. Plus, Cici and I are thinking of doing a fitness boot camp one weekend.' Before Danae could get a word in, she added, 'No, don't say anything about how I've never done any exercise up to now!' Then she laughed, a slightly harsh laugh.

Methinks the lady doth protest too much, thought Danae. Speaking the truth harshly before anybody else did was an age-old defence mechanism. There was no point in explaining this to Mara, though.

Instead Danae said, 'That sounds lovely. I've always wondered what exactly a boot camp is. Is it military instructors yelling at you to do sit-ups on the spot?'

'I sincerely hope not,' said Mara. 'I can't do any sit-ups at all, and I'll be able to do even less if someone is shouting at me when I'm trying!'

They talked for a little longer, and then, claiming that she had to get ready to go out for the evening, Mara said goodbye, promising to phone her aunt soon.

'You could come to Avalon for a visit,' Danae suggested. 'The feathered Mara would love to see you.'

Mara laughed, a genuine laugh, at that.

'I hope the poor hen hasn't been dumped by her boyfriend, too.'

'There's no rooster here,' Danae replied. 'They only cause problems.'

Mara laughed that harsh laugh again. 'Ain't that the truth! I'll come soon, I promise.'

Danae hung up, convinced that all was not well with her niece. But she would wait until Mara came to her. That was her way.

Cashel Reilly was having breakfast on the thirty-fourth-floor terrace of the Sydney Intercontinental when he got the phone call. He liked eating on the balcony and staring over the harbour, watching the ferries cruising silently beneath him, passing the armadillo scales of the Opera House.

He'd drunk his coffee and eaten his omelette, and was reading the *Sydney Morning Herald*, having skimmed both the *Financial Times* and the *Strait Times*. It was only half seven, yet the club floor was already busy with business people having meetings and making phone calls.

Cashel disliked breakfast meetings. He preferred to enjoy his meal and then talk, rather than do both at the same time. His first meeting was at half eight in the office on George Street and his assistant had already left him notes.

His business was varied and remarkably recession-proof. Not that he didn't occasionally dabble in high-risk investments, but the bulk of capital was tied up in the nano-technology firm in California, the enzyme research here in Australia, the computer intel business that spanned the globe. Gifted with a mind that roamed endlessly, he invested in the future, forever seeking new angles and new business opportunities, and it had made him a very rich man.

The plus of being so successful meant that any mild recession-led diminishment of his wealth was a mere ripple in the pond of Reilly Inc. He'd put the chalet in Courchevel up for sale not because he was strapped for cash but simply because he hadn't been there in years. Rhona had been the skier. She'd loved nothing more than decamping to the chalet for weeks at a time, skiing all day and putting on her glad rags to party all night.

Cashel had enjoyed skiing. He was strong and agile, which helped, but he couldn't get worked up over it the way she did, endlessly pacing herself on black runs.

It was one more thing that separated them. In the beginning, they'd happily told each other that 'opposites attract'. By the end, they'd realized that opposites might attract but building a life together when you had so little in common was another matter.

He still owned the house near Claridges in London, the apartment in Dublin, a penthouse in New York on the Upper East Side, and the apartment in Melbourne, an airy fourth floor appartment off Collins, where he would wake to the somnolent rattle of the tram cars. Melbourne with its trees and boulevards reminded him strangely of home. On the face of it, Avalon was nothing like the city, yet there was an inescapable sense of history that they both shared.

Nowhere was that sense of history stronger than in the De Paor house.

Cashel could vividly recall the first time he'd seen the house properly, as a tall, skinny nine-year-old accompanying his mother as she went about her work as a cleaner. He'd been there before then, of course. Climbing the crumbling De Paor walls was a rite of passage for the boys in Cottage Row, where he and his younger brother, Riach lived. The Cottage kids, as they were known in the local national school, were always up for mischief, some worse than others. Cashel remembered the time Paddy Killen's older brother got himself arrested for breaking and entering. Paddy had been delighted with this infamy, but Cashel's mother had sat her two sons down on the kitchen chairs and told them that if they ever did anything like that, the police wouldn't need to lock them up: she'd have killed them first.

When his phone buzzed, he answered without so much as a glance at the screen. Few people had his private number.

'Cashel,' said his brother's voice.

He knew immediately that it was bad news.

'What is it?'

'It's Mam – she's dead.'

Cashel felt as if his body was in freefall down the side of the giant hotel.

'Tell me,' he said hoarsely.

'Massive heart attack in her sleep. Dolly found her.'

Cashel paid for Dolly and three other nurses to take care of his mother. He'd wanted Anna to stay in her own home, even if the dementia meant she no longer recognized it. At least his money allowed him to do that much for her.

'It doesn't seem real,' Cashel said to his brother. 'Despite the dementia, despite everything, she was *there* . . .'

His voice tailed off. Their mother had been so strong, so courageous, like a lioness protecting her sons. Their father had been a man with a penchant for the bookmaker and the local pub. His bad back meant he wasn't in work often, and any money he got, ended up in the pub or the bookie's cash register. Without Anna Reilly, Cashel knew that he and Riach would have had no warm house, no education, nothing.

'I know,' said Riach, his voice soft. 'Not real at all. But we knew this day would come, Cashel, and it's better for her. She'd have hated this half-life, not part of this world and not part of the next one either.'

Cashel stood and leaned over the balcony, staring down towards Macquarie Park where people were walking, their lives untouched by his tragic news. He wanted to scream it out, to tell everyone what had happened. Cashel Reilly, once-divorced man of forty-six, regularly on rich lists and in financial columns for his business acumen, felt as if a part of him had been ripped out.

'I'll be home as soon as I can,' he told his brother. One of the benefits of having a private jet. 'Will you do the notices in the paper? We can talk about undertakers and all the rest when I get there.'

He found himself shuddering at the word 'undertakers'. The world of death was upon them with all its traditions and rituals. Cashel had a sudden vision of St Mary's in Avalon, sitting in the pew beside his parents at Sunday Mass.

'Don't fidget!' his father would hiss, and Cashel's mother would put her hand – soft, despite all the work she did – into his and let him know that he hadn't really done anything wrong, that a bit of fidgeting was normal.

And now she'd be lying in St Mary's in a big dark box. He'd be there mourning her without anyone to put their hand into his, and he knew how much that would upset her – how much it had upset her for so many years – that he was alone.

Today, it upset him too. And it made him think about Tess Power.

Anna had always loved Tess. There had been no issue between the woman who cleaned Avalon House and the daughter of the house. There might have been in many of the other big houses, but not there. It was partly to do with Tess and Suki's father, a man who genuinely didn't discriminate between those with money and those without. He was unlike most of his class in that respect.

Mr Power was cut from different cloth. He cared about people, from the men who worked on the estate, trying to stop the ravages of time and the weather from destroying the beautiful old house, to people like Cashel's mother, who cleaned and sometimes took care of Tess and Suki. He always addressed Anna respectfully as 'Mrs Reilly' and spoke to her as if she were a duchess. And Anna, though she came from the poorest street in the village, spoke back to him in the same way. So it was no surprise that Anna and Tess were close.

But Cashel didn't want to think about Tess Power. Not after all that had happened. He hoped she wouldn't have the nerve to come to his mother's funeral. The lady of the manor bestowing her presence on the funeral of a mere town person . . . He shuddered; no, he didn't want to see her there.

October was not a good time for boutiques in small villages – or so said Vivienne, proprietor of Femme, the high-fashion boutique next door to Something Old.

The Christmas frenzy of wanting something new to wear hadn't yet started and everyone was saving for Christmas presents.

'The number of people I've had in this morning who rattled through the sale racks dismissively, then marched out again. It's so depressing,' Vivienne sighed. 'They don't even look at the full-price stock.'

She'd stuck the 'Back in five minutes' sign on the door and dropped into Tess's for a cup of instant coffee and a moan. The two of them had been shop neighbours for ten years. Vivienne had done marvellously during the boom years when wealthy women thought nothing of paying a hundred euros for a sparkly T-shirt or twice that for a long, bewildering skirt with trailing bits here and there. Now, Vivienne said, they wanted a whole outfit for the same hundred euros.

Tess boiled the kettle and spooned coffee into cups in the back part of the shop and listened quietly to Vivienne's lament.

The past couple of years had been tough, no doubt about it.

Once upon a time, she used to close the shop for the whole of January and open up again in February, with new stock, the old stock rearranged, and a spring in her step after the rest. She hadn't done that for the last two years. These days, she couldn't afford to close at all.

At least when the place was open, people came in, bringing warmth with them.

She carried the coffees back into the shop, having decided against telling Vivienne that a customer had bought a sweet 1910 marcasite brooch only that morning. Vivienne would take it personally.

'No news?' asked Vivienne.

'Not a scrap,' said Tess, smiling. It was a trick of hers: smiling fooled people into smiling back at her. It was infectious; a bit like yawning at dogs.

Vivienne perked up. 'They're doing a special offer in the supermarket,' she said. 'Two instant meals and a bottle of wine for twelve euros. Of course, Gerard hates instant meals.' Gerard was Vivienne's husband, a man who could be relied upon to bail the shop out when profits were low.

Tess was used to Vivienne's rants. She never let on that she too worried about money, that there was no one to bail her out, and now even the capital her father had left her had dwindled, despite its relative safety in the post office. Staring her in the face was the knowledge that before long she might have to give up Something Old and join an auction house – if she could find one that would have her. She didn't have a degree in fine arts. Her college experience a million years ago had been in general arts. Her knowledge of antiques came not from books but from her love of old things and an affinity for them, but she had an expert eye and could generally tell a fake from the real thing.

'Are these the best biscuits you have?' Vivienne said, eyeing the plain biscuits.

'Sorry,' said Tess. 'I did have a pack of amaretti biscotti, but they're all gone.'

'I need chocolate,' said Vivienne, getting to her feet. 'I'll nip down to Ponti's for a pack of chocolate ones. Back in a moment!'

It was ten minutes before she returned. After all that time, Tess expected her to turn up with cupcakes from the delicatessen and a couple of milky coffees from Lorena's Café. However, when Vivienne arrived, panting from the walk up the hill to Something Old, she carried nothing but a pack of chocolate biscuits.

'I got stuck, talking to Mr Ponti,' she said, collapsing on to her chair. 'Apparently, Anna Reilly died. One of the nurses found her dead this morning. Mr Ponti reckons it was a mercy, given how bad she was. I suppose the older son will be home for the funeral. I've met Riach, obviously, and his wife, Charlotte's lovely, but I've never set eyes on Cashel – except in the papers. He's a fine thing, I have to say. Is that bad of me? Saying he's good looking when his mother's only died? I suppose it is. Can you boil up the kettle again, Tess? This coffee's stone cold.'

But Tess was no longer listening. She was thinking of the woman she'd known since she was a child, who'd been a friend to her even after the split with Cashel.

Nineteen years had passed, yet it remained as painful as ever to think about him. Tess closed her eyes, as if that would block out his face.

She saw him on television sometimes, talking about business. He looked as if he'd filled out over the years, with broad shoulders to go with his great height. He'd had a beard for a while, giving him a hint of Barbary pirate with his midnight dark hair and the slanting eyebrows over those expressive brown eyes.

On the day he'd told her how much he hated her, he was leaner, his face still youthful and full of hope.

When she looked at pictures of him now she saw someone who'd been knocked by life and whose face had taken on a wry, slightly wary expression as a result. The dark eyes were permanently narrowed and there were lines around them that should have made him appear older but somehow only succeeded in making Tess wonder if there was much happiness in his life.

His mother had come to see Tess a couple of years after she married Kevin. Zach had been a toddler at the time, and Anna had brought him a little sweater she'd knitted. It was blue with the red outline of a train embroidered on to it. Anna was a wonderful knitter. Tess could remember Cashel, tall and strong, in a cream Aran sweater his mother had made him. Tess used to lie against him and trace the complex patterns of stitches, marvelling at both the intricacy and the feel of his body through the wool. Everything had been so simple then, dreaming of the day Tess and Cashel would marry, Suki would be First Lady . . . And then it had all gone wrong . . .

Taking the little blue sweater from Anna, she had blurted, 'It's lovely,' before dissolving into tears. Without a word, Anna had gently picked Zach up from his beanbag, dressed him in the tiny sweater, and handed him to his mother. It was the only thing which soothed Tess in those days: holding her beloved son and burying her nose in the fine tufts of dark hair on his small head.

There was no need for them to be strangers, Anna had pointed out in her matter-of-fact way. Just because Cashel had stormed off saying he would never speak to Tess again, didn't mean Anna had to follow suit.

'We've known each other too long for that,' she said in her firm, strong voice.

Anna Reilly had been unlike anyone else Tess knew. There were plenty of women with husbands who spent every waking moment in the pub and thought work was an occupation for those poor souls without an aptitude for betting on horses, but Anna did not allow this behaviour to beat her down. She was going to raise her boys as best she could, with or without Leonard Reilly's help, and if that meant cleaning other people's houses and scrubbing their doorsteps, so be it. The jobs she did in no way defined her. Her strength defined her.

Over the years, Tess often wondered whether Cashel knew

that she and his mother had remained friends. In subtle ways, Anna would let her know when Cashel was home, and Tess understood that she wouldn't be welcome in the house on Bridge Street until he'd gone.

'You should have seen some of the houses he wanted to buy me,' Anna joked when she showed Tess around it the first time. It was bigger than the place on Cottage Row that Cashel had grown up in, but not too big.

Through Anna, Tess had followed Cashel's career from afar. At no time did Anna ask why it had happened that way, why had she broken Cashel's heart. And Tess never tried to explain, for she felt certain that Anna wouldn't understand. If it had been her darling Zach whose heart had been broken, Tess knew she'd find it hard to forgive. And yet Anna had been part of her life since she was a child; part housekeeper, part babysitter when it was required. She realized that Tess wasn't heartless or stuck up, or any of the things Cashel had called her.

She'd been distraught when she first saw the signs of Anna's decline into dementia. To ensure the old lady got the help she needed, Tess had phoned Riach, alerting him to the problem.

Like his mother, Riach held no malice for her. He was the one who made sure she could continue to visit his mother without revealing her surname to the nurses Cashel had hired.

'Cashel would go mad if he knew you were visiting her,' Riach told Tess.

'I know,' she said, her silvery-grey eyes cloudy. 'But it's not his business. It's about me and your mother. We were friends.'

Now Cashel would surely be returning for the funeral, and for the first time in many years, they would come face to face.

Assuming Riach thought she should attend the funeral.

Suddenly Vivienne broke off munching through the biscuits, having spotted someone walking towards her shop window.

'Excuse me, Tess,' she said. 'It looks as though I have a customer.'

The moment she was gone, Tess went to the back room to make a phone call.

Riach's mobile rang so long, she thought she'd have to leave a message, but just as she was steeling herself for the voicemail announcement, he picked up.

'Riach, I am so sorry. I just heard about Anna. You must be devastated.'

'I am – we are,' he said. 'I knew it was coming, but it still hurts. I want to cry, only I keep thinking how she'd hate me to cry.'

'She was a very strong woman,' Tess said, 'but she'd have wanted you to mourn her, so cry away.'

'Yeah,' he said, and Tess could hear the slight hitch in his voice.

'Riach, I would like to be at the funeral, but only if you think it's all right for me to come,' she went on. 'I don't want to cause any more pain. You've enough to deal with, without me—'

Riach interrupted her. 'She'd have wanted you there,' he said.

'What about Cashel?'

'Cashel will have to get over himself,' Riach said shortly. 'This will be a day for my mother and the people she loved.'

Tess unexpectedly found she had a lump in her throat.

'She did love you, you know,' he said.

'I loved her too,' Tess said, beginning to cry. 'I'll miss her so much. I know it's better that she won't have to endure the living hell she was in—'

'That's what I said to Cashel,' Riach interrupted her. 'I don't know if he agrees, though. She was the one person he could come back to, you see. I've got Charlotte and the kids, he has no one.'

There was silence. A long time ago, Cashel's *someone* had been Tess.

'You should be there, though,' Riach went on. 'I'll call you when it's all organized. You'll have to see him, but I'll tell him you're coming.'

Tess wasn't sure what was worse – Cashel knowing in advance that she was going to his mother's funeral, or him suddenly seeing her there after all these years.

That evening, just as Tess was locking up the shop, Kevin sent her a text.

We need to talk, the message said. Are you in later?

She had an inkling of what he wanted to discuss. The depression in the building trade meant that even brilliant carpenters like Kevin – Tess had to admit that he was a genius at what he did – weren't able to find work. Before he'd left, they'd sorted out the finances in a general way, neither of them touching the joint account but agreeing that, since Kevin would be living basically rent-free in his mother's little apartment he could afford to put more money into the mortgage. Clearly that was now becoming too much.

She dialled his number. 'Hello, Kevin. The answer to your message is yes,' she said into the phone. 'I'll be in later tonight – where else would I be going?' she laughed.

And on the other end of the phone there was a slight nervous chuckle that didn't sound like her husband at all.

'Yes. Where,' he said.

'It's about money, isn't it?' Tess said finally. 'Go on, tell me. You want to change things. Listen, Kevin, maybe . . .' she paused, on the verge of saying, *Maybe this has all been a mistake, maybe the separation has shown us what we really needed to know: that we were supposed to be together* . . .

Something stopped her.

'But we'll talk about it tonight,' she said breezily. 'Do you want to have dinner? We're having shepherd's pie – not very exciting, I know, but I made double last week so I'm defrosting.'

'I'm not sure . . . I'll probably already have eaten,' said Kevin.

'OK,' Tess replied, startled. Kevin loved her shepherd's pie. Anna Reilly had taught her how to make it. And even though Tess could hardly claim to be a *cordon bleu* cook, she had mastered all the simple dishes she'd learned from Anna. 'Fine,' she said. 'What time do you want to come up? Before dinner or after? If you want to come after, could you bring some biscuits? I've run out and there's nothing nice in the house to go with tea.'

'Maybe after,' Kevin said quickly. 'And when Kitty's gone to bed we can talk.'

It had been a strange day, Tess thought as she closed the shop and started to walk home with Silkie dancing around at her feet. The odd tone in Kevin's voice. The news of Anna Reilly's death. The thought of Cashel returning to Avalon. It had all shaken her.

In the nineteen years since Cashel had left, they'd met only once: a horrible stand-off in the pharmacy, he clutching at what had to have been one of Anna's prescriptions, she trying to choose some small present for Vivienne for her birthday. It had felt like touching the live wire on an electric socket. Tess had been rooted to the spot, staring up at Cashel's dark, stormy eyes. Stormy was the only word for them. He had lost that air of warmth and kindness he'd had when he was young. No, that was all gone. As he looked back at her, his jaw set, every inch of his body had been tense with repressed anger.

Tess had been about to say something, to break the horrible cycle. It was so long ago, she wanted to say, can't we be friends? After all the time we spent together and being each other's first love . . . But as she'd opened her mouth to speak, he'd given her a look of such venom that she'd felt it as intensely as if he'd pierced her side with a sword, then he'd turned and walked out.

And now he'd be back for Anna's funeral. Nevertheless,

Tess had to go. She wouldn't be frightened away by him. Anna was her friend, her dear, dear friend. She had to go for her sake, and her father's. He would have wanted her to go. That was what the Powers did. No matter how uncomfortable something might be, they went through with it anyway.

So no matter that Cashel would be glaring at her with those stormy eyes of his, Tess was going to be at that funeral.

On the way home, Tess stopped by her mother-in-law's house to collect Kitty. Helen minded Kitty two days a week and Lydia, a childminder, picked her up from school the other three. Occasionally Kevin would finish work in time to drop Kitty home, but most of the time Tess went to get her.

Kitty loved going to Granny's after school, not least because Granny was not too fussed about homework being done and was all too eager to fill Kitty with her home baking. As a result, come dinnertime Kitty would have no appetite, so she'd stare at the vegetables on her plate and moan, 'I am not even a teeny-weeny bit hungry and I am not eating broccoli.'

Kitty wanted her mum to come into Granny's and stay a while, as she often did, but today Tess felt so weary from the double-edged sword of hearing about Anna's death and the thought of Cashel coming home and glaring at her, she couldn't face it. 'Sorry, Helen,' she said. 'I'd stay for a cup of tea, but I'm absolutely zonked tonight.'

'No problem, love,' said Helen. 'See you tomorrow, chicken,' she added, planting a big kiss on Kitty's head.

At home, Tess checked her daughter's homework, put the shepherd's pie in the oven, sorted out vegetables, did a bit of tidying, emptied the dishwasher. All the normal everyday stuff. Zach came in tired from his day in school with a bag of books so heavy that Tess didn't know why all schoolchildren didn't have major back problems.

'It's fine, Ma,' Zach protested, 'I'm strong.' He held up a muscle and flexed it. She laughed. He *was* strong. How amazing to think her baby had turned into this seventeen-year-old-giant.

'I'm strong too,' said Kitty, flexing her skinny nonexistent little-girl muscles.

'Yes, you are, darling,' said Tess. 'Super strong. And you'll get even stronger if you sit down here and eat your dinner.'

'But, *Mum*, it's shepherd's pie. I hate shepherd's pie,' moaned Kitty.

'Last night you said you hated roast chicken and you promised you'd be really good and eat your dinner tonight,' Tess pointed out. 'Come on now, you made a pinkie promise.'

If you hooked baby fingers and said 'pinkie promise', there was no going back on your word. A pinkie promise could not be broken.

'OK,' moaned Kitty, with all the misery of someone being forced into a ten-mile trek in the dark.

Zach wolfed down his dinner and came back for seconds, while Kitty pushed hers around the plate. Tess was too tired to argue with her.

'Eat one bit of broccoli and you're done.'

'Do I have to?' moaned Kitty.

Tess gave up.

She was washing the dishes when the doorbell rang.

'That's your dad,' she said. 'Will you get it, Zach?'

Zach hurried out to open the door. A few seconds later Kevin appeared on the threshold of the kitchen looking awkwardly around him as if he needed to be invited into the room.

'Come on in, Kevin, sit down. Do you want a cup of tea? Did you bring any biscuits?' she asked.

'Erm, yes. Here, they are.' He handed a package to Tess formally.

What was wrong, she wondered. He looked uncomfortable and unhappy. It had to be money. One of his big jobs had been cancelled, that must be it. How were they going to cope?

Paying the mortgage was hard enough already. Now, with her business down on last year and Kevin's income taking a dive, it was hard to see how they could manage. Maybe she really would have to give up the shop and try to find other work.

Kevin sat at the table and chatted to Zach and Kitty. He was like his old self with them, and that made Tess feel better. Children needed a father and she needed . . . Well, she liked having him around. She wasn't *in love* with him, but she did care about him, and perhaps that was enough. All this talk about pure true love that would survive anything and still be as fiercely strong twenty years later – that was just fairy-story rubbish, or maybe movie-story rubbish. In movies, people adored each other for ever. Of course, in real Hollywood life, staying together for even seven years was considered a record-breaking marriage.

But in Tess's life, normal life in Avalon, perhaps loving and respecting the man you were married to was enough. Everyone got irritated by their husband or wife. Everyone sometimes wondered if there wasn't more to life. For a brief second, she thought of that wild passion she'd had with Cashel, then she reminded herself: look where that had got her. Wild passion didn't last. Wild passion ended badly. No, security and love and raising a family together were the things that counted. She resolved to say it all when they were alone. As she made the tea, she rehearsed in her mind how she'd explain it:

Kevin, I'm sorry, I was wrong about the whole separation thing. It was a stupid idea, but it's shown me that we should be together after all, that what we have is wonderful. Please come back and we'll start again.

By the time the tea was ready, Zach was gathering up his gigantic bag ready to trundle off and do his homework.

'Kitty, upstairs and get into your jammies,' said Tess. 'And don't forget to brush your teeth. Then you can come down and watch twenty minutes of Disney Channel before it's time for bed, OK?'

'OK, Mum,' said Kitty, running across to give her father a huge hug on her way out.

Instead of launching into whatever was worrying him as soon as Kitty was gone, Kevin stared deep into his cup, as if the secrets to life were contained therein.

'I know what you've come to talk about,' Tess said. 'I understand. I mean, it's difficult, obviously it's going to be difficult, but other people have been through worse. We'll manage somehow.'

Kevin looked up at her, incomprehension in his eyes. 'You know?' he said.

'Well, yes,' she said. 'I guessed: the finances. We have to do something, don't we? I really think I'm going to have to close the shop and get a job somewhere else.'

'Oh Lord.' He went quite pale, which was no mean feat because Kevin's face was always weathered from being outdoors. 'That wasn't what I came here to say,' he said.

'Go on, then.' Tess took another biscuit. He'd got them from the deli. A local lady named Madeleine made them and she really was the most marvellous person at baking. Her Christmas cakes were much in demand; the last couple of years she'd baked one for Kevin and Tess, wonderfully decorated with sugarcraft Santas, reindeers and penguins – all manner of Christmas things that Kitty and even Zach adored.

'It's not about money,' Kevin said. He took a huge breath. 'I've met someone else.'

'What?' Tess stared at him in utter bewilderment.

'I didn't mean it to happen this way,' he said, 'it just did. I don't want to hurt you, Tess, or the children, but the fact that we separated and the fact that I met someone means that separating was the right thing to do.'

Her language skills finally came back to Tess. 'What do you mean, "the right thing to do"?' she said. 'We separated to see if we wanted to be together . . .' she could barely get the words out, '. . . not to go looking for other people.'

'I wasn't looking,' he said. 'It just happened.'

'Nothing just happens,' hissed Tess.

'Well, this did.' He ran his hands through his hair. It was always spiky. No hair product would ever make it flatten down and it grew like crazy. Once a month he went to the barber and got a short back and sides: three weeks later, it was wild as a bush again.

'Who is she, this someone you met?' Tess said. She pushed her tea and biscuits away from her. She didn't want any form of comfort as she took in this horrendous turn of events.

'Her name is Claire. Her parents moved to Avalon about a year ago. She's lovely. She's an illustrator – you'd really like her.'

'Oh God, I can't believe you said that!' Tess said. '*I'd really like her*? Why? Is she like me? Does she have kids? Is she married? Divorced? What? Tell me.'

'She's a bit younger, actually,' Kevin said. 'And no, she doesn't have children – although she'd love to. One day.'

And that's when Tess thought she was really going to lose it. 'A bit younger?' she asked, enunciating every word carefully. 'Exactly how much younger?'

Kevin moistened his lips. 'She's twenty-nine,' he said.

'Oh my God, twenty-nine!' Tess got up and began to pace. 'She's twenty-nine. She's Claire. She's an illustrator. Don't tell me: she's got long blonde hair and wears cool skinny jeans and goes to rock festivals?'

'Well . . .' began Kevin.

'She is, isn't she? Why? Why did this happen?' Tess said.

'I did some work in her mother's house and I met her. And as to why it happened . . .' He held his hands out in supplication. 'I don't know why. All I know is that I met her, we had an instant connection and we went out. We've been out three times now – not here though. We've never been out together in Avalon. I didn't want people to talk,' he added, his tone pleading. 'You know what this town is like. We went into

Arklow, but people are going to see us together soon and I wanted you to know.'

'And it's serious?'

Kevin couldn't meet her eyes. 'Yeah,' he said, 'it's serious.'

'Do you know, I thought you were coming up here to tell me that you were having even more financial problems than we had been already and . . . oh . . .' Tess shook her head. 'I didn't know what you were going to say, but not that. That wasn't on the list.'

'I'm sorry,' he said. 'The thing is, how do we tell the children?'

'What do you mean, *we* tell the children?' she demanded.

'Well, we have to.'

'*We* don't have to,' said Tess grimly, '*you* have to. And do you know what, Kevin, right now I think you'd better go. Just go. Get out of here.'

He got up and crossed the room, turning back at the door to say, 'I'm really sorry, Tess. I never meant for it to turn out this way . . .'

'Just go,' she said wearily.

After he'd gone, she sat with Kitty through twenty minutes of something on the Disney Channel, although Tess would never have any memory of what it was: she was in shock. Instead, she held Kitty's hand and tried not to cry. She wouldn't let it all out in front of her daughter, she couldn't. This would devastate the children. Zach had hated it when his father had moved out, and even though Kitty had coped in her own childlike way by asking for a kitten, she was like all young kids and hated change.

Tess had worked hard to make the separation appear perfectly normal by saying things like: 'Grown-ups sometimes live apart for a bit and then it all works out again.' How could she explain this? *Nothing* would explain this. Her family had broken into two pieces – and it was all her own fault.

At two a.m., when she had finally given up on sleep, she rang her sister in Massachusetts.

'I don't understand it,' Tess whispered, not wanting to wake the children. 'What's gone wrong? We tried counselling. All the magazines and books say that when people love each other, counselling fixes it. When that didn't work, I read that separation can shock you back into realizing what you might lose. You know: it's make-or-break time. Kevin didn't want to try that, it was me who said let's give it a go, separation could work.'

'That's bull and you know it,' said Suki, who was an expert markswoman in shooting straight. 'Listen to me, Tess. I may have screwed up more relationships than you've had hot dinners, and I made a mess out of *my* only marriage, but I get the two facts that have been eluding you for the past few months: separation never leads to anything but break-up and *people change*. When you met Kevin, you were vulnerable.'

They were both silent and the gulf of the Atlantic Ocean felt huge. The two of them were the only ones who really knew just how vulnerable Tess had been back then. Vulnerable almost wasn't the word. Tess had felt so horrendously alone. Her sister was in America, her father was dead, Cashel had gone and there was nobody else in her life.

'You needed to be rescued. Now, you're a grown-up. If any rescuing needs to be done, you do it yourself. So you've changed. When Kevin met you, he loved being the strong silent type who could take care of you. But you don't need him the same way any more. That's probably why he's fallen for this Claire girl. She thinks he's the strong man who's going to take care of her, and he loves that.

'And what those magazines and books of yours didn't tell you,' Suki added in a dictatorial voice, and Tess could imagine her sister saying this in a lecture on the differences between the sexes, 'is that men are far less likely than women to stay alone after a break-up. I can't recall the precise statistic off-hand, but a high percentage of widowers remarry within a year of their wife's death. The same isn't true of widows. Men don't like being on their own, honey, and you sent him off into the wide, blue yonder on his lonesome.'

'He was living in the granny flat behind his mother's house,' Tess hissed, 'in the same town as me and the kids. He said he couldn't wait for the separation period to be over because the minute we were apart, he knew we ought to be back together!'

'What about you?' Suki asked.

She'd always known the right and hardest question to ask, even when they'd been kids.

'I was changing my mind,' Tess admitted slowly. 'It's been lonely.'

'I know what that's like,' Suki said quietly on the other end of the phone, so quietly that Tess only thought she'd heard it. Any other time, she'd have dived in and asked Suki what was wrong, being the good sister, trying to help Suki sort out another tangled romance in her hectic dating life. But tonight she wanted it to be about her. Tonight, Tess needed Suki to put that fabulous brain to use and help her sort this mess out in her head.

'I was used to being married, Suki. Used to waking up with Kevin, used to the stuff he did. Now, I have to do everything – the grocery shopping, the cooking, sort out all the school stuff, work out all the bills. And Kevin gets to play couple-in-love with his child girlfriend. Whom *I'm going to really like*, apparently.'

Tess exhaled and lay back on her pillows miserably. 'I still can't believe he said that.'

'Honey, I wish I could help you but—'

'Yeah, but you're three thousand miles away and you're broke too. I get it,' Tess said sadly. 'We should offer our services to some marriage counselling clinic. They could use us on their posters: *Meet the Power Sisters, whatever you do, don't do what they did – that way you'll be happy.*'

'There's one thing you never mentioned,' Suki went on as if she hadn't been interrupted. 'Love. You haven't talked about love, Tess. You miss Kevin and all that, but is your heart broken because he's not there, or is it broken because there's no one to share the chores and no one in your bed at night? Only you can answer that. If you decide that you do love him, then you have to fight the child girlfriend for him.'

For the first time that evening, Tess laughed. It was hysterical laughter, and once she started, she found she couldn't stop. She tried to muffle her laughter in the pillows.

'I'm sorry,' she said, coming up for air. 'I had a vision of me and this lovely twenty-nine-year-old in hand-to-hand combat in the main square. Me whacking her through the pub window, bare-knuckled.'

'Tell me when that bout's scheduled,' Suki said drily, 'and I'll book the first flight home.'

Winter

Chapter Five

Coffee was Suki's drug of choice these days. A silky Colombian macchiato with a hint of soya foam from the small coffee shop down the block. She'd pick up a cup to go and then take it out to the porch at the back of the house. Once a fine, albeit small, clapboard house owned by a local potter, it was prettily decorated and had several storm lanterns hanging from the porch roof. There was also an old peeling swing seat with a cushion that probably pre-dated the last ten political administrations, but it was the perfect place to sit in with her coffee and smoke the first of her ten cigarettes of the day.

The radio had forecast a fierce nor'wester that morning, and in the jungle of a backyard, the skinny trees shivered in the wind. Gardening was not Suki's strong point.

Compared to the old cottage she'd got in the divorce settlement from Kyle, the view was nothing to speak of. There, she'd looked out over the fine sand of the beach, watching as the waves rolled over driftwood. She used to collect interesting pieces of driftwood; they complemented the pale blue of the cottage walls and blended nicely with the various bits of nautical paraphernalia Kyle's mother's decorator had added to the cottage when they'd first moved in.

In this house, with its wallpapered walls and mustardy cream paintwork, the driftwood looked dirty. It was all a matter of setting.

Another difference was the skyline: no Richardson had lived within hailing distance of the neighbours for decades. Neighbours were what poor people had. The rich could afford glorious isolation, and their cottage had been suitably solitary, the only one on the beach.

Here, on the edge of a small estate in Falmouth, Massachusetts, she had another line of houses behind hers. Rather than look at them, she stared up into the sky as she blew smoke out and sipped her coffee. It was a good time of the day for thinking.

Today, she needed to get groceries, pay some bills online and progress a little further with the book.

It wasn't moving.

'Do you write all the words?' a woman had said to her at a cocktail party once. This had been back in the days when Suki had felt loved by the world, so she had merely smiled kindly and said, *'Yes, I write all the words.'*

Today, she'd have been less kind: *'No, the Word Fairy comes in the night and does them. I just read them through in the morning to make sure she's written enough. By the way, you need to go back to your village, 'cos they're an idiot short.'*

The Word Fairy wasn't working at all these days.

Growing up in Ireland, she'd never been a morning person except in the summer holidays, when shafts of morning sun would slant in through the holes in the curtains in her bedroom. Sometimes, Suki would get a cup of tea from the kitchen – summer was the only time Avalon House wasn't arctic – and then climb up the back stairs to the third floor, where a window led out on to the ersatz Norman battlements. Nobody but she and Tess ever went up there. Suki used to scatter her cigarette butts everywhere, until Tess brought up an empty baked bean can and it became the ashtray, occasionally emptied when it was overflowing. They had dragged two old cushions up to the window and on nice days, she and Tess could sit in comfort, hidden from the world, and gaze down from their lofty position at the top of Willow Street. They could see the comings and goings of Avalon, could see the line of caravans in Cabana-Land and the rocky spur to the right where children loved to explore in the daytime and where young lovers liked to make out at night.

Suki liked being near the sea. There was a claustrophobia in being land-locked. Sea and trees, they were her lodestones.

The beach at Avalon was so beautiful, the curve of the sand on one side, tailing off to a tiny cove covered with smooth rocks that shimmered in the sun. Valley of the Diamonds, it was called.

Once, a boy had taken Suki there. She hadn't let him go all the way, whatever he told his friends. Suki Power was lots of things, but stupid wasn't one of them.

Cigarette finished now, she made her way wearily upstairs to her office.

The office was really a glorified cupboard. Two years ago when she bought the house, the realtor had enthusiastically described it as 'the nursery'. Suki had shot him an angry look at this description. Did he seriously think she was looking for a place to settle down and raise a family at her age? But the realtor was, she realized, a self-absorbed young man who was operating on auto-pilot, trotting out the same spiel whatever the house, whoever the client:

. . . through here the kitchen/diner, and look, an original wood-burning stove! And upstairs, conveniently placed next door to the master bedroom, a nursery!

She no longer walked into the tiny room and thought of it wistfully as the nursery. Even though she railed against older mothers, there was still a tiny place inside her that mourned her own childlessness.

But she was beyond that ever becoming a reality. These days, the 'nursery' was more of an office-cum-torture chamber. The place where she went to suffer and stare at a blank screen, wondering how to fill the endless pages that stood between her and the next tranche of the advance from her publisher – money she needed so desperately.

When she emerged from the wasteland that had been her life on the road with Jethro, Suki had been broke. Not a penny remained of the divorce settlement from Kyle Junior; it had either gone up their noses or on her back, indulging a penchant for ridiculously expensive clothes, jewellery, cosmetic treatments to make her look younger. The pretty Maine cottage she'd been given as part of her alimony had been sold to pay the debts she'd run up, splashing money around, settling bar bills with bravado to show that she was a famous feminist writer and not just another groupie hanging around with TradeWind. Except that's exactly what she was – another groupie.

What shamed her most was that she hadn't come to her senses and walked out. She'd hung on until Jethro had tired of her and tried to pass her along to someone else.

The thought of that night still made her feel sick. The following morning, she'd packed her bags and gone.

Out of the ravages of all that, she'd tried to rebuild her life. One of the few old contacts prepared to return her calls was her agent, Melissa, who somehow landed her a two-book publishing deal.

The advance was about a quarter of what she'd got on her last contract, and that was for one book.

'You're lucky to be getting this much,' Melissa had said with customary frankness. 'I suspect they've agreed to publish your feminist politik book on the basis that, come the day you write the bestselling "I married into the Richardson clan, then toured with Jethro and TradeWind and came out the other side", they'll make their money back and then some.'

'I'll never write *that* story,' said Suki quietly, thinking that she wasn't entirely sure she had come out the other side of either of those periods in her life.

'*Never* won't pay the bills, honey,' Melissa pointed out. 'Keep it in the back of your mind. We can talk about it when you come to New York for our meeting with the publishers.'

Suki had no intention of devoting any part of her mind to that particular project. But in the meantime, another book had forced its way to the forefront of Suki's mind: Redmond Suarez's book on the Richardsons. If he lived up to his reputation and succeeded in digging out all her secrets, Suki knew she'd fall apart completely.

It was late afternoon when Suki finally admitted defeat, having deleted just about everything she'd written that day. She went down to the kitchen and found Mick, still wearing the T-shirt he'd slept in, the one with his band's logo on the front. His eyes were heavy with sleep, as though he'd not long got up. Mick was muscular, tall and admiring – just Suki's type. He was also, she had begun to suspect, more than a little hung up on her relationship with Jethro and TradeWind. She wondered if she was a trophy girlfriend for him: '*I'm dating Jethro's ex.*'

Maybe not. But he was becoming quite proprietorial. Last night, when she'd told him she was flying to New York to meet with her agent and publisher, he'd immediately started dropping hints that he wanted to come with her.

It seemed he hadn't given up, because his first words were: 'We need a little vacation, babe.'

He was sitting at her pine kitchen table, studying Mr Chan's Takeout Menu as if there was a possibility he would deviate slightly from what he always had, which was chicken chow mein and peanut noodles. Suki teased him about it all the time, but today she found his careful perusal of the menu irritating.

Neither of them had money for a 'little vacation'. Any more than they had the money for takeout every damn night of the week. Mick couldn't cook anything except barbecue, which he thought should be added into the Constitution as an amendment: 'Every man should have the right to grill in his own backyard and down a few cold ones at the same time,' he liked to say.

He rented a ground-floor apartment in an old house two blocks away and he didn't have a proper outdoor grill, just a makeshift one that ruined at least half the food. His friend, Renaud, band drummer by night and tax accountant by day, had a propane grill, and a decent backyard to go with it.

Mick and Steve, the bass guitarist, liked to bitch about Renaud, saying he wasn't a real rocker because he had a 'civilian' job. They were true musicians: they didn't do day jobs.

Suki was expected to agree with this assessment, but the more the bills came and the more it seemed as if Mick was living off her ninety per cent of the time and contributing nothing, the more she envied Renaud's wife, Odette, who had the money for facials, a personal trainer and perfect nails.

A month ago, Mick had moved a lot of his stuff into her house. Now he was subletting his apartment.

Suki knew that if they stayed together, she'd have to be the one who earned the money. Which was about as modern feminist as it got.

She also knew that she'd never be able to mention the fact that she was the breadwinner, any more than she could tell Mick that his band was going nowhere.

Instead, she was expected to attend any gig they managed to get and stand at the side of the stage clapping and whooping over-enthusiastically. Anything less would upset Mick.

'I don't think you liked the show,' he'd said once, early on, when Suki and Odette had been talking near the bar instead of frantically leading the applause.

'I loved it,' said Suki automatically, because that was what you did with performers. Only promoters and managers got to tell the truth, Jethro once told her. He'd been remarkably knowledgeable and clear-sighted about the industry, for all his drug-absorption.

'Honey,' she told Mick now, 'New York is business. You know the cost of hotels there. I'm going to fly in and out the same day. Let's have our vacation another time.'

He picked up her cell phone to call the takeaway.

'OK,' he said. 'You want boiled or fried rice?'

Manhattan had once been Suki's favourite place in the world. The glitter, the hum of excitement, the sense that *anything* was possible. She'd arrived the summer she was nineteen and she couldn't wait to get her first waitressing job, didn't care that she had to share a barely furnished house with eight other Irish college students in the Bronx. She was there – in the city that never slept. And she, Suki Power, was going to conquer it.

She'd been back to Manhattan many times during the years when *Women and Their Wars* was on the bestseller lists, and while she was with Jethro. Sometimes, they stayed in Jethro's vast apartment on Park Avenue, but more often they flitted from hotel to hotel. Jethro was addicted to hotel living. He didn't know how to boil a kettle and, if he thought about it at all, probably assumed the sheets were thrown in the garbage after being taken off his bed every day. He'd lived a normal life once, but that was a long time ago. He'd been a star so many years that he couldn't or wouldn't remember it.

Today, as the forever altered skyline came into view from the airplane window, she knew that another love affair was over. New York had moved on without her. Younger people with clear, unbroken hearts now stalked the glittering city. Strangely, this made her feel older than any line on her face did.

Her appointment with the publisher was at two and she was meeting her agent, Melissa, for lunch beforehand.

'I'll order something for us in my office, Suki. I've got a West Coast conference call at twelve. We won't have time to go out,' Melissa informed her when it was all being set up.

Suki knew what that meant: the Suki Richardson account made so little money, taking her out to lunch was no longer financially viable.

The old Suki would have raged about being treated badly. The new Suki said 'fine'.

She had a long way to go to become the goliath she'd once been, if she could ever get back there.

When the adrenalin was flowing, Suki felt a match for anybody: when she'd been on television all the time, when boys in Avalon had lusted after her, when she was Kyle Richardson's wife, when she was with Jethro . . . But for herself, *in* herself, she didn't know the last time she'd felt truly confident. That scared her like nothing else. If she could no longer fight, what would become of her?

The offices of Carr and Lowenstein had once occupied half of a suitably grand brownstone, but when they'd joined forces with a theatrical agency, they'd all moved into a glass tower. Suki spent the time in the elevator on the way to the forty-fifth floor fighting vertigo, a feeling which worsened when she stepped into the sheeny lobby, which was all reflective surfaces, to emphasize how high up they were. The reception had just-big-enough olive trees in planters in every corner and the silvery-green walls were massed with photos of the agency's most famous and highest-earning clients.

In the Jethro days, he told her the record company people put photos of TradeWind on every wall of their office and played their latest album whenever they visited.

'Flipped the switch to play another band as soon as we left, man!' pointed out Stas, the band's lead guitarist.

'Sure did,' agreed Jethro, unconcerned. 'That's business, nothing personal.'

Suki saw no photos of herself on the walls of Carr and Lowenstein. Not even an itty, bitty one. And it did feel personal.

The receptionist, a Cosmo-girl vision dressed in nude shades with Lincoln Park After Dark nails, didn't bother to feign a polite smile as she took Suki's name and told her to wait. The receptionist knew everything. Who was on the up, who was on the way down.

No picture on the wall and no smiles from Cosmo-girl. It all told a story.

Suki sat on a couch and felt the panic rise. Her career was over. She was broke. There was nowhere left to go and the most dangerous man in the dirty biography business wanted to write about her and the Richardson family. Suki didn't want all the mistakes she'd made in her life turned into trash-biography horror. It would destroy any credibility she'd got left.

The terror which had been building since Eric Gold first told her that Redmond Suarez wanted to write the book exploded fully into Suki's body.

'Which way is the women's room?' she asked Cosmo-girl.

'Straight down the hall and second left,' said the girl with barely a flicker in Suki's direction.

Tess would have introduced herself and made the girl smile, Suki thought. Tess was beautiful and yet she'd had that gift of being able to stop other women from hating her. Suki had never mastered it. Men loved her, women were wary of her.

Why was she thinking about Tess so much? It had to be all the worry over the book and how it all linked up. The past, Avalon, all the things she'd tried to forget, all the secrets.

In the women's room, she locked herself in a stall, put down the toilet seat lid and sat. A Xanax for nerves, some Tylenol for the headache that was rumbling at the base of

99

her skull and one of her prescription antacids to quell the bile that seemed to rise so easily these days. She washed it all down with her bottle of water. That all these ailments were stress-related didn't pass her by, but Suki knew there was no easy fix when it came to stress. She was broke, so that stress wasn't going away anytime soon. And the book . . .

The women's room door slammed and Suki got up, flushed the loo loudly to imply she wasn't in there taking cocaine – which she would have been, back in the day – and came out.

She slicked on some lip gloss and walked back up the hall as if she hadn't a care in the world. *Act as if*, she thought.

Melissa Lowenstein was a tall, striking woman who favoured tailored pantsuits worn with a single large piece of costume jewellery. Today's was a striking orange Perspex brooch on one lapel.

'Suki, great to see you,' she said, shaking hands.

Melissa didn't go in for continental air kissing. 'Gives some men the wrong idea,' she'd told Suki once. 'Kissing can make them think it's fine to put a hand on your butt. Kissing blurs all the rules. So I keep it simple. No kissing anyone, no touching – and no messing if they overstep that line.'

Suki found this approach strange. She liked seeing the flicker of admiration in men's eyes, liked using her sexuality as part of her personal arsenal of weapons. But it was different for Melissa, she realized: Suki was the talent, the performer, whereas Melissa had to do deals with men. Totally different.

At Melissa's small boardroom-style table, lunch was set up for two: some deli cold cuts, bagels, salad and diet sodas.

They sat and helped themselves, even though Suki wasn't in the slightest bit hungry. The Xanax was kicking in and now she wanted a strong coffee, preferably a macchiato with foam, and a cigarette, then she'd relax totally. But instead she made up a plate of salad and poured herself a diet drink.

'How's the book going?' Melissa asked.

Suki had already worked out how she was going to answer this.

'Slowly,' she said. There was no point in lying to Melissa. She was about to explain all the issues which were clouding her head: money worries, the damn Suarez book, and point out that if she was earning more money, then she could concentrate . . .

'What's wrong?' rasped Melissa, bonhomie gone, suddenly looking panicked. 'You've given the publishers the outline, Suki. That's what they've paid for. Reuben is a big fan of yours, he turned down *Women and Their Wars* all those years ago and he still regrets it. That's money in the bank for you, but the publishers won't keep waiting for ever. Past glories have got you this far, now you have to deliver – on schedule. My ass is on the line with this. Your due date is in three months and they've had nothing so far. What's going on?'

Suki could feel the hand holding the glass of soda shake at Melissa's lengthy outburst. The fear rose in her again.

'It's Redmond Suarez,' she said. 'He's writing a book about the Richardsons. He's interested in me. I'm so stressed about all of this, I just can't write.'

The words, once blurted out, had the effect of making Melissa sit back and smile with relief.

'Suki, relax, honey. This is good, better than good. This is a publicist's dream. I get that you're worried. Nobody wants a guy like that writing about them. Suarez is a sewer rat – but people are interested in sewer rats. No matter what he says, it will be good for your profile. A little of that high-class Wasp stuff can only do you good. Plus, Reuben is going to flip with joy. He's always had a thing for the old Republican Mayflower types like the Richardsons and he'd like nothing better than to see them red-faced with embarrassment – if WASPS *can* go red, that is. Money can't buy it!' She beamed. 'This is all good. Why didn't you tell me before?'

Melissa began eating her bagel again and Suki somehow

found the strength to put her glass down. 'I need a coffee,' she said. 'I can't eat.'

Melissa flipped a switch on the desk phone and asked for coffee. 'Hurry, Jennie, we've got to be out of here at forty after one to get to Box House by two.' Then she turned back to Suki. 'So,' she continued, 'what have you heard about the Suarez book? Have you talked to the Richardson family about it yet? I presume they know? Bet they do.'

'I haven't talked to them,' Suki said, 'but they'll know. They always know everything.'

That she knew for a fact.

By the time they got to Box House Publishing – another monolith of sheeny glass – Suki had drunk two coffees, plastered a nicotine patch on her arm in lieu of cigarettes, and taken another half Zanax. She was feeling no pain and the face she examined in her compact mirror was looking good. Tranquillizer-induced good, she knew, but that was fine. Who cared where the relief came from, right? She raked her blonde hair back from the widow's peak in place of combing it, and applied more eyeliner and fire-truck red gloss.

'Is Suarez interested in the Jethro years?' Melissa asked as they went up in the elevator.

'Not sure,' said Suki, unconcerned in her happy bubble. 'Not yet, anyhow. Jethro's people would have the lawyers on to him like a shot. It's always hard to nail down facts with bands like TradeWind. The tabloid rumours are so wild, nobody cares what another biography would say. Jethro never speaks, never denies, never apologizes.'

She knew that from personal experience. When Jethro had moved on, she'd never heard from him again, despite their having shared a bed for more than two years.

Today's meeting was with her editor, the marketing team and the cover department. They were all at least fifteen years younger than Suki and Melissa, but Suki tried to tell herself she didn't care. When she'd started out as a writer, these kids were still in strollers. How could they know what she stood for with their talk of modern covers and what people wanted?

It turned out that they had heard about the Suarez book and everyone was pretty perky at the prospect.

'It's what people want to read, the inside story,' breathed one particularly young girl in opaque pantyhose and a skirt so short she'd have been told she was 'asking for it' when Suki was young.

Suki had railed against the 'asking for it' mantra all her life. Women should be able to wear what they want, be what they want. But as she'd found to her cost, it hadn't quite worked out that way. When you looked like you were asking for it, you sometimes got it – and that had the potential to destroy you.

Decades on, female politicians were still criticized for what they wore, though nobody would do that to male ones. Yet here were these young women with careers wearing clothes that seemed to say *one more inch and you're at my crotch*.

Suki shook her head to rattle these crazy thoughts out of it and tuned back in. They'd moved on to the subject of e-books, blogging tours and the fact that Suki's interesting past made her a person of interest to both the books and feature pages.

She continued to intermittently tune in and out until the meeting came to an end. Still in a Zanax-induced daze, she made her way back down to street level. On her way to hail a cab, she passed a gaggle of young girls wearing what looked to her like fancy dress costume: dark pantyhose, tight denim shorts, unflattering sneaker boots, long open shirts and skimpy stomach-baring T-shirts with writing on them. The clothes were not revealing as such, but they did, Suki realized, high-light the female body. Some guys laying cable watched the girls and Suki watched the men. She had never worn clothes like that when she was their age, but the body-conscious dresses and high boots she'd dressed in back then were designed to achieve the same result.

After the no-nonsense style of Melissa, who'd made such a statement, Suki felt almost shocked by the girls. And she was unshockable, wasn't she?

In *Women and Their Wars* she'd written about female empowerment and the glass ceiling. At the time, it had been a hot topic. Not any more. Though the glass ceiling remained, no one seemed interested. Feminist writers had devoted entire books to topics such as body image, sexuality, the power of motherhood – and what difference had it made?

Young girls still chose clothes that would make men want to sleep with them. Older women wanted to have both a career and babies. Women of all ages wanted to look attractive to the opposite sex and not show any sign of growing old, ever. Nothing had changed at all.

Suki held out a hand to hail a passing cab. When it drew up, she saw her own image reflected in the windows: a woman with a nest of tousled blonde hair and full lips stained with red gloss. The perfect image of wanton sexuality.

In the back of the cab, she wiped the excess red off with a tissue.

The plane was delayed and she had to wait an hour at the gate with nothing to read but notes of the meetings and a magazine she'd bought that morning. She liked the empowering stuff and snippets about mindfulness or meditation. She didn't *do* any of it; so far as Suki was concerned, reading about it was enough. The articles calmed her, as if the information was seeping into her bones.

One day, she promised herself, she would give this stuff a try. Maybe when the book came out and she had some money. Perhaps then she'd go to Avalon and spend time with Zach and Kitty. They were growing up and she was missing so much of it. She'd been close to Zach when he was younger: he'd been so sweet, so wise, despite being a kid. Suki had felt the warmth of both Tess and their father's kindness in the boy and she'd adored being with him.

But she hadn't been home for a long time. There were phone calls at Christmas and birthdays, but she knew he was slipping away from her. Once kids grew up, they moved on. She didn't want to lose him. She still had time with Kitty because she was young.

Yes, when her book was done, assuming she managed to dodge the bullet with the bloody Suarez book, she'd go to Avalon and move in with Tess for a while. Practise yoga and mindfulness, meditate on the beach, stuff like that. She smiled at the thought.

Another delay announcement was broadcast, so she phoned Mick, who sounded grumpy when she told him that she was going to be home late.

'Why don't you go out for a session with Renaud?' she suggested, like a mother suggesting a new toy to an irate toddler. Easier to have him sinking a few beers than waiting for her and getting annoyed.

'I guess I could do that.'

The after-effects of the drugs and the energy she'd had to summon up for the day, had left her feeling exhausted. Suki kept her bag protectively close on her lap, wrapped a light shawl around her shoulders and let herself sink into the airline gate seat as far as its hard back would allow.

Jethro and the band had their own jet. There was no hanging around boarding gates when you were travelling with TradeWind. Her mind went back once more to that first time she'd met Jethro, that instant connection on the television show and then that kiss in his dressing room, after he'd thrown everyone else out, his hands holding her face so tenderly.

His music wasn't the only lure for the fans; Jethro's looks were a huge part of the appeal. Tall, almost menacing in his beauty, except for that wry, crooked smile; the jet black hair swept back from his forehead, and the Sioux bones he'd inherited from his mother defining the tanned face. He was so fiercely stunning that Suki had wanted to touch his face to see if he was real or if clever make-up had created those incredible shadows and high bones. But he wouldn't let her touch him.

His was the only touch allowed. His hands on her body, feeling for her breasts under the silk shirt, making her not care who was on the other side of the dressing-room door or what they might think. Just wanting him.

'No,' he rasped, face buried in her breasts. 'Not here – my hotel.'

'I thought you had to fly to another gig?' she said breathlessly, watching as he grabbed his jacket from a chair, checked the pockets for his smokes and took her hand.

But the jet could wait. There was time to go back to his hotel before they had to race off to Pittsburgh.

As they left the television studios, Suki felt the exquisite buzz of being with a man everyone recognized, a rock god at a time when there were many such gods. But Jethro wasn't a man on self-destruct mode. Beneath all the stage make-up and tattoos, including a snake writhing up one arm and around his carotid artery, Jethro had more in common with Suki's former father-in-law, Kyle Richardson Senior, than he did with his fellow rock gods. Like Kyle Senior, he knew precisely what he wanted and was hell-bent on getting it, no matter who got hurt along the way.

Surrounded by bodyguards in suits – otherwise Jethro said, nobody would be able to tell the bull-necked roadies from security – they were escorted to a black limo. Through the smoky glass, Suki saw the screaming fans held back by the barrier, and as the car pulled into traffic she leaned back, feeling safe, cocooned, *special*.

Jethro sprawled across the back seat and Suki, unsure now and wondering whether she had made a hideous mistake, sat nervously near the window. She could smell her own sweat through the Shalimar she'd drenched herself in that morning. Studio lights made everyone sweat and she pressed her arms firmly to her sides lest the inevitable wet patches on her amber silk shirt were visible.

'Do fans turn up like this every time you're on television?' she asked, trying to ground herself in normality. She could still get out of this, this *madness* that had possessed her during that frantic kiss in his dressing room. Television made people crazy, it was well known. The studio lights, the notion that you were smiling into millions of peoples' homes; it was all pure madness.

And then, to have someone like Jethro growl that you were the sexiest thing he'd ever seen . . .

She stole a glance at him, his roman profile staring straight ahead, jet black (dyed?) hair raked back from his high forehead. He must wear contact lenses, she decided, peering a bit closer because he wasn't paying her the slightest bit of attention. Nobody's eyes were that green; a lucent green like crystal from the bottom of the Mariana Trench.

'You still thinking of backing out?' he murmured without looking at her. He reached into a compartment beside him, took out a bottle of champagne and glasses, then deftly popped the cork with all the skill of a sommelier.

When he passed Suki her glass, the look of pure lust in his eyes made her feel all the heat and excitement come rushing back.

'Just one,' she mumbled. 'I have a thing on tomorrow . . .' She was babbling now, particularly as he slid across the leather seat to get closer to her.

'Cancel it,' he said flatly. 'You'll be in Pittsburgh tomorrow. With me.'

'I can't cancel it,' she said, suddenly irked, despite the inky liquid pooling inside her groin. How dare he tell her to cancel something!

Jethro drank some of his champagne and then he was right

beside her. His face with its hard lines was close to hers, and then his mouth was opening hers, and she could feel the coolness of his champagne coursing into her mouth. She'd heard of liquid kisses but nobody had ever done it to her before, and suddenly she pulled herself away, drained her own glass, then dropped it and pulled his face close to hers with both hands, and spilled a sliver of cold bubbles into his mouth. She could feel his throaty growl rather than hear it because they were so close, chest to chest, and it didn't matter that she smelled of fresh hot sweat and Shalimar: he was the same, a raw animal smell and something musky and expensive.

He drained the last of his drink, then held the bottle to her lips.

'Who needs glasses?' he said, mouth closing on the soft curve of her neck.

At the airport in Martha's Vineyard, she had to wait in line for fifteen minutes to pick up a cab.

'You wanna share one?' said a guy in a business suit in front of her. Suki sized him up; business man out of town for work, expense account dinner in front of him and a bottle of whatever he liked. Probably fancied a little fun on the way.

'No, thank you,' she said in her steeliest voice.

When the cab pulled up in front of her house, Suki got out slowly. The street was quiet, the way suburban streets were in winter, with most of the kids inside, no teams of laughing teens playing softball in someone's front yard, no drone of a lawnmower or the bark of a small dog being walked by a gaggle of little girls who'd squeal with delight when the dog peed.

Suki shivered at the November cold and let herself into the house. She was cold a lot of the time now, apart from when she had the hot flushes and her core body temperature seemed to reach meltdown levels. She was fed up with this damn hormonal thing but she wouldn't give in to it. No way, sister.

She was going to beat it at its own game with agnus castus and the dong quai she got from the Chinese medical centre in town. Taking replacement hormones was like admitting it was all over: welcome to Cronesville. She would not do it. She was still young, still fertile, still beautiful.

The house had the appearance it always had when Mick was home all day. The sports pages of the newspaper had been dumped on the floor beside Mick's recliner, which in turn, was facing the flat-screen plasma, an item she hadn't wanted and which Mick couldn't afford, but he'd got a loan from the bank for it. She could smell takeout from the kitchen and knew, without looking, that he'd have left the boxes on the table.

She resisted the impulse to tidy up. First, she needed to get out of her dressy clothes. Lord knew, she didn't have many elegant clothes left. The designer outfits she'd once worn were all out of date and too small. This messiness with her hormones had thickened her waist, and she hated that.

Upstairs in their bedroom, she stripped off and pulled on her sloppy velour sweatpants and a GAP sweatshirt she'd once bought for Mick, not realizing that denim was his preferred choice in all clothing.

There was a note on the bed: *Baby, gone for beers with Renaud. Might be late. Xx Mick.*

She smiled at the kisses and the term of endearment. *Baby.* No woman who got called 'baby' could be turning perimenopausal. He loved her, and she loved him, even if he was the worst housekeeper she'd ever met.

Still smiling, she went downstairs, ignored the cartons on the kitchen table and poured herself a glass of chilled white wine from the fridge. On a hook by the back porch door were a few heavy rugs Suki used when she wanted to sit on the porch swing seat on winter nights. Snagging one, she went outside, wrapping herself up in the rug. It was nicer on the porch when she lit the candles in all the tiny storm lanterns, but it took ages and she was too tired. When Mick sat out with her, he made sure he had music playing, sometimes bluegrass, more often rock. For Suki, music just reminded her of the hurt she felt, so when she was alone, she sat in silence.

Closing her eyes, she let wine and nicotine sink into her. When she was a teenager, she'd sit out in the orchard in the evenings, sneaking a cigarette after dinner. Sometimes their cat, a small black creature called Raven, would join her, weaving around for attention.

Tess had rescued the cat from the woods one day, a tiny scrap of a thing thrown into a sack with the top tied.

Of course, they'd kept her. Nothing in pain was ever sent away from Avalon House.

Tess had saved the cat and named her, yet Raven had chosen Suki to be her beloved mistress. Suki was careless of the cat's affection and that appeared to suit the cat just fine.

Raven was long gone now, buried with all the Avalon House animals in the tiny pet graveyard outside the orchard wall.

Suki's eyes filled with tears. This was ridiculous, she thought, stabbing out her cigarette and then wiping her eyes with the back of her sleeve.

She kept thinking about home, about Tess, about Avalon, and it was stupid. Smart women didn't look back, they looked forward. Right?

Chapter Six

M ara had thought going to Jack's wedding was painful: but going into work and seeing him with Tawhnee every day *after* the wedding was far worse.

'I feel as if I've disappeared into a black hole,' she told Cici miserably. 'I'm there but I'm not there, not in Jack's eyes, anyway. I've just realized that it wasn't the most thrilling job in the world. Yes, I was lucky to have a job at all, but I loved it because of him. Now it's torture.'

It was torture to go into work each day, feeling 'ordinary' and having the beautiful, long-legged Tawhnee swanning past, with every man's eyes upon her.

It was torture to feel every woman in the place – except Tawhnee – urging her silently on, giving her thumbs-up signs across the office and silent hugs in the kitchenette.

She was invisible to every man and an object of pity to every woman.

Mara had never felt like a beauty queen, but when she'd been with Jack, she had felt loved for who she was. Once the love had been taken away and paraded so openly in front of her as so obviously false, she was bereft.

'You're great,' Veronica had said one day at lunch, which had turned into a women-only zone where all the anti-Tawhnee and anti-Jack people congregated and bitched about how short Tawhnee's skirts were, how tight her blouses were, how ludicrous her false eyelashes were . . .

'Yes, totally OTT,' agreed Sean, who was gay, and therefore allowed into the women-only zone. '*She* wears so much make-up, she's like a tranny.'

'Whereas *you*, Mara,' went on Veronica, 'are classy, individual, clever and . . .' she searched for another word.

'Not a Ferrari,' supplied Mara. 'Apparently, Tawhnee is a Ferrari and I am . . . nobody knows, but I assume I'm a clapped-out old banger. A Ford Cortina with two hundred thousand miles on the clock? Something ordinary, anyway.'

Everyone stared at her.

'It's what the guys were saying the day I found out about Jack and Her. She's a Ferrari, therefore hotter than hell, and I'm not. They couldn't come up with anything else for me.'

'Ah.' Everyone got it.

Sean poked her with his fork. 'Call yourself ordinary in that rig-out?' he said, and everyone, including Mara, laughed.

In an attempt to cope with her misery she had made an extra-special effort with her clothes. That day, she'd chosen an emerald green vintage Dior-ish swirling skirt worn with a black patent belt around her hourglass waist with a beret topping off her red curls.

'Without the clothes, I'm ordinary,' Mara said sadly.

Sean held his hands over his eyes dramatically: 'I don't want to see the *without the clothes* version,' he said. 'Tried it once and didn't like it. Keep the clothes on, dearie.'

But despite all the moral support, Mara's spirits were low. She came to the conclusion that her job and the daily proximity to Jack were to blame.

'I know it's mad to give up a decent job these days, but I have to,' she'd said one night to Cici, when they were in the DVD shop, pootling around the shelves as they decided what to rent. 'I love Galway, you know I do,' Mara said to her

112

friend. 'But everything about this place reminds me of Jack and I need to get away.'

As soon as she said it, Mara felt the rightness of the decision. She'd go away – and not home, either. She'd brought Jack there, she'd brought him proudly into the family home with the hope that he was hers for ever. No, she felt too raw to run home to her parents. She'd go to Avalon and Danae; Jack had never been there. It would be clean, virgin territory, un-tainted by Jack.

'Leave Galway?' The words finally got through to Cici, who was toying over a rack of DVDs featuring men with guns in their hands, chiselled faces and torn T-shirts showing taut six-packs. Cici had no interest in guns, as it happened.

'I've got to leave my job,' Mara went on. 'It's hell going in there every day and seeing her looking stunning and thinking that, if I looked like that, I'd be married to Jack.'

'Just shows you he's a moron,' muttered Cici. 'But you can't leave Galway. What'll I do?'

'Sublet my room,' said Mara decisively. 'Give me six months to wash Jack out of my hair and who knows what I'll feel like then.'

'But I'll miss you,' Cici said, beginning to look panicked.

'I'm going to Avalon to my aunt, Danae. You can come to visit – you'd love it.'

Cici turned away from the men-with-bared-torso DVDs. 'Beaches,' she said. 'That's what we need. Or *The Bodyguard*.'

'No,' said Mara. 'Let's rent *Aliens*. I want to watch the bit where Ripley gets to go after Mama Alien with a flamethrower. That's the way I feel about men right now. The next man who comes near me is going to get a blast of the flamethrower.'

'Should I phone the local police station in Avalon and warn them you plan to run amok with your flamethrower?' Cici asked.

'No,' laughed Mara. 'Don't bother. I'll tell them myself. Or I'll get a sign for the top of the car.'

*   *   *

113

Mara was on her own that Friday night and she'd planned a glass of wine, chocolate and an evening with the remote control.

Cici and a few of the gang were going to see a film, then have dinner at a new Mexican restaurant.

'You need to get out,' Cici said.

But Mara had no interest in *out*. She could only just bear being *in* if she watched one of the endless crime series on TV, where evil stalked and complete nutters came up with ever more inventive ways to torture people.

Cici thought all the serial-killer shows were weird and believed the people who watched them were even weirder.

'What do you get out of watching that stuff?' she asked, mystified.

'Comfort,' explained Mara. 'No matter how bad I feel, it's better than the people being tracked by the killers. Plus, the detectives always work out whodunnit in the end, which is also comforting. Bad deeds are punished. That's a nice thought.'

So she was alone, with a box of chocolate finger biscuits and a glass of rosé that night at eight when the doorbell rang.

Shuffling along in her sloppy home sweatpants and slippers, Mara went to the door and peered out through the peephole.

Jack.

He'd come to tell her he loved her, she knew it.

Thank God, thank God. Her giving in her notice had clearly been the tipping point.

But he mustn't see her like this.

'Hold on,' she yelled, 'just on the phone . . .'

At high speed, she raced into her bedroom, ripped off her saggy sweat clothes and pulled on the silky dressing gown that hung on a hook on the door. At the mirror, she dragged a brush through her hair, squirted some grapefruit perfume on her cleavage and rubbed lip balm on her lips. She'd do.

Anyway, he wouldn't be looking at her, he'd be kissing her frenziedly, telling her he loved her, that it had all been a big mistake.

'Coming!' she yelled.

She opened the door and smiled at Jack, who looked so heartbreakingly familiar that she thought she'd cry with the sheer joy of seeing him there.

'Oh, hi, it's you,' she said. *Play it cool*, she told herself.

'Can I come in, Mara?' he asked.

'Of course.'

She let him in and shut the door gently. She loved the door at that moment. *Loved it*, loved everything and everyone. A smile filling her face, she followed Jack into the living room. With Jack in it, even the room seemed to glow. Certainly, Mara felt herself glow with a happiness she'd forgotten she could feel. He was coming back to her. As she'd known he would, in her heart.

The room was very tidy. One of the plusses of no longer hanging around with Jack meant that she had a lot of time for housework. She'd discovered a previously unrecognized obsessive compulsive disorder in herself. She liked the magazines on the coffee table to lie at an exact right angle to the edge of the table and she felt very upset when there were crumbs anywhere in the kitchenette. She didn't need to light candles or dim the lights to make it very attractive: another plus of being manless was that she tried to make the place look as pretty as possible to cheer herself up, so the candles were already lit. The big minus was the box of chocolate fingers on the coffee table, with at least three-quarters of them already devoured. But Jack had loved her appetite. Besides, he probably wouldn't notice.

'Would you like a glass of wine?' she asked. Somehow she managed to turn off the TV, paused halfway through *Criminal Minds*. Where was the remote for Cici's music system? Romantic music was what she needed.

'No, I don't want any wine, thanks,' he said, and sat heavily on the single armchair.

Mara had thought he might sit on the couch, and she'd sink on to it beside him. Still. She smiled, picked up her wine glass and took a sip, while scanning around for the music remote. There it was. She scrolled through the remote to find something slow and romantic, Cici's movie love themes. Perfect.

Then Mara sat down on the couch, curled her feet elegantly up around her and draped the silky dressing gown to what she hoped was its best effect. How many times had they curled up on this very couch, kissing languorously?

'How have you been?' she asked softly.

This was bound to be hard for him. She wanted to make it easier.

He said nothing, simply stared at her, which meant that Mara could stare right back and drink him in. His blond hair was ruffled up on one side, she noticed lovingly. He must have come straight from work; he was wearing a suit, the grey Italian one, the tie pulled askew. His face looked thinner and the blue eyes watched her carefully. She loved this man, Mara thought. Like nobody had ever loved before.

Coolness flew out the window.

'I've missed you so much, Jack,' she said quickly. 'I thought I'd die without you. It's a half-life, you see, without you.'

She got up and sat on the edge of his armchair, ready to sink into his arms when he said it. *I love you, Mara. It's all been a terrible mistake.*

She reached out to touch his face but he grabbed her wrist suddenly, hurting her.

'No,' he said roughly.

He leapt out of the chair in his haste to get away and Mara stumbled back towards the couch.

With one hand, he pulled at his hair. He wasn't looking at her now, but down, he was looking down at the floor.

'I didn't come here for this, Mara,' he said.

Then he looked up at her face and Mara saw what she hadn't allowed herself to see before: embarrassment.

'I'm really sorry,' he began again, still facing her. 'This isn't easy for me, but I have to do it because it's my fault. You leaving could be seen legally as constructive dismissal. You know: you didn't want to go, but the pain of seeing me with Tawhnee made you give in your notice. Six months down the road, you might decide to sue Kearney Property Partners, and I can't let that happen. The business is in enough trouble as it is. We'd fold if we had an unfair dismissal court case.'

From inside the jacket pocket of the lovely Italian suit, he took some papers.

Unfolding them carefully, deliberately not meeting her eyes, Jack put the papers on the table.

'You don't have to sign now. You can get your lawyer to look them over—'

'I don't have a lawyer,' whispered Mara as it all became clear to her.

He hadn't come to tell her he loved her: he'd come to tie up all the loose ends so his business would be protected.

And she'd thrown herself at him, ignoring reality, convincing herself that he still loved her.

She pulled the silky robe tighter around her. It wasn't an item of clothing designed to cover – it was made for revealing, but Mara no longer wanted to reveal herself to him. She tied the sash so tightly that it bit into her.

'You should go,' she said, her voice shaking.

'Look, Mara, I never meant for it to end up like this,' he began.

'GO!'

Her raised voice startled both of them.

It seemed to do the trick. Jack gave her his helpless look, an expression she recognized from times when he hadn't managed to sell a property. She wished she hated him. It would be easier.

But for the moment, she only hated herself.

'You'll look at the papers?' he asked.

'I might,' she said evenly. 'Now, go.'

Mara realized what a sensible plan it was for people not to be permitted to carry handguns, because if she had one, she would absolutely have shot Jack at that moment. She wasn't sure *where* she would have shot him, but it would have been somewhere very, very painful.

She didn't watch him leave, although she felt the blast of cold air when he opened the front door. It was a bitterly cold evening and to maximize sea views in their elderly apartment block, each front door opened on to a balcony that got the full blast of wind from the Atlantic. Suddenly, Mara hated the apartment because every part of it held memories of Jack.

When he was gone, she finished off her glass of wine and began to eat the rest of the chocolate fingers in the pack. *Aliens* had gone back to the DVD rental shop, but somewhere she had a copy of *Terminator 2* where Linda Hamilton got really muscley and beat the heck out of lots of people. That was exactly what she needed right now.

Chapter Seven

*D*anae's routine on a Saturday morning rarely varied. She'd collect her shopping basket and walk down Willow Street into the town, stopping at various places to buy food for the weekend and occasionally pass the time with some of the other shopkeepers. Nothing too personal, just talk about the weather, a subject which enthralled everyone.

'Will it rain, do you think?'

'The forecast said gales, but you can't trust what they say. Always wrong. My husband's cousin has a pig that always predicts the weather – goes into his pen if it's going to rain, stays out if it's fine, and if frost is due, he runs to the back door and tries to get in.'

There was always something to be discussed when it came to weather and it made the perfect subject for someone like Danae: you could talk all day about it and never reveal a thing about yourself.

One of her favourite stops was the new wool shop, where she'd go in and touch the beautiful silky skeins of wool and wonder what she'd make next. She loved knitting, loved the meditative quality of hearing the needles clicking together, feeling the wool slide through her fingers in the age-old tradition.

Avalon's wool shop, Rudi & Madison, was on a cobbled

lane off the square and it was painted a pretty lavender colour that drew the eye. The owner, Sandra, who was gentle and kind, had named the shop after her two dogs. Anyone who loved dogs that much was a good person in Danae's eyes. Danae felt she could be friends with Sandra, but she was anxious about getting close and saying too much. She wasn't good with people: it was safer to stand back, wasn't it?

'Morning, Danae,' said Sandra, as the shop bell tinkled over the door. 'How are you, pet? We've got some new silvery speckled pure wool, lovely for Christmas cardigans or things like that, and gifts, too – you could make beautiful scarves. Or imagine a lovely Aran sweater with sparkles in it; wouldn't that be a great gift for a friend?'

'Yes,' said Danae, smiling. It was a genuine smile, even though there were few people in the world she called friend, and what Christmas presents she gave went to her family, who were probably quite sick of knitted things. Nevertheless, she dutifully went over and looked at the beautiful wool. It was indeed a lovely shade of pewter grey with little silver flecks running through it.

It would suit Mara; she could knit a lovely, lacy scarf for her, a small present that would be sitting on her bed when she arrived. She was happy that Mara was coming, but now that her arrival was imminent, Danae was feeling a little anxious. She wasn't used to living with anyone for any length of time and Mara hadn't said how long she'd stay. Probably not for long, Danae decided. She'd be off looking for work somewhere – Dublin, London or Australia: that's where the young people were going. No need to worry, really.

A scarf would be a nice gift for her. Mara adored clothes. The girl was a veritable magpie when it came to all that vintage stuff. Things Danae used to call second-hand, back in the day. She had bought plenty of second-hand clothes herself over the years. There had been a time when all her clothes came from the Lifeboat Shop round the corner from her and Antonio's flat, ekeing out the few pennies to keep herself dressed so that nobody would know she had so little money in her purse.

'Isn't it lovely?' said Sandra again, reaching out and touching Danae, as if she could sense her pain.

Danae jumped. She wasn't used to being touched. Quickly, she pulled herself out of the past.

'Gosh, yes,' she said. 'I think I'll make a scarf, a couple of scarves. My sister-in-law, Elsie, might like one too. Although maybe in a different colour. Do you have any soft lilac shades?'

As she watched Sandra pack the wool into a bag, Danae thought how small her Christmas list was: something for her brother, Morris, a gift for Elsie, something for Stephen, their son, and for Mara, and then a gift for Belle. That was it: that was her circle of friends and family. Without them, she'd have nobody. Morris and Elsie were so lovely to her, always asking her to stay with them in their pretty house in Dublin for Christmas, but Danae had never gone. She had her hens and Lady to take care of, she explained, making sure to let them know she was grateful for the invitation and that she considered it an honour to be asked. Truthfully, she'd have loved to spend Christmas with them, but she always found it such a sad time of year and she didn't want to inflict her sadness on them.

Christmas was a time of extremes, she felt. If you were happy in your life, the world reflected that back to you and you felt only happiness and joy in the festive season. If your life was lonely and sad, then you felt it ten-fold, because all around you were smiling people, while you stood there in your sadness, not a part of it all, feeling like the loneliest person on the planet.

Belle usually asked her to the hotel for Christmas dinner, but Danae had gone a couple of times and found it an uncomfortable experience: she was too used to remaining on the outside of things to get into the madcap camaraderie of the hotel's holiday dinner. There were silly hats, crackers, charades, and at least one person commandeering the microphone to

121

sing what would turn out to be a mournful song about the old days. Then Danae would feel as though she was going to cry, and she'd leave, wishing she'd stayed home in front of the fire with Lady.

'There we are, all packed up,' said Sandra cheerfully. 'I hope we'll see you for the turning on of the Christmas lights the first Wednesday in December.'

'I'm not sure,' said Danae, when in fact she was sure. She wouldn't go.

She left the knitting shop with her purchases in her bag. There was only one more thing on her Saturday-morning agenda, and that was to drop into the Avalon Hotel and Spa to meet up with Belle. They'd become friends many years ago when both of them were new to the town. In those days some of the older folk had looked upon newcomers as blow-ins who wouldn't properly be part of Avalon until they'd been there at least thirty years.

'We're nearly there,' Belle used to joke, 'eighteen and counting. Another ten and they won't call us newcomers any more.'

After a time, though, it ceased to bother her. 'I don't really care what the aul ones think, do you?' she'd said to Danae recently. And Danae had laughed.

'You know full well I don't care what *anyone* thinks,' she said. 'They all think I'm mad anyway.'

'Oh, that's for sure,' Belle had replied, 'you're the hermit lady who runs the post office and lives up high at the end of Willow Street. Sure, *you* have to be mad. No husband, no child – I was going to say "no chick nor child" but I'd be wrong there. Goodness knows, you've enough chickens.'

Danae had felt a stab in her heart when Belle said it. 'No, plenty of chickens,' she'd replied bravely.

She loved that Belle said what other people were afraid to say. Nobody else would voice the thought in her presence, though she was sure they all considered her odd, living way up there with only her animals for company.

Saturday mornings the two of them would share a quiet cup of tea and a scone in Belle's office. They'd chat about their week and Belle would usually try to persuade Danae to come out somewhere over the weekend.

If it was a trip to the cinema or a meal out, just the two of them, Danae would generally agree to it. But she didn't like anything that involved going out with other people. In the early days, Belle had thought it was because she was shy. 'How can a shy person run the post office?' she'd demanded. Belle liked to get to the bottom of every mystery.

'I'm not shy,' Danae had said. 'I like my own company, that's all. I'm not good in crowds. I don't like lots of friends.'

'I love loads of friends,' Belle had said. 'Friends are what keep you going, Danae. When poor Harold died, I'd have gone mad if it wasn't for my friends telling me it was all right to be angry with him for leaving me. Telling me it was all right to want to spend days in my nightie, staring at the television, eating biscuits like there was no tomorrow. Friends get you through stuff like that. How can you say you don't need friends?'

'I didn't say I don't need friends,' Danae had said, a little sadly. Harold sounded so lovely: no wonder Belle missed him. 'I said I'm not good with lots of people.'

It had taken eighteen years, but Belle had got the hint. Now the pair of them went out perhaps once a month to the cinema and then to dinner afterwards. Belle had given up trying to make Danae meet new people. When Danae had told her the whole story – well, most of it – she'd understood why her quiet, dark-eyed friend was happiest on her own.

'Well,' said Belle, when they were sitting down in her office with tea and beautiful scones in front of them, 'what's the gossip? Any wild excitement in the post office this week?'

'Nothing really,' said Danae. 'I told you Mara's coming to visit in a few days?'

'Yes, that's great,' said Belle, who was truly delighted. She'd

123

only met Mara a few times, but she thought it would do her friend good to have someone staying.

'And I heard that Anna Reilly passed away,' Danae went on.

'I heard that too,' said Belle, who heard all that happened in Avalon within moments of it happening. 'Poor Anna,' she said. 'She was a great woman – strong.'

'True,' said Danae. She'd both liked and been slightly nervous of Anna Reilly. Before she'd succumbed to the dementia, Anna had always struck Danae as one of the few people who might discover her secret. There had been something in the way Anna looked at her with those shrewd, blue eyes, as if to say, *What's your story? What's your sadness? Tell me.*

Danae found people like that unnerving. She didn't want to tell anyone her secrets. She merely wanted to live in peace and forget about the past.

'I met her daughter-in-law, Charlotte, yesterday evening,' said Belle. 'God love them, they're all very upset, even though Anna had long since ceased to be of this world. Dementia really is the long goodbye, God rest her. But it's always a shock when someone dies.' Belle's own eyes got misty and Danae leaned over and put a comforting hand on hers.

'How about we go out tonight, to the cinema?' Danae said, and Belle looked at her in astonishment.

'Mother of God and all the saints!' she declared. 'I don't think you've ever suggested going out. Danae Rahill, what's wrong with you? Do you have a temperature? Is it the change of life?'

Danae laughed. 'I've gone through the change of life already, darling,' she said. 'No, I think it might be good for the two of us to get out so you'll stop thinking about dear Harold.'

'True,' said Belle, 'it'd be lovely to get out. But is there anything decent on? I only like thrillers if there are handsome men in them. And no weepies, either. Fun or gorgeous men, that's what I like.'

'Ah, there's bound to be something on in Arklow that'll fit the bill,' Danae said. She didn't let many people into her life, but when she did, she took good care of them. And she was going to take care of Belle. 'We'll look it up in the paper now and book it, right?'

The driver was silent. He'd tried idle chit-chat as they'd driven away from Cashel's Dublin house, but Cashel had told him that he'd be working in the back, making phone calls and reading papers, and the man had got the hint. In reality, Cashel had made his few phone calls half-heartedly. He didn't want to speak to anyone today. His assistants in the offices in Dublin, London, New York and Sydney had told people that he'd be out of contact for a couple of days. He had papers to read too. He'd long ago learned to read in the back of cars and limousines as he'd sped around the capital cities of the world. Driving had been something he enjoyed, but it was rare that he had the chance. Cashel Reilly's time was too precious to waste driving himself anywhere; instead, other people drove while he worked. Other people did everything for him. It was, he thought with amusement, only a matter of time before some genius came up with a system whereby captains of industry could get someone else to work out for them in the gym too, while they concentrated on making yet more money.

After a while he gave up trying to work, put his papers down and looked out the window at the changing landscape as the sleek, black car left the motorway and joined the road that would take them through Avalon.

Cashel felt, as he always did, the years peeling away. Nothing seemed changed here, and yet everything was changed now his mother was gone.

He and Riach had spoken on the phone early that morning:

'You'll stay with us,' Riach had said. 'Charlotte has a room ready.'

Normally, when Cashel went to Avalon, he stayed in his mother's house. The luxury home he'd bought for her in the town; a far cry from the cramped, damp-ridden cottage he'd grown up in. He'd wanted to build her a mansion – no, better than a mansion – but she'd laughed and said, 'Cashel, love, I'd be rattling around inside a place like that! No, a nice little house with proper central heating and no damp, that'd suit me.'

And because his mother was the one person he listened to, no matter what, Cashel had gone along with it. She'd had her little house, a lovely place with a beautifully landscaped pocket back garden, so she could indulge her love of flowers and plants in a way that she had never been able to in Cottage Row. There, all they'd had was a communal back yard lined with coal sheds and dustbins, where kids kicked balls around when they got into trouble kicking balls around on the street.

It seemed strange not to be staying in the new house tonight, but he didn't want to stay there without her. Tonight he wanted to be with his brother and Charlotte and their two beautiful children.

The driver came to a fork in the road and turned right, as Cashel had instructed. There were two ways into Avalon from this direction: the winding road along the coast, and the road that came over the hill. Cashel preferred the hill road with its view of the town, spread out like a cloak, and the beauty of the horseshoe bay with its white gleaming sands shining up at them. In the distance, on the hill, was the old De Paor estate and the beautiful woods surrounding Avalon House.

Cashel gazed at it for a few minutes. He didn't know who was living there now, who owned it, who'd renovated it. He knew nothing. He didn't want to know. His mother had known better than to raise the subject and then, in the last few years, she hadn't been able to. What did he care about Avalon House anyway? What did he care about the bloody Powers? Suki and Tess, who between them had managed to rip his heart out all those years ago. No, he didn't give a damn who lived there. That house was bad luck, bad luck to anyone who had anything to do with it.

Chapter Eight

Tess slipped into the back of the church quietly, not wanting Cashel to see her. She had spoken to Riach on the phone the day before and he had assured her it was all right for her to come to his mother's funeral.

'And Cashel knows about it?' Tess said, hesitantly.

'He knows,' was all Riach would say. And Tess could read what she wanted into those words.

That Cashel no longer cared, that Cashel was so grief-stricken it was immaterial, that Cashel had forgotten her . . .

The church was full, with people standing at the back. Tess made her way a little to one side so she could see Anna's coffin, which was covered in white flowers. Before the dementia had taken her, Anna had loved flowers and her garden. She and old Mrs Maguire, who used to run the butcher's shop, had both been avid gardeners; Tess had often found them discussing plants and cuttings together in Lorena's Café.

The whole of Avalon was in St Mary's church. Danae, resplendent in black velvet with a sombre hat upon her long, tortoiseshell hair. Belle from the hotel, doing her best to look funereal but failing because really Belle always looked as though she had stepped off the stage. Even Dessie from the pub was there, which was unusual because funerals meant extra business and he'd be busy behind the bar, getting everything ready for the mourners to pour and cheer themselves up with a few stiff ones as soon as the service was over. A feed of pints seemed to help so many people get over the pain of death, Dessie would cheerfully tell anyone who'd listen.

Tess was tall enough to see the Reilly brothers seated in the front pew. They towered over everyone else. Riach's head was dark and Cashel's . . . well, Cashel's was almost the same as she remembered from all those years ago: dark, but now with a scattering of grey. It was strange, looking at the back of his head from this distance instead of being beside him, touching him.

So many years had passed, but for a moment Tess felt again like the young girl she'd been when she'd fallen in love with him for the first time. She reached in her pocket for a tissue and found nothing.

'Here,' said someone, thrusting a bit of tissue into her hand. 'You need this. It's a terrible day, isn't it? But, sure, it's a mercy that the Lord's finally taken her, isn't it?'

'I suppose it is,' said Tess.

And it *was* a mercy. Anna Reilly was not the sort of woman who'd have wanted to be trapped in a body with her mind somewhere else. It was a sad end for such a vibrant, bright woman.

Father Liam was conducting the Mass and Tess rather thought that her old friend would have preferred the sweet Nigerian, Father Olumbuko, to conduct proceedings. Anna had never been conservative. She'd have liked the tall African priest with his gentle eyes, but she'd never known him, not properly. For the past three years, she hadn't known anyone, including Tess.

Funerals always made Tess think of other funerals, in the same way that weddings made her think of other weddings. Today, in the grand old church, she thought back to her father's funeral in St Ethelred's, up the road. To outsiders, Irish funerals must have seemed strange, with their enormous crowds. Funerals were done differently in other countries, with only invited guests and nobody daring to go to the graveside. But here in Avalon, everyone wanted to turn up to pay their respects, and graveyards were generally full of mourners, teetering on gravesides, wondering if it was terrible to walk across the actual graves or should they stand on the edges?

Death was a part of Irish life as much as birth was. The cycle of birth, death and rebirth was part of a pre-Christian, pre-Celtic Ireland that had lived on through the centuries. The rituals might have changed but the crowds remained constant.

Her father was so well loved that the whole town had turned out for his funeral, like today. Tess could remember her sister sobbing in the front pew as she knelt on one of the old embroidered kneelers. Suki had cried and sobbed and yet managed to check her mascara in the funeral car mirror as they drove back to the house, where tea, drinks and sandwiches were laid out.

'Dad loved a party,' Suki had said. 'He'd love this one. Did you buy enough drink, Tess? I might make us pink gins, wouldn't that be lovely? Dad would like that.'

At the time, Tess had been so grief-stricken that she'd simply gaped open-mouthed at her sister and said nothing. How could she think of making pink gins when their father was dead? Darling, darling Dad. But then that was Suki all over: try and find the fun element to everything. The fun element meant you could avoid thinking about the actual sadness.

For years, this had annoyed Tess beyond measure. Now, Tess felt sorry for her older sister. She didn't think Suki had ever mourned their father properly; had ever mourned *anything*, for that matter. Suki didn't do the past, she was too busy rushing towards the future with both hands held out, like a child about to receive a birthday present.

Tess looked round the church today, at the couples and families who had come to pay their respects. She had nobody with her.

A soprano launched into 'Panis Angelicus' and Tess felt the tears well up inside. Music did that to her, grabbed her heart and twisted it. She had to stop thinking like this. It was stupid, futile. She'd think instead of Kitty and Zach. She'd hugged Zach this morning before he'd gone to school and he hadn't pulled away and said, '*Oh, Ma,*' the way he sometimes did. It was as if he knew she was sadder than she should have been over the death of an old lady with dementia.

Seventeen-year-olds were supposed to be totally self-absorbed, and Zach could be that way at times. Yet he was remarkably intuitive. She'd never told him about Cashel or why Anna Reilly was a special link with the past, but somehow, she thought he understood. He was a wise old soul, as Suki liked to say. Pity Suki hadn't been to see them for so long, then, Tess thought crossly.

Finally, the funeral was over and the priests, the coffin and the chief mourners were coming down the church. Tess tried to hide behind the crowd of people because she didn't want Cashel to see her. She'd come to pay her respects to his mother, nothing more. The tradition at local funerals was for people to throng around the bereaved and offer their sympathies after the coffin was loaded into the hearse. Today, there were hundreds of people in a big crowd around the entrance of the church and it took Tess quite a while to emerge. She had no plan to go to the graveyard. Instead she was going to head back to the shop, which she'd shut for the morning. That was on her mind as she finally made it outside and looked instinctively towards the hearse where Cashel and Riach stood. At that instant, Cashel saw her.

Tess was in the middle of a group of people pushing out of the chapel and yet she still felt as if she was all alone with Cashel's harsh gaze upon her. Nobody else had ever looked at her the way he'd looked that last time, with revulsion in his eyes. And that was the way he looked at her now. Instinctively she winced as if she'd been struck.

'Sorry, sorry,' she muttered, as she tried to escape the group of people coming down the steps towards Cashel and Riach. But the crowd was moving as one and Tess was carried inexorably towards the two brothers. Catching sight of her, Riach smiled sadly, before realizing that his brother was standing like a piece of granite beside him. Riach reached out for her, leaning past the crowd of mourners. Tess clasped his hands in sympathy, but she was too aware of Cashel beside him, glaring at her, and she pulled away quickly without saying anything.

Turning back into the crowd, she jostled her way towards the steps of the church, where she could see an escape route. Her heart was pounding and she knew her face was red and flushed. She shouldn't have come. It had been a mistake. She could have mourned at Anna's grave another time.

Riach might have told Cashel she was coming, but that didn't mean she was welcome.

Tess barely saw the people she bumped into in her haste to disappear, until one of them spoke to her.

'Tess, how are you?' ventured Danae, having noticed her flushed skin and shocked expression. 'You look a little unwell.'

'I'm fine,' stammered Tess, even though she knew she was anything but fine.

She couldn't stop now. If only she could make it to the shop. Silkie would be waiting for her, she could hold her tight and sob her heart out, then she would be fine. Right now all she needed was to be as far away from Cashel Reilly as possible.

Cashel had often wondered what he'd do if he saw Tess Power again after all these years. He'd thought about it many, many times, wondering what he'd say to her. He simply hadn't thought he'd see her at his mother's funeral.

And in that instant, that electric glance had told him that it wasn't all over, that he'd never, *ever* forget.

He wasn't sure what he'd thought she'd look like: older, dried out, maybe. That's what he'd wanted. For her to have diminished for having turned him down. And yet she was none of those things. Tess Power looked older, naturally, but despite the black clothes in honour of his mother, she had a glow about her. Her fair hair curled as wildly as ever, but it was short now, probably some chic salon's work, a messy look that cost a fortune.

She looked strangely more like her sister Suki than she used to, a little like the photographs of their long-dead mother, despite the Power colouring. When they were kids, she'd always looked different, softer than other girls, and she still did, but there was no mistaking those cheekbones, the full lips. Being older suited her: her face had lost the puppy fat of youth, enhancing the elegant beauty that had been there all along.

He'd watched, stunned, as she'd come towards the group of people surrounding him and Riach. He had to hand it to her: Tess Power had guts.

That morning, Riach had muttered about everyone in the town coming, including 'all the old pals from school . . .'

Now, Cashel realized what that phrase had meant: Tess.

Mechanically, he shook hands and accepted condolences from the hordes of people lined up to talk to him.

'I knew your mother, she was a wonderful woman,' they all said.

'She'll be sadly missed in the village.'

'It's a mercy really, Cashel, she wasn't herself.'

He let the words flow over him. People did their best in times of pain, they tried to find the right things to say, but when you were hurting it was all so meaningless.

He remembered Tess and what it had been like all those years ago and the things his mother and Riach had said.

They'd done their best to console him, but that too had been meaningless.

'You've clearly made your mind up, so go. I suppose you'll forget her,' Riach had said nineteen years ago, none too confidently.

His mother had been more prosaic. 'If you want to go off and leave Tess this way, Cashel, then you must do it. Remember that I'm here for you. Avalon is here for you. Wherever you go, you can always come back. And wherever you are, you'll always have our love.'

That love was being buried today.

The funeral director, recognizing who was in charge, gave Cashel a nod to signal that it was time they left for the graveyard.

Cashel nodded in return. It was time.

A fine mist began to descend upon the graveyard as the ceremony ended. The gravediggers had moved forward to the edge of the grave, ready to start filling in the earth. Cashel couldn't remember the last time he'd been at a graveyard ceremony. When he was a child, many kids of his age had been to every funeral their mothers had been to. It was the Irish way: children were taken to funerals, perhaps in an effort to help them understand the cycle of living and dying. In the countryside, there was no escaping death – it was everywhere. Animals were born and died, the pig you'd played with as a piglet was killed and turned into sausages, the scrawny chicken who'd never been a good layer ended up in the cooking pot. And people went back to the ground, ashes to ashes, dust to dust.

Anna hadn't been one of the mothers who'd taken her children to the funeral of every Tom, Dick and Harry. But even so, Cashel had been to enough of them; he'd seen enough damp earth spilled on coffins. He was sorry now that they hadn't considered cremation. He hated the idea of his mother lying in the damp earth, food for worms. But today was the sort of day she'd have relished when she was well: the day with all her friends around her and her beloved sons, too.

Rhona hadn't come, although his assistant had emailed her with the information. He wasn't surprised; there had never been any real closeness between Anna and his ex-wife.

Riach was busy talking to people, saying the right things, his wife at his side. Charlotte was dressed in black, like they all were; she was indeed a fine woman, with short dark hair and small, dark eyes that viewed the world with kindness and wisdom. She was a good wife to Riach, Cashel knew that. His mother had never needed to worry about her younger son's choice in the marital stakes. She'd been so happy at Riach and Charlotte's wedding day ten years before.

They had got married in Rome – something which had pleased Cashel, because he knew there was no danger of bumping into Tess. It was stupid really. He'd been married to Rhona then, wealthy, obviously happy, with more money than they knew what to do with, and yet he couldn't stop thinking about the small-town girl he left behind. Only his mother had ever seemed to be aware of the fact.

'It all in the past, Cashel,' she'd told him as they posed for photographs.

Riach had cracked a joke about Avalon being a match for the glories of Rome, and immediately Cashel's mind had drifted back to his home town and all that was there.

'There's no point in looking back. Her life has moved on and so has yours,' his mother had said shrewdly.

'What do you mean, "her life has moved on"?' he'd asked, and then felt angry with himself for wanting to know. 'No, forget that I asked. I don't want to know.'

'That's good, then,' Anna Reilly had said. 'It would be a terrible shame to be here in the Eternal City with your lovely wife and continually be thinking of Tess Power, wouldn't it?'

Yes, he'd thought, but he didn't say it. Instead, he'd given a magnificent speech at the wedding lunch, talking about the wonderful times he and Riach had growing up in Avalon, omitting to mention their father's drinking and his devotion to the bookmakers, and leaving out the friendship both brothers had had with the Power family. Wedding speeches were as much about what you left out as what you put in, he realized.

Rhona had loved the wedding feast at the elegant palazzo. She hadn't been born into money, any more than he had, but she enjoyed spending it. He worked out that her Gucci outfit probably cost as much as the bride's wedding dress – probably a lot more, if he knew Charlotte – but then he had the money to indulge Rhona. And indulge her he did. Spending money on her was easy, easier than making their marriage work.

'Isn't it divine?' she said to him, as they circled the dance floor, her head resting lazily on his shoulder.

'Yes, it is,' he said automatically, wondering what was wrong with him, why wasn't he happy?

By the time they got divorced, the writing had been on the wall for years. Both of them had gone out of their way to avoid being together until, finally, there was no pretending any more: it was over. Cashel signed the divorce papers feeling like a failure – not something he encountered much in his professional life.

'Are you coming?' Charlotte asked him.

His sister-in-law put her hand on his sleeve and the touch unmanned him. Cashel felt the tears burn up behind his eyes. Here in Avalon he felt like the loneliest man in the world.

The after-funeral teas and coffees were held in the Avalon Hotel, and Cashel found people he didn't recognize talking to him at every turn.

'Hello, Cashel, I'm sorry for your loss,' they'd say, and he would thank them and wonder who they were.

He'd been gone so long, he knew nobody here.

135

And there was to be no escape from reminders of Tess, either.

An elderly lady with bifocals and a head of lovely silvery blonde hair hugged him and said she was sure he remembered nobody now, '. . . except the Power girls.'

Unable to listen to any more of this, Cashel shoved his chair back. 'I'm sorry, but I need to make some calls,' he said abruptly, and ignoring the startled expressions around the table he got up and left.

The driver he'd hired was outside reading a paper in the car. He looked up in mild alarm to see his client marching out with a face like thunder. Cashel waved him away and walked down the hill, not really knowing where he was going, only that he had to get away. The aroma of freshly ground coffee drifted across from a café on the square that hadn't been there in his day. Who was he kidding, he thought: *nothing* had been there in his day. Avalon was like a totally different town. Despite Riach and his family being there, Cashel felt as if the last true link to the place was gone. Riach could visit him anytime, anywhere. He'd send the plane for them. The kids would love it. There was no need ever to set foot in this town again.

A wave of grief for his mother swept over him. He hadn't been there for her. He'd paid for things, naturally, but he hadn't *been* there, hadn't been the person she'd call to ask about a fuse box or a shrub that needed to be cut back. Riach had been that person for her. Tess Power had taken all that away from him when she'd rejected him. Tess Power – it was her fault.

Cashel marched into the café, tall and brooding in his funeral suit, a formidable presence of wealth, privilege and expensive tailoring. Behind the counter, Brian took a step backwards. The big man looked as if someone had done something to upset him and Brian hoped to God that the person who'd done the bad thing wasn't him.

136

'Yes?' he said anxiously.

The man seemed to focus on him then, dark brows opening up.

Brian felt a relieved quiver in his legs, the way he used to in school when someone else was in trouble. It wasn't him, after all. The man in the suit wasn't angry with him.

'An espresso,' said Cashel, not sure why he was here at all. He didn't even want more coffee.

'You're here for the funeral,' said Brian, attempting a bit of light chat. His mother, Lorena, who owned the café, said he didn't do enough conversing with the customers, but it was hard. Brian didn't have the knack when it came to chatting.

At the mention of the funeral, the glower came back into the big man's face.

'Right, so,' said Brian, and busied himself with the coffee machine.

Cashel paid for his coffee and sat down at a window seat. The local newspaper had been left, folded incorrectly, on the seat beside him and for want of something to do, he picked it up and scanned it. News was the same the world over, he thought, long fingers flipping through the pages: communities raising money for charity, a politician no longer in power lamenting the state of the country, young athletes beaming for the camera as they posed with medals or a cup . . .

His fingers stilled as he turned to the back pages.

Property for sale: Avalon House.

After the funeral, Tess went back to the shop and opened up. She found that her fingers were shaking as she tried to undo the mortice lock at the bottom of the door.

'Yoo hoo,' called Vivienne from next door. 'How was it? Is that lovely rich son looking for an older woman to spoil? I can't promise much in the way of sex, but they're working on that female Viagra, aren't they? I could go on a pharmaceutical trial!'

Vivienne finally arrived at her door, took one look at Tess's stunned, now-pale face and said: 'That bad? Come in and sit down. You can keep the hordes of buyers happy and I'll get you a strong coffee.'

She installed Tess in a chair by the till, then locked Something Old and handed the keys to her. 'Nobody's come near us all morning. I doubt that a busload of rich tourists is going to turn up within the next five minutes.'

Tess was glad she was sitting.

Vivienne liked mad disco music from the seventies. She played her old CDs on a loop. Any day of the week, you could be sure of hearing 'September' or 'Disco Inferno' belting out from the shop. There were times when the seashore whooshing 'tranquillity' soundtrack from the beautician's upstairs was on extra loud and the disco beat had to compete with the odd whale or dolphin song. Today someone was singing a hit from thirty-odd years ago about how someone could ring their bell anytime, anywhere. In spite of her shock, Tess smiled. It was all wildly suggestive and she thought of how she hated the songs her kids listened to now because they were too racy for Kitty's ears. It was all a cycle really.

Would she look back on this day in thirty years, if she was around then, and smile at how upset she'd been?

Would she ever be able to think of Cashel without wanting to cry and tell him what had really happened?

No, she didn't think she would.

Vivienne meant well, but she wasn't someone Tess could unburden herself to. Suddenly she was overcome with the desire to talk to Suki.

It was eight on the East Coast, too early to phone, but she didn't care. She fished her mobile out of her handbag and dialled.

Suki was up.

'I'm sorry for phoning so early,' Tess said. 'I had a bad day.'

'What's happened, Primrose?' said Suki, using the baby name she'd given her sister.

Tess was Primrose, and Suki was Fleur. Flower fairies, their father said. They used to laugh at the very idea.

Tess burst into tears. She had no words left.

Chapter Nine

*T*he radio was the recently heartbroken woman's worst enemy, Mara decided. Yearning love songs made her want to cry; feisty numbers by female singers made her want to take up kick-boxing and drop-kick Jack into the next century; and talk shows refused to stay away from subjects designed to make her guts tighten.

She'd been prepared as she got into the car for the three-hour drive from Galway to Avalon. She had her iPod ready to go in case the radio signal went bonky and she was left alone with her own thoughts for any length of time.

But the iPod turned out to have been a double-edged sword.

It transpired that there wasn't a single album in her collection that didn't have a Jack-shaped imprint in it.

The time she'd listened to Adele while driving for a date with Jack the previous summer; a Kings of Leon song she'd heard on the radio one day when they were having lunch in a pub near the office and he'd stroked her knee and she'd felt so happy, so loved. Every note in every song seemed to be tinged with heartbreak.

She'd switched on the radio instead and found herself hit from another direction by a talk-show discussion about women playing Russian roulette with their fertility.

'. . . women do not have all the time in the world,' said the voice of doom in the shape of a fertility expert, lamenting the fate of women who turned up at his clinic at the age of forty convinced that a baby was merely a credit-card pin number away.

Another contributor challenged his assumption that women were deliberately putting off getting pregnant until it was almost too late, pointing out that many were the victims of broken relationships, who'd found themselves left high and dry in their thirties. If they didn't manage to meet a new man and start baby-making immediately, their fertile years would have slipped away through no fault of their own.

'Nobody plans for this to happen,' said the contributor fiercely. 'Fertility has a sell-by date and life doesn't always oblige. Women don't choose to be in this situation . . .'

Mara listened numbly, powerless to change the station.

This was her they were talking about. She'd wasted her fertile years on Jack. Worse, she'd let him break her heart so badly, she didn't think it would ever recover enough to let another man in. What was the half-life of a broken heart? Four years? She'd be thirty-seven, nearly thirty-eight before she could think of looking at another man. If Mr Fertility was to be believed, she'd have to start planning getting pregnant on the second or third date.

A crazy dating setting came into her mind: her and The Man, intimate in a restaurant, getting to know each other . . . and right before the waiter came to take their order, she'd drop the clanger:

'No, I don't really like red meat. I have a younger brother. Where do you come from in your family? Middle child, interesting. Yes, I'm from Dublin but I lived in Galway for a few years. Tell me, would you like a girl or a boy?'

A sign above the road promised coffee, beds and bathroom facilities.

Mara took the exit gratefully and flicked the radio off. If

141

there was a book shop in the town she was stopping in, she was going to buy a talking book. Anything to stop the music and the radio talk.

Mara had forgotten how lovely Avalon was, particularly the hill upon which Willow Street sat. The road steepened slowly and then widened out as the houses dwindled. There were more trees up here, the elegant willow trees and many magnolias that bloomed with a scent almost like honey in the early summer, she recalled. Danae had once told her that the trees on the street were cuttings from the magnolias one of the De Paor ancestors had planted on the Avalon House avenue years before.

The notion that the owner of a big old house would ever give anything away had fascinated: it didn't fit in with her notion of the Big House people.

'Avalon House has a gentle soul,' Danae said mystifyingly.

What was that all about, Mara wondered.

'What's more amazing,' Danae went on, 'is that the magnolias grew. These aren't the best conditions for them. But look, the whole of Willow Street is a magnolia paradise. Magnolias and willow trees everywhere.'

On a wintry day like today, it seemed as if the trees were curling around the houses, boughs close to windows as if protecting them from the sea winds.

Mara looked at the big old gates of Avalon House as she turned into Danae's gravel drive, and was immediately greeted by a flutter of red-and-white wings to her right.

A congregation of hens had gathered, beaks pressed against the wire of their run in anticipation of a visitor, squawking at the tops of their voices.

Only Danae would have a posse of attack hens, thought Mara fondly.

She got out of the car and Lady uncurled herself from the mat at the front door, silver-grey fur shaking with delight at this long-absent visitor.

142

The hens, outraged at someone else being greeted and not them, began to ruffle up their feathers to twice their normal size, clucking loudly.

Mara let herself into the run and was instantly surrounded by the gang of fluffy-bloomered girls, some angling inquisitive heads at her, others content to peck happily at her boots.

'Come in,' said Danae from the back door, 'or they'll peck higher up. They are dreadfully nosy and subject to none of the boundaries of normal hens. They want to come into the house these days.'

'Which one is my hen? Which one is Mara?'

'The little red one pulling at your skirt,' said Danae.

'Hello, henny pennie,' said Mara, picking her namesake up and holding her firmly under her arm.

The two Maras regarded each other solemnly.

The avian Mara did not look as if she'd been publicly dumped by a man anytime recently. She looked as if she'd had breakfast, an insect or two, and a few tiny stones. All was right in her world.

'If you had any advice for me, Mara, what would it be?' the human Mara asked.

The hen reached out and had an exploratory peck at Mara's jacket. Then another, a sharper peck this time, which hurt.

'Ouch. Go for what you want in life and don't take shit from anybody, is that it?' Mara set her namesake down. 'I think your hens have the secret of life all figured out, Danae,' she said, leaving the run to hug her aunt.

'Who needs a Zen Guide when you could have a Hen Guide,' Danae laughed.

Even though she'd barely arrived, already it felt comforting and relaxing simply being in Danae's place. Mara's possessions were out in the car, but there was no frantic rush to put everything away, no hurry to get the bag unpacked or to work out what everyone wanted for tea. That was how things would

143

have been in Furlong Hill, and it was very restful to be away from the hustle and bustle of her home.

Danae didn't even mention Mara's bags. If Mara had turned up without spare knickers or a toothbrush, Danae wouldn't blink an eyelid. She'd simply have produced something that would do.

She'd made an aubergine and goat's cheese pie earlier and it was heating in the big cream oven, filling the cottage with lovely aromas, while she and Mara sat on iron chairs outside the kitchen window, with the menagerie at their feet, pecking happily. Danae had brought out a couple of rugs to wrap round themselves to ward off the breeze roaring up from the coast, while a pot of tea sat in a hand-knitted tea cosy on a matching iron table. Mara would have quite liked a glass of wine, but Danae didn't seem to drink. Mara had never questioned this state of affairs, and she wasn't about to start now. Tea in mismatched hand-thrown pottery mugs was exactly the right thing to drink as they watched the tide sweep inexorably into the horseshoe curve of Avalon Bay and discussed the world.

'Would you have been happy with him, Mara, do you think?' Danae said tentatively.

'I was happy . . . I *thought* I was happy,' Mara amended. 'But he didn't know I wanted to marry him – which is an excuse, really, isn't it?' She looked down where a hen was sitting on one of her boot-clad feet. It was strangely comforting, and nicely warm into the bargain. She hoped hens didn't poop sitting down. 'I thought he'd know what I wanted,' she said. 'I knew all the things he wanted. I knew he wanted to go to Monaco to a Grand Prix more than anything. I'd thought we could do that on our honeymoon. I was thinking ahead,' said Mara sadly. She'd told nobody else about the Grand Prix. It was such an admission of futile love and she felt diminished even by saying it.

'Love turns the wisest of us into complete idiots,' Danae

144

said. 'We think we need love to complete us. And we don't. Trust me, we don't.'

All Mara's life, Danae had had the knack for saying the right thing at the right time. She'd been the one who told Mara that the beauty inside a person could shine brightly out of them; that mean girls at school might never suffer for their meanness, and wishing for them to suffer was not only pointless but personally painful. All good advice, delivered in a distant and somewhat reserved manner, as if she was making a special effort to say these things to Mara.

It had never occurred to Mara to wonder *how* her aunt knew all this stuff; that was simply part of who she was: thoughtful and wise, yet somewhat removed from it all. Choosing to keep her distance. Mara had always assumed that Danae enjoyed her almost monastic life.

Until that moment.

Trust me, we don't. Nobody said *that* without having learned it the hard way, through personal experience. Suddenly, Mara wanted to know how Danae had come by her wisdom.

She poured another cup of tea to give herself time. Despite their closeness and fondness for each other, she knew so little about Danae's life. Her dad's older sister, the calm, kind postmistress who loved her chickens: that was all Mara knew of her aunt.

'Oh, listen to me – Madam Know-It-All,' Danae said with a light laugh, as if she could read Mara's thoughts. 'Don't take my advice, Mara, love. Do what you want.'

She was changing the subject, but it was easier that way.

'I am going to recover from my broken heart, walk along the beach and write poetry,' Mara said dramatically. 'Really bad poetry that I'll send to Jack. I may throw myself into the sea a few times with misery . . . but it's a bit cold right now, isn't it?'

'Bitterly cold,' agreed Danae. 'If you want Jack's attention, throw yourself into the sea nearer his house, perhaps?'

145

Mara sniffed. 'Hell will freeze over. I wasted enough time on him. I'm not going to get hypothermia over him.'

'Good girl,' said her aunt. 'At the risk of sounding like a walking cliché, you're young and there are more fish in the sea.'

'I am off fish for good. No fish.'

'I bet your father told you to find a lovely man who'll adore you,' Danae said, tilting her head to one side as she studied her. Mara burst into laughter.

'Those were almost his exact words. How come he's such an innocent and—'

'—and I'm so bitter and twisted?' asked Danae wryly.

'No. Well, Dad is innocent,' Mara pointed out. She'd often marvelled at the difference between her father and his sister. Morris Wilson was a gentle man who thought well of the world and was assured of his happy place in it. Danae was wise, kind and gentle too, but she lived an almost hermit-like existence in Avalon. This place had always been Mara's sanctuary when she needed peace and tranquillity. Nice for a few days, but not necessarily somewhere you'd want to live. Yet this was how Danae spent her days: alone but for her animals.

Maybe that was why Mara had felt the urge to flee to Avalon, she mused. Everything happened for a reason and this was the reason.

Chapter Ten

Suki sat in the Petersens' great room in their holiday mansion on the Cape, a glass of Krug in one hand, and wondered why she'd come to the party in the first place. It had been a long time since she'd bothered with these sort of events: parties in huge mansions with waiting staff, the finest champagne on tap and exquisite canapés cooked by the finest chefs.

At least she'd found somewhere to sit – there were rarely enough seats at these affairs and there was nothing worse than standing for hours. Here, in her corner seat, she was signalling taking a break from the party. Here, she could simply watch.

After the divorce from Kyle, people had continued to invite her to parties because she remained a part of the great Richardson clan, and so far as hosts and hostesses were concerned, even a tenuous connection with Kyle Senior was worthy of a place on the guest list. For their part, the Richardsons hadn't cast Suki out, because they knew better than to alienate her; the last thing they wanted was a bitter divorcee who'd been privy to life on the inside telling the world all their secrets.

Back then, Suki had also enjoyed the status of a minor celebrity; a feted author appearing on chat shows and in the press.

But since she'd hit skid row, there had been no embossed, gilt-edged cards on her mantelpiece inviting her to dinners or elegant parties in the moneyed enclaves in Massachusetts.

So when she'd bumped into Missy Petersen in the health-food shop in Provincetown, the best one by far in the area, she'd been surprised when Missy had hugged her and said it had been too long.

'What have you been up to?' Missy said, tucking a strand of glossy, recently blow-dried blonde hair back with a perfectly manicured hand. Her engagement ring, a pink diamond the size of a conker, caught the light.

'Working on a new book,' Suki said pleasantly.

She'd always liked Missy: she was genuinely nice, not like some of the rich men's wives, who viewed all other women as competition.

'Oh, I don't know how you do it,' said Missy. 'You career women. I can't imagine what I'd do if I had to have a career. Charlie says I'd make a good interior designer, though. I have thought of it, you know.'

Rich women always wanted to be designers. Making a house look pretty was easy when you had a million-dollar budget to play with.

Suki smiled and prepared to move on. 'Lovely to see you, Missy,' she said truthfully.

'Do you know, I clean forgot to invite you to Charlie's birthday party,' Missy said. 'He's fifty-nine, can you believe it? He's planning something wild for his sixtieth, but you know men, they like a party, anyway. What's your address now?'

Suki dutifully gave it, thinking that it was a nice gesture on Missy's part but not expecting it to come to anything. Charlie, a money-mad alpha male, would nix her from the guest list if he saw her name on it. Charlie only wanted players at his parties.

To Suki's amazement, true to her word, Missy sent an

invitation: *Charlie's fifty-ninth, the run-up to the Big One. Come dressed up or come as you are.*

Suki didn't know what made her do it, but she accepted. However, she didn't tell Mick. He wouldn't like that sort of party, she reasoned: Chopin playing on the Bang & Olufsen, or maybe an actual string quartet. No, he wouldn't like it.

It wasn't that he wouldn't fit in, she told herself. It wasn't that at all.

She went to the salon and had her hair done; something she rarely did these days.

'A file and paint,' she told the manicurist. She couldn't afford the extra ten dollars for proper cuticle work.

Money – why did it always come back to money?

There was plenty of money in the Petersens' house, a timber-framed mansion on the Hyannis side of the Cape with more rooms than the Louvre.

Because this wasn't a 'big' party, Missy explained as she greeted Suki, they didn't have a marquee or anything. 'It's only us at home.'

'Home' was filled with modern art and enough odd sculptures to convince people that Charlie and Suki had artistic sense. In reality, Suki knew they'd have an art expert on the payroll, looking out for nice 'pieces' that would ensure they kept their place in the art fashion loop.

That was the trick when you had new money. Old money people could have paintings of the family home and deranged great-grand-uncles who'd had four wives and twenty-six children and had owned half of East Manhattan when horse-drawn carriages drove the streets.

New money people had up-and-coming artists and a selection of hideously expensive pieces to show how rich they were.

The Petersens at home turned out to consist of a collection of rich men scattered around the place, comparing their assets – or wives.

I should never have come, Suki thought again, accepting a glass from a waiter.

Sitting in her armchair, champagne glass in hand, she surveyed the room. It was a world she thought she'd left behind. Everyone here was rich or married to someone rich. The result was a roomful of people all hell-bent on outdoing each other while trying not to be too obvious about it.

During her years on the ultra-rich social circuit, Suki had noticed that the women generally fell into one of two tribes: the more ordinary women, who got by with a little regular maintenance, and the trophy second wives, for whom maintenance was a way of life. First wives tended to avoid standing beside second ones. The sole exception was one exquisite first wife, Delilah Verne, who managed to look younger than her forty-eight years, having been rejuvenated so many times that a second wife could no doubt have been assembled from the bits she'd had surgically sucked out of her.

It was Delilah who descended upon her quiet corner now, teetering on her platforms. Not quite Prada witch but not far off it, she was dressed in something designer-ish (Balmain?) that Suki knew had commanded a sum that would have paid her own household bills for three months.

'Suki! Hello!' trilled Delilah.

Class A or anti-depressant drugs, Suki wondered. Or merely the permanent ultra-happiness required if one wanted to stay married to a grumpy billionaire? Clark Verne, in common with most billionaires, was always grumpy. The amassing of money seemed to do that to people, a fact which mystified Suki. If she was rich, she'd be so happy she'd never stop smiling.

'Hello, Delilah,' said Suki, tilting her cheek to be air-kissed. Once, she'd thought it made sense to stay friends with people like Clark via their wives. Now, she couldn't really see the point of fake friendships.

'You look super, darling!' Delilah went on enthusiastically.

Suki flashed the regulation thank-you smile, and followed it up with, 'And so do you!'

They were not pals and never would be. For a start, Delilah didn't do women friends. Secondly, Suki didn't fit comfortably into any niche. She wasn't rich, but she wasn't one of the eager women hanging round the fringes of power, either. She'd had a very public career and wouldn't hesitate to remind men of that if they fell into a discussion of money and politics, ignoring all female interjections. That gave her a certain power, as did her former marriage. To these billionaires, Kyle Senior still represented the seat of power, and Suki had evolved various strategies to make sure they knew that separation from her husband had not meant separation from the Richardson clan: 'I dropped by the compound in Hyannis over the summer,' she'd say idly, and suddenly they'd all be hanging on her every word.

Suki knew she was pretty glamorous in her own right. The liaison with Jethro hadn't hurt in that regard. And her heavy lidded eyes with the death line of block kohl and the rippling hair told the world that she was a somebody. But the Richardsons bestowed extra glamour, no doubt about it.

Tonight, however, Suki was fed up with all the fakery. Truth was, she wasn't part of the Richardson clan any more. She was only invited to the compound on the rarest of occasions, and only then because Kyle Senior was a great believer in the old adage: 'Keep your friends close and your enemies closer.'

'I got a phone call from a friend recently,' Delilah said idly.

Suki waited.

'Well, not a friend, exactly. More of an acquaintance.'

Suki tried to maintain an expression of polite interest. As if she cared about Delilah's friends. A chat with her dermatologist about the latest laser treatment was probably Delilah's notion of female bonding.

'She's had a couple of phone calls from someone who's a researcher for Redmond Suarez. It seems the latest book he's working on is about the Richardsons . . .'

Suki could barely hear the rest of the conversation. She didn't want to hear it.

'. . . I said we were friends and, of course, you know them – after all, you married one of them! But I'd have to check with you first.'

Somehow, Suki's expression remained neutral.

'Yes, Delilah, he's writing a book about the Richardsons,' she confirmed, her heart fluttering with panic. Always better to sound as if you knew everything up front. Knowledge was power.

'I don't know much about it, but if someone wants to write a book about a great American dynasty, I'd hate it to be tawdry,' Suki managed to go on. 'You know how Kyle Senior and Antoinette value their privacy. The *Family* –' she deliberately emphasized the word in the way people said things like the *President* – 'want us to meet to discuss it.'

In reality, Antoinette had left a crisp message on Suki's answering machine that sounded more like a command than an invitation: 'Come to the compound on Tuesday afternoon. You can stay overnight. We need to talk about Mr Suarez and his nasty little book.'

Suki took Delilah's hand and held on to it. 'They will be so thrilled you didn't talk about them, that instead you came to me with this,' she said, smiling ingenuously.

If Delilah was discomfited by Suki's apparent calmness, she didn't show it. Botox, naturally. Delilah's brow was smooth as alabaster.

It was time for her to go.

'Thank you,' Suki said again, embracing Delilah's bony frame. 'I must phone Kyle and tell him this,' she added with a hint of sadness.

Last time she'd spoken to Kyle, they'd had a blazing row. But Delilah didn't need to know that.

Suki never drove up to the Richardsons' compound in Hyannis without feeling a sense of mild astonishment that she'd once

152

belonged there. The seat of political power, a bit down the road from the Kennedy compound. It was all heady stuff. Back in the day, the Richardsons had been friends with the Kennedys in spite of their political differences. Kyle Senior had socialized with JFK and Jackie, and Suki used to love listening to his stories about those far-off days before it all ended so horribly in Dallas. Of course she'd exhibited only idle interest. Nothing marked someone out as a rubber-necker more than 'Tell me more . . .' requests.

And yet all that seemed so long ago. Suki had lived many lifetimes since she married and divorced Kyle Junior.

Antoinette, the family matriarch, was seventy-nine now, with steely grey hair and a steely grey attitude. Her day uniform had never deviated in all the time Suki had known her: cashmere twinset, pearls and woollen skirt in winter, and silk or linen blouse and silk skirt in summer, also with pearls. Of an evening, she opted for crocodile pumps (never during the day – far too common), something in crêpe de Chine in a jewel colour, and a hint of face powder and lipstick that had probably been on her bureau since Roosevelt was in power.

Suki couldn't imagine Antoinette sitting in Dr Frederik's office asking for a top-up of Botox. Her frown lines presumably did as they were told, much the same way as the compound staff leapt to do her bidding. Worrying about physical beauty was for lesser mortals.

In her day, Antoinette had been what people called a handsome woman. Noble bones, a strong chin and a gaze that made her son quail. Nothing much had changed. Handsomeness certainly lasted longer than prettiness.

An uneasy truce had existed between Suki and her former mother-in-law since the first day they met. Suki's background – checked ruthlessly by Kyle Senior's private investigators – was certainly top drawer. Impoverished gentry, but gentry nonetheless.

Even Antoinete had been charmed by Suki's father, who

was the perfect example of an Irish gentleman landowner with more than a whiff of academia thrown in for good measure.

Adding to the patina of class, Suki could talk the talk about antiques, thanks mainly to Tess's interest in the subject.

'Daddy had a full set of Audubon prints, you know, but they had to be sold,' she might say, which was entirely untrue but impossible to check. Her father only remembered the things he'd had to sell when they'd had some special significance to the family, so should Antoinette ever ask if this was true, he could be relied upon not to recall one way or the other. Suki was clever enough to know that the best lies were the ones where you couldn't be caught out.

Her father had cried over selling the Walter Osborne portrait of his grandmother, but a growing interest in Osborne as a painter and the roof in the west wing falling in had coincided and it had made sound economic sense. She'd mentioned the sale of the Osborne too and had craftily added in a little Pissarro and a minor Watteau as well. She had no intention of letting her new in-laws spend too much time with her family, so it was safe to lie. For all Antoinette's much-vaunted blue blood, she hadn't grown up in a house with beautiful art, had she? She'd had to marry it.

Throughout the marriage to Kyle, Antoinette never ceased to remind Suki that she wasn't a suitable wife for her darling son.

In return, Suki got to slip little digs into her conversations with Antoinette. Like the time she'd meanly identified Antoinette's charming collection of floral bowls as fake Meissen rather than the real thing. Suki had absolutely no interest in antiques unless they were worth something and Meissen certainly was, so she could tell the difference.

Plus, during her one and only visit to the compound, Tess had told Suki she thought it was wonderful that Antoinette wasn't hung up on original everythings, but kept items of sentimental value like the Meissen copies. Tess, silly girl, had meant it as a compliment; she admired people who collected valuable and non-valuable things and displayed them side by side. It meant they liked what they liked, rather than what was expensive.

Suki knew Antoinette too well to fall for that. Clearly her mother-in-law thought those bowls were the real McCoy.

'I do adore Meissen copies,' she'd said, waving a hand over the display of bowls occupying pride of place in the formal drawing room. 'So very clever, and equally adorable, aren't they?'

Antoinette's lips had tightened imperceptibly.

The next day, the bowls were gone.

Life as Kyle Junior's wife was all about savouring such victories. It was petty of her, Suki knew, but her mother-in-law was equally petty – and Suki liked to win. She wasn't the matriarch, not yet. But watch this space, she seemed to be saying to Antoinette.

And then it had all ended when Antoinette found out. But by then, Suki's daydreams of becoming the next Jackie O had been dust for a long time anyhow.

The fierce animosity between the two women had not diminished with time. Suki and Antoinette still loathed each other, but these days they met so rarely that they could just about manage to put up with each other. Especially with Senior on hand to remind them to keep it civil.

'Nobody needs to know our business – understand, girls?' he'd growl in that gravelly voice that brooked no disagreement.

And the 'girls' had both toed the line.

As Suki approached the front door, she knew that, for today at least, Antoinette would have declared a truce where she was concerned. The Redmond Suarez biography was threatening the family and they needed to join forces to fight off the common enemy. After that, they could resume the old hostilities.

Mrs Lang, the housekeeper, opened the door with a frozen

155

smile on her face: 'Hello, Mrs Suki. Lovely to see you back again.'

'Mrs Suki' was the courtesy title decided upon by Antoinette once the divorce was final. It wasn't quite as bitchy as 'demoting' her to Miz Power, but was another telling detail.

'Hello there, Mrs Lang,' Suki said, marching into the hall, pulling her weekender suitcase behind her. She knew Mrs Lang didn't like her, but she didn't care.

As usual, the house smelled of money and beeswax polish. The antiques – all genuine, Suki was pretty sure because she'd looked – gleamed from constant dusting, while the pictures, all by major American artists, were beautifully lit. Two old leather couches – the sort of thing Ralph Lauren was famous for, but clearly a much earlier vintage than his iconic designs – sat on either side of the huge hall with tapestry cushions scattered upon them, decorated mainly with nautical themes and the American flag.

Suki went straight to her bedroom. She was always assigned the blue bedroom at the back of the house where they were no views of the sea. It was definitely one of the lesser bedrooms. Once you were put in a bedroom in the compound, it was your spot for life. She tidied up, put on a soft pink sweater and went down into the great room.

The lights were set Hyannis-style for November – Antoinette was a penny-pincher who insisted that no bulb could be of a high wattage. Consequently, the house was like an ill-lit restaurant and reading was impossible, except in places like Senior's study or your bedroom, provided you'd had the foresight to smuggle in a decent bulb. It had been many years since she'd stayed there, nothing had changed lighting-wise; fortunately Suki had brought a little battery-powered reading light, just in case. On the other hand, the wine was always good and she expected to imbibe well tonight.

The bad news was that Kyle Senior wasn't home yet. That didn't suit Suki. If there was one person who'd understand what this all meant, it was Senior. He was the one she needed to talk to before dinner. Senior liked his booze and, once dinner started, she'd never get to talk to him alone.

A swish of silk and a hint of Rochas Eau de Parfum in the sea-facing drawing room signalled the arrival of Antoinette Richardson.

'Good evening, Suki,' said Antoinette, a gracious smile fixed on her face. 'How lovely to see you. You do look well.'

Antoinette regally proffered both cheeks for a brief kiss, a habit picked up on travels to Europe. Though she would have preferred to shake hands, Antoinette was nothing if not an elegant hostess and her manners almost never slipped, not even when greeting the woman she considered had come close to ruining the political career of her first-born.

Greetings over, Antoinette withdrew, sat primly on a couch and gestured for Suki to do the same.

'What have you been up to, Suki dear?'

Suki smiled back. Two could play this game. Bloody bitch probably knew exactly what she'd been up to: living in that pokey house, struggling to resurrect her career and make ends meet. If Antoinette was half the matriarch she pretended to be, she should have made damn sure that anyone connected with the Richardson family didn't need to scrape a living by doing appalling lectures in cold college halls.

'This and that,' Suki replied, smiling as if she'd been accepting Pulitzers and heading the UN all the while, instead of worrying about money. 'And how are you, Antoinette? And Kyle Senior – how is he?'

'Fine, really fine. He's away tonight. Junior will be here any minute now though.'

Antoinette's face warmed when she spoke of her son. It always had. Junior brought out both the best and the worst in her.

Mrs Lang came in with the sherry tray. Antoinette disapproved of liquor being kept in any of her rooms, although

Senior insisted on a full bar in his study. So sherry was brought in before family dinners and cocktail trays before dinner parties.

Suki accepted a thimble of sherry with a smile. It was going to be a long night.

Half an hour of excruciating small talk later, Junior rolled up in his Porsche. Hearing the growling engine, Suki wondered if he'd brought his second wife with him. She didn't mind Leesa. She was beautiful in a very WASP-ish way, with a straight nose and a slim, boyish figure, and she was gloriously stupid. She was sweet to everyone, said things like 'I'm not a brain surgeon, folks,' and deferred to Junior like a child to Daddy. That was the only thing that annoyed Suki about Leesa.

Ten minutes later, Junior and his wife appeared, obviously having rushed down because Antoinette didn't like being kept waiting.

'Hello, everyone!' said Leesa excitedly, going over and giving Antoinette a big hug.

To Suki's intense surprise, Antoinette seemed pleased to see her daughter-in-law. There was a definite show of warmth as Leesa embraced her. Now this Suki couldn't figure out. She felt a frisson of irritation: Antoinette was the type of woman who would never approve of any woman her darling son was married to. Suki had always assumed that was why Antoinette had hated her.

And Leesa was precisely the sort of woman she'd have expected Antoinette to look down her patrician nose at. Even though Leesa had all the right connections, came from old money and had no aspirations for herself beyond taking care of Junior, she was entirely brainless and invariably had to be kept away from reporters at fund-raisers in case she said the wrong thing.

Yet Antoinette seemed to like her. Crossly, Suki drained her sherry and wished it was a double vodka tonic.

158

Junior was looking well. He was a tall, well-built man, tanned from lots of outdoor pursuits, and he had the same mane of leonine hair as his father. The difference was that Kyle Senior looked like the wily old lion that he was, while Junior was a slower, duller version. Not that this seemed to have harmed his inexorable rise in the direction of the Republican presidential nomination.

'Good evening, Suki,' he said, giving her a dutiful peck on the cheek. She could feel the frost in the air.

'Hello, Suki,' said Leesa, holding out a hand for Suki to shake, as if she were a duchess.

Suki felt herself getting angrier.

She could have been the wife who'd get Junior into the White House, not this idiot. Instead, she was being made to feel like a total outsider – and it hurt.

As usual, Antoinette didn't beat around the bush but got straight to the subject everyone else would have preferred to avoid.

'We must discuss this wretched book,' she said. 'I've had four telephone calls this week from friends who've been approached by his researchers. They're all saying the same thing: Redmond Suarez wants to hear "the real story" of the Richardsons.'

She paused while Mrs Lang came in with drinks for Leesa and Junior. Suki was outraged to see that they were getting cocktails. Leesa's drink looked suspiciously like a martini. Nobody had offered *her* a martini.

'I think we need someone we can trust to meet him and find out what he knows,' said Leesa.

'Don't be ridiculous!' snapped Suki. 'That's like saying, *We've got something to hide, so tell us what you have found out.*'

Antoinette interrupted. 'I think Leesa has a point,' she said. 'Not one of us, not one of the family. But we need someone who is loyal to us to meet with this Suarez.' She spat the

159

name out. 'Kyle Senior has some ideas on how to do this . . .'
She coughed and took a sip of the water on the small table
beside her.

Leesa got up and sat beside her mother-in-law, patting her
gently on the arm.

'Don't get all worked up, Antoinette, my dear. You know
what the doctors told you, you've got to take care of your
heart.'

'What doctors?' demanded Suki.

Junior looked lazily at her over the top of his highball glass.
'Mother had a minor heart attack last month,' he said.

'You should have told me!' said Suki, shocked.

'I wanted to keep it very private,' Antoinette announced.
'Keep it in the family—'

'I was family once,' Suki said quietly. She stared at her
former mother-in-law and ex-husband. Both of them knew
why she was no longer a part of the family, and she needed
their help to keep Redmond Suarez out of her life too.

Perhaps they needed reminding of the past.

'*Immediate* family,' Junior said coldly.

Suki knew then that she hadn't been imagining the polar
blast she'd felt when he'd said hello. She was truly on the
outside now, it seemed. They'd obviously decided that she
had sunk so far down the totem pole that what she knew
couldn't hurt them.

Well, she'd get him back. He knew what had happened,
he had to know that it hadn't really been her fault. And if
he'd given her a decent divorce settlement, then she wouldn't
need to scrape to make a living. She bet bloody Leesa had
never done a day's work in her life.

'Suki, you mustn't be upset,' soothed Leesa, sensing the
anger raging inside her but misunderstanding the reason.
'Mother didn't want anyone to know, and the easiest way to
keep it quiet was to tell nobody, that's all.'

Suki forced herself to smile. 'How are you now, Antoinette?'

she asked, as politely as she could. 'Was there any damage to your heart?'

That was a joke – Antoinette had a heart of cold, black stone, so how could that be damaged? Suki had a sudden vision of herself leaking the news of Antoinette's heart attack to the papers. She could see the headline now: *Antoinette Richardson Has a Heart – Doctors Astonished.*

Antoinette talked about how awful it had all been and how she was so grateful to Junior and – she smiled up at her doting daughter-in-law – to darling Leesa for being there for her. Jacqueline and Anastasia, Junior's younger sisters, had both been away at a wedding in Europe when it happened, so Antoinette had had to rely upon Leesa for so much.

Jacqueline and Anastasia were always away. Both had married rich men and spent their time trailing round the world on endless holidays with friends. Suki didn't know what they had to take holidays *from*, since neither of them had worked a day in their lives.

When Mrs Lang came back into the room to check on drinks, Suki ordered a martini.

'Make a strong one, Mrs Lang,' she muttered grimly. 'Make it a Kyle Senior Special.'

That was code for double measures of everything. Suki had never asked for such a thing in the Richardsons' house before – that was the prerogative of Kyle Senior – but she didn't feel like playing the dutiful ex-daughter-in-law right now. A martini with a powerful kick was what she needed.

When dinner was ready, the four of them made their way to the dining room and sat in state at the huge dining-room table.

The food was good, but there wasn't enough wine. Suki emptied her glass quickly and had to wait an age before anyone filled it up. They were on to a cheese and fruit course before the subject of the unauthorized biography was raised again.

161

'Father says that nobody –' Kyle stared hard at Suki – 'nobody is to cooperate with this man.'

Suki glared back at him. 'I have no intention of cooperating, and I'm insulted at the implication that I might,' she snapped. 'It's not as if I don't know where all the bodies are buried in this family, but I have never spoken about any of that, to anyone.' She paused purposefully and looked Antoinette straight in the eye. There was a silence and then Antoinette intervened.

'Of course nobody is suggesting that you would do something like that, Suki,' she said. 'Kyle is merely reiterating his father's wishes. Nobody in this room would do anything to upset the family, we know that. But other people, other people don't have the same loyalty. Loyalty is something that is sadly missing today. I've often said that. When I was young, loyalty was one of the most respected virtues, but not today, sadly.'

'My grandpa always says that loyalty is so important,' echoed Leesa virtuously.

'I believe in loyalty,' said Suki, looking from Antoinette to Kyle. 'As long as people are loyal to me in return.'

She'd had enough. She couldn't understand why they'd summoned her, unless it was to intimidate her. She got to her feet. 'You must forgive me, everyone, I am overtired and I think I'll go to bed.'

Unable to endure one more minute with them, she said goodnight and went to her room, where she sat on the bed and tried not to cry.

The Richardsons were so much more powerful than she was. Compared to them, she was a nobody. If the truth came out, they could easily twist it so that she came out the villainess. One way or another, the family would come up smelling of roses, while her name would be mud.

Chapter Eleven

Stanley the estate agent had no gush left. There was, he had learned, no point. People either had the money or they hadn't. And if they hadn't, no amount of gushing and going into raptures over beautiful club fenders, stone fireplaces and plaster mouldings that had once been painted delicately by hand with gold leaf was going to make a difference. No, the sort of person with the money to buy and restore somewhere like Avalon House would not be susceptible to having their head turned by a eulogizing estate agent.

That certainly seemed to be the case where Cashel Reilly was concerned. An alpha male with knobs on, in Stan's estimation. He'd arrived from Dublin in a Maserati Grand: a sleek, dolphin-grey, quite subtle-looking Maserati, but a Maserati nonetheless. Everything he wore, everything about him, reeked of money, power . . . and precisely zero patience with not getting his own way.

'Have you been here before?' said Stan, cautiously, wanting to figure out which way the ground lay. If what he'd heard was true, and Cashel Reilly really had grown up in the area, perhaps he'd lived here at some stage. It wasn't as if there were any other houses in the town that fitted the profile . . . But no, the Powers had lived here. Stanley was a blow-in and didn't know all the families properly. Perhaps Mr Reilly had visited a childhood friend who'd lived here. But looking at Cashel's stony face, Stan decided it would be inadvisable to ask.

'Yes, I've been here before,' said Cashel.

Clearly a man who never used more words than necessary.

'I won't do the spiel then,' said Stan.

'No,' agreed Cashel.

Stan used to love showing these old Irish houses in the days when people actually had money to buy them. It gave him such a buzz, pointing out all the original features to some delirious client with money to burn and an urge to spend it on historically correct plastering and historically correct painting of fiddly ceiling mouldings. They'd thrown money at these houses, *thrown it*. Now, you couldn't shift this type of place for love nor money. Most clients didn't have the wherewithal, and the ones that did weren't about to spend it on some run-down pile without the benefit of central heating or modern plumbing.

Stan took a risk.

'Since you've been here before, do you want to walk around yourself while I wait in the hall?'

He was rewarded with the glimmer of a smile.

'Good plan,' said Cashel. 'I know my way around.'

There wasn't a lot of furniture left in the old house, but Stan found a shabby-looking kitchen chair and pulled it out to the hall, sat down and began to go through his text messages. This Reilly fellow certainly seemed like the sort of bloke who had enough money to buy Avalon House, but whether he would or he wouldn't, who could tell?

Having long since learned that what would be would be, Stan applied himself to his phone:

Yes, love, home for dinner, fish pie would be great, xx Stan

*   *   *

What astonished Cashel most was how different the house felt. As a child, it had been like some magical palace, home to the amazing Power family, Avalon's gentry. Whether they were broke or not was immaterial: they could trace their ancestors back hundreds of years. Most people in Avalon would be lucky if they could go back three generations. The Reilly clan did not have a particularly long or noble family tree. When he was a teenager, that had upset him. Mainly because, by then, he had got to know the Powers and was aware of their long heritage. And felt slightly diminished by it.

Suki and Tess could boast a lineage of noble earls and kings. He and Riach were descended from a man who lived his life in the bookmaker's shop or the pub.

Now, he was proud of his rootlessness. Proud of the lack of rich relatives. Everything he had achieved had been a product of his own hard work. There had been no family money to help him on his way.

Whenever he was invited to give talks to groups of youngsters on how he'd got where he was today, he'd conclude by telling them:

'It's not who you are that matters. It's what you do with who you are. The blood running through your veins is the only blood that matters. When you go out into the world, you have the chance to leave the past behind.'

It was strange how the past seemed so close now as he began his tour of Avalon House.

He started off in the ground-floor drawing room, purely because it was one of the rooms he'd never seen as a child. The left side of the house had always been off limits, according to his mother and Tess. They were the grand rooms, relics of a bygone age when there had been parties and balls up here on the hill. He'd imagined glamorous titled ladies and gentlemen wandering around in evening dress, listening to scratchy gramophones and talking about hunting and estates in the colonies – the way he'd seen people behave at parties in the movies. To a boy whose mother had to clean other people's houses to keep food on the table, it had seemed an alien and mysterious world.

Stalking past Stan the estate agent, sitting engrossed in his phone, he made his way to the kitchen. That was the room he'd always liked best; a big room, built in the days when many people had lived here, gentry and servants. The huge ovens remained, but the hooks from which saucepans and serving cloches had hung were all gone. Sold, he wondered, or stolen?

Being in here brought it all back though, especially seeing that familiar table, so big it was more like a refectory table from a monastery. He ran his hands over it, feeling the wood, willing some electrifying jolt of memory to leap up into his fingers, but there was nothing. After school, he and Tess used to sit here doing their homework while his mother cooked on the big gas stove. She didn't know how to cook the sort of food that Tess's father was used to, so she stuck to the food she knew: peasant food, like bacon and cabbage, barley and lamb shank stew. The food that Cashel had grown up on.

He used to help Tess with her homework. He was five years older and it was fun to help her; she was so sweet, so grateful. Suki, her older sister, never helped in any way. Not that Suki was ever big on homework, even when it was her own. She had made a name for herself in school, a name for being wild, untamed, not caring. She hung around with the most dangerous kids, the ones who had left school and were serving apprenticeships or working with their fathers. She didn't want to be tied to people her own age, oh no. Suki Power had always wanted to be different.

He walked into the big scullery at the back, where the eggs used to be kept in the water glass to keep them fresh. The meat safe was kept there, a big green painted metal cage where piles of meat would sit on the shelves. Every time the dogs came past, they'd put their paws up and whimper and someone would have to slap them down. It was here in the scullery, the least romantic spot in the whole place, that he'd first kissed Tess.

It had been so innocent and unexpected. Because she was younger, he'd never seen her in that way. He'd loved her, but it had been the sort of love you feel for a kid sister; they got on so well, teased each other, laughed, joked.

And then came that summer day.

He'd been away, working in Dublin. When he arrived home, the house was empty, so he'd headed up to the Powers' hoping to find his mother. Instead, he'd found Tess. She'd turned eighteen while he'd been gone. The skinny little kid with the lanky legs, the questioning eyes and the hair tied back in an untidy ponytail had vanished. In her place was a new Tess: taller, with a woman's curves, and the face of a woman, with beautiful rounded lips. His mother had been nowhere to be seen, so he'd stood in the scullery with Tess, feeling strangely dumbstruck in her presence.

She behaved as if nothing had changed between them, chatting happily about leaving school, about her plans to go to college, about how Suki wanted to drop out of college because she was fed up to the tonsils of boring old studies. 'You know,' she said, laughing, 'same old same old. And what about you? What's it like in the big city? Come on, tell all – are there any fabulous girlfriends on the scene? Your mother will be delirious! She wants you to settle down, you know, Cashel. She wants the patter of tiny feet. Have you found your perfect woman up there in the city?'

Cashel remembered how he'd looked at Tess in that moment and thought with utter astonishment that *she* was the woman, how could he have not seen this before? Maybe it was the distance that had made it obvious. She'd grown up, he'd been away: suddenly he'd come back to this new woman.

'No,' he muttered, 'no women.'

'Oh, go on,' she said. 'I don't believe that for a second.'

'No really,' he said. 'What if I was saving myself for someone?'

'Someone in Avalon?' she said. 'Tell me – who? Not Suki, please.'

He'd roared with laughter at that. No, not Suki. It was no secret that Cashel and Suki didn't get on. They squabbled like two fighting cats whenever they were in the same room.

'There might be a girl,' he'd said idly, moving closer to her, wondering if she could see it in his face, in his eyes. He didn't want to shock her, but surely she must feel it too, that electricity in the air?

She'd turned away from him, opening the meat safe to take out a leg of lamb for dinner. It looked heavy. He'd gone to help her, naturally. What else would he do? And their fingers had touched. That was when she felt it too, and she let go of the wrapped meat so that he was left holding it alone. Tess stared at him and said his name, although he couldn't hear her; he just saw her mouth the words as if she'd been saying them into her mirror for years.

Cashel.

And he'd leaned forward and placed a kiss on her forehead because he didn't want to frighten her, after all.

It was crazy to buy a house because of a scullery, but he wasn't buying it because of that. No, Cashel Reilly hadn't become as rich and powerful as he was today by doing things on a whim. Instead, he told himself he wanted to buy the old De Paor house as a declaration, a declaration that said *I wasn't good enough for the daughter of this house nineteen years ago when she rejected me, but now I've returned, and this house that the Powers lost, that has been gone from the family all these years, I can come back and buy it, just like that. With one phone call, I can have the money here.*

That was satisfying. The part of him that understood

feelings and emotions and the dangers of letting revenge live on inside for ever, told him it was a mistake. But some deeper part, the animal part that was still hurt, told him it was the right thing to do.

Stan was busily scrolling through texts. It was a great time to get some work done. Arrange a time for a valuation, sort out who'd show the old Moloney place tomorrow. Property was a nightmare, these days, make no mistake.

'I'll take it,' said Cashel.

Stanley felt his mobile phone fall out of his hands and clatter to the marble floor, where the battery pinged joyously out.

'Right so,' said Stanley, collecting himself and the scattered bits of his phone. *Remain calm at all times* was a good mantra for estate agents. They'd have champagne in the office when the sale went through. It had been years since they'd sold anything this big, years.

'You'll want it all done quickly?' he ventured.

These alpha businessmen types wanted everything done quickly.

'Of course,' said Cashel. 'I want to get the work started as soon as possible.'

Stanley thought of recommending his brother-in-law, master builder and currently unemployed, but thought better of it. He'd wait until the ink was dry first, then see about mentioning Freddie.

Less than a mile away, Kitty was doing her homework at the kitchen table, writing out her sums with the lead pressed so deeply into the paper that yet another pencil was in danger of breaking off. The pages underneath were all similarly engraved with sums from previous copybook pages. During homework time, Tess spent many moments wielding the pencil sharpener.

'How are you doing, love?' she asked, bending over her

daughter to see how she was doing with her multiplication. Maths had never been Tess's strong point, so she had to mentally run through each sum, using her fingers as an abacus, to see if her daughter was right.

'Super. You're nearly finished,' she said.

Kitty made a 'yeuch' noise in reply.

'I hate sums,' she grumbled.

Tess had spent enough hours at parents' events in the school, listening to the latest educational theories, to know that between the ages of eight and nine was when children decided what they 'loved' or 'hated', often based on the most random things.

She went straight into the recommended spiel: 'But you're so good at sums, Kitty,' she said brightly. 'Look at the lovely report you got last summer.'

Not entirely convinced, Kitty went back to indenting her pencil on to her copybook. 'When's Dad coming? He hasn't been for dinner for ages. Why not? Are you fighting? What is for dinner – I'm starving.'

'Your dad's been busy, Kitty,' Tess lied, wishing she had her own pencil to stick into something. She'd left Kevin two voicemail messages telling him he had to figure out what to tell the children, and he hadn't replied. 'We'll see when he can come over, shall we?'

'But we haven't seen him in ages,' Kitty went on. 'He didn't bring me home from Granny's once this week.'

Tess had been grateful for that. It would have been too much to find Kevin sitting in her home mere days after he'd told her he was in love with another woman. But presumably this was all part of his avoidance-of-anything-difficult plan.

Clearly, Kitty knew something was wrong. Tess was pretty sure that Zach sensed it too, even if he hadn't said anything. She would have to talk to Kevin and get him to agree to tell their children. Left to his own devices, Kevin would just carry on saying nothing.

And wait for her to do it.

'I'll phone Dad now, then,' Kitty decided.

Tess sat helplessly at the table.

Kitty was back in two minutes, the portable in her hands: 'Dad wants to talk to you,' she said. 'He's taking us out to dinner on Friday, to Mario's!'

Mario's was a pizza restaurant, and Kitty's favourite for the chocolate fudge desserts.

'Great,' said Tess. Perhaps he was planning to do it then.

'Tess, help me out on this,' he pleaded, the moment she got on the phone. 'I'm not sure how to begin,' he said sadly. 'I don't want them to hate me, and I don't want to hurt them.'

Tess flattened down all thoughts of saying 'It's a bit late for that now.' She was culpable too, she knew. But despite that, it was a bit rich for him to want *her* to tell Zach and Kitty about Claire so that they could all be happy families together.

'How about Friday night?' she said pleasantly.

'We should do it together,' he insisted.

Tess hesitated. Perhaps that would be best. A united front might help Zach and Kitty understand that, even if parents split up, they were together for their children. 'Fine,' she said. 'But you're paying.'

She might have gone to bed that night and actually slept, if Helen, Kevin's mother, hadn't phoned right after Kitty had been put to bed.

'Tess, I had no idea,' she said, her voice catching. 'I had no idea, honestly. It's all such a shock.'

'I know,' Tess soothed, wondering why she was the one doing the soothing.

'I thought you were mad to separate in the first place,' Helen sobbed. 'Now look what's happened: he's got this new woman. Oh, Tess, it's not right – not right for you, Kitty or Zach. Look at what all this separation nonsense has done!'

'We both agreed to the separation, Helen, so it's not all Kevin's fault,' Tess said, trying to say something comforting because she knew that Helen adored her and the children.

'Yes, but you separated to fix things,' wailed Helen, 'not to find new people.'

Since this was largely what Tess herself thought, she hadn't the heart to argue with her mother-in-law.

For the next ten minutes, Helen cried over the phone while Tess tried to find a way to end the call.

'She's only a young girl, you know,' Helen sniffled. 'I don't know what's got into him. Would you take him back, Tess, if it ended with this girl?'

Tess breathed out slowly. 'Helen, love, it's gone beyond that,' she said, wondering if it really had gone beyond that. Could she take Kevin back if he asked?

Her mind flickered, as it so often had of late, to Cashel.

That had been real love and real passion, she realized now. A tornado of emotion compared to what she'd felt for Kevin. If she took Kevin back, it would be agreeing to a life of gentle, kind benevolence with him, the two of them returning to sharing a home but leading separate lives in so many ways.

Seeing Cashel at his mother's funeral had made her remember the fierceness of her love for him. If only he hadn't abandoned her, things might have been so different.

'But now everyone knows,' Helen went on. 'I've never even set eyes on her, but when Agnes Ryan phoned me to say she'd seen my Kevin kissing this girl on the street outside the café, I was so shocked that I rang him straight up and asked him. That was the first I knew of it.'

Tess simmered. So much for the not-upsetting-you-by-bringing-Claire-out-on-the-streets-of-Avalon schtick.

'Oh well, it's out in the open now,' Tess said. 'Helen, pet, I have things to do, perhaps we can talk tomorrow?' *You might need to bail me out of jail for murdering your son for*

172

not telling his own children when other people have seen him snogging this woman in the town square.

She'd have to tell Zach now. News like that would be all around Avalon at the speed of light. Someone on Zach's bus in the morning would be bound to have heard. He ought to know the facts himself.

Wearily, she went upstairs and knocked on Zach's door. 'Can I come in?' she whispered.

As usual, a moment passed before he got up and opened the door. Tess wasn't sure exactly what he was doing in there, but whatever it was required privacy, and it was her job to give it to him. The room smelled of socks, teenage boy and the new deodorant that he was spraying like there was no tomorrow.

'Sure,' he said.

He was dressed in an old faded sweatshirt and jeans. They both sat down on the bed and Tess was silent for a moment, wondering how the hell she was going to broach the subject.

'What's up, Ma?' he said. 'You look like somebody's died.'

'No! Don't be silly,' she said, going into mummy mode.

Mummy mode meant that if the sky was falling in, Mummy would say, '*No, it'll be fine. We'll sort it out. There's bound to be a solution somewhere.*'

'When your dad came over the other night, he had something important to talk about.'

A wary look stole over Zach's face. 'He wants to get divorced?' he said.

'Well, not exactly. Why did you think that?'

'He's been different the past month . . . happier,' Zach said. 'Before, he used to keep saying how much he missed being at home, and I felt angry at you for the whole thing. But then, he was really happy. I figured it out. He's seeing someone else.'

Wish you'd told me, Tess thought. *Then I wouldn't have been the last to know.*

173

'You're very intuitive,' she said, patting his arm and repressing the desire to lie on his bed and cry. 'I suppose there's always the risk that this could happen when two people split up . . .'

'But you weren't supposed to split up. You didn't need to split up,' Zach said. 'That was your idea. I heard you talking about it.'

He sounded angry now and Tess felt the weight of guilt upon her.

'I thought it was the right thing to do,' Tess said.

'Not for us, it wasn't,' Zach said accusingly. 'Not for me and Kitty. We were a family, *before*. Now we're not.'

'I'm sorry.'

'Whatever,' he muttered.

Tess tried to put her arm around him, but he shrugged it off.

'Do you want to meet her?' she asked.

'No,' he snapped. He put his headphones into his ears, which was teenager-speak for 'conversation over'. Normally that would have been Tess's cue to deliver a mild lecture on rudeness. Tonight, she let him be.

They sat together on the bed for a few moments, Zach with his eyes closed, then Tess got up and left the room, closing the door quietly.

He was right: it was her fault.

Chapter Twelve

It had been nearly two decades since Danae had lived with anybody; two decades of being on her own in her cottage in Avalon with her animals and her beautiful garden for company. She didn't realize how much she'd grown used to this until Mara came to stay.

At first, it had been novel to have Mara around the place with her vitality and her energy. Mara was forever cheery. Even being dumped by the man she'd loved hadn't dimmed her light. Danae was astonished at this and wondered if perhaps Mara secretly cried in her room at night, sobbing over pictures of Jack. Danae suspected that, in Mara's place, that's what she would have done. She would have felt so devastated to be rejected by a man who'd been so important.

But if Mara was feeling utterly broken-hearted, she wasn't showing it. No, there was this amazing strength inside her niece; it must be something to do with being brought up in such a happy family, Danae decided.

After a while, however, Mara's presence began to – well, Danae decided, there was no other word for it: to *irritate* her.

Mara was so cheerful all the time and so at home, sharing the place. Not that she took advantage – no, not for a second. She did all the housework, every chore, cooked meals.

'Well,' said Mara, 'I'm not out working and you are, so it's only fair.'

She bought the groceries out of what must have been a dwindling supply of money and Danae fretted over this. Danae had fretted over money her whole life.

'No, it's fine really, Danae,' Mara said. 'I'm a good saver, you know. I'd money in the bank, plus I've been sending my CV off all over the place looking for work, although not many people are employing former estate agents these days.'

Even this didn't seem to dim Mara's enthusiasm. 'I was thinking of looking around here for work. Do you know of anyone who might need someone to help? Part-time, to dip my toe back in the water. It's a good time of year to get part-time work, people tend to need more staff in the build-up to Christmas, so I might be able to get a bit of shop work or something. I'll do anything, I don't mind: sweep floors, scrub, iron – you name it.'

Danae had laughed. 'You're brilliant,' she said. 'Nobody can say you don't know how to work.'

'Oh, I know how to work, all right,' Mara said. 'I was fabulous at my job.' She turned quiet and reflective for a moment. 'Cici told me I was mad to leave, but I couldn't go on working there. It felt wrong. It was the principle of the thing. And . . . and then I couldn't look for money from them for some sort of constructive dismissal case. No, that's not my way. Jack marrying Tawhnee was a sign, that's all. I had to move out.'

'A sign?' asked Danae, interested.

'Oh yes,' said Mara. 'I'm a great believer in signs, aren't you? It's like . . . I dunno. A parking space is a sign, right? Someone's terribly friendly to you in a shop – that's a sign, isn't it? There are lots of signs of happiness and good things out there, you have to be on the alert for them.'

And that was probably one of the big differences between the two of them, Danae thought to herself. Mara was exuberant, full of life, brimming with a gentle confidence. She was warm to everyone; warm in a way Danae was afraid she never could be.

There were several things about having Mara staying with her, Danae reflected, that made it hard. One was the simple physicality of having another human being about the house, even if that human being was a wonderful, loving, kind, thoughtful guest, like Mara. Another difficulty was the sheer contrast between them. Mara could walk into a room where she knew nobody and ten minutes later she would have made firm friends with at least half the people there. Danae, walking into the same room, would watch carefully from the sidelines. That was what she did: watch carefully. That was what she'd done for a long time. It was probably too late to change now.

But the biggest problem to do with Mara's presence had nothing to do with their different personalities or getting used to sharing a house with her – it was the matter of how to keep Mara from finding out about her monthly trips to Dublin.

'You're up early,' said Danae in surprise as Mara emerged from her bedroom in her pyjamas, hair tousled. She had counted on Mara still being asleep when she set off.

'Yes,' said Mara, 'it must be the country air. In Galway I could sleep for hours at the weekend, but here it's different.' She yawned, 'Cici would laugh if she saw me up at . . .' she looked at her watch, '. . . half seven on a Saturday morning. Where are you off to at this hour?'

Was it her imagination, Mara wondered, or did Danae really look a little furtive this morning? There was definitely something different about her. On days when she wasn't going to the post office, Danae's uniform seemed to consist of a comfortable skirt and a sweater, possibly accessorized by a scarf or a long flowing cardigan. Today she was much more formally dressed, in neatly pressed trousers, a blouse and jacket.

'I have a few errands to do in . . . erm . . . Arklow,' Danae said, looking flustered and uncomfortable.

No, Mara hadn't imagined it, there was something going on. Her imaginative mind ran over the possibilities: Danae was sick and she was going to an appointment with the hospital . . . No, that was crazy – what hospital or consultant had appointments on a Saturday? Honestly, she was being paranoid.

'OK,' said Mara. 'What time will you be back? Do you want me to do anything?'

Again Danae looked furtive. 'I was writing you a note, asking if you'd mind throwing a bit of feed to the hens at about five? Round them up before it gets dark and lock them in. I'll probably be back by . . . by dinner time.'

Mysteriouser and mysteriouser.

Mara nodded. 'No problem,' she said. If Danae had secrets, that was fine by her.

Ten minutes later Danae set off in the car, leaving Mara sitting at the kitchen table with Lady staring up at her, those hypnotic, wolf eyes watching adoringly. Mara loved Lady, she was such a beautiful dog, so affectionate, content to sit beside Mara and Danae and occasionally put a questing nose up for a little pet, as she did now. And as Mara sipped her coffee, she wondered what her aunt was up to, what she had to hide. And then she told herself to mind her own business; everyone was entitled to their secrets.

Danae felt rattled as she took the Dublin road out of Avalon. She hated lying, it had always felt wrong to her. Up to now, she'd managed without ever having to lie; she just didn't tell people things, and that worked. But Mara was changing all that, Mara was making it harder. Living with another person was tricky. That was the word, Danae decided.

Now that Mara was living with her, Danae felt she owed her niece some explanation. But she couldn't, she couldn't talk about it, it still hurt too much. No, it was easier to keep it to herself. Mara would leave soon enough. She'd been talking about going to London some time, and then Danae would be there alone again. Why go through all that pain unnecessarily? No, no, she would be better off keeping quiet till then.

Of course the other problem was that Mara was so very sociable and she was determined that Danae would be sociable too. In the few short weeks that Mara had been living there, Danae had been out five times to the cinema with Mara and Belle.

'Belle – she's your best friend, isn't she?' Mara had enquired within a day or two of her arrival. Danae had been shocked. How had Mara noticed? Not that Danae had such a thing as a best friend really, but if she did, Belle was it.

'Well, I suppose she is,' said Danae, trying to appear normal.

'OK, there's a great film on in Arklow, what do you think, will we book it for Friday night? Maybe have something to eat beforehand – pizza, Chinese? What do you think?' Mara had said, making it all sound so terribly normal.

Belle had been delighted. 'I don't know how you managed to get Madam here out of the house twice in one month,' she'd said as she sat in the front of the car while Mara drove them into Arklow.

Mara giggled. She'd told Danae that she thought Belle was a riot, but she wouldn't want to get on the wrong side of her. Belle looked tough.

'Now, tell us, have you taken a vow of chastity since this desperate Jack fellow left you?'

Mara didn't seem to mind Belle talking about Jack. Perhaps because Belle would probably knee Jack in the groin if she so much as set eyes on him.

'No, but there's a lot to be said for a vow of chastity,' Mara pointed out. 'I mean, with chastity you never have anything to do with men, which in my current state of mind sounds like a very sensible plan altogether.'

179

'Ah no, men are great as long as you can give them back to their mummies afterwards,' said Belle, with a riotous laugh. 'I'm only kidding, Mara,' she added. 'I don't care for the ones under forty: they know nothing. They are unformed under forty. Aren't they, Danae?'

Sitting in the back of the car, squashed because there was no room for her legs, Danae nodded, as if she knew.

'Totally, yes, I agree,' she said.

Then, there'd been the impromptu night out that came about after Mara had gone into the café and met up with mad Vivienne from the clothes shop. Apparently Vivienne had said Tess Power needed a good night out because she was wasting away in the house watching the television in misery and somehow that had resulted in Belle, Mara, Danae, Vivienne and Tess ending up in the town's Italian restaurant laughing, giggling, talking until one o'clock in the morning.

Jacinta Morelli and her sister, Concepta, had sat down beside them at closing time and joined in the chat, bringing over coffees and plates of delicious biscotti. Danae couldn't quite remember how long it was since she'd been out past midnight. It felt odd to meet people like Tess and Vivienne socially. She'd been so stiff at first, she felt like the postmistress behind her plexiglass. Without the safety of that dividing screen there was a sense of being vulnerable, laid bare to their gaze. Not that anyone else appeared to feel that way or even notice. But it had been difficult for Danae.

From the beginning, Tess and Mara had got on like a house on fire. 'So you're not wasting away or withering away up there on your own watching television,' Mara had said, tipsy on three glasses of wine.

Tess had laughed so much she nearly cried. 'Is that what she said to you? Vivienne, you've got to stop telling people that I am wasting my life, just because Kevin has a lovely girlfriend.'

'Whom he met when you were having a trial separation,' Vivienne said loudly.

'Say it more loudly,' Tess said, 'I don't think the diners at the far end of the restaurant heard! I'll get you a megaphone next time.'

And Danae had put a hand on Tess's arm and squeezed it, because even if Tess was able to joke about it, she knew it must hurt unbearably still. Tess had looked at her gratefully as if to say, *Yes, I can joke about it but there's a lot of pain in there nonetheless*. Danae, who knew a lot about pain, had smiled back warmly in return.

Danae joined the motorway that would take her to Dublin. There was so much different about her life now that Mara shared it. It was so much fuller, so much more fun. It made her realize what she had been missing and the loneliness that she'd go back to, once Mara was gone. But it was easier not to tell her, easier to tell nobody.

'It's strange, Mum,' said Mara on the phone to her mother one evening. Danae was off on her solitary walk with Lady, climbing the hills, something she did come rain or shine, never mind that it was pitch dark this time of year. 'I love her, and I know she loves me, but she's not that comfortable around people, and I never noticed that before. I suppose in the past I'd never stayed here for longer than a weekend. Now, having been here for a while, I see how reserved she is. If ever I offer to do something nice for her, like doing her hair – you know how good I am with hair – she can't accept it. It's as if she doesn't like people helping her. And then she went off last Saturday and she wouldn't tell me where she was going. It was very strange.'

On the other end of the phone there was silence.

'Mum, are you there?'

'Yes, I'm here,' said Elsie. 'Mara, you know things have been difficult for your Aunt Danae.'

'You see, that's it,' explained Mara. 'I know there was some terrible thing in the past with her husband when he died and everything, but I never really knew what it was because you didn't tell us. Whatever happened to her then, it's like she's closed off. I mean, what did happen, Mum?'

There was another silence, which was in itself very unusual because Elsie was not a woman given to great silences, as the rest of her family would testify.

'Mara, that's not my story to tell,' said Elsie. 'It's up to Danae to tell you that, and she's a very private woman. She'd be terribly upset if you brought it up, to be honest.'

'But what if his anniversary happens while I'm here and I don't say anything and she'll think I'm being horrible and ignoring it? I mean, if I had been married and my husband had died, I'd want people to remember it. Go on, you've got to tell me what this is all about.'

Elsie clammed up. 'Pet, I can't go into it, that's all I'm saying.'

'And how am I supposed to ask her about it then?' Mara demanded. '*What would you like for your dinner, Danae? We could have spaghetti Bolognese or perhaps some of that lovely vegetarian quiche I made yesterday, and oh, by the way, will you tell me all about your husband?*'

'For heaven's sake, Mara, you're a terrible child,' Elsie groaned. 'Look, I'm no good with this sort of thing. Ask your father. And tell me, what's the story about Christmas? Are you coming to us?' There was a faint hint of pleading in her mother's voice.

'Well, I'm sure *I* am,' said Mara. 'And I'll try to get Danae to come this time.'

Danae had never come before, despite the offer always being there.

'But it would help if I knew . . .'

'Leave Danae be. If she doesn't want to come, she won't come,' said Elsie quickly. 'As long as she knows the invitation is always there.'

'I'll definitely try and get her to come this year,' said Mara. 'Leave it with me.'

There was no more to be got out of her mother on the subject. By the time she put the phone down, Mara had heard all the latest happenings on Furlong Hill, how the O'Briens opposite had got bay trees exactly like Elsie's and how violently annoyed she was with them.

'They copied us on the stone cladding and now the bay trees too! Well, that's taking it too far,' said Elsie, ominously.

Mara grinned. Her mother's life-long battle with Mrs O'Brien across the road always made her smile. But when the call was over, Mara went back to thinking about Danae.

Rafe Berlin sat in the window of the café on the corner of Avalon's main square and watched the girl with the green felt hat get out of her car. She was wearing weird clothes, he reckoned: a crazy red skirt with embroidery, alpine boots, a green coat cinched in tight around her waist and that hat. It was like a pancake stuck on her head. But the face made up for the mad outfit. Like a naughty angel with her dark red fringe in her eyes, amazing big eyes with lots of dark eye stuff smudged around them, making them shine out like jewels in that freckled face.

And now she was stomping over to the café.

Clearly plugged into her own personal music, she shimmied over, hips and shoulders moving to a beat he couldn't hear. She didn't care if she was half dancing as she walked. Rafe grinned. Cool chick, oblivious to what anyone else thought: exactly the sort of girl he liked.

She marched in and went up to the counter.

Deciding he needed a refill, Rafe downed his coffee and followed her.

She even smelled good, he decided as he stood behind her: something cinnamon? Did they make perfume with cinnamon in it? She was a small girl, and he liked that too, not being overly tall himself. He liked everything about her.

'Hi,' he said.

She whirled around, stared up, and he got a blast of those eyes. Viridian green, he decided, and flashing with anger.

The angry eyes said: *Don't talk to me, stranger.*

She turned away with a flick of the dark red curls and gave the cakes on the counter further consideration.

Rafe was wildly entertained. He *loved* this. He hadn't met a girl this sassy since he'd left New Zealand.

'I said hi,' he said.

The curls jiggled and she stared at him again. The green eyes raked him and she ignored him again.

'Nice day,' he went on.

This time, she turned round slowly.

'Honey,' she said, the glare ongoing, the eyes staring up at him, 'I am Not. In. The. Mood. OK? Capisce?' Her gaze swept over him again, taking in the worn work jumper and the stockman's overalls. 'Whatever "no" is in your language, cowboy.'

'Vulcan,' he murmured.

'What?'

'Vulcan, that's my language.'

The eyes narrowed. 'Like Dr Spock?'

'No, Mr Spock. "Live long and conquer" sort of thing,' he said. 'Dr Spock gave baby advice.'

'If it's advice you're after, I've got some for you: leave me alone,' she said with a smile that could strip paint from a door.

'Yes, miss, can I help you?' said the guy behind the counter, carefully ignoring the atmosphere.

'Large take-away cappuccino with an extra shot of espresso, please,' she said politely.

Rafe approved even more. None of this 'skinny cappuccino' rubbish.

'Are you a tourist?' he asked. He had never seen her before, he was sure of that.

'No,' she said, 'I'm an outreach worker with a care in the community centre and we're rounding up all the local weirdos with a particular emphasis on ones who chat up women in cafés.'

'Would you need handcuffs for that?' Rafe said conversationally.

The freckled girl didn't bat an eyelid. 'I'm packing heat,' she said, patting her hip as if a gun nestled under her coat. 'And if that doesn't work, I've got a staple gun in my handbag. Few men are immune to the staple gun.

'Ouch.'

'You bet.'

She whirled back again and paid for her coffee, purposefully ignoring Rafe.

'Isn't she something else, Brian,' sighed Rafe, watching her shimmy over to the door, coffee in one hand. 'I could eat her all up.'

'It would be like eating a piranha,' said Brian, who'd never had any luck with women.

'Ah, Brian, she *said* no. Inside, she was interested, I can tell.'

'Don't know how you can tell,' said Brian. 'I've never had a clue what women are saying. It's all in code.'

Mara stomped out with her coffee in her hand, irritated by the man in the café. She was fed up with the male of the species: always on the hunt, even if it was only for fun. Pity Cici wasn't here though, he was precisely *her* type: all scratchy designer stubble, messy hair and, if that cow-minding outfit was anything to go by, not the sort of man who'd worry about his clothes too much. Jack had been a regular fashion hound, keen to have the hottest jeans, the *now* watch. The guy in the café probably chose his clothes of a morning by sniffing things from the laundry basket to see what would do. Still . . .

She angled her head as she got into the car to see if he was watching her. He was. He was something, there was no doubt about it. Probably had the local girls eating out of his hand with his flirty remarks. Not her. She'd had it up to her teeth with men.

She gave him one last filthy look.

I am not interested, she said telepathically. *The next man who gets close to me will end up with terminal injuries. OK?*

She turned on the ignition, let the talking book she'd got from the library switch on, and headed for Dublin.

Mara's home was a two up two down in a quiet Dublin city street. The end of Furlong Hill where the Wilsons lived was home to families who'd lived there for donkey's years, while the other end was lined with shops, bars, and the chip shop Mara had adored when she was a youngster. Even now, she judged fish and chips by the standards of Rizzoli's and the velvety taste of Mrs Rizzoli's battered onions. Nobody else could compete. And curry sauce for the chips. It was funny how many of her early dates had taken place in Rizzoli's. The lads in her secondary school hadn't been too adventurous when it came to dating. It was either the pub – difficult to get into when they were under-age – or Rizzoli's, where you could sit at a table nursing a Fanta and sharing a single plate of chips and sausages for hours on end and Mrs Rizzoli wouldn't throw you out. She'd understood young love.

Mara felt the pangs of hunger as she drove past Rizzoli's. Listening to Becky Sharpe's adventures in *Vanity Fair* had taken her mind off both Jack and the fact that she'd only had a coffee and that bun for breakfast. For a second she thought of the man she'd met in the coffee shop. He *had* been cute, she had to admit, but she was off men.

Mara parked outside her family home, switched off *Vanity Fair* and smiled, as she always did, at the stone cladding her parents had scrimped and saved for months to install on the front of the house. It was pale grey and 'classy', as Mara's mother like to say. Not like the O'Brien's cladding, which was a yellow colour and entirely unsuited to Furlong Hill in Elsie Wilson's opinion.

'They're copying us,' Elsie had been saying for years.

Mara's dad simply patted her arm and said, 'Ah, now, Elsie, imitation is the sincerest form of flattery. You have great taste, that's all. God love the O'Briens. What would they do if they didn't have you to look up to?'

Mara's mother had never been entirely convinced by this line of thought. The latest addition to the Wilson frontispiece were a couple of bay trees in pots. Elsie had got her husband to nail down the pots, just to be on the safe side. Then she had watched through narrowed eyes as the O'Briens suddenly decided that bay trees were the fashion.

Grabbing her handbag, Mara wriggled out of the car.

Number 71 was as gloriously unchanged and comforting as ever. The moment you were inside the door, there was the aroma of something cooking. In the hall was a pretty arrangement of crimson winter roses on the small hall table that Elsie had carefully covered with decoupage many years before. Mara knew her mother would have got the roses cheap from a flower seller in town at the end of the day, but she'd arranged them beautifully with bits of greenery from her own garden. Not having any money had never stood in the way of Elsie making their home beautiful. For a second, Mara wanted to cry. Standing here in her childhood home, the pain of Jack's defection and wedding hit her anew.

Home was where you came to cry.

Mara had never told her parents that she and Jack were going to be married. But she'd been so sure that they would end up together, and that sureness had seeped into every conversation she'd had with her parents over the past year or so.

Jack had been to 71 Furlong Hill to meet her parents and

little brother. They'd even slept together in Mara's old bedroom – an unprecedented event in the Wilson household. It was immaterial that Mara was thirty-three and her boyfriend was thirty-eight. No, it was the principle of it having a single daughter sleep with her boyfriend under the Wilson family roof.

Elsie went to daily Mass and liked to say the rosary once a week. She never pushed religion upon her family, but they all understood Elsie's devotion to the Virgin Mary. Letting Jack stay over had been a huge concession on her part.

And now Mara was back home, boyfriendless, having slept with said man and with her heart broken to boot. Great result, thought Mara. She was glad she'd decided to go to Avalon for a while before coming home: she'd have burst into floods of tears if she'd come here first. Here, Jack's defection felt worse than ever.

She could hear the hum of the television from the sitting room. When Jack had been there, she'd seen the disapproval in his eyes at the amount of time her family spent in front of the box. Meals were often eaten on trays on their laps while watching the soaps. The Wilsons didn't go to the theatre or frequent art galleries. They didn't do any of the things that Jack's family did.

He'd said nothing, except that her father was 'salt of the earth'.

Mara had once been to his family home in Galway – modern, detached, with a lawn cut by a smiling man from Slovakia – where there was always someone round for dinner, where the walls were lined with books and where someone would play on the piano after dinner or else a conversation would start up about a show they'd all seen, a book tipped to win the Booker, a new play.

'Nobody can ever better the genius of Synge's *Playboy of the Western World*,' Jack's mother might say when she'd had her single martini with an olive in it.

188

A martini. Mara had stared open-mouthed the first time she saw the martini jug and the way everyone had just the one. Her father liked a glass of Guinness of an evening, but he'd never have it at home. He'd have it in Fagan's down the road, where he went with his pals to talk about the racing or the state of the country and how it had all been different in their day.

Her mother didn't drink, having taken the pledge when she was twelve. She was proud of her Pioneer pin: a sign of abstinence.

Mara was sorry she hadn't taken a pledge and got herself a Man Abstinence pin.

'I saw enough of what drink does to people,' was all Elsie would say. But she didn't mind Mara opening a bottle of wine for Jack when he was there, and never said a word about the new wine glasses coming into the Wilson home. They were bigger and more delicate than the ones Elsie kept in the good china cupboard, which were exactly like the ones they had for events in the bingo hall, where Elsie might have an orange juice.

With shame, Mara remembered feeling that her family were somehow inadequate beside Jack's. No martinis before dinner, no talk of books and plays, no proper wine glasses.

How stupid and disloyal she'd been. Her family were wonderful, while Jack had turned out to be a complete fake.

She pushed open the sitting-room door.

'Mara, my love!' Her mother got to her feet and in a second, Mara was in the familiar and comforting embrace.

Elsie smelled of Blue Grass perfume, the only scent she'd ever worn. 'I like it. Why would I want anything else?' she always said.

'I sat down to watch Dr Phil and he was talking about family – how's that for coincidence?'

'Oh, Mum,' said Mara tremulously. 'It's lovely to be home.'

*   *   *

That evening, there were many conversations about Jack, Tawhnee and what had gone wrong. Opinion was mixed in the Wilson household about whether Jack was a cheating, conniving pig (Mara's father), or an innocent man hijacked by a sultry beauty (Mara's mother). Mara found herself trying to keep the peace between the two warring factions. She abandoned the effort when her brother Stephen mentioned that he'd met Tawhnee on a trip to Galway, where he'd joined Mara's work crowd in the pub. He thought she was 'hot'.

'How can you say she's hot?' demanded Mara, vexed. 'She ruined my life!'

Avalon had dulled the pain for her: here, it was as fresh as ever.

'Exactly my point,' said Elsie, who was bending over the oven, checking on her scones. Nothing like a bit of home baking to mend pain.

'Don't go letting Jack off the hook, now,' insisted Mara's father. 'He was the one who took our beautiful daughter and ruined her.'

'He didn't exactly ruin me, Dad,' said Mara, getting anxious. 'Ruin' sounded like a throwback to the days when evil men had their way with young women and then left them in the lurch. After which no decent man would have anything to do with them.

Maybe it had been a mistake to tell them everything. But how could she have kept it from them?

'I never liked him,' said Stephen from his position on the floor, where he was getting mud out of his football boots.

'You never said a word to me!' said Mara.

'He didn't like to, I'm sure,' said her father grimly, shooting Stephen a fierce glare.

It appeared that after Jack's visit to Dublin, the Wilson household had done nothing but speculate as to when Jack would ask Mara to marry him.

'Well, she *is* hot, you can't deny that, Mara,' said Stephen, head still bent over his boots, oblivious to the dark looks from his parents.

Mara could tell from the tone of his voice that he was visualizing Tawhnee. She'd seen this happen to many other men, many other times. Jack included. Why was it that tall, slim women with enormous breasts had this effect on men? Was the male of the species really so easily distracted with physical things?

'Does she have any sisters . . . ?' asked Stephen.

'Oh God,' muttered Mara crossly. He was only twenty-three, after all. Twenty-three-year-olds did not necessarily think with their brains. They weren't always loyal, either.

'Sorry, sorry,' said Stephen, recovering. 'I wasn't thinking. Really sorry, Mara.'

'Oh, it's all right, Stephen,' Mara sighed. 'You're not alone: I don't think there was a single man in Kearney Property Partners who didn't lust after her. In the beginning, Cici said I wasn't being fair because she was so beautiful. Cici reckons beautiful women have it really tough because all other women suspect them of stealing their men.'

'That Cici is a bright girl,' said Elsie firmly. 'She knew which she was talking about, that's for sure, certainly when it came to that bitch.'

The other three members of the family gasped in shock: Elsie Wilson did not swear or utter vulgarities of any kind, so for her to come out with such an expression was highly unusual.

'Ah, Mum,' said Mara, conscious that the pain she felt on her behalf had poor Elsie in a muddle. 'There's no need to be upset. Cici wasn't defending Tawhnee, she said all that before Jack ran off with her. Plus, he probably wasn't the man for me anyway.'

'He certainly didn't deserve you,' declared her father with thinly veiled anger.

'I know,' said Mara soothingly, and she realized that instead of her family consoling her, she was trying to console them. That was the way it had always been in the Wilson family: wound one of them and you wounded them all.

By bedtime that night, Mara decided she needed to get away early next morning or she'd go mad. All evening her father had alternated between treating her with kid gloves and telling her men were like fish in the sea.

'Or buses,' said her father. 'Always another one along soon.'

Mara thought of the number 45, which came up their road. It had been notoriously unreliable ever since she could remember. If men were like the number 45, she was in big trouble.

'Dad,' began Mara, desperate to change the subject, 'I wanted to ask you something. It's about Danae . . .'

Seeing the look that passed between her parents, Mara could tell she wasn't going to get any more from him than she had from her mother.

'Do you have five minutes?' Danae asked Belle on the phone the following morning. 'I need to see you.'

'Absolutely,' said Belle, with the confidence of a woman who knew that minions would do her bidding in her absence. 'I'll drop over, will I?'

'No, not here,' said Danae.

'Are you all right?' asked Belle suspiciously.

'I'm fine, but I need to talk to you.'

'You sound rattled,' said Belle, her suspicions growing. 'Are you sure something's not wrong?'

'No,' said Danae.

'Oh, right,' said Belle. 'Something *is* wrong, but you're not going to tell me over the phone. Fine, when can you come over?'

'I was thinking of shutting the post office now,' said Danae.

'Jesus, Mary and Joseph and all the saints!' said Belle in alarm. 'It must be something very serious. We'll go into a corner of the coffee shop – no, better yet, the bar. I'll have a big pot of green tea ready. No one will disturb us in there.'

'Actually, I think I might have a strong coffee,' said Danae.

'Jesus, Mary and Joseph!' Belle said again. 'I've never seen you drink coffee in your life.'

'Today is one of those days.'

Danae felt nothing like her normal self. She hurriedly shut the post office. It was half ten in the morning, hours away from her normal half-hour lunch break. She didn't think she'd ever done anything like this in all the years she'd been post-mistress; not even that time when she had the terrible flu and had to keep rushing in the back to go to the bathroom. No, nothing stopped her doing her duty. But today, she simply couldn't cope. Not after the phone call from Morris.

She'd had an inkling of what Mara was up to when she'd casually said, 'I'm going to set off for Dublin today, drop in and see Mum and Dad, stay overnight. I feel a bit guilty, you know, 'cos I did come straight to you from Galway, and you know my mam, she worries, she needs to see me.'

'Of course,' Danae had said, thinking this was a great idea and what a lovely girl Mara was, always thinking of others, so kind and generous and always happy.

Plus it would be nice to have a night on her own again.

And then this morning Morris had phoned. Even before he said anything, she'd had the strangest prickling of anxiety that something wasn't quite right. Morris almost never rang on the private line in the post office.

'Hello, love,' he said.

'Hello, Morris,' she'd replied. 'Why do I feel this isn't just a social call?'

'Oh, well, it's not,' he said. 'Mara's here, as you know, and she's been asking questions about you. Nothing horrible – you know she loves you, worships the very ground you walk on, Danae – but she knows there's something not quite right and she wants me to tell her.'

Danae closed her eyes and leaned against the wall for strength, because otherwise she might have sunk on to the carpet in the back office. 'Oh, Morris, I suppose she has to know, but I wish she didn't, I wish nobody ever had to know.'

'You did nothing wrong,' Morris said. 'You did the only thing you could, Danae. Nobody could blame you for that.'

'But they do,' she said quickly, 'they do. His brothers. His mother. She blamed me until the day she died. She never forgave me. And his brothers – they hate me, hate the sight of me. And him . . . Oh, Morris, I don't want Mara to know, I really don't. And if she has to be told, I should be the one to tell her.'

'Well, you should have thought of that before she set off all the way up here. Now she's determined to get the information out of myself or Elsie.'

'Did you tell her you were going to ring me?' Danae asked quickly.

'No, I didn't. I'm not that much of an eejit,' said her brother spiritedly. 'It's your secret, it's your story to tell.'

'Oh heck,' said Danae. 'Let me think about it. Can you put her off for a little while?'

'I'll do my best,' said Morris.

'Fine,' she said. 'I'll ring back.'

And then she'd rung Belle.

Belle greeted her in the front lobby of the Avalon Hotel and Spa, looking resplendent in her normal hotel outfit of crisp black suit, cream silk shirt and a large flower brooch pinned to one lapel. Even this bit of girlish femininity couldn't detract from the steeliness behind Belle's smile.

'Come on, into the bar with you,' said Belle, and marched her through.

Coffee arrived, filter coffee, in a beautiful silver pot.

'I didn't think you'd be wanting a shot of espresso or anything like that,' Belle said. 'Certainly given that I've never seen you touch a drop of the stuff in all the years I've known you.'

194

'No,' said Danae, 'I don't normally. But I feel so shaken now and this might help.'

'I don't know about that,' said Belle. 'It might give you the jitters. You could be climbing the walls in five minutes with all the extra caffeine in your system . . . but I suppose you know what you're doing.'

Belle busied herself pouring coffee, leaving Danae to add a drop of milk to hers.

'Right – spill,' said Belle. 'I've only got fifteen minutes. There's a couple coming in who want to talk about their wedding in two years' time. The function manager is off today with a sore throat. I'll give her a sore throat when I see her! But anyway, we don't have long. What's wrong?'

'It's Mara,' said Danae slowly. 'You know I love her, and it's been wonderful having her around but—'

'But difficult,' interrupted Belle. 'Of course it's been difficult! Sure, you've been living on your own up the side of a hill for donkey's years. Of course it's going to be difficult to have another human being there with you. Is that what this is about? Do you think it would be easier if she didn't live with you? If she went somewhere else in Avalon? I'm sure we could sort something out.'

'No, that's not it at all,' said Danae. 'Granted, it is tricky living with someone when you've been living on your own for so long, but Mara's so easy-going and lovely. She keeps trying to bring me tea in bed, and in the evening she cooks and insists on doing all the washing up. I feel quite spoiled. It's strange.'

'Course it's strange,' said Belle, 'when no one has looked after you in a very long time. So if it's not Mara, what's the problem?'

Despite her anxiety, Danae grinned. No matter what the situation, Belle could be relied upon to get straight to the point. There was no going off on tangents for her.

'She wants to know about Antonio.'

'Oh, right,' said Belle slowly. She looked carefully at her friend's face. 'And how do you feel about that?'

'I don't want her to know,' said Danae, as if this was perfectly obvious. 'I don't like anybody knowing.'

'I can vouch for that,' Belle said grimly. 'How many years did I know you before I managed to drag the truth out of you?'

'It's so painful, and people are bound to think worse of me. It's easier if nobody knows.'

'Of course,' said Belle with an edge to her voice, 'it's much easier if your friends haven't the slightest clue as to what your life has been like and what you've suffered and how difficult it is to live with it every single day of your life. Oh sure, much better if nobody knows. I agree with you there. In fact, I would say there are psychologists as we speak saying, "*Oh yes, vitally important and painful things in people's lives should remain buried for ever, then we'd all be much better off."*'

'Oh, for heaven's sake, Belle, don't go off on one,' said Danae. She added a teeny bit of sugar to her coffee and took another sip.

She'd forgotten how nice coffee tasted. The richness on her tongue. Antonio, being typically Italian or half-Italian and half-Irish, had loved his coffee. They'd been drinking espressos and Americanos long before the rest of the country got round to finding them fashionable.

'The thing is,' Danae said, choosing to ignore her friend's mild sarcasm, 'Mara has now hightailed it off to Dublin to get the truth out of her father, and I don't want him to tell her. Before I came to see you, Morris rang me to say that Mara wanted to know what had happened. It's all my fault, I should never have let her come to stay here, I should never have suggested it.'

'I'll tell you what you should do,' said Belle firmly. She reached out and took one of Danae's slim hands in hers. Belle's hands were big and strong and there was a pearl ring on one of them, her engagement ring and a wedding ring from her last husband. Her first marriage had been a disaster – hence her slightly cynical views on young love and early marriage. But she'd loved Harold, her second husband, dearly, even though rumour had it in the town that he'd died under mysterious circumstances – a rumour that enraged Belle every time she heard it. 'Cancer's very mysterious all right,' she used to say grimly. Anyone who mentioned the rumour in her hearing never repeated it again; Belle made sure of that. She held on to Danae's hand tightly.

Danae's hands were long and slender and her jewellery was of a totally different type. On one hand, she had a strange silver ring with a beautiful turquoise stone in the middle of it. Her nails were never painted, merely filed short. She had sensible, workmanlike hands, and they were cold. Bad circulation, some might have said. Belle preferred the old adage of 'cold hands, warm heart', because she knew her friend had one of the warmest hearts ever. And yet it had been frozen for so many years because of the past.

'What I want you to do is ring Morris, get him to put Mara on the phone, then say that when she comes back, you'll tell her the whole thing.'

'I can't,' protested Danae.

'Yes, you can. It's about time you shared the load. I knew it would be good to have Mara living with you. I knew she'd not rest till she found out.'

'You're like a bloody witch,' said Danae crossly.

'You're calling *me* a witch?' laughed Belle. 'You with the long, streaky hair with the grey bits in it and the mad jewellery! You do realize that half the aul fellas up the mountains think you're the witch, living on your own up there with that wolf-like dog and all the hens.'

For the first time Danae roared with rich, true laughter.

'Oh Lord,' she said, 'wouldn't it be great to be a witch if you could cast spells to make yourself happy and spells to make other people happy. Sadly, no, I'm no witch, as you well know. Just a little sad right now.'

'You know the old saying, "A problem shared is a problem halved"? There's a lot of truth in it. You've been keeping people out for a very long time, Danae. Now you need to let Mara in. What do you think she's going to do? Hate you? Think any less of you? Course she's not! She knows who you are. And if you tell her the whole story, the whole, truthful, painful story, trust me, she'll understand.'

Danae nodded. She pulled her hand away and started searching in her handbag for a tissue. She almost never cried any more. She didn't know how: it was as if all her tears had been cried out years before.

Belle handed her a tissue. 'I've got a box of them on standby for the engaged couple. You'd be surprised at how many brides-to-be start weeping when they think about the wedding day. The grooms generally start to weep at the price of the wedding day, but the brides get all moony and delirious once they see the ballroom and we talk about the whole thing. Then, when I show them the wedding suite, well, it's a toss-up between tears and swooning in ecstasy. Most of them want to book in there and then, stay the night and have a go at everything. That Jacuzzi bath is a brilliant thing; I'm so glad I got it installed. Anyway, you've got your orders. I know what's good for you, even if you don't. So you're going to take my advice, aren't you?'

Danae wondered how anyone ever managed to resist doing a single thing Belle ordered them to.

'Yessir,' she said, and she meant it. 'That's what I'll do. I suppose she needs to know sometime. And if she runs away from Avalon, screaming . . . Well, I'll have to get used to that.'

'If you think Mara's going to run away screaming when you tell her the truth, you don't know what sort of girl your niece is at all,' said Belle.

Back in the post office, Danae phoned Mara's mobile and left a message.

'Mara,' she said tiredly, 'I'll tell you all about it. But give me some time to get used to the idea, OK? I'll tell you, eventually, OK?'

That night, Danae lay in bed and thought about the past. She spent so much of her time trying hard not to think about it, but it was always there, every single month when she drove to Dublin: waiting for her in ambush.

Danae was not a woman for clutter. Her home had a few beautiful pieces she'd picked up over the years – a bit of driftwood from the beach, a lovely earthenware jug made by a local potter, some blue glass that she sometimes sat flowers in during the summer – but there was very little junk. It was the legacy of a childhood spent moving around, never staying in one place for long. Her mother had taught her there was no point in having much stuff because it only got in the way when you needed to get out in a hurry.

'Better to be able to throw your few bits into a suitcase and be off,' Sybil would say, as if this was a great gift.

Danae didn't know any other way to live. The tenement on Summer Hill was where they'd lived the longest. Not that they put down roots there or made friends among the neighbours.

'We're better than the likes of them,' Sybil would say, 'never forget that.'

She never went to the laundry with the other women on washing day. Instead, she washed her lovely silk lingerie herself, draping it over a chair in front of the fire.

'They'll never have seen a pair of silk cami-drawers in their lives,' Sybil would say, holding up a delicate peach garment with its exquisite lace.

Danae knew what the other women made of her mother. She'd heard them talking: 'Thinks she's Lady Muck,' they'd say. 'All fur coat and no drawers.'

199

But they were wrong. Regardless of what she might say, Sybil didn't really consider herself above everyone else. The reason she tried so desperately to cling to a sense of superiority was because it was one of the few things left to her. Dignity was long gone. The men had taken that.

Big Jim was the first that Danae could remember. She must have been about three or four back then. She'd thought he was her daddy, because they all seemed to live together and other children had daddies. Then one night he came home in his cups and hit her mother such a clatter that she flew clean across the room and landed against the window like Danae's beloved rag doll before sinking to the floor.

'Daddy!' shrieked the little Danae.

'I'm not your father, you stupid child,' he'd hissed at her. And then he left.

Danae had rushed to her mother's side. But Sybil was made of the sort of stuff that said you didn't cry, you didn't need to be comforted. No, you got up on your own two feet.

'I'm fine,' she said, dragging herself up by the curtains, wiping the blood off her mouth with one hand. 'Do you know, I think it's time we moved out of here.'

'But, but . . . we like it,' Danae said fearfully. It was small, but she had her little bed in one corner, behind the chest of drawers, with the curtain around it. And she had her rag dolly, her only toy.

'No,' said her mother. 'The rent won't be paid now, with him gone. Time we were off.'

Two small suitcases and a small valise was all it had taken. Danae had had to drag one of them, small though she was.

'Quiet now,' her mother said as they crept down the stairs. 'If you wake the landlord, there'll be hell to pay.' Sybil laughed, quietly. 'Whatever's to pay, we haven't got the money for it.'

They'd made it out safely that time. Then on to the next place, the next town.

Sybil came from better stuff, she told her daughter. There

were many stories about the good times in the past. Lovely times with servants and beautiful clothes and lovely meals. Always enough to eat.

'Too much,' Sybil would say. 'Far too much. The waste!'

Danae's mouth watered at the thought of food you could waste. They were living on a thin soup made of bones that her mother had beseeched from the butcher, saying it was for the dog. *But we haven't got a dog*, Danae wanted to say, but she knew better. Her mother was also adept at digging up a few vegetables here and there from other people's gardens.

'They won't miss them,' she'd say. 'Isn't it a kindness to let someone else share a little of your good fortune?'

Each time they moved, Danae had brought her few books with her. Two on the lives of saints – her mother had been going to throw them out; the dratted nuns had given them to her. 'Fling them in the fire,' she'd said, 'we might as well get some use out of them.'

'No,' cried Danae, 'I like them. I like to read.'

So the lives of the Little Flower and Maria Goretti had been saved, along with the story of Edel Quinn and a copy of *Wuthering Heights*.

'You're a curious little thing, with your head stuck in a book there,' said Mr Malcolm, one of the nicest men her mother had met up with.

'I like to read,' said Danae carefully, not really looking up into his eyes, because you never knew what sort of man Mother might bring home. Sybil never knew herself; that was the problem, Danae was beginning to see.

Sybil had never been what you would call a reliable narrator. All the stories of her past had to be taken with a pinch of salt because she was inclined to make her own role bigger or smaller, depending on circumstances.

When Danae had fallen out of the cot at the age of one, Sybil had barely been in the room at all, for goodness' sake! A woman couldn't spend her entire time watching a baby:

she needed a bit of time to do her hair. The cat had taken much of the blame, on that occasion. When a chip pan caught fire and the whole house had been in danger of burning down, Sybil had risked life and limb to rescue her darling daughter. Any talk of the fire brigade's involvement was glossed over, along with their reprimand for having two chip pans and a frying pan all going hell for leather on the one gas stove with the kitchen curtains flapping around nearby.

The fact that Danae had been left with a small burn on one leg was something she should be grateful for. If it hadn't been for her mother's speed, she could have been a lot worse off.

Sybil liked to be the heroine in every story. She was never happy until she was in the spotlight. It had taken Danae years to realize all this.

And then into their lives had come kind, jovial Bernie Wilson. He wanted to marry Sybil. Marry her and make an honest woman out of her, now that the baby was due.

Widows with children, Danae heard other women in the flats talking, were more likely to marry again rather than widows without children.

'Men like ones who've been broken in, who know the score. And with chisellers, they know the score.'

But Bernie wasn't like that: he was special.

Sybil was full of grand names for the baby, something to rival Danae.

'Could we not have something nice and simple?' said Bernie, 'I was thinking Morris, if it's a boy. That was my father's name, God bless him. And maybe Alice, if it's a girl?'

The baby had been Morris. Lying in her bed in the little cottage in Avalon, Danae recalled those years when she'd lived with Bernie and Morris as the happiest of her life. There had been stability then; a stability she'd never known before.

But for all her lack of clutter, on top of Danae's big old wardrobe there were three boxes of things from the past.

In the first box was the diary she'd been asked to keep.

The second contained her wedding dress, carefully wrapped up in tissue paper – something she'd never been able to throw out.

In the third were her white satin shoes from the day, and her bouquet, also wrapped in tissue paper. She hadn't thrown it. Somehow, in the wildness of the day and the excitement and the great drama of entering the Rahill family, no bouquet had been thrown.

Perhaps that had been the bad luck that marred the day, Danae thought. But no, the bad luck had been written in her life long before that. The bad luck meant she chose men the same way her mother chose them, for all the wrong reasons. Except her mother had finally found a good one in Bernie. Whereas Danae had made the worst choice of all right at the outset.

When she got home from Dublin, Mara hugged her aunt and said, 'Whenever you're ready to tell me, Danae, tell me. I love you, I wanted to understand so there wouldn't be any danger of me hurting you inadvertently. The last thing I wanted was to upset you.'

Danae had stood in her niece's embrace and closed her eyes.

'You didn't hurt me, love. I'm scared to talk about it. It was not a good marriage, not a good childhood either. That's why your father and I are so different, because we have different fathers. Bernard, your grandfather, was a good man. Morris was lucky.

'It was different for me when I was a child. Life was painful and my marriage was painful, that's why I didn't tell you. Give me a little time to get used to the idea of talking about it, and I'll tell you. It shouldn't . . .' she paused, thinking of what Belle had said, '. . . be a secret.'

Later, she took down the box with the diary and the cuttings and all the various bits of paper relating to what had happened, and she laid them on her bed. They were all tied up with a black ribbon and Danae didn't even want to undo the package. Opening it would be like letting a bad spirit out. As if the box was a genie's lamp and undoing the ribbons was the spell that would release it into the world.

No, Mara could do it. As soon as Danae got up the courage to give the box to her. Mara could read everything, and then she'd know.

Because Danae didn't think she had the heart to tell her beloved niece the whole story.

Chapter Thirteen

*D*id everyone in Avalon know, Tess wondered as she walked
down the town to pick up a few groceries for dinner. Was
everyone staring at her thinking, *Poor Tess, her husband has
left her and found someone else?* Tess herself was never a person
for gossip. It was partly her father. Dad had never been a
gossiping sort of man. He'd quite happily walk into the village
shop in the morning with scenes of wildness going on all around
him and ignore it. Suki had once said that if half the town had
been seen frantically kissing the other half of the town, he
wouldn't notice. He'd just go in and say, 'Good morning, lovely
day, isn't it? I'm sure I saw a red kite out there this morning.
Very unusual. Thought they were gone from Ireland. Terribly
exciting!' And then he'd wander off with his newspaper, not
even looking at the scenes of bacchanalian craziness around him.

Consequently, Tess worked on the theory that life could be
difficult and that you never knew what was going on behind
the curtains. She'd learned this partly from living in the big
house all her young life, when outsiders would assume the
Power family ate off the finest Sèvres china with silver cutlery,
when in fact they were all sitting around the kitchen table
shivering like whippets in the cold, hungrily tucking into Anna
Reilly's Irish stew.

When they'd finally sold Avalon House and she'd come to live in the village in the beautiful little house she still lived in, she knew people were talking about her, but there was pity in their eyes when they looked at her because she was well liked. And there was pity in their eyes now. She was convinced of it whenever anyone looked at her.

Poor Tess Power, the last to know. Split up from her husband. And what was that story about a trial separation they both agreed on? That was clearly a ruse. No, Kevin must have left her and gone out and found himself a younger model.

The women would feel sad for her and the men . . . maybe the men would think that Kevin had got it right, trading in forty-something Tess for a younger model.

In the butcher's she looked at various cuts of meat, knowing she really needed to choose the cheapest for Sunday lunch. Maybe lamb shanks, she thought. Cheap, and if they were cooked slowly enough, they fell off the bone and made a beautiful stew. Yes, lamb shanks, she thought.

'How are you, Tess?' said Joe the butcher, in his normal friendly tone.

'Fine,' said Tess, knowing she sounded brittle and wishing she didn't.

'Great,' said Joe, 'what can I do for you today?'

She gave him her order, all the time wondering what he thought or whether he knew.

In the cake shop, she bought some Rice Krispie slices for Kitty's lunch. On Fridays the children were allowed to bring in something sweet, and Tess generally managed to bake something during the week. But she wasn't able to concentrate. Her mind kept flitting off whenever she thought about anything normal. Flitting off into the craziness of Kevin and Claire and what it all meant. What had she done? The whole thing was her fault. She'd let him go. And had he really loved her at all?

'Hello, Tess,' said the girl behind the counter in the cake shop.

Tess's mind went blank. What was her name, what was her name? Erm . . . Sophie, yes, Sophie.

'Hello, Sophie,' she said gratefully. 'I'll have two of those Rice Krispie cakes and one French stick, please.'

It was dreadful to be buying those cakes when they were the easiest thing in the world to make, but she felt so tired at night, so weary. And once dinner was over and washed up, she only had the energy to sit blankly in front of the TV and look at it, not really taking anything in. Staring into the middle distance. She was doing her best for the children. When she was with them you wouldn't think there was anything wrong, you wouldn't think that her life had been ripped apart. No, Tess Power would not let her beloved children down. And no matter what people were talking about, she would show the stern Power backbone.

'Thank you, Sophie,' she said with a bright smile.

Let people talk: they would see that she was well able for anything the world threw at her. Groceries bought, she turned and headed back up the town, towards the shop. She saw Danae on the way and waved hello at her. That was the nice thing about people like Danae. They weren't garrulous. Wouldn't offer an opinion. Wouldn't say anything. Danae, Tess decided, was probably the only person in the entire town who you could sit and have a cup of tea with and she'd never ask a single personal question or offer a personal detail in return. But then, Tess thought, Danae had always struck her as a lonely figure, someone on the outskirts, not quite a part of Avalon. No, it was easier to be talked about and live in the town like a normal person, even if your husband had run off with a twenty-nine-year-old illustrator. Easier to do that than live in the half-life of loneliness.

Vivienne had been minding the shop for the half-hour while Tess was out buying dinner.

'Someone came in and was very interested in that little round table with the darker inlay,' said Vivienne excitedly. 'I told her you'd be back in half an hour. She said she'd come back.'

'Oh Lord,' said Tess. 'They often say that, but they don't mean it.' She was quite used to people coming in, examining things, promising on their mother's life they'd be back in half an hour when they got the money from the cash machine, and then never appearing again.

'No, she looked like she really meant it – and I can tell,' said Vivienne. 'Hasn't been a bad day at all, you know. You sold those teacups and I sold four, *four* of those new skirts I got in, so it's been a good day.'

Yes, thought Tess. It's been a good day. Let's concentrate on the positive and not mention Claire or wonder if everyone in town knows that Kevin's now in love with her. She knew all too well that once Vivienne got started on the subject of Kevin and Claire, there was no stopping her.

Vivienne had very firm views on how she should treat Claire.

'Ignore her,' she'd said, when Tess had broken the news to her. 'You shouldn't meet her. She's beneath you. She's a child.'

'She's twenty-nine,' said Tess, finding herself in the odd position of defending Claire. 'And she's not a child. When I was her age, I had a child and was married,' she added.

'You should steal him back, give her a taste of her own medicine,' said Vivienne heatedly.

Again Tess had to intervene. 'She didn't steal him, Vivienne,' she said tiredly. 'He was . . .' She paused; she wasn't sure exactly what Kevin had been during the trial separation. Was he like a library book in the recently returned slot, which was where everyone in the library seemed to go first, as though the fact other people had chosen them somehow made the books more interesting. Kevin had been in the recently returned slot and Claire had picked him up. Tess really had nobody to blame but herself.

'I know what you should do,' pronounced Vivienne, 'you

should start dating that gorgeous Cashel hunk. That'd make Kevin jealous. Actually, forget making Kevin jealous: go off and date Cashel. I would.'

'I told you,' Tess said, 'Cashel and I have history, there's as much chance of him dating me as him dating the man in the moon or the woman in the moon, whatever in the moon.'

No, Tess thought, best not to get Vivienne started on that subject. 'Thanks for minding the shop,' she said brightly. 'I'd better put my shopping away and get ready for when Miss Small Round Table turns up.'

'Great,' said Vivienne, and marched back into her own shop.

Alone, Tess thought how much easier it was to be angry than sad. If she let herself be sad, she fell apart. Anger was far more productive. Anger had got her through telling Kitty the news.

Kitty had taken it better than her brother.

'Does that mean that you aren't married any more?' she asked. 'Will you be getting a divorce?'

Tess knew that many of the children in her daughter's class had divorced parents, for which she was grateful, but she had never planned on being one of them.

'Not yet,' she said cheerily. 'Daddy says Claire is a lovely person.'

She had no idea how she managed to say it without wincing but if it would spare her daughter distress, she could do anything.

Kitty put her small head to one side, considering. 'I like having Daddy living here,' she said. 'Can't he move in here with Claire?'

'No, darling, he can't. That's not the way it works. He'll live with Claire and it will be your second home, with another bedroom and everything.'

'Can I take Moo with me when I stay over?' Kitty asked.

Tess felt the anger flood through her at the prospect of

another woman putting Kitty to bed and tucking Moo in beside her.

'Of course, darling,' she said.

'OK,' said Kitty thoughtfully. 'Is Claire pretty? As pretty as you, Mummy?'

Anger left to be replaced by love. 'I don't know,' Tess said, snuggling her daughter close, 'but Daddy and I love you best, remember that. We will always love you best. That's what Mums and Dads do.'

Tess and Kevin were communicating by text message. It seemed easier. Texting made Tess less likely to want to kill Kevin for his thoughtlessness in forcing her hand with Zach, who was behaving moodily, as if it was all his mother's fault.

They want to meet Claire, Tess texted.

I'd love that, wrote Kevin.

I want to be there, Tess replied.

She didn't really want to be there, but she did want to inspect this woman who was going to have access to her darling kids.

A date was set, and in a fit of brilliance, Tess decided that a neutral location would be best for the first meeting with Claire.

Good idea texted Kevin back.

He'd have said 'good idea' if she'd suggested a moon meeting, Tess thought with a flash of humour. So it was that she, Kitty and Zach were to meet Claire at the Avalon Hotel over Sunday lunch.

'Lunch is a good plan,' said Vivienne. 'It's a buffet in there and you'll all be busy organizing food and such, that way you'll get round the awkwardness of it.' She looked at Tess's wry face.

'OK,' Vivienne amended, 'it won't be *quite* as awkward. And it'll save on cleaning bills too – less chance of you throwing a plate of food all over Kevin if you're out than if you're at home.'

Even Tess had to laugh at the image this conjured up.

Then Kevin phoned, sounding worryingly grave.

'I need to talk to you, Tess,' he said. 'Face to face.'

'Fine,' she said wearily. 'Come tonight. After dinner.'

Tess rapidly ran through the things he might have to say: *I want to move to Reno to get a quickie divorce so Claire and I can marry?* Divorce in Ireland was notoriously slow and took five years. Or would it be: *I want to bring Claire to live here too – we can all be happy, surely?*

'Daddy, Daddy,' yelled Kitty, launching herself at him that evening.

'Hi, Dad,' said Zach, and stopped texting to bump fists with his father.

There was talk of how Kitty was doing in school, was she sitting next to Tamara, who was mean and stole her pencils while Miss Stein did nothing about it. Then there was chat about the football with Zach until, finally, Tess shooed her children away, telling them that she and Dad needed to talk on their own.

As a great concession, she made tea and put the plainest biscuits they had on a tray without bothering to open them or even add a plate.

'So,' Tess said.

Kevin, sitting on the furthest seat, squirmed a bit.

'Well, it's . . . it's very difficult,' Kevin said. 'I'm not really sure how to tell you this, and over the phone wasn't the best way, that's for sure.'

God, maybe he was broke. Maybe he *did* want to move to Reno and get the quickie divorce so he could marry Claire. Zach and Kitty would be devastated.

'What is it? Spit it out,' she said. 'It can't be anything worse than what's gone before. Plus, I've got to get Kitty to bed in the next hour, and you know how hard that is.'

'Claire's pregnant,' he blurted out.

There was a brief interlude where Tess thought that, *yes,*

this was a difficult thing to say, and then the information went from her brain down to her solar plexus and she felt as if she'd been punched.

'Claire's having a baby?' she said, and even as she said it she knew it sounded stupid. Claire was having a baby.

'Yes,' he said, sighing heavily. 'It wasn't planned or anything. She's on the pill and she was sick one night and . . .'

'I don't want to know the details,' Tess said. 'Exactly how pregnant is she?'

'The doctor says eight weeks,' Kevin replied.

Tess was silent. Eight weeks. Eight weeks of the baby growing inside her husband's new girlfriend's womb, which meant Kevin and Claire had been an item for a lot longer than he'd initially implied. OK, she could be calm and deal with this.

'How are we going to tell them?' she said. 'Zach's already barely talking to me. He blames *me*.'

'Well, I don't know,' he replied. 'I thought maybe you could sound them out, you know, before we announce it, because it really is the *end* of you and me, and that's going to be hard for them to take.'

'I think that when you started going out with Claire, *that* was the end of you and me,' Tess replied tightly.

'Well, a baby makes it absolutely final, doesn't it?' said Kevin.

'Oh my good lord,' Tess said slowly. 'Do you realize that this means we have to introduce Zach and Kitty to Claire and explain that she's pregnant all in the same go?'

'We don't have to tell them that she's pregnant,' Kevin said. 'You know, we could let them meet her and then maybe a couple of weeks later say she was pregnant.'

'Like Zach cannot do sums? He's seventeen, he's going to work out that she was pregnant when he first met her and he's going to be very annoyed at the subterfuge. He's not a child, Kevin,' Tess pointed out. 'Kitty may be too young to understand the ins and outs of it all, but Zach isn't. We owe it to him to tell him. No,' she said suddenly. 'YOU owe it to him. In fact, you can do it now. I'm taking the dog for a walk.'

She simply couldn't bear to stay near Kevin another minute. 'I'll see you at the weekend,' she said, getting to her feet. 'Bye.'

Out in the hallway, she grabbed her coat and Silkie's lead and called up the stairs, 'Kitty, I'm taking Silkie out for a walk. Zach, keep an eye on your sister – Dad wants to talk to you, and then he's going. I won't be long.'

She needed to be alone for a few minutes, to cry.

Silkie was thrilled with this unexpected treat, even if she shivered when they got out into the icy winter evening and felt the frost in the air.

In the darkness of the street, Tess allowed herself to cry. As tears ran down her cheeks, melting cool on to her face in the bitter air, she stopped trying to hold it all in.

Tess didn't want any more children, not really. After all, she had darling Zach and her beautiful little Kitty. Yet as she edged closer to her forty-second birthday, she'd begun to realize that her chances of ever having a child again were growing slim.

That thought brought grief, a type of mourning for something precious now lost.

To add to that grief, here was Kevin, able to have a baby with Claire. Young, fertile Claire. Never before had Tess felt so old.

She walked slowly up Willow Street almost without thinking, some internal magnet pulling her homeward.

It was a clear night and above, the stars glittered brightly. Tess thought of the nights she'd walked up the hill with Cashel at her side, laughing as they walked arm in arm, stopping every while to kiss because it almost hurt not to. Had she ever been that young and foolish?

Chapter Fourteen

Suki had travelled all over the world and she collected things on her travels. Not the sort of knick-knacks other people might collect. No, Suki collected amulets and precious stones, talismans from other cultures. Tiny jade buddhas, a little brass goddess she'd picked up in the Far East that somebody said had come from Bhutan. 'It's the goddess of hope and fertility,' she'd been told. She wasn't sure she needed the fertility, but the hope, she certainly needed that.

From trips to South America she had pre-Columbian gold-plated amulets. 'Show me the feminine ones, the ones for female gods,' she'd told the guy in the shop selling them. He looked surprised, maybe no one else had ever asked him this question. Usually tourists wanted the colourful lizards and the strange-shaped men who looked as if they were dancing to some unseen music. But Suki wanted something specific, something for joy.

There was no joy.

'This one—' Suki said, pointing to something that looked like a heart with beautiful scrolls on top of it.

'This is for long life,' said the man.

'I'll take it,' said Suki.

From Canada she had beautiful Inuit dreamcatchers, with

tiny shell wolves carved on them and dangling feathers; from the Native American reservation near Four Corners in the US, she had beautiful turquoise necklaces and bracelets on leather thongs.

And when she wasn't shopping for her amulets on her travels, she was trawling for psychics. Stopping in some rural town on a book tour, she would ask any locals she met – the concierge, the maid doing her room, the staff in the bookshop – if they knew of anybody. The men were often startled by such requests, the women less so. Women understood the need to find out what the world had planned for them. To find out if it would all work out OK, if you would live long and be happy – which sounded like something Captain Kirk might say.

At the coffee shop she went to some days when she was visiting the other side of Falmouth, where the good bookshop was, Suki had seen a sign for a new psychic. It was a plain notice, nothing fancy, not even well written. A travelling woman, Suki suspected, in the trailer park, far out of town. Definitely the wrong side of the tracks. Suki always felt at home in trailer parks. She'd gone out with a guy once who'd come from a trailer park; he'd felt the difference between them was a chasm, but it hadn't seemed that way to Suki.

'I spent a lot of time in the trailer park in my home town,' she told him. 'Cabana-Land.' She said it the way she'd always said it, like it was slightly dangerous, because it had been. For sixteen-year-old Suki Power, daughter of Avalon House, Cabana-Land definitely spelled danger, but she'd managed to sidestep trouble many times.

'You just like roughing it, you rich broad,' the guy had said, and he'd dumped her, his pride seriously dented. And that made Suki feel ugly and unloved. If her allure wasn't able to overcome his basic insecurity, then she must definitely be losing it.

The trailer park on the outskirts of Falmouth, Massachusetts was the sedate sort of affair one would have expected: hidden behind lots of trees, screened off from the highway. When Suki had phoned to ask for directions, a young man answered, perhaps the son of the woman. The directions were pretty simple: second row, the trailer at the end, on the right-hand side. At least these days her car wasn't the sort to attract attention. She drove a subcompact, an old one at that. Nobody would look twice at it. And when she pulled up outside the psychic's trailer, which boasted a red Thunderbird no less, her car blended in nicely.

The door of the caravan was opened by a teenage boy, the voice on the phone.

'Mom's in the back,' he said, before moving past her to go outside.

Suki had often wondered why so many psychics and fortune tellers were poor when they theoretically had a gift that could have made them rich. If only they could predict which horse would win a race or which lottery numbers would come up. She'd been told that it didn't work that way; those who had the gift of sight couldn't use it for themselves, only for other people. And if you managed to make enough money doing that, great.

This woman was probably Suki's age, though she looked older. A bad dye job had turned part of her hair rich red, the roots greying. The woman looked at Suki, taking in her face and her clothes. Suki had instinctively dressed down. She didn't want to be the femme fatale today or wear any of her designer clothes, things she'd bought a long time ago. People in trailer parks might not be able to afford Michael Kors originals or Donna Karan dresses, but that didn't mean they couldn't recognize them.

Suki fingered her pre-Columbian necklace with the talisman for long life.

'Sit down, please,' said the woman.

They were in the living-room part of the trailer, all veneer wood, plaid cushions. There were no crystal balls around. Although the woman had very old and well-used tarot cards to one side, she didn't touch them.

'It's a hundred and ten dollars for a reading,' she said to Suki.

'Fine,' said Suki, and passed the money over.

'When was your last reading?' the woman asked her.

'I can't remember,' Suki said truthfully. She genuinely didn't know. When she'd left Jethro, she'd been to see so many people: angelologists, fortune tellers, psychics, shamans . . . Once, she'd got her hopes up over a woman who was supposed to be 'am-aa-zing', in LA parlance. It turned out the woman worked out of a small premises on Hollywood Boulevard, wore a pink fur wrap and cowboy boots with rhinestone jeans. The day Suki turned up, the psychic was clearly out of her mind on drugs.

'Wow, you're kinda blue today. Blue haze around you. I like it,' the woman had slurred. 'Do you like it?'

At the time Suki was so desperate to make sense of it all, desperate to know when the pain would go, that she'd almost stayed. But she realized that a woman who was obviously hallucinating might not give her what she wanted: clarity about the future. That she had a blue haze around her was not exactly the kind of insight she'd been looking for.

'I'd guess it's been at least a year since I've seen anyone else,' she said now.

'You have an addiction,' the woman said bluntly.

Suki stared at her, thinking of the years with Jethro and the drugs. There had been lots of drugs. Suki wasn't entirely sure what they'd all been, because it seemed so un-rock'n'roll to ask. She'd swallowed all kinds of little tablets and, well, who knew what the heck they were, they just kept coming, along with lines of coke and vast hash cigarettes fat as cigars. But she'd been able to give them up. Had given them up the day she finally regained some of her pride. The day she'd walked out of the beautiful hotel in Memphis with nothing but a collection of suitcases to show for two years of her life, and nobody to help her into a cab, apart from a disinterested concierge who'd clearly seen many dishevelled women leaving in the wake of rock bands.

'No,' the woman said, 'not drugs, not drink – men. Powerful men, that's your drug.'

Suki stared at her, astonished. Nobody had ever said this to her before. The woman was clearly as crazy as the girl in the pink fur wrap. It didn't make any sense.

'You didn't come for fancy language, did you?' the woman asked.

'I came to see if I could finish my book, get some money and get my life back on track,' Suki blurted out without meaning to. She tried not to tell them anything: that way, you could tell pretty easily if they were genuinely psychic or merely clever mentalists.

'You will,' the woman said thoughtfully, 'but not in the way you expect it to happen. You have to face your demons first. You try to pay them off with jewellery,' she gestured at the amulet and instinctively Suki grabbed it. 'That will only work when your spirit is well. There are two wolves inside you. The wolf who leads you to pain, and the wolf who leads you to happiness. Which wolf will prosper?' The woman smiled as if this was a story she had told a hundred times before. 'The wolf you feed.'

'But how can I do it?' Suki asked, feeling desperation rise. This wasn't going the way she'd expected at all. She wanted to hear that it was going to be all right, that she *was* strong enough, that she would find success, and maybe a little bit of self-respect and possibly some fame and money. Damnit, she wanted money because she hated being poor, she'd been poor too long. And now it was back again, gnawing away at her insides the way few pains ever could. She didn't want to shrivel into old age in poverty, she knew what that would mean. Going home to Avalon at best, ekeing out an existence on State benefits, thinking of what could have been.

'I can see lots of futures for you,' the woman said, 'but you must deal with the spirit inside. Let go of the addiction, and then you can be the woman you want to be. What did you expect to hear? To beware of dark strangers? Always wear the colour green?'

The woman reached for a packet of cigarettes, tapped one out, lit up and inhaled with the practice of a forty-a-day smoker. For once, Suki didn't feel like a cigarette.

'You're not a run-of-the-mill psychic are you?' she asked.

'I'm a psychic who can't follow her own advice,' the woman said laconically. 'Look at this place.' She gestured around her. 'It's no palace. Bad men: that's what I go for every time and it's brought me nothing but trouble, despite seeing all that I can see. And I can see, sister. But every time you think it's going to be different, doncha? That's it,' said the woman. She motioned with the cigarette hand that it was time for Suki to go.

Suki was at the door of the trailer when the woman spoke again.

'Oh yeah, you need to call your sister.'

'What's wrong?' asked Suki anxiously.

Her reply was a shrug. 'That's all I saw. Call her.'

Suki left. She didn't see the teenage boy and she wondered was he the only thing left from a lifetime of bad men. She slammed the door behind her, took out the keys to her car, backed out of the road and sped on the highway back to town.

Ring your sister and *Give up powerful men.* That was it? Well, what did you expect for $110?

After twenty-six years of poverty, Suki Power Richardson had loved having money. It wasn't hers, essentially, it was her husband's. But she got to use it, to spend it. And spend it she did. She had accounts at all the big stores: Saks, Bloomies, Bergdorf Goodman. She found that she didn't really like the old rock-chick clothes she'd worn for years, she'd been kidding herself when she said she preferred old jeans and scuffed leather jackets. It turned out that she loved new, elegant clothes made from luxurious fabrics that clung to her hourglass figure in all the right places and cost more than a month's rent on her old apartment. Her failsafe tight black polyester pants went in the garbage and she bought beautifully cut pants off the rack at Donna Karan, along with marvellously draped jackets, and rabbit-soft knits. Her shoes were Italian, her fair hair was no longer given added oomph with a store-bought highlighting kit applied in a washbasin in her apartment: she went to a chichi hair salon where ordinary joes couldn't even *get* an appointment.

Kyle loved to see her spending money on her appearance.

'You need to look the part, honey,' he'd say. 'Daddy always says, "Look the part, son, and they'll think you are the part."'

For the first year of their marriage, Suki didn't care what 'the part' was, she was simply pleased to be able to indulge in an orgy of spending. After a childhood of scraping by in draughty old Avalon House, it was like being released from prison and relishing the freedom. She bought art for the walls of the house on D Street, perused antique auctions with a gimlet eye and repainted the hall four times before she'd achieved the right shade of subtle grey. She bought flowers – too many for the house, sometimes. But she didn't care about the excess: the Richardsons had serious money; nothing she could do could put even the slightest dent in it.

She and Kyle went to charity balls, dinner parties, and Republican party fundraisers where the wives of party bigwigs wore Chanel suits and worked the room. Even Antoinette seemed to be thawing towards her. Suki had been brought up

220

in an important Irish mansion, she was clearly from upper-class stock and she knew how to behave.

But as Tess might have told them all, Suki got bored easily. She became fed up with statements referencing Kyle Senior. Daddy had an opinion on everything: he said it was a ludicrous idea to buy a house in Taos as Suki was suggesting instead of a cottage in Newport where Daddy wanted them to buy.

'It's none of his business where we buy,' Suki shouted at Kyle as they stood at their matching his and hers sinks in the cream marble bathroom en suite.

'Oh, come on,' said Kyle angrily. 'You're not that naïve are you? I thought you prided yourself on your intellectual abilities, Suki. It's like listening to a Renaissance painter saying he doesn't want to paint what his patron wants him to paint. My father pays for it all!'

This last statement, and the way Kyle had hissed it at her, stuck in Suki's mind: did his father's absolute control over the whole family rankle with Kyle, or was he merely angry that she'd threatened to upset the applecart?

She flew to Taos to look at properties in spite of them all and then received an irate phone call from Antoinette.

'If you continue with this nonsense, Suzanne—' only Antoinette refused to use the nickname Suki had had since she was three – 'you will upset my husband. And we don't want that now, do we?'

'Don't we?' said Suki truculently. 'What do I care if he gets upset?'

There was silence on the other end of the phone.

Finally, Antoinette spoke. 'Kyle said you'd say that. Personally, I thought you were too clever, but I can see I overestimated you. Kyle Senior and I control you, whether you want to admit it or not. That goes for everything: from where your children go to school to whether you holiday in Europe or on the Cape with the rest of the family.'

Suki felt rage overwhelm her. She wasn't sure which part of the conversation infuriated her most: the fact that her husband clearly told his mother everything, or the veiled threat that Antoinette and Kyle Senior could stop her going home to Ireland for the summer, because she wanted to be in Avalon again and was fed up with Massachusetts and its social set.

'Oh, and the house in New Mexico – don't even bother. You won't get a red cent for that. You'll summer with us. Perhaps, in time, you might get a cottage of your own on Martha's Vineyard. That's it. You're a Richardson now, Suzanne, and you play by our rules.'

Boredom wasn't something Suki was used to, but in the gilded cage the Richardsons had constructed around her, boredom dominated her daily life. She wasn't expected to do anything other than look beautiful at functions, know all the right people, do a little charity work, have her hair done expensively, learn how to make small talk at elegant dinner parties and never, as Antoinette explained to her, say anything controversial, even as a joke: 'There are no jokes in Washington.'

At this, Suki had thrown her head back and let rip with a great, throaty laugh, but Antoinette had stared at her, stony-faced.

'I am not joking,' she said. 'Junior has a very good chance of a Senate seat and he needs a wife by his side, not a loose cannon. I can see that in you, Suzanne – a certain wildness. It must be the Irish blood.'

Suki could take Antoinette's insults because she always managed to get her own little barbs in. However, saying anything about her Irishness inflamed her.

'My ancestors were living in a castle when yours were still . . .' Suki searched her mind for some suitable retort, 'digging for vegetables in a field somewhere, and on your knees at night praying for redemption.'

Antoinette glared at her. 'I will not lower myself to your insults,' she said.

'Oh, but you can insult me and that's fine, is it?' said Suki. 'We all know the truth, don't we, Antoinette: I'm the one with the blue blood in this family.'

In truth, Suki didn't really care about the Power name or what it meant. Her father had been proud of his De Paor ancestry, but proud in a gentle way. Proud to be able to trace back his family, and yet deeply sad that a succession of feck-less Powers in the past had frittered away the family fortune. As a result, the Powers had lost the ability to keep their lovely home, had lost the ability to take care of the people of the village. Her father would have been a philanthropist, if only he'd had the cash. So Suki hadn't been brought up to think that being a Power meant that she was better than anyone else. But if it riled Antoinette, then she would remind her at every opportunity.

Angry, she went off and signed up for a course in Women's Studies and ostentatiously left the books lying around. *The Feminine Mystique*, Mary Wollstonecraft's *A Vindication of the Rights of Woman*. Incredibly, she found herself fascinated by the writers, by the work. She had always thought she was living a very different life from other women because she'd left her home and had to make a living for herself in America, yet it turned out she was only doing what countless other women had done before her. And like countless other women, she'd succeeded in marrying well, but not wisely.

Kyle didn't like her studies.

'For God's sake, what are you doing with all those damn books?' he said. 'You've finished with school, you don't have to go back to it.'

Kyle was not bookish in the least, despite his father's attempts to get him to keep up to date with happenings around the world. Kyle Senior was a voracious reader of non-fiction, particularly biographies and accounts of war. He'd never served in the military and yet he thought like a military commander, Suki realized. If he hadn't been such a cut-and-dry bastard, she might have admired him.

It didn't help that the slow push to get Kyle Junior's feet wet in the world of politics was beginning to gain momentum.

'Children,' said Kyle Senior, 'you need children. The wife isn't enough.'

Suki was in the room while this conversation was going on and she sat, quite astonished. 'Talk about me as if I'm not here, Senior,' she said. 'Absolutely fine. I'm a brood mare, am I?'

Kyle Senior laughed. 'Yes, honey, I guess you are. And we're looking for sons.'

That night Suki went out on her own to a bar across town and proceeded to get very, very drunk. She arrived home at two in the morning, having danced the night away in a jazz club and extricated herself with some difficulty from the very good dancer who'd wanted to take her back to his place. 'I can't, my husband wouldn't like it,' she'd managed, which was strange because the old Suki would have leapt at the chance.

'You're drunk,' Kyle had said as she'd thrown herself into bed, clothes on, her mascara sliding down her face.

'Yeah, I am,' she said. 'So what?'

The next day she'd felt sorry. She loved Kyle. It wasn't his fault that his family were pigs and treated her as if she was nothing but an accessory in a political campaign.

'Maybe we should have a baby,' she said.

The baby-making plan brought them closer together – at first. Six months down the line, and still no baby, it was a different matter.

'Maybe we should go see Dr Kennedy?' Suki had suggested. 'There's lots of tests you can have these days and stuff you—'

'We will not go to the doctor to discuss this,' said Kyle,

his nostrils flaring. For a second, he looked exactly like his father. Oddly, Suki found this a turn-on.

'OK,' she said. 'Let's give it another few months.'

But nothing happened. Kyle started to spend nights in a different bedroom, said he couldn't get to sleep at night, he didn't want to wake her, but Suki knew the real reason. He couldn't bear to make love to her any more. He could barely get an erection when he came near her. In their desire for a baby, somehow Kyle Junior had been emasculated.

She began going out on her own more, hanging out with women from her college course. Nobody on the course had any money, but Suki would buy them all drinks, cocktails. 'You're gonna love this one,' she'd say. 'It's a Long Island Iced Tea and it is fantastic.'

Carlotta, a fiery Latina on the course, wanted to write a thesis on racism and stereotyping of Hispanics in American culture. Her father had threatened to disown her. 'He wants us to fit in,' she said, dark eyes flashing. 'I do not want to fit in, I want to be myself. I do not want to be put into a box I need to fit.'

'Me neither,' said Suki.

'And you drink too much, Suki,' said Carlotta, 'if we are being straight with the truth.'

'Yeah, thanks for telling me, honey,' Suki said. 'You might drink too, if you had my life.'

'You might drink if you had *my* life,' countered Carlotta. 'I pay for this course by cleaning houses at night. Maybe I clean yours too?'

'Oh, gimme a break, Carlotta! We're supposed to be in this together.'

'Money separates us,' said Carlotta. 'Don't forget that, *chica*.'

Kyle Senior rang her up. 'I want you to stop this ludicrous college course immediately,' he said. 'From what I hear, it's all rubbish about women's rights, that tired old turkey. You've got plenty of rights, you don't have to work, you've got money to buy clothes. What else do you want?'

'A life,' said Suki sarcastically. 'A life where I'm not the Richardson family brood mare.'

'If you can't have a baby, you're not much of a brood mare, are you?' said Kyle Senior.

'What do you mean, if *I* can't have a baby?' said Suki. 'Who says it's me? Your bloody son can't even get it up when he sees me.'

She wondered if she'd gone too far, but Kyle Senior never shied away from plain talking.

'We'll have to make sure he does then,' he said. 'But I don't want you going out at night with your girlfriends, going to bars. There are rumours starting, rumours about you having fun in bars. Inevitably, sooner or later somebody will pick up on the rumours and start to wonder whether you're playing around. No Richardson wife plays around. So you be *very* careful, because I'll be watching you.'

'There's nothing to watch,' snapped Suki, and slammed the phone down, but she felt frightened. Kyle Senior was not a man to cross.

Chapter Fifteen

The days following Kevin's revelation, outwardly Tess continued to drive Zach to the bus, take Kitty to school, and carry on with her daily business. Inside, Tess wondered was the whole separation disaster all her fault and thought that if only she could have kept her mouth shut, if only she'd been happy with *I love him most of the time* love, then she, Kitty, Kevin and Zach would still be a family. Then Zach wouldn't have to put out the bins in an attempt to be the man of the family, Kevin wouldn't have fallen for Claire, and she wouldn't be consumed by the most unbelievable rage she'd ever experienced.

Despite her best intentions, a great vat of anger was boiling inside her over Kevin and Claire.

'I'm so furious with him for doing this to the kids and to me,' she said to Vivienne. 'How could he?' Tess paused because the last bit was the hardest: 'And I'm angry with myself for almost pushing them together! *I* made this happen. *Me!*'

Zach wasn't talking to her at all, as if it was all her fault.

I didn't tell Kitty. We need her to get used to the idea of Claire first, Kevin texted.

Wonderful, thought Tess. *Now* he turns into the concerned parent.

Then she felt guilty – Kevin had always been a good parent. And he loved Zach and Kitty. He probably was doing his best under difficult circumstances. She needed to meet him to discuss what they did next.

The problem was that Kitty was desperately keen to meet Claire.

'She had to go away,' fibbed Tess, which earned her a furious glare from Zach.

'It's not my fault, Zach,' Tess said to her son later.

Only to have him hiss: 'Isn't it?'

'If Gerard did that to me,' Vivienne said, 'I'd take him to the cleaners in the divorce courts. I'd be more than bitter, I'd be furious.'

Under the circumstances, Tess felt that bitterness was allowed, except that, having met a few bitter divorced women, she wasn't in any hurry to join their ranks.

They were the women who divided life into two chunks: Before the divorce and After the divorce. Everything in the After category, be it global warming or a stock exchange crash, could be blamed on the departed husband.

We had no holes in the ozone layer until he left me!

Much of the stock in her shop had come from these perpetu-ally enraged women. It was astonishing how many of the husbands had failed to collect their belongings after they left.

'This was *his* mother's,' one ex-wife said furiously, holding up a particularly fine piece of Chinese pottery.

In the interests of legality, Tess enquired whether the woman was entitled to sell the pottery. It was a valuable piece. Perhaps her ex-husband's lawyers would need to be contacted . . .

'I got the house and everything in it!' hissed the woman, making Tess think, not for the first time, that the antique business was not your average job.

It was almost easier dealing with bankruptcy sales, much as Tess hated those. Having been through it herself, she found it unbearable trying to make a profit from people who were forced to sell everything they owned.

'No, Vivienne, I'm going to concentrate on the business,' Tess said. 'I need it now that we're not getting back together. I'll have to hire someone to work here occasionally so I can attend more auctions and go off round the country to executors' sales.'

'You should find a new man. That would show bloody Kevin what a mistake he's making,' Vivienne said. 'There's that lovely Cashel Reilly, he's not married. A nice millionaire – or is it billionaire? Either way, you could do worse.'

'I told you, we dated years ago and it ended horribly,' said Tess miserably.

'Oh, that was years ago. People move on. He's been married since, he's got over you. And besides,' Vivienne said, returning to a well-worn theme, 'if you made even the slightest effort, Tess, you'd look fabulous. I've never seen a woman less interested in her appearance.'

Tess wasn't even mildly insulted by these words because Vivienne had been saying them for years. Ever since they'd been shop neighbours, she'd been pushing Tess to have her hair cut properly, wear make-up and, obviously – befitting advice from a woman who owned a clothes shop – to dress beautifully.

'I could do so much with you, Tess,' Vivienne would say regretfully. 'Look at you, you're slim and tall. Most women would kill for long legs like yours, and such a narrow waist. And heavens, Tess, your hair! You've got to stop going to Eileen's to get your hair cut. Eileen can only do blue-rinse shampoos and sets. Her version of the pixie cut makes you look like someone went at your hair with sheep shears.'

'Stop with the compliments,' said Tess drily. 'I don't think I can take any more of it.'

'I've only got your best interests at heart,' said Vivienne. 'Now that you're a single woman, you have to make more of an effort. At least go to the beauty salon and get your eyelashes tinted, seeing as you won't wear any eyeliner or mascara or anything. You're like my sister-in-law, Gladys, determined to live her life without a bit of lipstick passing her lips.'

'You hate her! You always say she's a complete cow,' said Tess, finally insulted.

'Oh, you know what I mean,' sighed Vivienne. 'You're anything but a cow. You're one of my best friends and I love you dearly, but I don't know why you persist with this sheep farmer from the back of beyond look. You're beautiful; you could be so stunning if you made even the slightest effort. It's as if you want to look like some old boot so that no man will ever look at you again.'

And there it was finally, the thing that really hurt Tess.

She quickly moved the conversation on to something else because Vivienne had touched a nerve. Kevin had never said anything to her in all the years of their marriage about dressing up or wearing eye make-up, and that had suited Tess. Suited her too much, she realized now.

'Of course, hunky Cashel is going to be around much more now that he's bought the house.'

'What house?'

Vivienne paused. 'Avalon House,' she said reluctantly.

Tess nearly dropped her cup of tea.

'You hadn't heard? Oh hell, I'm sorry, Tess . . .' Vivienne flailed around, trying to find the right words. 'I honestly thought you'd know, that someone would tell you . . .'

'Why would anyone tell me?' Tess said. 'It hasn't been my home for years. It's nothing to me now.' She put down her cup and gave Vivienne a brief hug. 'Sorry, love, I'm going next door to shut up shop. It's been a tough few days.'

She almost ran out of the shop and into her own. Silkie, who'd followed her into Vivienne's, ran after her and looked up in alarm.

'Come on, darling,' said Tess, getting to her knees and

burying her head in the dog's silken coat the way she had with her animals as a child, 'let's go home.'

She'd had enough.

But the wheels of business move on and the next day, Tess knew she couldn't miss the year's biggest antiques auction. She had to find some fresh stock – as cheaply as possible.

In the past few years, Tess had got used to closing early when she needed to go out to an auction because she could no longer afford to hire anyone. But with Christmas only a month away and the books looking so bad, she was nervous of losing a day's trading. Danae's gorgeous niece, Mara, whom she'd *loved* on their night out, seemed like the perfect stopgap: she was looking for work, and she was happy to fill in for one day.

Mara said she had worked in property, and Tess prayed she'd be OK holding the fort for a small, unusual antique business. Though it helped enormously if the person had even a vague knowledge of antiques, Tess had descriptions of everything in the shop on the tiny luggage labels she used for the prices.

She was due at nine. Bang on time, there was a knock on the door.

Tess looked up to find a vision in the shop doorway.

For the occasion, Mara had dressed in an exquisite arrangement of vintage, figuring that this was one job where old clothes would be an advantage. She wore a 1950s butter yellow dress with a Peter Pan collar, a tiny waist and whirling skirts. She had a fluffy white mohair cardigan draped over her shoulders and carried a white hard-frame handbag.

'Mara, you look wonderful!' she said.

'Thank you, Tess,' said Mara, and stepped into Something Old.

That night in the restaurant, Tess had decided that Mara had a glow about her, like she was lit up inside. Tess couldn't quite put her finger on the exact cause, whether it was Mara's rippling mane of auburn hair or the huge green eyes that looked at everything with such interest. Today, she was the same: glowing and smiling, looking as delighted at the possibility of a day's work as she might have been over being head-hunted for some glamorous corporation.

'You're wildly over-qualified for the job,' Tess said. She knew of Mara's career history but looking over her CV now, she could see that was definitely the case.

'Oh, you must read my reference,' Mara said cheerfully. 'The ex-boyfriend I was telling you about: he wrote it. They were all terrified I'd sue them or him, so from the reference, you'd think I'd personally run the entire office single-handedly for three years.'

She paused thoughtfully. 'I could have too – run the office, that is. But property is not the job to be in right now. Too many people selling their beloved homes in misery for half of what they'd bought the place for, and you still have to demand commission. Horrible. I'd probably have been made redundant soon anyhow.'

'I'm not sure the antique business is much better,' Tess said. 'A lot of my current stock is from people who've been forced to part with pieces they've had in their families for decades and they've looked as if they wanted to cry as it went out the door.'

'So kindness is a necessity if anyone comes in with something to sell,' Mara said quickly. 'Trust me, I can do kind.' A wistfulness crept into her voice. 'I'd have gone mad if not for other people's kindness over the past couple of months. Henry James said kindness was the most important word in the English language. He was right.'

'Do you know anything about antiques?' asked Tess briskly. She didn't want to talk about people's kindness or how she melted into a puddle of tears when she experienced it. It was easy being strong as long as nobody said anything gentle to you: that was when the floodgates opened. There was definitely something magical about Mara: she made people open up. Tess hadn't been crying much at all these past few days: she'd trained herself not to.

'Oh look!' in an instant, Mara had swooped on one of the rosewood jewellery cabinets (a stunning piece for displaying jewellery, but for sale if the correct price was reached), and pointed to a dainty Art Nouveau brooch displayed on a velvet choker on an old gold papier-mâché bust.

The brooch was so tiny that it would get lost worn any other way, but the sinuous silver lines made a perfect adornment to a choker, exactly like the one in the old oil painting of Great-great-great- (Tess forgot how many greats were involved) aunt Tatiana from Avalon House, although in the painting, Tatiana was wearing a vast diamond choker which had come from the Tsar's court in the 1800s. Pity they'd never been able to find that necklace in Avalon House when they had to sell everything, Tess thought wistfully. It was one of those priceless pieces, with a maharajah's diamond in the centre of it and a whole history surrounding the necklace. It would be worth hundreds of thousands. But even though she and Suki had searched for it, they'd never found it or Great-great-great. . .aunt Tatiana's alleged hiding place for her gems.

As soon as she'd seen the lovely brooch, part of a job lot, Tess had known how beautiful it would look worn as a choker and set against black velvet.

'That is so beautiful,' Mara breathed. 'And where you have it is perfect. I feel like it's on a lady's dressing table and she's about to cast off a silky robe so she can dress for a fabulous party, cover herself in Chanel No. 5 and . . . oh, I don't know – what would she be wearing for something of this period?'

Tess grinned. 'I take it all back,' she said. 'You don't need to know anything about antiques if you can make them come alive like that.'

'It's not me!' exclaimed Mara. 'It's you, the way you display everything. It all looks like a room in a beautiful house where you want to wander into each corner and discover . . .'

Seeing it through someone else's eyes, Tess looked around at her little kingdom.

Without her realizing it, she had created a microcosm of Avalon House in the two rooms of Something Old. There was the gentleman's library section where the hunting prints, the wine-drinking paraphernalia and the old leather-bound books lay, the way they had in her father's library, even though the valuable books had all been sold. There was the ladies' boudoir area where silver-backed brushes and jewellery sat alongside glass bottles from every perfume era, and where beautifully speckled foxed antique mirrors made everyone's reflection look hazily lovely. Even Tess, who didn't have much time for admiring herself in mirrors, looked twice when she caught sight of her reflection in them.

And the larger pieces of furniture at the back of the shop: the bookcases, portraits, giant Victorian vases, old travelling steam trunks, ornate chairs. Every piece could have fitted into her old home and looked as though it belonged.

Tess felt her eyes brim. She thought she'd left Avalon House and all its memories behind, when what she'd done was recreate it in her shop.

She shook herself and got on with explaining the till to Mara.

The next day, Mara walked up the last bit of Willow Street and in through the rusting but imposing gates till she was on the avenue leading to Avalon House. Danae had said it was like walking under a canopy of shimmering greens in the summer, as the branches from each side met in the middle. In winter, the bare branches reached out to their friends, as if waiting patiently for the first acid-green bud to appear. Mara knew nothing about gardening apart from admiring

234

whatever it was that Danae did with her garden, but even she could see that the vast acres Avalon House sat on hadn't seen a lawnmower or a leaf blower for many years. It was a wild place, with tangled bushes and great clumps of ivy climbing the trees, strangling them.

What would it be like to live here? Would life be infinitely better if you were born master or mistress of this place instead of being the ordinary girl from Furlong Hill? A girl who lived here probably wouldn't have to try too hard to forge a life. Someone like that would have instantly divined that Jack wasn't serious. And then again, she knew Tess, knew a little of her history. It seemed as if being born into such a noble family with noble bricks and battlements around you meant nothing. People were still people, whatever their birthright.

Cashel Reilly stood by the entrance wearing a cashmere navy coat. He was very tall and good looking, if you liked that dark, brooding type of thing. Mara once had, but she was over it. Besides, he was too old.

'Hello, I'm Mara Wilson, I'm here for the interview,' she said.

'You walked?' said Cashel in surprise.

Mara's very-professional-person-looking-for-a-job look was immediately replaced by a wry smile.

'My aunt lives outside your gate,' she said. 'Hers is the last house on Willow Street. This is the country, not LA: people walk here.'

'True,' said Cashel, recovering. 'In fact, that's what we're going to do now: walk round the place.'

He set off at a brisk pace, despite the wellington boots he was wearing. Mara, who was wearing flat boots herself, struggled to keep up.

'I liked your CV and your application letter,' he said.

There hadn't been many suitable applications. If he'd chosen a big city firm to find someone for him, he'd have been inundated, but he wanted to keep this local. It felt right doing it that way, and Mara Wilson had been the only local applicant.

'Can you take decent notes?' he asked, beginning to speed up, opening the door into the house.

'Yes, if I'm not running like a hare after you,' Mara said. 'Would I have to follow you around?'

'I usually pace in an office,' Cashel admitted. 'We'd need to find an office in town.'

'We'd need an office full stop,' Mara said. 'I can't operate out of here.'

They'd reached the old hall, which Cashel scanned rapidly. He couldn't imagine that broadband had ever been installed in Avalon House.

'Good point. Look into it. Something in town, big enough for both of us. I won't be there much, but I'll need my own office.'

'Any special chair or desk requirements?' Mara asked. 'Does your chair have to be some wildly expensive leather gizmo in the ten grand range?'

Cashel looked at her suspiciously. Was she being funny?

'People can be very specific about what they like,' Mara said, as if she had read his thoughts.

'Surprise me,' Cashel said – a statement that surprised him. Normally, he assumed total control. Most of the staff in his various offices had been with him long enough to develop a sense of his preferences and knew better than to bother him with the details, but he hated it when they got it wrong.

'Does that mean I've got the job?'

Cashel looked at his new executive assistant in charge of Avalon House. She looked smart, streetwise, and she said what she thought, a quality he liked.

'Yes,' he said. 'Don't disappoint me. I like you on instinct, and I'm rarely wrong. See that I'm not.'

'Okey doke,' said Mara cheerfully. 'I'll get working on an

office, architects – unless you have someone in mind – and builders. The best, I'm guessing?'

He nodded. 'I don't like being ripped off, though,' Cashel said grimly.

'Understood, loud and clear,' said Mara.

They walked around the ground floor and Cashel found himself speaking slowly so Mara could take notes, rather than rattling off instructions in his normal shotgun manner. He didn't know if it was this spiky, unusual girl who was having that effect on him or the fact that he was in Avalon House – the house he now owned.

Here, in the town where he'd grown up, he felt different, less like the captain of industry who expected minions to jump when he said so. If he sent Mara off scared, doubtless he'd get a reputation in the town for being a rich bastard, one of those people who'd let wealth change them beyond recognition. And he didn't want anyone to think that, because it wasn't true.

Money had changed him, to a degree. The absence of it was a nightmare, and he knew that, because he'd grown up that way. But having money didn't necessarily change the person you had been from the start.

A billionaire Swiss friend had put it wonderfully when he said that having money merely emphasized what you were all along. If you were a poor son of a bitch, you'd turn into an even worse son of a bitch with money. But if you were fundamentally decent, then you'd stay that way – simply with a nicer bank balance.

'One question,' Mara asked, when they'd spent an hour walking around the house, talking, with her taking copious notes all the while. 'Is this to be your home, or are you doing it up to sell?'

Cashel didn't look at her.

He seemed a million miles away, in fact. It was as if he had to drag himself back to the present when he finally answered her: 'I don't know. Yet.'

When Mara had left, Cashel walked around the house and looked at it. It didn't matter how much money you had if you weren't happy, he knew that all too well.

And he knew that the Power family had loved each other, even though there wasn't any money to go round. They were never too proud to be friends with the locals. Well, maybe Suki wasn't friends with all and sundry, but that was because Suki had always been wild. Even so, the wildness didn't come from her thinking she was a cut above anyone else. If anything, it was a fierce desire to do better that made her wild. To get herself out of Avalon. To be rich and famous.

But old Mr Power and Tess – even *thinking* of her name upset him – those two never thought they were better than anyone else. Maybe their ancestors would have thought so. It would have been bred into the De Paors: *You are better than all the townsfolk. They are there to do your bidding.* But old Mr Power and Tess weren't like that.

He remembered Tess, years ago, getting angry with him as they passed through the gallery where all the portraits were. She had noticed that he was walking cautiously, as though he might get into trouble for being in this part of the house.

'Would you stop comparing our backgrounds, Cashel, please,' she'd said. 'You know, your mother knows, *we have nothing*. We've barely been able to pay for electricity for the past three years. There's no money in this house. Stop looking at it like it's something different. It's a big house, nothing more. So what if my father can trace his ancestors back for decades? What does that mean in real terms, exactly? *You're* the one who's making it different.'

These days he couldn't seem to stop thinking about her – not surprising, given that he was buying the house she used to live in. The house she'd lived in when he first kissed her. The house she'd lived in when she betrayed him.

He made a note to himself to talk to Mara in the morning.

Not a penny was to be spared when it came to Avalon House. It was to be the best of everything. The very best.

Within weeks, Cashel found a strange peace in walking around the grounds of Avalon House. Mara had sourced a company of local tree surgeons, who were diligently examining the trees in the avenue. Some of the beautiful magnolias would have to come down, they'd told Cashel, because they were diseased.

Mara had also found a landscape gardener who specialized in the restoration of old gardens, and even though Cashel had meant to be in a meeting in London the morning she arrived, he'd found himself cancelling so he could join in on the walk around the grounds.

The gardener, a formidable lady named Judy, was in her sixties and wore sensible tweeds and a waxed jacket that looked at least as old as the house. She had a brusque manner and a small dog snapping at her heels, and Cashel found he was delighted to lope along behind her and Mara, wearing wellington boots and a heavy coat.

'There's a lot of work to be done here,' Judy said. 'Really serious work. It looks as though none of this has been touched for nigh on thirty years.' Her tone conveyed the disgust she felt for those responsible.

'It's true that the place has been neglected,' said Mara, who'd begun to research the history of the estate diligently and had learned how, thanks to her feckless ancestors, Tess had lost her home. And now the poor woman was struggling to hang on to her shop, as well as having to cope with her husband leaving. Though Judy was clearly the sort of woman who brooked no opposition to her views, Mara felt she owed it to her new friend to provide a more sympathetic account of Avalon House's recent history:

'For the past eighteen years, the house has been empty. The previous owners – the Powers, who'd owned Avalon House since its inception – lost all their money, so they hadn't the

239

resources to do anything to stop it becoming more and more decrepit.'

Cashel found himself compelled to intervene, although he didn't know why he was sticking up for Tess's family. 'These huge houses are a nightmare to run,' he said. 'It's the same story all over the country: grand old houses that were once the envy of everyone, handed down the generations until there wasn't a ha'penny left to maintain them, for all that they could trace their ancestors back to the year dot and had the portraits in the hall to prove it. Not that it matters who your ancestors are, or anything,' he trailed off.

'Yes,' said Judy, maintaining her brisk pace. 'I can see that. I've come across many similar cases in my work. I take it you want to make sure this garden is restored in keeping with the property?'

'Absolutely,' said Cashel, and he found himself wondering why he'd said anything positive at all about landowners in trouble.

It was as if he was standing up for Tess, Suki and their father, and the fact that they hadn't a ha'penny. Bizarre. He kept pace with Mara and Judy, shortening his long strides so the other pair could keep up. Mara shot him a couple of interesting glances but he ignored them. There could be something on her mind, he decided. Mara was not like any other assistant he'd ever had before. In fact, he'd probably have fired any assistant who behaved as Mara did toward him. Not for any insubordination or lack of ability – far from it, she was marvellously efficient, clever, capable of thinking on her feet and coming up with fantastic ideas – but she didn't kowtow to him at all. Of late, however, Cashel had changed; he found Mara's attitude refreshing. It was as if she was saying, *You may have lots of money and be my boss, but you're no better than me, sweetie.*

Cashel Reilly, who'd grown up feeling exactly the same way, admired that sort of spirit.

While he found Judy a joy, he couldn't cope with being present for too many of the architectural meetings. The architect, a slender, respectable young man named Lorcan Reed, had been highly recommended, having been involved in the restoration of many such period houses. But after hearing him expound at length on the need to ensure that all renovations and improvements remained absolutely in keeping with the various periods of the building, Cashel had decided that Lorcan Reed was an almighty bore. The architect was also intent on getting his own way, which immediately put Cashel's back up as he was accustomed to people deferring to his preferences, especially when it was his money they were spending.

Whether it was a question of choosing a particular flooring, a certain type of wood or stone, Cashel's choice would invariably be rubbished by Lorcan as historically inaccurate:

'With all due respect, in this part of the house it simply has to be parquet flooring,' he would splutter, becoming even more earnest when he was trying to make a point. 'I mean, there can be no other choice.'

Mara looked at Cashel, one eyebrow raised and the slightest hint of a smile playing around her lips, which were some wild, red colour today. He wondered where she got those mad lipsticks. They never seemed to fade. It was as if Mara decided *Today I shall be wearing bright red and it shall be bright red from morning 'til night.'*

'Will you bail me out when I kill that bloody Lorcan?' Cashel asked her when the architect was gone. 'He is so determined to have his own way.'

'I know somebody else like that, but I can't think who . . .' said Mara.

Cashel swotted at her with his giant pile of papers 'Make me a coffee, madam, and stop teasing. After a couple of hours listening to him drone, I think I need a kick-boxing session.'

'Kick boxing?' she'd asked. 'I'd no idea you were interested in that. I saw you as more of a weights man. Or a marathon man. Yes, I can see you doing marathons, never giving up. Oooh, the iron man – have you ever done one of those?'

He grinned at her properly this time. 'You really are a minx,' he said.

'Have I overstepped the mark?' Mara enquired. She did sometimes wonder whether she overstepped professional boundaries in her dealings with Cashel, but they got on so well that this wasn't an issue. Leaving Kearney Property Partners after what had happened with Jack had changed her. The part of Mara that was always irreverent and determined to be her own person had come fully to the surface. No matter what job she was in, she was going to be herself, her ordinary self. She was not going to reinvent herself in order to conform to other people's notions of what she should be, what she should wear, how she should behave, not worry over whether her boyfriend approved of her mad clothes, for example. She shook her head as if to dislodge the thoughts. No, let's not go there.

'Are you going to join the land of the living any time soon?' Cashel enquired. 'My espresso is ready.'

'Sorry,' she said. 'My mind was elsewhere. I was picturing you doing the marathon after a very long bike ride.' Her eyes twinkled at him. 'Worn out, begging for mercy.'

'Yeah,' he said, 'I really believe that.'

Restored after his espresso, Cashel set off to find Freddie, the master builder.

Striding round the house in his wellies and hard hat, eyeing things up and pulling a pencil from behind his ear to adjust his calculations on a scrap of paper, Freddie was a delight to deal with. He had lived in Avalon his entire life. Though younger than Cashel, he knew Riach and pronounced him 'sound', which appeared to be the highest praise there was in Freddie's estimation.

He was less enthusiastic when it came to Lorcan.

'He'd drive a sober man to drink,' Freddie had been heard

to say on a few occasions, according to Mara. He never said it in Cashel's hearing though. No, Freddie wasn't that stupid. It would be an awful mistake to insult the client by letting on you thought the architect should be locked up somewhere. Preferably with padded walls and something to draw on.

'It's a fine house,' Freddie would say wistfully when they were standing outside looking at the sweep of Avalon House in front of them. Then they'd turn and look at the avenue of trees, where the tree surgeons were busy at work, and over to the gleaming sweep of Avalon Bay. Because it was winter, the hard landscaping Judy was overseeing had to end early, but Cashel and Freddie would often linger after the workforce had gone home just to appreciate a spectacular sunset or the beauty of the view from Avalon House.

For all that Cashel was a very wealthy man and the new owner of Avalon House, because he was Avalon born and bred, Freddie looked upon him as an equal.

'Sure they were different times then,' Freddie might say, 'times when the landed gentry had land and money and the rest of us, ah sure, we had nothing. My father used to get fierce angry over the injustice of it all,' Freddie went on, 'the haves and the have nots made him a bitter man. A bitter man,' he repeated. 'He was always thinking of what we down there in the town had and what the rich people up on the hill had. And sure, for all I hear, near the end, they didn't have two pennies to rub together.'

'True,' said Cashel, 'true.'

'And it doesn't matter whether you live in a castle or a hovel. What matters is that you have a bite to eat, a fire to warm yourself at and a bit of love. What was that old saying from the bible . . . ?' Freddie could talk for hours in this manner, and Cashel found he liked to listen to him. '"Better a dinner of herbs and love than a stalled ox and hatred within." I think that was it, anyway,' said Freddie. 'For all the teachers who tried to get it into my thick skull, I can't remember much of the aul catechism, but it was something like that.'

Cashel grinned. 'I know what you're saying,' he said. 'My own family didn't have much, either.'

He was waiting to see what Freddie knew about his humble upbringing – but then, Freddie must have known, given that he knew Riach. Whatever he knew, however, Freddie was too wise to mention it.

'Ah, we were all the same back then,' was all Freddie said. 'No arse in our trousers.' He laughed. 'Look at us now, two fine men with jobs – aren't we doing great?'

Yes, we are, thought Cashel to himself. And on the surface, it all looked great. So why didn't he feel great?

Chapter Sixteen

*H*er addiction to hot chocolate with Danish pastries for elevenses would have to go, Mara decided as she drove down Willow Street in the direction of Lorena's, the best café in Avalon. She could feel her waistband getting tight and, now that Christmas was coming, she didn't want to have to watch what she ate. Mara loved Christmas. The only problem was working out where she'd be for it.

Danae was clearly much more comfortable with her around and Mara had begun to wonder if she'd stay in Avalon for Christmas Day itself and then drive to Dublin the next day.

At the back of her mind was Danae's secret: Mara was consumed with a desire to know about her aunt's past. Would Danae ever tell her?

All these thoughts flooded Mara's mind as she wound her way down the town to look for a parking place in the central square, which was already full of vehicles double parked in the rush up to Christmas. *Only two more shopping weeks to go!* said signs stuck outside the butcher's shop, where tinsel and illustrations of happy turkeys on platters were painted in primary colours above real slabs of meat.

'I miss you,' Cici had said mournfully on the phone the night before. 'We had such good times together.'

'I miss you too,' Mara said. 'But I couldn't stay. It was all too painful, everything reminded me of Jack. Anyway,' she added, determined to haul the conversation away from dangerous territory, 'bet you're having great fun with all the Christmas parties in full swing.'

'It isn't the same without you,' Cici said gloomily. 'Everyone says so.'

Mara was briefly gratified by this information. At least the friends she and Cici hung around with missed her.

'Nobody wants to go dancing because they say going out's too expensive. Despite that, they all go round to each other's flats and drink cheap beer or the latest Lidl wine offer by the crate. Next day, it's alcohol-induced depression and even less money all round. At least dancing doesn't give you a hangover.'

'That's because we danced without having to have six cocktails each,' Mara said virtuously. She hadn't had so much as a drop of wine since she'd been staying with Danae, who never drank anything but water and green tea.

'I saw Jack and *Her* last week in Eyre Square: Tawhnee,' Cici said the name in a rush, as if she had to say it fast or she wouldn't be able to say it at all. 'I wasn't going to tell you, but they were arguing. I thought you'd like that.'

'Arguing?' Mara said faintly. Unless there was a gun, blood and a body lying in the gutter, it would take more than 'arguing' to make her happy. In fact, the only way she'd be happy was if Jack had been seen dragging himself to the train station, bleating '*Mara, I must see her, she's the love of my life, I made a huge mistake, if only she'll forgive me and have me back . . .*' while Tawhnee screeched '*No!*' while clinging on to him and somehow looking much less beautiful in the process. In fact, Mara decided, Tawhnee had become Scrawnee. Her boob job had flopped and she was no longer skinny with a huge bust but skinny with a droopy bust . . .

'Yeah, he was smoking and she was shouting at him, saying he was supposed to have stopped.'

'And you could hear all this?' For a moment, Mara wondered if Cici had gone insane with a type of single-white-female stalker thing.

'They were shouting.'

Mara was surprised. She and Jack had never shouted at each other, he wasn't that sort of man. Raised voices weren't in Jack's repertoire. When he wanted his own way, he played the trump card of flashing his charming smile and Mara fell in with what he wanted. His other trick was to shrug and go missing for a day, which sent Mara into spirals of despair, thinking he'd left her because of her demands – not that she'd ever demanded much. When he'd eventually saunter back in, she'd apologize for anything – the sinking of the *Titanic*, the Icelandic volcanic eruption, *anything* – because she was so relieved to have him back.

'It looked to me as though not everything's rosy in Jack's world,' Cici said smugly.

'Oh, it doesn't mean anything, Cici. I'm not surprised he's back on the fags. She'll get used to it. Women will get used to anything for Jack.'

She had.

'But, you know, it proves they're not happy . . .' began Cici.

'It proves they argue,' Mara said quietly. 'Couples do.'

'You should come back,' Cici said. 'The city's boring without you and I miss you.'

'Miss you too, but I need some time away,' Mara said.

She couldn't tell Cici that she didn't know if she'd ever be able to live in Galway again, to revel in an atmosphere that was at once both medieval and very, very modern. Galway was where she'd finally found love, only to discover that it hadn't been love after all, not for him at least.

It wasn't exactly female warrior behaviour, to run away

from the scene of the pain, but she felt a peace living in Avalon that she knew she wouldn't feel in Galway.

And she was healing in Avalon. Healing took time. So did her job, which she loved.

A delivery truck began to back out of a parking space ahead of her and Mara grinned. It was a sign. Parking spaces that became vacant as you drove by were always a sign.

She hopped out of the car, paid the meter fee and marched off to Lorena's with a spring in her step.

Avalon had embraced the festive season with what Danae described as its usual exuberance. There wasn't an eave that hadn't been adorned with Austrian-ski-village-style fairy lights, and a Hollywood producer doing a remake of *A Christmas Carol* would not have been let down by the amount of red and white adorning every shopfront.

Mara smiled as she passed Reagan's bar, which stuck out like a sore thumb with its single limp gold star stuck to the door, looking as if it needed a dose of decorative Viagra to perk it up.

'Billy Reagan hates Christmas,' Danae had explained to Mara. 'Christmas Day is one of two days in the year when he has to shut. If he could get a couple of beds into the back snug and pretend the place was a hotel, so he could have a hotel licence and serve drink, he'd be in heaven. The only reason he's hung that gold star is as a concession to Belle – our lady mayoress sent all the local businesses a memo on the importance of Christmas decorations.'

There was no queue at Lorena's this morning, but the café was jammed and Mara pulled off her ugly but warm frontier-style hat with the two floppy ear flaps. A girl could only take being a slave to fashion so far when it was a degree above freezing. Shaking her mane of flaming hair, she looked around for a seat. There was one left at a table for four, where two women sat opposite each other and chatted, while on the third chair sat a man, head bent, engrossed in his magazine. Perfect.

Brian behind the counter mumbled 'hello', which was the equivalent of an effusive greeting from him. He was so painfully shy that Mara felt sorry for him, therefore she always did all the talking for the two of them.

'Morning, Brian. Isn't it a lovely day? I love the low December sun when it comes. Lifts your spirits, doesn't it?'

Brian mumbled something in reply and Mara's eyes spotted the Swedish cinnamon buns that Lorena, Brian's mother, had recently begun selling. Giving up Danish pastries didn't mean she couldn't try Swedish buns, did it?

'I think I'd like one of those buns, too, Brian,' Mara went on. 'Very bad for me, I'm sure. Or is that the low-calorie version?'

Mara's eyes twinkled as she looked up at Brian, and he smiled nervously back, then hurriedly turned away to busy himself with the coffee machine.

'I'll grab that empty seat before anyone else gets it,' Mara added, and wriggled through the crowded café to the single vacant spot.

'Is there anybody sitting here?' she asked.

'No – sit away,' said one of the two women, before turning back to her friend to resume their conversation.

The person opposite lowered the motorbike magazine he was reading as Mara plonked her bag on the seat and began removing her winter parka, a giant duvet-like garment that looked ugly but felt snug. From out of nowhere, a big masculine hand reached across to help her wriggle out of the coat.

She blinked as she saw who it was. The flirtatious Kiwi cowboy. He wasn't wearing his ridiculous hat today, which was why she hadn't spotted him first.

The idea of having her elevenses snack as a takeaway suddenly appealed, but Mara decided she wouldn't be run out of the café on account of a man. She'd had enough of fleeing the vagaries of men, thank you very much.

'I can manage to get my coat off,' she snapped, and did some more struggling with the parka.

The café was so full with tables jammed next to each other that the long duvet coat thwacked at least three people at nearby tables before Mara had it under control.

Crossly, she stuffed it on to the seat and marched off to get her coffee, looking all the while for another place to free up.

At the counter, she paid Brian, smiled thanks and took her small tray grudgingly back to the table.

She sorted herself out and was about to take a bite of cinnamon bun, when the two women decided they were leaving. Mara and the Kiwi Cowboy were alone at the table.

He put his magazine down and smiled at her.

'Hi, Red,' he said, in that velvety Southern hemisphere accent.

Honestly, she thought, was he ever going to take the hint? She was Off Men.

'Don't bother,' she snapped.

'Do you hate all men or is it just me?' he asked engagingly.

Mara was about to snap, *It's just you*, but held her tongue. Ignoring him, she concentrated instead on checking the sugariness of her chocolate.

Cici would definitely like him, Mara decided. He was much more her style. Mara liked the lean, elegant types like Jack, men who wore nice suits and had an aura of elegance about them even when they wore casual clothes. Cici had always gone for the macho guys with big muscles; the type of men who exuded animal magnetism and probably played sports morning, noon and night. That was this guy to a tee.

He had that sort of face, marked by smile lines and fresh air. He'd probably never used moisturiser in his life.

'I'm only making polite conversation,' he remarked.

'Well, don't,' she snapped, inwardly shocked at herself. That had been harsh. OK, Jack was a bastard; that didn't mean all other men were. She had now veered from mildly brusque to downright rude. 'Sorry,' she said. 'That came out all wrong.'

250

Mr Cowboy said nothing, but he continued to smile at her. She struggled to think of something to say – a rare phenomenon where Mara was concerned.

'You're clearly not local,' she decided upon. 'Do you live here or are you passing through?'

'I live here,' he said.

'What do you do?' Mara asked.

'I run a business with my brother – custom-made motor cycles,' Rafe explained.

'Oh,' said Mara. She knew precisely nothing about custom-made motor cycles. She had a vague recollection of Jack watching some American TV programme about it once. But he wasn't a bike sort of man. No, Jack was a Porsche sort of man. That's what he really wanted: a Porsche. He was determined to own a 911. A red one, with a black leather interior.

Mara wasn't sure about red for a car, particularly a sports car. It seemed a bit flashy. Loud. But then, who was she to comment on vehicle colours when she was the proud possessor of a bright green Fiat Uno? Bright green was more of a happy statement than a shiny, red sports car. That was a bit of a macho cliché, surely.

'And what do you call the business?' she asked.

'Berlin Bikes,' he said. 'That's my surname: Berlin. Rafe Berlin.'

'Oh, like the city! Cool! I like that,' said Mara.

'I could show you around,' Rafe said.

'I'm too busy to be shown around,' Mara said quickly, and then realized she had ventured right back into ultra rude territory again. Where men were concerned, it was as if her manners had been surgically removed the day Jack dumped her. A Dumpectomy. 'Sorry, that came out wrong. It's simply that I have a lot of things on. I've taken a mad busy new job.'

'What do you do?' asked Rafe, which was a reasonable

question under the circumstances. Mara toyed with a variety of answers: a trapeze artist in the circus, a burlesque dancer, a secret agent – but if she told him that she'd have to kill him. She went for the truth.

'I . . . I used to sell houses, I worked in a property agency. Now I'm working for the man who's just bought Avalon House – and living with my aunt, who runs the post office here.'

Damnit! That was far too much information to give away. She'd definitely never make it as a secret agent. One hot chocolate and she'd spilled everything. Secret agents had to be able to drink treble vodka martinis and lie brilliantly.

'Kind lady, long dark hair, lots of cool jewellery – that's your aunt?' said Rafe.

Most of the bike stuff was delivered by couriers and turned up in giant vans or lorries. The post office wasn't a place he was overly familiar with, but he was prepared to become their best customer if it would help him get to know this crazy girl whom he was liking more with every moment. He liked the rudeness of her, the sheer difference. Rafe had had girls throwing themselves at him since he was fifteen. This quirky girl was different.

'Rafe Berlin, nice to meet you,' he said, holding out a hand.

Mara took it. 'Mara Wilson,' she said, before fixing him with a gimlet glare. 'Are you married? Engaged? Going out with anybody? The father of a passel of children, perhaps, on the run from paying maintenance?'

'What's a passel, exactly?' Rafe enquired.

'I don't know,' revealed Mara. 'Loads. So, are you any of those things, otherwise connected with another woman?'

'No,' said Rafe truthfully.

Mara narrowed her eyes at him. 'Tell me the truth,' she said, channelling her inner secret agent.

'That *was* the truth,' Rafe said. 'Why? Have you recently fallen victim to some married dude with a passel of children who won't pay maintenance?'

252

The brief flicker of pain behind Mara's eyes told him he wasn't too far from the truth.

'Sorry,' he said, 'didn't mean to be intrusive.'

'No,' said Mara, apologetic, 'it was my fault. I have been giving you the third degree.'

'Why do they call it the third degree? Everyone says that around here,' said Rafe. 'I don't get it.'

Mara shrugged, 'One more weird Irish custom you'll have to get used to,' she said. 'Us Irish are a mysterious race with a proud tradition of being poetic and given to flights of fancy.' There, that all sounded mad enough to put him off her.

She gestured as she talked and he liked looking at her. Liked the way her eyes lit up. Liked the way those red curls bounced around and the lips, in that glossy fire-truck red, moved as she spoke, like she was creating a story out of thin air.

'What brought you here, Rafe? Seems like an out-of-the-way place to start a business.'

'It's a long story,' Rafe said, his merry eyes looking sombre. 'My brother was badly injured in a bike accident. I came here to help him keep the business going.' He pushed back his chair. 'Gotta run, Red. Would you like to have dinner with me?'

Mara was momentarily at a loss for words again. She stared at him. 'Dinner?' she repeated.

'Yes, dinner,' said Rafe. 'A meal we Kiwis traditionally have in the evening. Is there a mysterious Celtic way of saying this perhaps?'

She smiled at him for real then. Mara's smile had the power to make anyone fall in love with her. Rich, warm, marvellous. 'You're asking me out to dinner?' she said, as if the whole idea was both unexpected and totally delightful. 'Dinner.'

Some madness possessed her. Dinner with another man: yes, that was the way to de-Jack her soul.

'Dinner . . . I think I'd like that.'

253

'And you can tell me about the married man with the passel of children.'

'Not married at the time, though he is now, which is the problem – he didn't choose me as the bride,' said Mara. 'Please, let's not talk about him at all.'

'Fine by me,' said Rafe. 'Any weird food allergies, before I decide what to cook?'

This left Mara nonplussed. 'You're going to cook for me?'

Jack didn't know how to do anything but heat microwaveable meals or cook steak and baked potatoes. Red meat or 'pierce the film and microwave for four minutes on high'. Nothing in between.

'I love cooking,' Rafe said, with a grin that revealed white, even teeth. His eyes were a hypnotic grey blue.

Going to his house seemed a bit risky, though.

'No, let's eat out,' she said. 'If you're really nice, you can cook me dinner next time.'

As if there would be a next time.

Rafe drove the jeep down the drive and parked it outside the workshop. He always felt a surge of pride when he looked up at the big sign on the doors: BERLIN BIKES – CUSTOM MADE MOTORCYCLES.

So far as the locals were concerned, this was simply a small business run by the two Berlin brothers. But to bike aficionados, Berlin Bikes ranked up there with Orange County Choppers. The Berlin brothers had more clients in the US and the rest of Europe than anyone in Avalon would believe.

Jeff's jeep was in his spot and Karen's car was parked up at the house. The house itself was lit up. Karen had the gift of homemaking. When she and Jeff had first moved in, the house had been nothing but an empty shell; five years later, it was a home. With Christmas approaching, string lights twinkled from the eaves, while Scandinavian-style decorations made the wooden interior cosy and bright.

Only the other day Karen's mother had rolled up with yet another bag of red gingham hearts to hang on the tree, causing Jeff and Rafe to exchange amused grins.

'I'll never understand these Avalon women,' Rafe muttered.

'Best not to try to understand them – just love them, that's my advice,' Jeff said.

Jeff's love for an Avalon woman was the reason they were all there. She'd been pregnant with their first child when he had the accident. Not many people survived motorbike collisions with drunk drivers, so Jeff was lucky to be alive, but the spinal injury he'd suffered had left him paralysed from the waist down.

It changed all their lives. Jeff and Rafe had originally planned to set up their own business in California, home of custom-bike culture. But with a husband confined to a wheelchair and a new baby, Karen needed the support of her family in Avalon. So Rafe had given up his dream of life in Los Angeles and the brothers had set up Berlin Bikes in the small Irish town instead.

'You're looking pretty pleased with yourself,' Jeff said, pencil in one hand as he expertly rotated his custom-made wheelchair round the specially lowered design table where he was working on a new commission from a guy in Switzerland.

Rafe grinned. 'You could say that, bro. I've met this amazing girl in the coffee shop . . .'

On Saturday morning, Mara had the most marvellous lie-in. Waking to a sunny but crisp December morning, she put on her fluffy socks to go into the kitchen in search of coffee. There was no sign of Danae. It had to be one of her mysterious Saturdays, Mara thought, with a little irritation. Why wouldn't Danae confide in her? What secret could be that bad?

Noticing a book lying in the middle of the kitchen table, she pulled it towards her and opened it.

Danae was on a familiar journey, one she'd taken every single month for the past eighteen years.

Normally she drove straight to the nursing home. On her arrival she'd go into the kitchen, where she'd make herself a cup of tea and the cook would give her a bowl of soup or whatever the residents were having for the day. They all knew Danae well, she'd been going there so long.

Today she'd been too tired to complete the journey without a break. Instead she'd stopped along the way for a cup of tea and a scone that she covered with butter and jam, to give herself a hit of sugar. Anything to pep her up. The thought of darling Mara reading her diary left her feeling absolutely shattered.

She was a slow driver and it was twelve o'clock by the time she drove up the manicured driveway to Refuge House. It was a charitable trust nursing home, so any money that was made from the inhabitants went straight back to the old-fashioned building with two modern wings on each side. Beautifully maintained, warm, kind, loving. If a person needed nursing home care, this was one of the best places to have it. Danae knew that. A lot of her salary went into making sure that Antonio would be looked after.

When his mother, Rosa, had been alive, she'd contributed. After she died, no more money had come in from the Rahill family. Danae knew it was because Antonio's brothers wanted *her* to shoulder the cost of keeping him in a private nursing home. After all, it was thanks to her that he'd ended up there.

In the front hall, the smell was the same as always: the vaguely institutional smell of cabbage and cleaning products. Every surface gleamed. The floors were polished. Each rung of the staircase to the first floor had been burnished till it glowed. Up there lived the ambulant residents and the elderly who were in full command of their senses. There was a scent of beeswax mixed with lemon oil in the air.

256

Antonio was downstairs in an area that nobody called the locked ward. It was simply 'downstairs'.

'My husband's downstairs,' a person might say if they met Danae in the visitors' room and she'd nod, knowing what that meant.

Downstairs was where people who needed twenty-four-hour care lived. These were the patients with dementia or brain injuries; they would never be able to live on their own. They only got out into the garden under supervision. Gentle walks with kind members of staff. So for their safety, the downstairs was locked, but nobody called it that; it was part of the ethos of Refuge House.

There was a receptionist on duty who looked up when she came in.

'Danae, how lovely to see you,' she said, before pressing the buzzer that allowed access to the rest of the building.

The code to get in downstairs was a rotating one. There were three separate four-digit codes; if you tried the first one and it didn't work, you'd try number two and then number three. Today it was number two. The door pinged open and Danae went in.

It was always busy downstairs. There'd be music playing, sometimes jazz, sometimes dance tunes from the 1950s and 1960s. The people with dementia loved those songs. Music was often the last sense to go. People who didn't know who their family were and couldn't recognize themselves in the mirror – their eyes would light up when they heard Elvis singing 'Wooden Heart'. They'd smile and try to dance a few steps clumsily across the room.

There was always lots of dancing. Finola, a small blonde nurse, was a great one for taking people up and giving them a whirl around the floor. Everyone loved Finola with her bubbly smile and her warmth. Today, Finola was feeding one of the oldest residents, a lady called Gwen who seemed so small and shrunken it was hard to believe she was actually able to breathe. She sat in a chair, her body cushioned against the hardness of the frame by a large sheepskin. Danae had often thought that the very, very old were like the very, very young. Babies were cushioned by sheepskin in beautiful buggies and frail old people needed to be cushioned when they were close to death.

'Hi,' said Danae quickly, keeping going. She didn't want to stop today. She didn't have the heart for smiling or chatting with any of the people who'd become her friends over the many years she'd been visiting.

There was no sign of Antonio. It was too cold for him to be out in the garden. The garden doors were shut, anyway. In one corner, the movement therapist was leading a small class; they had castanets and ribbons and were waving them wildly to the beat. They all looked so happy, gazing at their therapist's face.

Danae turned into the corridor which led to Antonio's dormitory. She peeped in, not wanting to intrude. Appropriate privacy was important in a place like downstairs. People were bathed and fed and taken to the toilet and had incontinence pads changed when required, but a person's dignity was important, the director had always said, and Danae agreed with him.

There was only one man in the dorm, lying on his bed, his eyes closed, although Danae knew he probably wasn't asleep.

In his bed, turned away from her, was her husband of thirty-five years. She took the chair and sat beside Antonio and reached out and held his hand, the way she had so many times before.

His brain injury had been so catastrophic that Antonio did not recognize her. He never would. The blows that had completely destroyed much of his brain had robbed him of all cognitive awareness. Yet when he lay sleeping, he looked exactly like the Antonio of old, merely an older version. The hair was grey along the temples where it had once been glossy black. Lines of age were etched into his face. Apart from that, he looked the same.

It was when he was awake that the injury became obvious: his mouth drooped to one side, his eyes looked at her with total incomprehension.

She sat holding his hand, stroking, hoping the morphine was taking away some of the pain he must be feeling. There was no drug for the pain she felt. There never would be. Science wasn't that good. Guilt and agony reached places that no pharmaceutical could touch.

It was hard to explain fear to people who had never experienced it. True fear wasn't jumping out of your seat at a tarantula in a scary movie or the thing under the bed in some horror flick. Such things had nothing to do with fear. To a degree, Danae had known fear in her childhood. A well-founded fear that she and her mother wouldn't have the food and shelter they needed to survive. That was clear and present in her childhood.

But the fear with Antonio: that was a different sort of fear entirely, a fear that bleached into her very bones.

Before they were married, he'd seemed like a different man – happy, merry, kind, good-humoured, full of life, the sort of man everyone wanted at their party.

'Let's have Antonio along, he'll sing us a few songs and play the piano,' people would cry.

Danae loved that. She was the girlfriend and then the fiancée of this wonderful man. Antonio Rahill, half-Italian half-Irish, with flashing dark eyes, gypsy dark hair, pale skin. Black Irish, they called them. Thanks to his mother, he could speak fluent Italian. His second name was Luigi. A Calzone family name for decades. Antonio's Irish father had wanted his son's first name to be a good, Irish saint's name, like Anthony. His mother had resisted. By way of compromise, he was christened Antonio.

He may have had a saint's name, but Antonio was no saint. Danae hadn't known that when he proposed, slipping the small ring with the tiny diamond in the claw setting on to her finger. The happiness she'd felt at that moment was over-whelming. This man loved her, loved her enough to marry her. There was to be none of the pain her mother had gone through, no succession of men. She would build a life with this one man, the man who loved her.

They had no money at first. After they married, they lived in a top-floor flat where the decor was at least twenty years out of date. But it was clean and dry, and it had great views out over the city.

She was a dreadful cook, Antonio would say.

'Get my mama to teach you,' he'd say, and she'd promised she would.

Danae could do any number of things with eggs, because in the bad old days, she and Sybil could always afford a few eggs. Omelettes, scrambled eggs – you name it, she could do it. With the help of Rosa, Antonio's mother, she began to broaden her repertoire. Rosa was delighted that her son's new bride wanted to learn how to cook like a proper Italian wife.

The first time she had showcased her newly acquired Italian cooking skills, Danae set the formica table with a sheet as a table cloth so they wouldn't have to look at the horrible blue-and-yellow pattern. She lit two red candles, got out their best glasses – a wedding gift from Antonio's uncle, who owned a restaurant. She'd struggled hard with cannelloni. For dessert, there was tiramisu, Antonio's favourite. Or rather, his second favourite. The dish he loved most was sweet cannoli, but Danae wasn't to attempt that one, Antonio insisted. There was no point. She could never reach the culinary heights of his mother. And Danae, who was used to being in second place, meekly agreed.

Danae had asked Antonio to bring some wine for this

special occasion. She rarely drank herself, but the glasses were ready. A jug of water was on the table. The oven was set on low with the cannelloni keeping warm inside. Having checked and doubled-checked that everything was ready, Danae waited patiently.

Seven came and went, eight, nine . . . She began to worry that something must have happened. Eventually she rang the restaurant, fearful that she'd made a mistake and tonight wasn't the night they'd agreed on, maybe he was still working. But no, he'd left hours ago. So she sat on the couch, a second-hand couch from another of Antonio's uncles, until eventually she fell asleep.

She woke with a start to find him standing over her, and her first instinct was to smile and reach her arms out and go: 'Oh, darling, I was worried when you didn't come.'

And then something inside her, some instinctive reaction, made her pull back a fraction.

The man who was glaring down at her didn't look like her husband. He didn't have the warmth in his eyes, the smile on his face. No, this man was different. He was Antonio, and yet not him.

'Where's my dinner?' he growled.

The words, *It was ready at seven o'clock when you were supposed to come home*, died on her lips. She knew that this would not be the correct thing to say. Faded memories of fear surfaced.

Danae moved carefully off the couch, sliding away from him, as if the slightest touch might somehow inflame him. Afterwards, she never knew where the instinct came from, the awareness that there was danger here.

'I'll get it ready for you, darling,' she said.

She wished she'd bought a bottle of wine herself. Perhaps that might have calmed him. But judging by the smell of alcohol on his breath, he'd been drinking already. Maybe more would make him worse; she didn't know.

She set the dish on the table. The edges were burnt. Carefully, she served it up, her hands shaking.

He hadn't moved from the couch. He stood staring at her, following her every move.

'There,' she said, putting down a simple tomato salad drizzled with olive oil, the way his mother made it. 'I hope you like it.'

The matches were on the table and she tried to light the candles, but her hand was shaking so much that she couldn't quite do it.

'Can't you do anything right?' he snapped.

And then Danae was frightened, a pure cold fear that started deep in her belly, turning her bowels to water, making her stomach clench, creeping up her chest so that every muscle in her tightened, every part of her was coiled, ready to escape.

'Maybe you could do it, darling,' she said, turning to him.

'Don't look at me,' he hissed.

He moved so quickly that he was beside her in an instant. The first blow went to the side of her head, and the pain that immediately followed was mingled with the strangest ringing in her ear.

She couldn't compute, her mind couldn't make sense of this.

She'd been hit, but how? Not by Antonio, not the man who loved her, he couldn't have done this. She must be wrong, this must be a nightmare and any minute she would wake up.

The second blow went to her stomach, felling her. He was taller than she and much more powerful. His fist in her stomach sent her flying backwards, against the cooker. As she fell to the floor, her head bashed against the oven. Collapsed on the floor, one leg straight, one leg bent beneath her, her stomach spasmed with pain. Her head was ringing with the strength of his blows. She still couldn't make sense of what had happened. Then she looked up at him again and he started kicking her.

When she came to, she had no idea what time it was, although the moon was shining in the windows and the oven was humming away on low. She tried to lift herself off the floor, but it was impossible. Every part of her body felt sore. As if someone had stood on her, tried to squash her flat like an ant. Nausea overwhelmed her, greater than the headache pounding through her head. Summoning all her strength, she pulled herself up. One eye couldn't seem to focus properly and she kept blinking. The rooms were dark, the only light came from the moon outside, but she knew she wasn't alone in the apartment – she felt his presence.

When she had managed to drag herself to her feet she stumbled to the kitchen sink and splashed cold water on her face, hoping to revive herself, hoping that the coolness would make the pain go away.

She couldn't move her left ankle properly and she didn't know why until she realized it was swollen and there was a boot mark across it. Moving slowly so as not to wake him, she made it out of the kitchen and down the corridor into the tiny bathroom. Staring at her from the bathroom mirror was a horror story. Her face swollen on one side, lip split from something he must have done after she passed out. Gingerly she pulled up her blouse to see the beginnings of a huge bruise around her stomach, bruises on her arms, and in the bathroom light she could now see the marks on her legs too. Her ankles were swollen beyond belief.

Even with the bathroom door closed, she could hear Antonio snoring. It had always been a joke between them, how much he snored.

At the dinner to celebrate their engagement, his mother had announced: 'My Antonio, always he snore! He wake us all up. Now he can wake you up.'

The family had laughed. It seemed like a million years ago. As if it had all been a dream. Or maybe this was the dream? But Danae knew this was no dream; this was her new, horrible

263

reality and the fear possessed her, the fear of what would happen when he woke up. The fear of telling anyone.

And if she did tell, who would believe her? Antonio was the epitome of a hail fellow well met, a charmer. Everyone loved him. Nobody would believe he could do a thing like this. She could hardly believe it herself.

Wincing with the pain, she took a towel and a facecloth and tried to cool down her bruises and wipe the blood off her face. Apart from her face, he hadn't hit her anywhere that would show. Shaking, she found the jar of aspirin she used when she had her monthlies and took two, fearful that she'd drop the glass of water, her hands were shaking so much.

Carrying the towels into the living room, she used them to make up a bed on the couch and laid herself down there, as comfortably as she could in her pain. Tomorrow, it would have to be different. Wouldn't it?

In Avalon, Mara sat outside with the hens at her feet and Lady leaning against her, and struggled to make out the words through the tears in her eyes. Danae's diary was the saddest thing she'd read in all her life.

The psychiatrist wanted me to write this. I don't trust psychiatrists that much. I used to. They were doctors and doctors were gods.

Like I used to think anyone with a degree was brighter than me. I hadn't been to university. I'd barely been to school, what with the way we moved when I was a child. My mother didn't have much faith in education.

'Life is the best university,' she'd say, tapping the side of her nose.

The first psychiatrist was very young.

The last one was older, a man, kind and gentle, brains bursting out of him. He even had one of those big foreheads where it looked as though the brains needed more room than most people's did. And yet, he didn't really know. He said things to me, but I could tell from his eyes that he knew I was clever and that there were no absolutes. He said that once. Those exact words. 'There are no absolutes.'

That was when I realized that nobody knew anything for sure. It was all guesswork. Guesswork made up of history and science, past cases and studies, but guesswork all the same.

Nobody knew what had been going on in my head or in Antonio's head. They could postulate till the cows came home, but nobody knew for sure. That was when I began to realize that we were all clinging to the rock, hoping. Everyone was the same. Some people had better rocks and a better foothold, but it was all a matter of clinging on. Once I understood that, I began to get better, although I didn't know it at the time.

I have nobody to visit. There's only one person I'd like to come, my brother, but I told him not to. I don't want him to see this place or me in it. The lack of dignity would shock him.

Sleeping in a ward with other women, no privacy, wearing a rag-tag collection of clothes because someone's always stealing yours. At one time, I'd have thought there was no dignity in living like that, but it isn't a worry to me now. I know none of that has anything to do with dignity.

The people here are trying to help us. They are tough but nice. Nobody hits you. Nobody on the staff shouts at you. They're trying to give you back your actual dignity, which means giving you back your mind and your soul.

That's dignity. All the rest, like peeing with the toilet door open, is immaterial. Did you know that when your mind goes, so does your soul? Like a dandelion blown in the wind, it floats away.

I had a visitor from the shelter today. Mary. She wears red a lot, that's what I remember most: huge red cardigans wrapped around her and red necklaces. Her hair is yellow from a home-dye kit, something my mother would be scornful of. Mary is the kindest woman I have ever met. She hugs me and I try to let her. I don't think I deserve hugs. I am stiff in her embrace and I know it. I try, really I do, but this kindness almost hurts. It's wrong. I cannot have it.

When I cry, she has tissues in her pockets. She's always had a never-ending supply for the never-ending tears.

'You deserve to be loved,' she says to me. It's exactly what the older psychiatrist has been saying.

Mary has no education except for running the shelter, but she knows as much as he does.

When Mary goes, I sleep. They're trying to get my medication right and that means lots of changing doses. This week, the drugs are making me even more tired than usual. I have to nap all the time. I lie on my bed with my eyes closed. I can blot out the noises around me. It's safe here. Even though that banging-head woman is wandering around, the only one she wants to hurt is herself. Another girl came in today, half-crazed with pain. She's in a room they have under camera surveillance all the time in case she tries anything. So I am safe. Safe in the nuthouse. If I could laugh, I would.

In the shelter, where I felt safe for the first time in years, we talked about our lives and our men. I said I'd never got used to being hit. Used to the idea, sure, but the pain and the fear was as bad every time. Except I knew I deserved it. He said I did. He said I couldn't spend any money. He kept the housekeeping money and it was doled out every week. None to spare, none to let me buy a lipstick: 'What do you want with lipstick? You think another man would look more than once at you? I'll make sure no man looks at you, bitch.'

One woman had lived with her husband for twenty-seven years before she ran away to the shelter. Her son wouldn't take her in. He blamed her for not leaving his da years before, blamed her for putting him through the fear of growing up in their house.

'I couldn't tell him how trapped I felt,' she said, crying. We all comforted her and we all understood.

You're trapped, like the mouse that a cat's playing with. Paralysed with fear. You believe all the things he says to you.

You believe you're worthless. Eventually, you reach the point where he doesn't have to be there for you to believe it. A little voice in your head tells you non-stop: 'You are a worthless piece of shit. You deserve this. You drive him to this. It's all your fault.'

One woman lost two babies to her husband's boot. She'd had six kids by then, it was all she could do to cope, and she didn't know how she'd manage with seven. She told herself it was God's way of making sure she didn't have to cope with rearing another child.

I never had to cope with rearing my own baby. The first one I lost, I thought he'd be a boy. I felt it. Nobody did the trick with the ring on a piece of thread over my belly or said I was carrying low or high and that meant a boy or a girl. I didn't have women friends to say or do these things. Antonio didn't like me having friends. Friends got in the way.

It was all about control, I began to understand.

Control and fear was how they kept us under their boots and their fists. The beatings were just a way of reinforcing their control.

We'd been married six years when I lost the baby. He wanted sex off me and I was so tired, bone weary. I guessed I was somewhere near three months along. That's when you're tiredest, the books from the library said. I hadn't been to the doctor about the baby. Our doctor said he hated treating me, seeing the bruises and the scars, when I would do nothing.

'But my husband's a good man, Doctor,' I'd say. I didn't add that it was me who made him do it and I had to stay with him, to take care of him.

I'd never refused Antonio sex before, never dreamt of it. Who knew what he'd do? I didn't refuse him that night either. But I couldn't pretend the way he liked, and he began to slap me.

The slaps could be the worst. He wouldn't stop slapping. He didn't even have a drink on him. Stone-cold sober, he was.

'It's that fucking brat inside you, isn't it?' he roared.

The fear that night was the worst. It wasn't just me any more, it was my baby. Did you know that, even at three months, your hands aren't big enough to protect your belly?

I must have passed out with the kicks. When I woke up, he was gone and I was lying in the bed, with the pain of losing my little boy deep in my belly.

The second baby was at the end. I didn't know I could still get pregnant then. He punched me in the belly and I lost it.

That was the night something in me changed. Like a light switch going on.

The taxi driver said he wouldn't charge for driving me to the shelter.

'No, love,' he said as he helped me in, then went back to get the few bits I'd taken from the flat. 'It's on me. He ought to be locked up, your fella. Locked up.'

Mary in the shelter was the first one I saw, and she got me straight to the hospital. She held my hand all the while, and when I woke up, when they'd scraped what was left of my second baby out of me, she was still there.

Mary didn't say: If you'd left him, you could have saved your baby. But I was thinking it, and I was saying sorry to the baby.

The police went looking for him, but Antonio was always clever. Someone tipped him off and they couldn't find him.

I knew he'd come after me, but Mary said I was safe. We used to sit on the fire escape looking out over the city, and she'd say he couldn't touch me any more.

I believed her. I believed them all.

And then he found me.

Afterwards, the police wanted to know how he'd managed to locate the shelter, because not that many knew where it was, but when he was in a rage, Antonio was capable of anything.

It was nighttime when he came. It was cold and I was sitting up with another girl in the big room with the fire. All of a sudden I heard him screaming my name, and I thought I must be going mad.

'Danae, you bitch, where are you?'

Then he was there, and the other girl ran to get help, and I was on the floor with him on top of me, choking me.

'I'm going to kill you, bitch,' he said. For a moment, I thought: let him. And then I remembered the baby coming out of me and I reached for the coal shovel.

I kept hitting him until his hands fell away from me.

Mary came running into the room with a baseball bat, but she didn't need it. Whatever I'd done to Antonio was well done by then.

Mara was waiting for the sound of Danae's car on the drive. It was evening when she finally arrived. She approached the door uncertainly, looking at Mara with anxiety in her eyes.

Mara threw herself at her aunt and enveloped her in a hug.

'Oh, Danae,' she said, 'I wish I'd known. How awful it must have been to live with this for so long.'

'I shouldn't have tried to defend myself,' Danae said, closing her eyes with relief. Mara didn't hate her after all. 'The police would have come, he'd have been put in jail.'

'Only to get out again and hurt you again,' said Mara angrily. She couldn't bring herself to say Antonio's name. 'You did the only thing you could have done. And that's why you've been punishing yourself all these years, isn't it? Living alone, keeping away from people . . .'

Danae nodded. 'The guilt kills me. Guilt over not having left him sooner, so my babies would have stood a chance. Guilt over what I did to Antonio. No matter what he did to me, I was alive and he was as good as dead. I couldn't live with that.'

'Have you never considered counselling?'

'Apart from six weeks in a psychiatric hospital because I went into a numb state – catatonic, they called it – no,' Danae said. 'They were kind to me in there, but nobody could understand. I had as good as taken Antonio's life away. His family never forgave me. Never. It was all my fault, they said. Your father and mother have always been wonderful. They understood my need to be left alone.'

Mara hugged her aunt even tighter. 'You poor darling, Danae. You've got me now, I'll do my best to help you from now on. You shouldn't have to cope with all this pain on your own.'

Chapter Seventeen

There was no protocol for meeting your husband's newly pregnant girlfriend. No book of handy hints. Tess had thought of doing a little Internet surfing before the meeting, but what keywords would she type into the search engine?

Forty-something bitterness versus twenty-something nubile happiness?

What to wear rather than how to behave would have been on her sister Suki's list for sure.

But then Suki always knew how to dress for the occasion.

Tess was the opposite. When in doubt, she inevitably wore the wrong thing.

And so it was that Sunday afternoon. Tess found herself wearing old fawn corduroy trousers and a dark brown turtle-neck sweater that somehow leached all the colour from her face, apart from the two spots of high colour on her cheeks. She took down her hair, realized she hadn't washed it that morning and her roots were greasy, so tied it up again. What was the point in looking good? Kevin and Claire were a done deal.

But Tess had recently wondered if it was time to make an effort. She had a few grey hairs in the blonde now, and stress had given her purple shadows under her eyes.

Downstairs, she caught sight of herself in the hall mirror. In this ensemble and with tied-up hair, she felt like the picture of a dried-up old prune who'd let her husband out of her sight and then watched him run away to sunnier, more youthful climes. Was there a fairy tale about that? The Stupid Older Woman? All older women were stupid or evil in fairy tales. Only the young and pretty females were treated kindly. Tess was theorizing whether this could be an idea for Suki in her new book when Kitty appeared with her woollen winter coat on, a purple furry handbag in one hand and an excited expression on her small face.

'We're having marshmallows, aren't we?' Kitty asked for at least the fifth time that day. The marshmallows were very important. Kitty liked to try to melt them into the hot chocolate on her teaspoon, drowning each one until it was a puddle of pinky-brown sludge and then sucking it up.

'Yes, with marshmallows,' said Tess cheerily, because no matter how many deranged thoughts were going through her mind, she wouldn't expose her children to them.

'Goodie,' said Kitty happily. 'Do you think Claire will have hot chocolate too? The baby might like it.' Despite Tess' horror at having to tell Kitty about the baby, Kitty was delighted with the news and told everyone.

'That's a very good idea,' Tess said evenly. 'Milk is good for babies. I drank lots when you were in my tummy.'

She managed a smile. It hurt like hell even to think about it, but this baby would be Kitty's half brother or sister.

Which made her feel mean and nasty. She wasn't the sort of person who felt anger towards an unborn child, was she?

Yet somehow, she did feel upset about it all in ways she didn't even want to think about.

She quashed those feelings. Today wasn't about her, it was about Kitty and Zach.

It fell on Tess's shoulders to make sure Kitty and Zach saw the baby as a good thing and not as a child who could conceivably get more of their father's love because he would be living with the baby's mother.

On the Internet, she had read scads of information on blended families and on welcoming new brothers or sisters into a complex mix. She was determined she wouldn't wreck it all with bitterness. She had separated from Kevin. She could not blame him for finding someone else or having a baby with that person. Exactly *how* she was to achieve all this was another matter entirely.

She checked her watch. It was a quarter to five. They should be leaving.

'Zach,' she yelled up the stairs. 'It's time to go.'

Zach, Kitty and Tess were to meet Kevin and Claire in the hotel coffee shop at five.

She put the white knitted hat on Kitty's head.

'Coming,' mumbled Zach, taking the stairs two at a time.

Antiques were easier than people and relationships. Antiques never asked personal questions or said, 'Surely you can't expect me to pay a hundred euros for this bit of old junk?' whereas people did. Sadly, antiques were harder to sell these days.

Thankfully, Zach was now speaking to her again. Tess suspected it had something to do with his new girlfriend, a tiny sprite of a thing from his class in school who was named Pixie and lived up to the name. Pixie had short, dark hair, wore boyish clothes and slightly Goth make-up and was both beautiful and very nice.

The final plus was that Pixie's parents were divorced and she had two sets of new siblings from each side, something she treated as entirely normal.

Tess could imagine Pixie telling Zach that his mother must be going through hell right now and it wasn't her fault his dad had a pregnant girlfriend.

Tess wanted to get down on her knees to thank Pixie for whatever it was she'd said to Zach, because he was being his normal sweet self again.

'Sorry about, you know, earlier, Ma,' was all he'd said. 'It's been kinda tough.'

Tess had hugged him. 'I understand,' she said. 'It's been tough on me, too, love.'

Now, she walked into the plush surroundings of the hotel lounge bar where afternoon tea was being served and looked around, feeling a tight knot of anxiety inside her. The place was busy and she couldn't see Kevin. Perhaps he'd chickened out. Perhaps she should have chickened out.

'Mum, it's Dad!'

Kitty's small, warm hand pulled away from her mother's as she raced across the busy room to her father. He was sitting at a prime corner table with a girl who looked both nervous and incredibly young. Very slim, Tess could see, and with no sign of any pregnancy bump under a pink mohair jumper with sequins on the outside. Claire was pretty; that lovely combination of fair hair, blue eyes and skin that tanned easily. As she rose to her feet to greet Kitty and Zach, who'd moved on ahead of his mother, Tess decided that Claire looked like a radio station's music festival DJ.

It was easy to imagine her with tanned legs emerging from denim cut-off shorts and a floppy hat on her head at any festival.

Beside her sat Kevin, who was hugging his daughter and then Zach.

'Tess, you're here.'

Tess knew she'd walked over towards the table, but it was as if her body had moved of its own volition. The whole scene felt a little unreal. This girl was going to be Kitty and Zach's step-mother.

Be strong, Tess said to herself. Be a grown-up.

'Hello, Claire,' she said with steely calm, and held out her hand. 'I'm Tess.'

'It's so lovely to meet you,' said Claire, getting to her feet and knocking over her glass of juice. 'Oh no, shit. Oh, sorry!'

Hand clamped over her mouth at having used bad language in front of a child, Claire went pink.

'It's fine,' said Kitty, settling in beside Claire and looking at her jumper with interest. 'Mum says that all the time, don't you, Mum? I have,' Kitty added in conspiratorial tones, 'heard her use the f-word.'

Zach laughed, while Tess wondered whether to laugh or cry.

'Kitty,' she said, 'behave yourself.'

While Kevin, also red-faced, tried to mop up the juice, Tess sat down in a seat across the table. She could do this.

'So,' she said brightly, with a hint of Montessori teacher talking to her new class, 'now that you've met Zach and Kitty, tell us all about the pregnancy. You must be so excited.'

It wasn't the way she'd planned to play it, but now that she was here, it seemed like the only way to go. Straight and up front.

'. . . er, we don't have to talk about that now,' said Kevin, who was just entering the puce-faced stage of embarrassment.

Tess looked at her husband and felt terribly annoyed with him. He was responsible for this – she might have wanted the separation, but the pregnant girlfriend was all his doing. The least he could do was act a bit more mature over it all.

'Kevin,' she said, 'let's keep this simple and honest. It's hard enough as it is.'

'I'm so sorry,' blurted out Claire, 'I never meant all this to happen. I didn't know, really . . .' Her lovely blue eyes filled with tears.

Pregnancy hormones, Tess decided.

'You didn't do anything wrong,' Tess said, with emphasis on the word *you*. Kevin, on the other hand, she wasn't so sure about. Did she or didn't she have an old ceremonial sword in the back room of the shop? She might skewer him with it one day soon.

'Drinks?' said a waitress, arriving pad in hand.

'Yes, thank you. We're all thirsty,' said Tess brightly to the waitress.

'Hot chocolate with marshmallows,' piped up Kitty.

'Tea,' for me said Tess. 'No, strike that, I'll have a glass of red wine.' They could walk up the hill home. A glass of a nice red might help.

'Me too,' said Kevin hastily.

'Sweetie –' began Claire, big eyes turned towards him. 'You said . . .'

'Make that a mineral water,' Kevin amended.

Beaming, Claire looked at Tess. 'He's not going to drink during the pregnancy. You never know when something might go wrong and he'd have to rush me to hospital, and he can't drink and drive.'

Tess nodded, thinking that she'd have a lot to tell Suki on the phone tonight. 'Very sensible,' she murmured.

Somehow, they all got through it. Kitty drank her hot chocolate without melting any marshmallows, occupied as she was in discussing Sylvanian Families and her love of pink things with Claire, who also loved pink things.

'I have a lot of Sylvanians, don't I, Mum?'

'I used to too,' Claire said. 'My little sister got them after me, but I'm going to get them from her for the baby.'

'The baby could have some of mine!' Kitty said. 'You can see them all when you come to our house to visit.'

Tess decided that a second glass of red wine might help.

Even Zach unbent after some time spent in Claire's company.

She was so sweet, and strangely innocent, that it was impossible to feel any hatred towards her. And why should they feel hatred towards her, Tess pondered, as she watched Kevin and Zach talk about football, while Claire entertained Kitty by discussing what bands she liked. Claire really hadn't done anything wrong.

At the end, Kevin paid and Claire hugged everyone, including Tess.

'You've been so nice to me,' she said and it looked as if she might cry again.

Up close, Claire's skin was so very clear and unlined and she smelt of a sweet, floral perfume. Beside her, Tess felt about ninety.

'Babies have a way of making things right,' Tess said.

And it was true. A new person was coming into this world and it was connected with her and her children. She would do the right thing. That was Tess Power's way.

A few days later, she wasn't feeling quite so well inclined towards Claire. Kitty hadn't stopped talking about her and Zach kept saying she was 'really cool', which was high praise indeed.

Family, thought Tess, determined to do the right thing, she had to create a new family: a blended family, because that's what they would be when Claire had the baby. How bizarre to be a blended family. Up until now she'd only read about such things in magazines. Tess's favourite was the magazine with the psychologist answering questions; she could clearly recall a letter from a woman who'd loathed the idea of her precious children spending time with her husband's new wife, or rather her ex-husband's new wife. Now that was going to be her. At the time, Tess had never dreamt that she might one day find herself in that situation, so she'd read the letter and the advice in a calm, dispassionate way. Never take it out on the children, they must be allowed to see both parents, without bitterness, without rancour – that would have been the old Tess's view of it all.

But now that it was happening to her, it was different. Despite liking Claire on one level, the thought of her having weekends with Kitty was like a bullet exploding into Tess's stomach. The sort of bullet that left you bleeding slowly to death on the inside.

Kitty adored Claire and was so excited about the idea of the baby.

'Mum, you've got to knit things for the baby, it's really important. Claire can't knit, she doesn't know how to make babies' cardigans and things. You know, like the ones I have that I put on my teddies now. Please say you'll make some. I know you're busy, but we could get the wool together. On the phone, Claire says yellow and white are good, because we don't know if it's going to be a boy or a girl.'

Tess was one of those people who couldn't bear to sit still; she was always doing something, even in front of the television. Zach used to joke that theirs was the only house with actual darned socks. She'd flirted with tapestry, and they had a few tapestry cushions, but knitting was a lifelong love. It was true that Kitty's dolls and teddies had a wardrobe of beautiful little tiny garments, knitted lovingly by Tess when Kitty had been the size of a baked bean in her womb.

'Gosh,' said Tess, and she felt the pain of the bullet inside her, 'I'm very busy these days. Do you think Granny Helen might do that, or even Claire's mum?'

Another granny. Tess had entirely forgotten about the whole concept of Claire's family and the fact that she would come with her own parents. Kitty would have another granny, sort of.

It was like a labyrinth: complex and never-ending.

'That's so clever of you, Mum!' said Kitty, delighted.

Kitty was so full of love, forever blurting out the first thing that came into her mind. She was a Leo, like her father, and there were no secrets with either of them. Kevin had never been able to tell a lie to save his life, a quality that Tess had always found admirable. And Zach was somehow the same: she could always tell what he was thinking, just by looking at his beloved face.

She was a Pisces: opaque, as Suki used to say.

'Nobody will ever know what you're thinking, Sis.'

Right now, Tess was glad for that quality. She didn't want her darling Kitty to know what she was thinking: it was so horrible and bitter, Tess felt ashamed of herself. What sort of letter would she come up with for the magazine's psychologist? *I'm almost forty-two, my ex-husband's girlfriend is pregnant and both my children are delighted about it. Oh yes, and I'm broke and bound to be even more broke when my ex-husband and his girlfriend try to find a house to live in.*

Money, thought Tess: it all came back to money. No matter how many times she added it all up, her dwindling income and whatever Kevin was paying in maintenance wouldn't be enough to pay the bills.

Nobody had money to spend on antique trinkets any more. Keeping the shop open through the winter months when there were no tourists around simply wasn't viable. The few trips she'd made out to private executors' sales and auction houses had yielded nothing that said 'Ming vase – wildly undervalued'. Instead, there was the sad sense of people's treasured possessions being sold to pay bills and buy food.

She was beginning to wonder whether she'd have to sell the house in Avalon and move into something smaller. It wasn't something she wanted to do, but it might be the only option left to them.

'You can't move,' Suki said on the phone that night. 'You love that place. It's special.'

'The bank don't care how special it is,' Tess said sadly.

The following morning, Suki sat up in bed with a jolt. She wasn't sure what had woken her, but she was wide awake. A glance at the clock beside the bed told her it was half seven in the morning. Half seven and still dark. She moved out of the bed quietly so as not to wake Mick, who was lying beside her. He ought to be paying rent, she thought; he stayed over so often. It wasn't that she invited him, he just came over and then it was too late for him to go home after a few beers. The arrangement didn't really suit Suki any more. She felt used by Mick. His idea of contributing to the household bills was to stump up for a couple of takeouts a week and to buy beer. He never bought wine or anything she'd like to drink. God, how was she going to say it to him? Once, she wouldn't have had any problem getting rid of a guy. The old Suki would have simply bundled up all his stuff, thrown it at him and said, 'Get out.' But the new Suki, the new tireder, older Suki, didn't have the energy for the fight.

She went quietly downstairs. The heating had come on so at least it wasn't freezing. Bad snow storms were promised, but they hadn't come yet. Suki had no interest in a white Christmas, or a white anything. She didn't like the snow, it made her feel trapped.

Having made herself a cup of coffee, she lit a cigarette and sat down at the kitchen table. She needed to work on her book today, but she felt so tired. Maybe she should go back up to bed, turn on her bedside lamp and read. She had so much research material to go through.

Back upstairs, she got quietly into bed, lit another cigarette, sipped her coffee and made herself comfortable. It was as nice a way to start the day as any. Mick shifted in his sleep, perhaps woken by the scent of nicotine. She looked at him, one muscular, tattooed arm over the bedclothes, thrown out towards her, as if reaching for her in his sleep. And at that moment she was struck with a memory of the past, a moment in time when she was with Jethro, towards the end. And despite the fact that she was in her own warm bed in the present, she shivered.

In the beautifully lit bathroom of the huge suite in the hotel in Memphis, Suki stared blearily at herself in the mirror. Last night's eye make-up was smeared on her face. She never took it off now – why bother? It was easier in the morning to wipe of the excess, put on a bit more and then you were set for the day. Her hair was shorter than it had been when she'd met Jethro first: shorter, blonder. She looked young.

She peered at herself in the mirror. Yeah, definitely, young. That plumping-up stuff on her cheeks had worked. She looked hot, definitely, *and* thin; who needed food when you could have your pick of any drug imaginable? Lately, her stomach had been giving her trouble. She kept feeling like she wanted to throw up, she was all bile and acid on the inside. She couldn't really face alcohol or drugs. Last night, only Jethro practically throwing it down her throat had made her drink that Jack Daniels and Coke. She felt sick again. Maybe something else would take the edge off? A line of coke, a Bloody Mary . . . something.

Or tea. She laughed at herself in the mirror, standing there in her black silk panties and nothing else. A cup of tea suddenly seemed gorgeous. Like the tea Cashel's mum used to make, with some of her scones. Oh wow, that would be fantastic. Suki wondered if she could call room service. Yes, she would, even if it was the middle of the night. What else was room service for?

She looked at the huge watch she wore: gold, encrusted with diamonds. Jethro had given it to her. It was very flashy, not the sort of thing she normally liked to wear, but hey, she was a flashy rock chick now. She walked back into the bedroom and saw Jethro lying there on the huge bed, sprawled out like a starfish, the way he always slept.

'You take up the whole damn bed,' she used to say to him.

'Yeah, well, get your own bed,' he'd say.

And then she saw the girl: a tangle of chestnut hair, long, long hair and naked, beautiful, burnished tanned back. One of Jethro's arms was resting on her back and he must have been waking up or coming to, because his hand began to slide up and down the girl's silky skin. Suki stood transfixed in the bathroom doorway. She didn't remember any girl. She remembered . . . yeah, she'd gone to bed early on her own and she'd heard Jethro come in, but she was so tired, she'd pulled a pillow over her head. He hadn't woken her up, the way he so often did after a gig when he was all partied out and needed sex to remind himself that he was a rock god.

'Hiya, honey,' he said, finally sitting up in the big bed. Except he wasn't talking to Suki, he was talking to the mystery brunette. She turned around to face him. She was so beautiful and so young. Suki felt as if the stiletto heels of her Manolos were piercing her heart.

'Mornin', honey,' said the girl, reaching over to Jethro. His hand cupped her breast and he moaned appreciatively.

'No, baby,' said the girl, 'let me,' and she was sliding down the bed, under the covers, while Jethro rolled over, groaning in appreciation.

Suki couldn't bear it: he'd brought another woman into their bed.

She'd heard rumours of other women on this particular tour.

'Jethro isn't the sort of dog to stay faithful for too long,' Leona, one of the make-up girls, had told her. Suki hadn't listened. She was everything Jethro wanted. OK, so she wasn't a twenty-four-year-old babe, but she was famous in her own right, intelligent, fierce, passionate. She was *someone*, and that's what he wanted, not some identikit beach babe with enhanced breasts and long legs.

At that moment, Jethro opened his eyes properly and saw her standing there. His face, that famous face that had graced millions of album covers and posters, creased up into a big smile.

'Hey, Suki, honey, where did you get to? Come on, join us! I got you a little surprise.'

'Join you?' she said, feeling an unbelievable headache start to pound into her temples. 'What are you doing with that other woman in our bed?'

'Ah, come on, honey, don't get all heavy on me. It'll be fun, you'll like it.'

'I won't like it. I'm not into that shit,' she managed to hiss.

But Jethro wasn't listening, he was lost in erotic fantasy land.

Suki turned and ran back into the bathroom, slamming the door and locking it. She stood under the shower, washing herself clean. She was sure she had some tranqs in her toilet bag; if not, Jethro was bound to have something in his. Never very much, he never carried too much, he had people on tour to do that for him, in case anyone searched his stuff and he got held up. That would never do. The tour was about money, and Jethro was the cash machine. Someone else would take the rap for transporting his drugs and they'd be royally rewarded for it. That was how rock stars did it.

She found a tranq, popped two. There was nothing in Jethro's bag except the remains of an empty baggie of coke. Wrapped in the bathrobe, she marched out of the bathroom, desperate not to look at the bed and hear the moans. The suite had a separate dressing room and she pulled on some clothes. Then, with her hair wet and clinging to her skull, she marched out, went to the lift and went down to the fifteenth floor, the club floor, where there was breakfast all morning. None of the band or the tour entourage were there. But the manager was: a wily, skinny guy, named Nico.

'Hey, Suki, what's up?' he said.

Nico liked Suki, he liked the fact that Jethro was sticking to one woman for a while. It was good for the band. There had been a few instances with girls of dubious age, sixteen-year-olds who looked twenty-five, and that was hard to handle. But now that Jethro was hanging out with Suki, it was good. She seemed to be keeping him on the straight and narrow. Well, as straight and narrow as Jethro could ever be, given the large amounts of alcohol and drugs that he consumed.

But Suki didn't look too good today. Without her hair all fluffed up and without the war paint properly applied, she looked her age. Definitely forty-something, despite all the botox and fillers and the eye lift.

'Hi, Nico,' Suki said, grabbing herself some water and drinking it straight down.

'You're up early,' Nico said. 'Do you wanna sit with me?'

Suki looked at him, wondering whether she could confide in him. She and Nico got on really well. Plus he knew she wasn't the sort of person to go and dump Jethro and sell her story to the tabloids the way so many other girls had tried to do.

She sank into the chair opposite him.

'Coffee?' asked a waitress.

'Yeah, loads of it – strong, thank you,' Suki growled. She started to light up a cigarette.

'Not in here, I'm afraid,' said Nico.

'Aw shit,' Suki said. She put a couple of lumps of sugar in her coffee.

'You look tired,' Nico said.

She'd tell him, Suki decided. 'Jethro has another woman in our bed,' she blurted out, and then felt stupid. She shouldn't have said anything. Now she'd look like a sad loser who couldn't keep her man.

'Ah.' Nico poured some more coffee into his cup. 'That tends to happen with Jethro. I would have liked to have told you, but . . . y'know, sometimes people don't like to be told these things. They have to find them out for themselves,' Nico said delicately. 'That's the way he is. I've known him for twenty years and that's the pattern, Suki. You can stay or you can go, but if you stay, you gotta put up with that.'

'But he's never done that before, not to me. I mean, why now?' Suki wailed. 'We're so happy, everything is great.'

'He gets bored.'

Suki took that one. It felt like a body blow, but she took it.

'And he likes . . . younger girls, sometimes. Not the teenage ones, but the early twenties: the ones who'll do anything so long as they can say they've been to bed with Jethro.'

It was the word 'younger' that did it.

'Younger women,' she breathed. 'I thought I was enough for him.'

Nico looked at her pityingly. 'Nobody or nothing is enough

for Jethro,' he said. 'You wanna stay on the tour, you need to remember that. He wants it all.'

After an hour, she went back to the suite, let herself in quietly and walked into the bedroom. Jethro was lying in the bed, looking happy, smoking a cigar. She hated the smell of cigar smoke. He didn't smoke many but, when he did, it always signified that he was in a particularly good mood. And today, it wasn't her who had provided that good mood.

'Jethro,' she said, determined to be calm, 'we need to talk.'

'About what, honey?' he asked, a dangerous glint in his eyes.

'About the fact that you had another woman in our bed. I can't live with that,' Suki said. She felt herself growing stronger with every word. 'It simply isn't acceptable, Jethro. You and I have a great relationship; we can't mess it up with other women. And how disrespectful is that to me, to bring her into our bed?'

'Honey,' he said, and this time his voice was the low throaty growl that had so captured her the first time they'd met, 'this isn't *our* bed, this is *my* bed. I allow you to sleep in it. Whoever else I want to bring in – that's my business. If you don't like it, you can get out. Stas says he's always fancied having a few rounds with you.'

Suki stared at him, horrified. Stas was the band's guitarist. She considered him a friend, but much as she liked him, she didn't fancy him in the slightest. Stas had always joked that if he wasn't in TradeWind he'd still be a virgin.

She looked at Jethro in horror. 'What do you mean, go to Stas? After all that we've been through? After all this time, after all these years.'

Jethro stared at her, uninterested. 'I'm bored, honey,' he said. 'So you can either take what I'm offering . . . or get out.'

Suki tried to gather her dignity about her. She looked at the man lounging in the bed, the face and body that so many women wanted, and realized that it was over. She couldn't stay with him if he brought other women into their bed.

The calmness of the tranquillizer allowed her not to break down and cry.

'OK, Jethro, if that's the way you want it, fine. Goodbye.'

She walked into the dressing room and started packing, half hoping he'd come in and say, '*No, baby, I didn't mean it, I'd be lost without you. None of those twenty-four-year-olds can talk with me late into the night. They're not like you – super bright, clever, funny . . .*'

But he didn't come.

When she'd gathered her stuff together, she hauled it out into the hall. There were ten bags in all. Everything she'd amassed in her time with him. Finally, she took off the big watch. It was one of the few things he'd bought her that was actually valuable, and she threw it at him in the bed.

'You can have this for your next girl,' she said.

And then she left, head held high.

Suki got out of bed and went downstairs to make herself another cup of coffee. Then she sat outside on the deck with blankets wrapped around her and thought about the psychic she'd met in the trailer park.

Addicted to powerful men, she'd said.

Suki tapped out a cigarette and lit up. The woman had been right. Suki had always been waiting for some guy to fix it all – and she still was. Even with no-hoper Mick, she kept praying he'd get a decent job and support her. So much for her feminist principles! She might have been talking the talk but she'd never really walked the walk. Instead, she'd moved from one man to the next all her life. And that had to change.

Chapter Eighteen

Mara was flinging Danae into Avalon's social scene as if her very life depended upon it.

First up was the town meeting to discuss what last-ditch efforts they could make to salvage Christmas, with shoppers staying away in droves thanks to the recession. It was being held in the town hall and as mayoress, Belle was in charge.

On the agenda were a series of festive-themed shopping nights. Mulled wine and nibbles, and a choir singing carols had worked a treat the previous Christmas. This year, there had been resistance to the idea, led by Dessie, who feared his takings might suffer if drink was being given away for nothing.

'We aren't all runnin' fancy hotels, making a fortune,' Dessie protested, with more than a whinge in his voice. 'Sure, I'm only breaking even. I don't hold with all this prettifying the place for Christmas. I have the odd decoration and that'll have to do you. I'm not shelling out money for any old tinsel or other daft things.'

Others had protested that, with takings down, they couldn't afford to contribute either. Now, with shoppers going elsewhere, it seemed they couldn't afford not to.

Danae, who wasn't open in the evening and had no real reason to get involved, was reluctant to attend the meeting, but Mara had insisted.

'We're a part of this town,' she said, 'and we're going.'

Danae was entirely astonished to find that she was enjoying getting out. She didn't quiver with nerves when she put her hand up to say she'd donate money for wine and some spices for the mulled bit.

'Thanks, Danae,' said Belle, who was thinking of ways of dispatching Dessie into the great hereafter. 'At least *some* people understand the concept of community.'

'Dessie's not the worst, Belle,' Danae said. 'He doesn't see the bigger picture, not the way you do. This is a wonderful idea for the town, you're a marvellous organizer.'

Ruffled feathers smoothed, Belle relaxed.

After the meeting, Danae found herself sitting in the café with a coffee and a scone, surrounded by people she'd been acquainted with for years but had never really known. Mara was there in the middle, chatting away.

'. . . well, it's different for her because Brenda *works*!' shrieked someone, and they all roared with laughter.

A private joke, Danae thought. Life was all about private jokes and you were either in or out of it. She'd always been out of it, one way or the other. But she was determined not to be on the outside in future.

Seeing Danae's confusion over the joke, Lorena from the café explained: 'It was something Margaret's husband said once. According to him, Brenda couldn't be expected to do normal things because she worked. As if we don't.'

'Tell me, is Brenda good looking?' asked Mara shrewdly.

Danae admired her niece for being a part of it all.

'Lord, yes! Stunning.'

'So she should be – she's got the time and money to have her hair done!'

*   *   *

Tess had gone along to the meeting but she'd felt like an interloper. Before long, she wouldn't have a shop any more. There was no point kidding herself: Something Old was teetering on the edge of bankruptcy. Nevertheless, she'd found herself swept up in the great exodus to the café. Tonight, Danae from the post office and a few other local women, including dear Mara, were deep in conversation at a table near the door. Tess walked past them quietly and ordered tea and a scone.

She had some auction house catalogues in her handbag but she didn't have the heart to read them. What was the point? She was nearly broke. It was only the thought that she had to get the shop and the family past Christmas that was keeping her going at all. Christmas was the final hurdle. For all their sakes, she had to keep the shop limping along a few weeks more. Then, in the New Year, she could consider her options and make decisions.

She ate her scone, drank her tea and found her eyes wandering again. It was odd how Danae seemed to be every-where now that they'd broken that barrier of politeness which encased so many relationships. Years of saying hello and nodding, and suddenly they were friends, and here was Danae, all over the place.

As if sensing that someone was looking at her, Danae's head lifted. She smiled as soon as she saw Tess.

'I wasn't avoiding you all,' Tess said when Danae sat down beside her.

'I understand,' said Danae. 'Sometimes it's nice to be on your own, isn't it?'

Tess nodded. She didn't want to confide in this lovely woman or she might cry.

As if she knew how Tess was feeling, Danae got to her feet again.

'I better get Miss Mara home,' she said. 'We both have work in the morning and she'd stay here all night if I let her.

Do drop in on us any time you're in the mood for a chat,' Danae added, feeling daring. She liked this new feeling of going out and meeting people.

Tess bent her head to her scone again, undone by Danae's kindness. She wouldn't cry, not here. She wouldn't cry because her business was going to collapse, her husband had found a new love, and the first man she'd ever loved had been back in town the last month and hadn't even come to see her, not once.

Danae was lovely, but she had neither husband nor children to cause her anxiety. She lived happily on her own most of the time; how could she understand Tess's pain?

Mara found that she adored December in Avalon, even though the ground was covered with a hard frost and Freddie the builder was forever muttering about how it was going to be a very long time before work on Avalon House could get underway, what with the frost and the rain and the prospect of snow. She loved it. There was a clearness to the air beside the sea, and when you were standing close to the house, with the protective circle of Avalon's woods all around, you could see down to the curving bay with the golden sands and the white-capped water where waves rocked under the stormy wind.

Her home in Galway had been right beside the sea – the Atlantic, that vast force of nature – and yet she'd never felt as close to it as she felt now. In Galway, she'd lived in an apartment block, somehow removed from nature. Here, she was in the middle of it.

Her car was not made for negotiating the slippery drive up to Avalon House during the cold snap, so she'd taken to leaving it at Danae's house and clomping her way up the avenue in her biker boots to meet architects and designers.

It was fun working for Cashel – manic, but fun. He demanded the very best and could afford to pay top dollar, which meant he generally got the best. Of course, these people, brilliant in their own fields, had very firm views. Since day one Lorcan the architect and Freddie the builder had been at war over the plans. The designer and his team were keeping out of it and, wisely, so was Mara.

'Best to let them fight it out amongst themselves,' she told Danae at night, snug in the beautiful cottage at the end of Willow Street. 'He chose all men. Isn't that interesting? Apart from Judy, the gardener, I'm the only woman on the team.'

'He chose you because you were good,' said Danae. 'That's the simple answer.'

'Yes, well, good and sensible,' said Mara, 'and keeping out of any rows. They can slug it out between them until Cashel steps in and decides one way or the other – not me. I'm not going to be living there, after all. Although I do wish I was,' she added wistfully.

The house would be beautiful when it was finished. It was beautiful now, even in its raw, unlived-in, unloved state.

'Imagine what it must have been like to live there hundreds of years ago,' she said, thinking out loud. 'It must have been like something from Jane Austen, all beautiful tea gowns and balls and . . .'

'Yes,' Danae finished for her, 'and tenants living outside on nothing but potatoes.'

'Don't ruin my fantasy world,' said Mara. 'OK, we don't have to go that far back then. I must ask Tess,' said Mara.

Next day, good as her word, she dropped into Something Old and asked.

For a moment, Tess said nothing, simply exhaled slowly. 'I lived there a long time ago,' she said finally. 'And I . . . I'd prefer not to talk about it. I'm sorry.'

Anyone else might have left it at that, but not Mara. Fresh from her success with making her aunt open up the pain of the past, Mara decided to press on. She refused to let Tess hide behind the facade of not wanting to talk about it. Bottling things up never helped, so she wheedled away, asking for more and more information until finally Tess gave up.

'All right, I'll tell you. What do you want to know?' she said.

'Well, first you could be so helpful to me, from the point of view of remembering what it was like in the old days. We don't have many pictures to go on – apart from a couple of the inside that Lorcan has tracked down – and it would be wonderful to have somebody working with us who knows what the house was really like when it was truly loved and lived in. It would really help Cashel, actually.'

Tess's laugh was a little harsh. 'Mara, one piece of advice: if I give you any information at all, you are not to tell anyone where it came from. Understand?'

'Yes, girl guide's honour,' said Mara.

'Were you a girl guide?' Tess asked suspiciously.

'No,' said Mara, 'but I can make a fire by rubbing two boy scouts together.'

Tess had to laugh. 'No, seriously,' she said, 'you can't tell anybody, particularly Cashel. He and I don't get on. He would be very upset if he knew you were asking me for advice about the house. Is that understood?'

'Loud and clear,' said Mara. 'That's interesting,' she added, giving Tess an arch look.

'Oh, Mara, you're incorrigible!' Tess said.

'Well, it *is* interesting,' said Mara. 'How very mysterious that you and Cashel don't get on. I've never heard you talk of him, and he certainly hasn't met you since he's been here, so this must all be in the past.'

'Sometimes,' Tess said, 'the past really is better left in the past. Now, I'll tell you about the house, but do not think you're going to cross-examine me about my relationship with Cashel Reilly, OK? Plus, I've no idea if we get on any more, because I haven't seen him for so long.'

Mara knew there was a story there and she was determined to get to the bottom of it.

There was no point asking Cashel; he was far too canny for even her wonderful wiles. And Danae was no help: 'I really don't know,' she said. 'It must have been before my time.'

Belle, however, was much more forthcoming. Belle, Danae and Mara were having dinner in the hotel brasserie one evening when Mara broached the question.

'What exactly went on with Cashel and Tess Power? There's something there, I can feel it.'

'Ah, well,' said Belle, 'there's a long story to that.'

'How do you know all this?' said Danae. 'I mean, you moved here around the same time that I did.'

Both Mara and Belle looked at each other in amusement.

'You're gas, Danae, do you know that?' said Belle fondly. 'The difference between you and me is that *I ask*. I have to know what's going on. When you run a hotel it's very important. I mean, I need to know who's fallen out with who, which families are feuding, so that when they all come in for dinner I don't put them near one another. The last thing I want is customers grabbing the ceremonial swords off the wall and starting a duel! When you're running a licensed business, you can't be too careful. When people get a few glasses under their belt, they're liable to decide it's time a long-term grudge gets aired.'

Mara patted her aunt affectionately, 'You missed out on the gossip gene, Danae. Unlike me and Belle.'

'I do not have the gossip gene,' Belle said haughtily. 'I have the mother of all gossip genes.' And she began to explain what she knew about Tess and Cashel. 'It's all a bit mysterious and nobody knows exactly what went on, but things looked very serious between Tess and Cashel for a time. Then suddenly it was a case of one minute they were engaged – and the next minute he was gone.'

Mara recalled the way Cashel had looked at her with narrowed eyes, heavy brows beetling, when she'd idly mentioned having worked in Something Old.

'Tess Power's shop?' he said.

For the first time, Mara had a sense of what it must be like to be an underling who had displeased Cashel Reilly by doing something terribly wrong. She hadn't done anything wrong, and what's more she wasn't afraid of him.

'Yes, I work for her occasionally. Lovely woman, very beautiful,' Mara said innocently. 'It's sad too, because she and her husband have split up. I think she's lonely, you know . . .'

'Can we stop talking about this and get on with our work,' Cashel had rasped out.

So it wouldn't be entirely true if she were to tell Tess that Cashel had evinced an interest in visiting Something Old. On the other hand, he hadn't said he *didn't* want to visit the shop either. The path of true love never did run smooth.

For a second, Mara thought of what Cici would say if she could see her.

'You're meddling, you mad thing,' Cici would say.

Mara didn't see it as meddling. It seemed wrong to stand by and do nothing while two people who'd once loved each other were leading sad and lonely lives apart, especially when it was obvious that they'd be just perfect together. She wished she had a magic wand to fix all past broken romances. But then, if she had a wand, she might have fixed her own.

Danae had found herself changing lately. She'd begun to talk to the people who came to the post office; like the Nigerian priest, who'd come in shivering from the cold despite being a strapping lad with huge muscles. Father Olumbuko was a recent arrival, and he was a joy. He spoke English like an Oxford graduate and had the kindest face. It soon became apparent to Danae that he understood people and felt great affection for them. The previous curate had been inclined to take the high moral ground on all occasions. From what Danae could see, Father Olumbuko appeared to share her view that there wasn't enough oxygen for sensible people up there on the high moral ground.

He'd given a blessing to a young couple who were marrying in the registry office because of an early, ill-fated marriage and divorce. Danae wasn't supposed to know about it, but she did.

Father Olumbuko wasn't supposed to know she knew, but he did.

'You are the eyes of Avalon,' he said to Danae when he came into the post office to buy stamps for his Christmas cards.

'As are you, Father.' Danae smiled at him from behind her plexiglass.

'But there is much to learn here,' he went on. 'Father Liam is a busy man.'

Father Liam was juggling a huge parish, dwindling resources and four crumbling churches.

'We have so many areas of pastoral concern,' Father Olumbuko went on.

He had the warmest eyes, Danae thought: like great, wise lights in that open face.

'Unemployment among local men has gone up,' Danae said thoughtfully, aware that, a month or so ago, she wouldn't have ventured an opinion at all. 'Women are better at facing it than men. I read somewhere about working on allotments being a great idea for men who are retired or unemployed. They feel better when they're doing something.'

Father Olumbuko's eyes lit up even more. He was a thinker, Danae could see. Once delivered, an idea wouldn't leave that clever mind until a solution had been reached.

'These wintry months are not good times for gardening in this country,' he said, with a small shiver. 'But perhaps, before we work on allotments, we could work on the common areas in the town.'

'The ground round the high cross is a bit raggy at the

moment,' Danae agreed. 'There's no money in the public purse for flowers, but we could plant bulbs for the New Year.'

'Crocuses and snowdrops,' said Father Olumbuko dreamily.

'Lovely,' agreed Danae.

She'd never have had a conversation like that with Father Liam, whose mind occupied a more cerebral plane when he wasn't worrying about parish finances. Give him a glass of sherry, and Father Liam could spend hours discussing angels dancing on pins.

Father Olumbuko's eyes suddenly focused on hers. 'Why are you not on our pastoral committee, Miss Rahill?'

'I'm not a joiner,' Danae replied simply. She'd used that phrase many times over the past eighteen years. It kept people at a distance, while saying nothing about her. But perhaps it was time to be a joiner, after all. Perhaps in the New Year she might consider getting involved in some of the local groups. 'And you may call me Danae.'

'Ah, the Greek princess who gave birth to Perseus, a child fathered by Zeus himself,' he said, then added ruefully: 'The benefits of a classical education.'

Danae was impressed. 'My mother loved the Greek myths,' she said. 'If I'd been a boy, I was to be Ulysses. Since you know my name, what is yours?'

'Edgar.' He bowed formally, and Danae found herself thinking that it was a shame Catholic priests were destined to a life of celibacy. This kind, interesting man would have made some young woman a lovely husband. Mara came to mind. But Mara kept insisting that she was off men for good, determined to obliterate the past. The young liked to run away from the past until they grew older and realized the past was always with you.

'We'll talk again, Edgar,' Danae said. 'Off with your stamps, now. I need a cup of tea.'

She must tell Mara all about it. Mara would be thrilled. Even if Danae had put her foot down over going to see a therapist – 'I had quite enough of them when I was in the hospital, Mara. I couldn't bear to see another one . . .' – she was venturing out into the world so much more.

But of course, tonight was Mara's date night with the New Zealand man. So much for being off men!

'It's not a date,' Mara kept telling herself as she got ready for her dinner with Rafe. 'It's only an evening out with somebody I've met in a new place, that's all.' And then inside her head came Cici's voice saying, *'You're putting a lot of work into something that isn't a date!'* Mara had to admit that was true.

She'd used the hot-oil conditioning treatment that made her hair all silky and glossy, and she'd spent quite some time on her make-up, flicking her eyeliner up very carefully, which, even though she was well practised at it, took time and a steady hand.

Smelling of a delicious combination of lemon and a faintly scented lavender body cream, she was ready to go, all dressed up in an outfit she'd bought for a date with Jack. 'You have no power over me any more,' she had told the blouse fiercely as it hung innocently on the hanger. It was green silk, fitted at the waist, cut low enough in front to give the faintest hint of creamy cleavage. It went with a dark olive tweedy pencil skirt. Jack had loved it.

'God I could rip that off you right now,' he'd said when she turned up to meet him in the restaurant. 'Who needs food? Let's go back to my place.' And they had. They'd left the restaurant without so much as a bite. Jack had thrown some money on the table and had whisked her off to his apartment, where he had indeed removed the outfit and made love to her.

Going out with Rafe would be an exorcism for the outfit. She'd stopped thinking about Jack as often as she used to; she was too busy, for a start. Nobody working for Cashel ever had time to be bored. But Jack's memory sometimes crept in when she was in bed at night, and she'd wonder if there would ever again be somebody to caress her, to kiss her, to nuzzle into her neck and say he loved her smell.

Mara jammed a brown felt hat on top of her curls and put on her coat, adding a scarf before marching back into the kitchen.

'OK, Danae, I won't be long – it's only dinner.'

'Have fun,' said Danae, beaming at her. 'I'm tired tonight, I might be in bed when you come back.'

It was only after Mara had kissed her goodbye, petted Lady and got into her car, that it suddenly occurred to her Danae was subtly saying: '*Stay out as long as you want, darling, nobody will be here to see it, it's up to you.*'

Morelli's restaurant in Avalon was busy when Mara walked in the door. She was ten minutes late; it had been hard to find parking and these shoes, though joyful to look at, were a nightmare to walk in – well, totter in.

She'd been in Morelli's before with the girls and Belle had filled her in on the facts. Gino Morelli had married into a huge Irish family and had set up the restaurant and it had been jammed ever since, people loving the combination of fabulous Italian cooking and the hospitality dished out by his wife Laura and her two daughters, Concepta and Jacinta.

Mara was embarrassed because she wasn't entirely sure which of the two sisters was on the desk this evening. The Morelli women all looked exactly the same: tall, with olive skin, dark eyes and long dark hair.

'Hello,' said Mara, smiling, hoping the smile might make up for her not saying the woman's name. 'I'm Mara – I was here a few weeks ago with my aunt and some friends. I'm joining Rafe Berlin tonight. I don't know if he's here already but I am a bit late.'

The dark haired woman behind the counter smiled. 'Hello, Mara, lovely to have you back. My sister Jacinta and I were saying only the other day what a lovely evening that was when you and the ladies invited us to join you. Mr Berlin is here. We've been admiring him already,' she said and one eyebrow lifted, 'if I wasn't a married lady, well . . .'

She left the rest of the sentence unsaid and Mara found herself grinning happily. He was good looking, there was no doubt about that, but this wasn't a date. If Cici were to ask her about it again, she'd explain: No. Date. Whatsoever.

With swaying hips, Concepta brought her to the table where Rafe was waiting and Mara had to agree with Concepta: Rafe was looking pretty good tonight. He stood up when she arrived and held back her seat. She was surprised, Jack had never done that sort of thing. Then he kissed her gently on both cheeks, European style. Mara found herself getting a bit flustered. *Definitely not a date,* she said to herself. *This is two people meeting for dinner. Modern people do this: have dinner, make friends with members of the opposite sex, it doesn't have to* mean *anything.*

'You look beautiful,' Rafe said, and this time Mara actually flushed.

'Thank you,' she said, and busied herself picking up the menu. 'Sorry I'm late, these shoes . . . and I couldn't find parking . . .'

'I didn't mind waiting for you,' Rafe said in that beautiful Kiwi accent. And the way he said it made Mara think what he was really saying was that he'd be prepared to wait a long time for her.

'So how have you been?' Mara asked, in a voice that sounded a little false even to her. She'd been aiming for matey, but it wasn't coming out quite right.

'I've been fine,' said Rafe. 'Looking forward to this, of course. I hadn't expected to wait so long for you to set a date.'

'I was a bit busy,' said Mara, which was an understatement.

'I figured that,' he said lazily, smiling at her in a way that was very date-like.

'Yes,' breathed Mara, flushing a bit.

This wasn't turning out the way she'd expected. He was acting like a suitor and she was responding. Boy, was she responding.

It was beginning to feel like a proper boyfriend/girlfriend dinner, and she was nervous now and conscious of him, how he looked and how he looked at her. Those blue eyes devouring her, not in a horrible way but in a loving, appreciative way.

She kept her head down, looking at the menu, although she wasn't reading it at all. It was a jumble of words and letters, pasta and basil and God knows what she was going to eat because suddenly she didn't feel in the slightest bit hungry and he was still looking at her, she could tell. She looked up.

'For God's sake, stop looking at me, OK?'

'Why am I not allowed look at you?' he demanded.

'Because you're putting me off,' Mara said. 'This isn't a date.'

'It isn't?' he asked.

'Well, no. I thought we were going out to dinner and you were going to fill me in on the town, both of us being newcomers.'

'I don't know about round here, but where I come from that's a date.'

'I told you, I have recently come out of a very hurtful relationship – well, hurtful when it ended,' Mara said. 'I'm not up for going out with anyone. My heart is broken, OK? Totally broken.' She glared at him.

'You are not wearing a totally broken outfit, and you do not look totally broken,' Rafe said. 'But forgive me if I'm wrong. Kiwi cowboys, such as I, have no clue what goes on in sophisticated Celtic warrior women's minds.'

She laughed at having her own words thrown back at her.

'I did not say you were a cowboy,' she said. 'Well, OK, I did. But you *were* wearing that ridiculous hat.'

'I went to Texas, I bought a hat, I like it,' he said. 'And

y'know, people have said in the past that it sort of suits me. Not that I'm really tall enough to carry it off.' And Rafe was grinning at her.

'Do not be mocking me, Rafe Berlin,' she said, but she was beginning to grin too. 'Fine, for categorizing purposes, it is a date. But a really, really, really early one. A sort of "we don't know each other at all and let's see if we even vaguely like each other" one,' Mara said. 'OK? Those are the ground rules.'

'Ground rules, right,' said Rafe. 'I will try and remember them. What are the other ground rules? Am I allowed to touch you? Was that double-kissing thing acceptable? 'Cos, you know, most women like that.'

'Do not do things to me that *most women* like,' she said. 'I am not *most women*. I want to be treated like an individual.'

'Fair enough,' Rafe said. 'I thought *you* might like it.' His voice was lower now and Mara found that she was holding her breath because she had liked it, liked it a lot. But she couldn't let him in, she was too hurt. It was too early. It was all wrong.

'How about we pick something to eat, and have our dinner and talk about stuff, and that'll be the first really-really-early embryonic date over?'

'Is there a time limit on this embryonic-date stuff?' Rafe asked.

Mara pretended to think about this. 'Mmm, it's a long time since I've done this. I think maybe two hours maximum. And then, you might escort me to my car – very slowly, because I'm wearing high-heeled shoes.'

'I noticed,' he said. 'I love your shoes.'

'But not in a shoe fetishy way, right?' Mara asked.

'No,' he agreed, 'not in a shoe fetishy way. I just like the way they make you sort of walk ... well, very nicely. Next subject,' Rafe said. He gave up on trying to explain how

301

attractive he found the way she walked, that instinctive little sway of her hips, the fact that all the men in the restaurant had looked at her and she hadn't noticed them at all. 'So after two hours I walk you to your car, shake hands with you and you go home. And if I'm really good we can do it all again next week?'

'That sounds reasonable,' Mara said.

By eleven o'clock, there weren't many other couples left in Morelli's. They'd shared a bottle of wine and Mara felt totally giggly and deliciously relaxed. She refused the waiter's offer of a complimentary Italian liqueur. 'Oh, heaven's no, I couldn't,' she said, 'sorry.'

'Me neither,' Rafe said. 'I feel a bit drunk really,' he added, 'which is odd on two and a half glasses of wine.'

'Me too,' Mara said, astonished. 'Why is that?'

He reached over and touched her hand on the table. He'd done that a few times and she'd let him. He was affectionate, liked reaching out and touching her. As well as her hand, he'd touched her face once when she had a crumb of breadstick on her mouth. And the strange thing was, she liked him touching her.

'I don't think I can walk you to your car,' Rafe said. 'You have to get a taxi. I should have picked you up in a taxi, but I didn't want to push my luck. Especially when it was hard enough getting you to meet me in a restaurant in the first place.'

Mara smiled, feeling mellow and comfortable.

'My last boyfriend almost never picked me up,' she said candidly. 'He'd just tell me to meet him somewhere. Once he wanted to meet up inside some fancy nightclub, which meant when I got to the door I had to pay the cover charge. It really annoyed Cici, my flatmate. She reckoned he was a tight git and he'd fixed it deliberately to save having to pay for me.'

'I'd say worse than that,' said Rafe, 'but I'm not supposed

to curse in front of ladies. I've never met somebody in a restaurant before; I've always picked them up.'

'On the back of your motorbike?' Mara asked playfully.

'No,' he said soberly. 'If I'm going to have a drink, I take a taxi. My brother's injury was caused by a drunk driver. That's why you are not driving home tonight, you are getting a taxi.'

'I wouldn't dream of driving tonight,' she said. 'I didn't plan to have anything to drink, that's why I brought the car. I mean, I don't ever drink and drive,' she said, anxious to convince him of the fact.

'It's fine, I believe you,' he said, 'but you know when something like that happens to you or someone close to you, it changes the way you think about things. I could never go out with somebody who thought it was OK to have a couple of glasses of wine and get into their car and drive home.'

'It must have been terrible, his accident,' Mara said.

'Horrific,' Rafe replied. 'He's my big brother. All the time we were growing up, he was like a god to me. To see him in that hospital bed and hear that he'd never walk again . . . It was pretty rough. He thought Karen should walk away from him, find another father for the baby, even though that would have killed him. He didn't want to be a burden. "A kid needs a dad who can stand up," he said.

'You know what Karen said to that?' Rafe looked off into the distance, remembering. 'She said she didn't care what had happened to him, she loved him, nothing could change who he was, and he was the man for her. And he's the most amazing dad in the world, which I keep telling him when I remind him of all the dumb things he said about needing to stand up to be a father.'

'He must be pretty special,' said Mara.

Rafe grinned at her. 'People say both the Berlin brothers are pretty special,' he said, with a slightly wicked grin. 'Let's get you out of here. In a cosmopolitan hotspot like Avalon, all the taxis will be gone if we don't get a move on.'

Rafe asked for the bill and when it arrived Mara made an attempt to grab it.

'We're going Dutch on this,' she said.

'No,' Rafe said. 'I'm sorry, but where I come from when a guy asks a girl out to dinner he pays the bill. You'll have to excuse my rough Kiwi cowboy ways, but that's what we're going to do.'

Concepta, who'd brought the bill, sighed a little at this masterful talk and shot Mara a glance that said: *You are one lucky girl.*

'OK,' said Mara, 'but I pay next time. I've got a job now.'

'We can talk about that later,' Rafe said.

He paid the bill and added a healthy tip. Mara had been craning her neck to see his tip and she was delighted. She hated bad tippers. Then he helped her into her coat at the door and somehow he was holding her hand as he led her out on to the street. When she immediately began to shiver in the bitter cold, Rafe put his arm around her shoulders.

'That sure is a nice coat,' he said, 'but I don't think it's warm enough.' A taxi cruised past and Rafe waved.

'The house right at the end of Willow Street,' Rafe told the taxi driver.

'You're not going to come with me? 'Cos the driver can drop you first and then me,' Mara said, getting in and then turning around and looking up at him.

He leaned in, his face close to her.

'You know what, Mara,' he said, his voice soft like honey, 'I don't think I can trust myself with you in a taxi.' And then he kissed her on the mouth, and Mara found herself leaning closer to him, her eyes closed, sinking into the kiss, feeling the controlled heat.

Suddenly he moved away, as if he ought to stop now or he wouldn't be able to at all.

'I'll call you tomorrow,' he said, 'is that all right?'

She could only nod at him in return. He shut the door and the driver sped off.

'He could have got into the taxi with you, love,' said the driver. 'I mean, I'm a taxi driver: there's *nothing* I haven't seen in the back of this car. Nothing. Besides, Willow Street's not that far away – he wouldn't have had time to get up to much.'

'Oh no, it's not like that at all,' Mara said. 'We barely know each other.'

'Yeah, right,' said the driver, his voice all-knowing. 'I'll say nothing then, but I know love when I see it.'

Mara sat back and closed her eyes, reliving that amazing moment when he'd kissed her. It had felt so right. *'Told you you'd get over Jack,'* said the Cici-voice in her head, *'told you that you would, you needed to get out and meet someone new, that's all.'*

'But I didn't want to meet somebody new,' Mara told the imaginary Cici.

'What was that?' said the driver.

'Sorry, talking to myself,' Mara said.

'Ah, sure, you're in love,' said the driver fondly. 'We do all sorts of mental things when we're in love, don't we? Hold on, I'll find a good station for you . . .' and he flicked around on the radio until he found a station playing soppy love songs. 'There you are,' he said, 'isn't that perfect?'

'Perfect,' said Mara, 'you're very kind.' And she listened to Lionel Richie singing 'Three Times a Lady' all the way home. But she was smiling all the way home, too.

Chapter Nineteen

*I*n the post office, Danae had spent weeks watching Christmas cards and Christmas parcels being posted off all over the world. Elderly Mr Dineen, who lived on his own in one of the sweet 1930s bungalows on Lincoln Terrace, was always very precise in his postings, never missing the posting dates for Canada, where his eldest daughter lived, Singapore where the youngest lived, and London, where his middle daughter lived. He was as reliable as a metronome, coming in with neatly packaged brown paper parcels for various grandsons and granddaughters scattered around the globe, the address labels bearing his handsome script. He was a widower, lived on his own, and Danae could never remember seeing him with any member of his family around the town. He never asked for advice, never attempted to make conversation beyond a polite, 'Hello, Mrs Rahill, how are you today?'

But Mara's influence was still working its magic on Danae. When Mr Dineen came into the shop with the last of his parcels – several small ones for London, addressed to Isabella and Amy, his twin six-year-old granddaughters – she couldn't resist saying: 'Are you visiting them for Christmas, Mr Dineen?'

The shock on his face immediately told her she shouldn't have said anything.

'No,' he said nervously and coughed a little. He began searching in a pocket for a handkerchief or something. 'I don't like flying, you see. My wife – my late wife, Doris – she liked it, but I'm nervous. That's why I never go.'

'But there are courses now to help people get over fear of flying.' Danae couldn't help herself. This had to be Mara's doing; the old Danae would never have dreamt of interfering. 'Or maybe the doctor could give you something to keep you calm for the flight. It's such a short flight to London, and it would be lovely to spend Christmas with your family, wouldn't it?' *God, why did I say that?* she asked herself. *What has come over me?*

Mr Dineen had found his handkerchief – a proper cotton one, no tissues for him – and blew his nose noisily. His face was flushed now.

'But you see, I . . . I would love to visit them, but . . . but I can't, and it's such a long way for the girls to come. Well, not for Yona, it's easier for her, but . . . but she says she comes all the time and I have to come to her – I have to be brave and try to get over it.'

Danae felt terrible. She'd opened a can of worms. The poor man was clearly terrified of flying and it sounded as though his daughter in London had issued an ultimatum along the lines: *We are not coming to you this Christmas; you must come to us.*

Remorse flooded through Danae. She of all people knew that there was nothing worse than other people interfering in your business.

'Of course. Flying can be very upsetting,' she agreed, as if she was on and off planes every day of the week. 'Noisy things, and it's worrying . . . especially as the plane's coming in to land or take off.'

'Which are the most dangerous times,' interrupted Mr Dineen eagerly, keen to go along with this version of events, the version where flying was a perilous endeavour, only undertaken by the foolhardy.

'Yes,' agreed Danae, 'you're probably right. So, what are you doing for Christmas?'

She'd done it again. For the second time, Mr Dineen's face flooded with red.

'Well, what I normally do, which is go to the Avalon Hotel, where Belle and her staff cook a very satisfactory Christmas dinner.'

Danae made a mental note to tell Belle that Mr Dineen thought the hotel's Christmas dinner was satisfactory, but then thought better of it. Belle would no doubt consider that a terrible insult.

All of a sudden, another bit of Mara-dom came over her. Danae knew what she could do to make up for upsetting poor Mr Dineen in this way, forcing him to admit he'd be having a sad and lonely Christmas dinner in the hotel.

'You should come to us,' she found herself saying. 'It will be myself and my niece, Mara, and the dog. We have hens, but they won't be joining us for Christmas dinner, although they might possibly look in the window.'

This was getting worse, she was making it sound like a madhouse. But Mr Dineen didn't appear to think so.

'That would be lovely,' he beamed. 'Lovely! What should I bring? Eh . . . Some wine perhaps?'

'No,' said Danae quickly, 'I do not imbibe myself.'

The poor man would want to bring something. She wracked her brains.

'A box of chocolates for after dinner, perhaps?' she suggested.

'And we might play board games,' he said eagerly. 'When I was a child, we always played Scrabble.'

'Scrabble! What a fabulous idea,' said Danae. 'Do you have a Scrabble set?'

He nodded. 'I sometimes play myself, although it's not really that . . . satisfactory.'

'I hope you will find our dinner satisfactory,' said Danae with a smile.

'I am sure, Mrs Rahill, that anything you cook will be exemplary,' he said.

'Just one thing,' said Danae, 'you must stop calling me Mrs Rahill. It's Danae.'

For the third time, Mr Dineen blushed, the rosy colour of one of Danae's precious tea roses in June – a sort of orangey pink, which was lovely on a rose, but not so good on an elderly gentleman.

'And I am Denis,' he said gravely, nodding.

'I'll give you my address, shall I?' said Danae, and wrote it out on a piece of paper.

'Willow Street. Of course, I know it. Doris and I used to go up there on walks and look at the old house. It was magnificent in its day,' he said mistily.

'Well, it's going to be magnificent again,' Danae informed him. 'Cashel Reilly has bought it and he's going to revamp it. In fact, my niece Mara, who's going to be at lunch with us, is assisting him.'

'Wonderful, wonderful!' said Mr Dineen happily. 'It will be like old times.'

After saying thank you again many more times, he left the post office and Danae was able to retreat into the back room. She sank down on her chair without even the energy to make herself a cup of tea to recover. Whatever had come over her? She knew. It was Mara. Mara's pernicious influence was changing her, making her all friendly and chatty, after all these years of keeping herself to herself. But it felt good. Danae smiled to herself. She had to admit it – opening up to the world felt good.

Danae arrived home that night feeling faintly sheepish. Mara was in the kitchen and the aroma of stir-fry drifted enticingly in the air. Lady sat at Mara's feet as she worked at the cooker.

'You're not going to believe this, Mara,' Danae began, 'but I seem to have invited three people to Christmas dinner.'

Mara spun round in astonishment. 'You did what?'

'I don't know how it happened,' said Danae, 'but first I found myself inviting Mr Dineen, and then I bumped into Father Olumbuko when I was locking up and I asked him too, but he said he and Father Liam would be eating together. So then . . .' Danae paused. 'Well, I totally lost the run of myself and asked Father Liam too. It's your fault,' she added, 'you and your introducing me to people and making me see people. Now look what you've done. Instead of you and I having a nice quiet dinner, we'll have to cook for a cast of thousands!'

Mara grinned. 'Three more people is hardly a cast of thousands,' she said. 'Besides, it'll be fun.'

In fact, Mara loved the idea. Normally she went home to Furlong Hill for Christmas, but Danae had been reluctant to join her. So, rather than leave Danae on her own, she had decided to stay in Avalon for Christmas Day and then drive to her parents' for St Stephen's Day. But much as she enjoyed Danae's company, Mara was accustomed to the hubbub of Furlong Hill, with a constant stream of friends and neighbours dropping in for five minutes to leave a gift and having to be shoved out the door six hours later having had too much eggnog. That was fun, that was part of Christmas.

Up here, in the little cottage at the end of Willow Street it would be a different, quieter Christmas, even with the dog around and the hens squawking madly in the window. Now, it would be fun, too, and she said so.

'I don't know about fun,' said Danae. 'I mean, you haven't actually met Mr Dineen or Father Olumbuko – although he is a very dashing and a charming young priest, and I'm quite sure he's good fun – but Mr Dineen is . . .' she hesitated, wondering exactly how to describe him, 'well, sort of fragile. He'll need a bit of looking after. Not to mention Father Liam, who needs a fleet of people to look after him, if truth be told.'

'Oh, that's fine,' said Mara, turning back to her stir-fry, 'looking after people is my speciality.'

Danae smiled fondly at her niece's back. It was true: looking after people really was Mara's speciality.

'Do you know,' said Mara, still stirring, 'another thought has occurred to me, now that we're going to be having this open-house thing. I've been thinking about Tess and her kids, Zach and Kitty. Things are going to be difficult for them this year, because Kevin will obviously spend the day with Claire and her family, leaving Tess at home with the kids, and possibly Kevin's mother – apparently she's refusing to go to Claire's. Every time I mention Christmas, Tess looks so miserable, as if she's absolutely dreading it. And you know,' Mara said earnestly, 'Kitty is such a little darling and Zach is a sweetheart, and I couldn't bear for their Christmas to be diminished. It should be full of fun and crackers and games around the table and Monopoly and silly hats and loud music, so they don't even notice their dad's not there. What would you say to inviting them here?'

First, Danae wondered how Mara managed to get all this information out of people so easily. Then, she looked around her beautiful, cosy cottage kitchen, filled with the simple furnishings and homely touches she'd put into it over the past eighteen years. It was calm and peaceful, but it had never seen crazy fun like the party Mara was describing. Maybe it was time that changed.

'You're right,' said Danae. 'You must see Tess tomorrow and invite them all, the mother-in-law included, and that darling little whippet too – no time to be lost!'

Tess Power, meanwhile, was sitting in her kitchen going over the books. She'd tried to give the business one last chance, even bringing in Mara for another two days while she went auction hunting – a decision which had turned out to be a sound investment, because Mara had the gift of selling things to people. She'd read the description that Tess had written on the luggage label attached to each item, and from that snippet of information she'd weave the most fabulous stories. If a customer happened to glance at a silver-backed brush from the 1920s, Mara would be off: 'Isn't it beautiful? Can't you just imagine an elegant lady, sitting at her dressing table while she . . . No, actually,' Mara would pause, correcting herself, 'while *her maid* brushed her hair the regulation one hundred times. And perhaps all the while she'd have been secretly dreaming of getting her hair shingled. You see, her father really wanted it long and she was being modern . . .'

Soon everyone in the shop would be listening, rapt, as Mara brought the past to life. People bought things in frantic haste after listening to Mara, which was wonderful. Unfortunately it would take more than Mara and her brilliant selling skills to keep Something Old afloat.

People simply had less money to spare, and even though there were far more antiques on the market because so many people were having to part with their treasures, many of them were way beyond Tess's budget.

The fabulous faded rosewood breakfast tables and silver-plated candlesticks she'd seen at the auction houses were too expensive for her. The Regency mahogany side cabinets probably wouldn't fit in the shop and, even if they did, she couldn't afford them. They were soon snapped up by other dealers, along with any sought-after pieces of Imperial ware china; items that she would once have picked up for a song were selling at a premium now that the Chinese were trying to buy back their heritage. The things that were left, like the sad-eyed portraits from the eighteenth century, nobody wanted to buy these days.

She needed a miracle: she needed a piece like the beautiful Chinese blue-and-white porcelain dragon dish that had been hiding in somebody's attic and had come out for sale at an auction with a 2,000–3,000 euro reserve price. It turned out that the dish was not only authentic Ming dynasty, but it bore the mark of Xuande, a fifteenth-century genius. That tiny

312

mark had changed everything: the dragon dish sold for hundreds of thousands of euros.

A success on that scale was what she needed. Instead, she'd come away with two exquisite bronze greyhound pieces. She knew it was crazy, and she'd paid too much for them, but their elegant, sad faces reminded her of the stone greyhounds that used to sit on either side of the front door at Avalon House when she was a child. They'd been among the last things to go and Tess could still remember her sorrow at seeing them loaded on to a dealer's lorry.

Now she'd have to sell them on because there was no way anyone coming to her door would be prepared to pay or even transport the two exquisite dogs.

Strangely, she couldn't help thinking about Avalon House these days, ever since Cashel had bought it.

There was talk of him all the time in the village. He wasn't Mr Reilly any more. No, he was *Cashel – Oh, Cashel's doing a fabulous job up at the house –* the local-boy-done-good, come home to spread the riches.

He was a total sweetie, insisted Belle from the hotel.

Tess thought that Belle had rather set her eye on Cashel. *Watch out, Belle,* she wanted to say, *he's not what you think.*

But she could say nothing. Instead, she found herself overcome with a terrible longing to go up to the house again, to walk around it, to step through the rooms laying her fingers on the doors and staircases she'd touched carelessly as a child. She wanted to make a pilgrimage around her childhood, to revisit that time in her life when things had been very different.

Except, she couldn't. She daren't go up there in case he saw her.

She might manage it over Christmas, because he was sure to be away and there'd be no workers there. Perhaps.

Right now, however, there were more pressing matters at hand: money, Christmas and her mother-in-law, Helen.

'Tess, I wanted to tell you I'm not going to go to Claire's

313

parents' house for Christmas. I simply can't,' Helen had said tremulously on the phone a few days before. 'It doesn't feel right, it's too soon, I'm not ready. You know me, I like to take my time over things and I don't know them and Claire's a sweet girl but it's so upsetting.'

'Well, you could always come here,' Tess had said, her guts clenching, knowing that a distraught Helen might not be the best addition to the household, given that Kitty was already desolate because Tess, Kevin, Claire, Zach and herself were not all going to be spending Christmas together.

'Why not?' she'd said tearfully. 'I mean, why not, Mum? They could come and stay. I'll move in with you and they can have my bedroom,'

'Well, I don't think that's a very good idea,' Tess had said gently.

It was wonderful that Kitty was so marvellously innocent and yet at the same time Tess couldn't shatter that innocence by explaining the truth or the facts.

'Claire wants to be with her mum and dad because she's having the baby,' Tess explained.

'But what about me?' cried Kitty.

Tess hauled her darling daughter on to her lap and held her tightly. Christmas was going to be difficult this year, no doubt about it.

She and Kevin had talked about it one night when he came up to dinner with the family.

Tess had decided that there was no point in keeping him away from the house in some act of rage – it was far better for the children to see their parents getting on like adults.

As Tess had told Zach and Kitty over dinner that night: 'We will always care for each other, but we will always love you two.'

And now it looked as if she'd be spending Christmas trying to console her mother-in-law too. Truly, life was strange.

Chapter Twenty

Cashel held the glass of mulled wine in his hand and stared out at the snow-covered valleys below him. It was truly picture-postcard here in Courchevel, yet Cashel had never felt less Christmassy in his life. They'd been skiing most of the day and now they'd come in at five when it was darkening. The scent of some amazing meal was wafting up from the kitchens. The luxury chalet – in the elite Courchevel heights of 1850, naturally – had a French chef, along with a seemingly endless supply of young locals in and out cleaning and tidying, while a married couple from the Philippines ran the whole place. Cashel had to hand it to Rhona. She knew how to pick a luxury destination for Christmas.

'Isn't it beautiful?' She was beside him, resting her hand on his shoulder in a friendly manner. 'You work too hard you know, Cashel,' she said. 'You should do this more often. Come away with us. Spend a few days doing nothing.'

'Yes, it's beautiful,' said Cashel automatically, because to say anything else would be rude. He didn't envy Rhona's existence, or even that of her new husband: a few weeks' work here and there, then a trip to St Bart's, another few weeks, then skiing perhaps. It was the sort of life Rhona had always wanted when she was married to him, and he could have given it to her from a financial viewpoint, but he wouldn't have been there with her. The drive to work – to keep working to hide any gaps in his life – was too strong in Cashel.

'Aren't you glad you came?' Rhona said.

'Yes, thank you,' he said, which was a lie because he wasn't glad at all.

When Rhona had phoned him, wheedling, saying that she and some friends were renting a luxury chalet in the French Alps for ten days over Christmas, she'd made it sound so wonderful.

'An escape, Cashel,' she had said. And those were the magic words. He wanted to escape from everywhere, but particularly from Avalon, which was casting its spell over him again. He had tried to stay away and let that Mara girl deal with everything and liaise with one of his assistants, but somehow he couldn't bear to leave it alone. He kept flying in, getting the helicopter down so he could look at the house, see what was happening, seek out Freddie and ask him why there wasn't more progress being made.

'Ah, well now,' Freddie said each time, scratching his head. 'These old houses are tricky, Mr Reilly.'

Cashel became *Mr Reilly* whenever there was a problem.

'We need to make the back of the house structurally sound before we can really get working. It's a huge old place, so that's going to take a long time. And even then, it's going to be slow. Like with the walls, for example: you can't throw up any old bit of plaster on the walls, you know. Myself and Lorcan, we're working to make it *authentic*.'

When Lorcan, the architect, started talking about making the house authentic, Cashel had to stop himself from letting fly with a left hook. Lorcan could bore for Ireland on the subject of authenticity. Any concept of making Avalon House into a home as well as a beautiful example of architectural heritage was entirely lost on him.

That's why Cashel left dealing with Lorcan to Mara. He

316

found himself getting very irritated by discussions over sourcing mouldings, plaster versus plasterboard, original slates that were nigh on impossible to find and would cost a small fortune in the event they did find them. He simply wanted it done. He didn't want to hear how it was to happen, *why* it was to happen and how far Freddie would have to go to get precisely the right thing.

Cashel had visited Avalon four times in the last month, which was unheard of, given his demanding schedule.

But the draw of home was proving too much for him. And he knew why that was. It wasn't so much Avalon House, much as he wanted it to be finished, to be able to look at this gleaming, beautifully restored house and think: *This is mine. This belongs to the boy whose mother used to clean the steps here and used to polish the brass.*

True, he wanted that fiercely, but there was another reason he kept going back to Avalon, a reason he didn't like to admit.

He'd seen Tess in town a few times and tried not to look, not to watch her long-legged walk, not to look at the curve of her cheek or to catch her eye. He wouldn't talk to her directly, no. Instead, he'd subtly questioned Mara about her, because he knew she helped out occasionally in Tess's antique shop. Being new to the area, Mara didn't have a clue about his history with Tess, so he was able to enquire idly about the Power family in general, throwing in the odd question about Suki and the girls' father, to make it seem as if he was interested in all of them.

'Is there a good living to be made from the antique shop, do you think?' he'd ask, and Mara would look up from whatever bit of paper she was scanning and say, 'I'm not sure, but times are tough, you know, Cashel. We're not all loaded like you. I think it's hard for Tess.'

If anyone else had spoken to him like that, Cashel might have fired them, but for some reason he could take it from

Mara. Perhaps it was because she was here in Avalon, and he became a different person in Avalon.

'Tess . . . did you say she'd split up from her husband?' he asked another time, trying to invest the words with the required combination of interest and lack of interest. Apparently, he hadn't managed it, because this time Mara looked up, stared him straight in the eyes.

'Yes,' she said. 'She and Kevin are very definitely separated, and now he's . . .' Mara paused.

'He's what?' Cashel urged, unable to help himself.

'His girlfriend is pregnant.'

'Oh,' Cashel said. That was unexpected, and hopeful in some strange way.

Tess Power was no longer officially attached. She was available, theoretically, and his heart jumped at the thought. And then he knew he was crazy because he and Tess were finished.

He'd said so many times over the years that he'd never look back. In a way, Tess had done him a favour. He owed some of his drive and ambition to her: heartbreak and rage were powerful forces and, with his own innate drive, he'd been ready to take on the world. He'd grown rich and powerful, so powerful that he could have almost anything he wanted. And he owed a certain amount of that to the one woman he hadn't been able to have.

'Cashel, there's someone I want you to meet,' said Rhona, dragging him out of his reverie staring blankly at the snow outside.

Beside his ex-wife was a tall brunette. She was slim and good-looking with an intelligent glint in her eye.

'Sherry Petrovsky, meet Cashel Reilly.'

'Delighted to meet you.'

Her handshake was cool and firm. She wasn't, he decided, one of the glamour-puss friends Rhona sometimes brought along for fun. After talking to her for a while, he soon realized that she was anything but.

She was a commodities trader in London.

'Tough job,' remarked Cashel.

'Yes, but I like it,' she said coolly. 'The biggest problem is the traders – they all want to be alpha dog and like to think my job is to be pack bitch.'

Cashel burst out laughing. From the way she spoke, he had no doubt that Sherry had no trouble handling a bunch of testosterone-fuelled traders.

'Hey, it's chilly standing here at the window, despite – is that *triple* glazing? Why don't we sit down,' suggested Sherry.

Cashel watched her as she led the way to a two-seater couch. She had a fabulous body, which spoke of getting up at about five in the morning to go to the gym, as traders started early and worked late. He began to like Sherry more and more. Maybe this holiday had been a good idea after all.

Across the room, Rhona caught Sherry's eye and winked at her. Sherry allowed herself a brief grin back. It was early days yet.

Sherry sat beside Cashel at dinner that night. It was his first night there, even though the others had arrived over the previous few days. Normally at these things he felt sort of different, an outsider for all his money. Shades of his insecurity, he knew; and he hated that, hated that there was any insecurity in Cashel Reilly, millionaire, entrepreneur, successful business man, but it remained nonetheless. With Sherry however, he didn't feel in the slightest bit uneasy. He felt comfortable around her. They knew some of the same people, moved in some of the same circles. But it wasn't that; no, it was the sense that Sherry had come up the hard way. She understood hard work and she understood not fitting in; partly, he reckoned, from being a woman in a man's world. There was no doubt about it, working in the city was definitely a man's world. But she was easy-going when she talked about her work.

There were no horror stories of *Playboy* magazine being passed around the office, rude emails or trips with clients to golf courses or strip clubs. Clearly Sherry had figured out how to deal with such things. She was comfortable with herself and he liked that. They talked easily, happily; it was rather like he was in a room with her and nobody else there. Once he caught Rhona grinning across the table at him, looking like someone who'd that instant figured out string theory. 'What?' he mouthed across at her.

'You two,' she mouthed back, pointing at him and Sherry in a most un-Rhona-like way. Normally, Rhona was very hot on the social niceties and would as lief point across a dinner table as she would talk about her upper brow lift. But it was clear she was happy that she had set up such a good match between her ex-husband and Sherry.

Funny that, he thought, raising a glass of red wine to her. She was happy that he had clicked with a girl she'd invited for him. Whatever else you might say about their marriage, at least they'd ended on amicable terms. How many ex-wives tried to arrange dates for their ex-husbands? Mind you, she'd done it a few times before with less successful results, but Rhona was a quick learner. She'd worked out his type soon enough. A go-getter, like him.

For a sliver of a moment his mind ran back to Avalon and Tess Power. Tess was very different from Sherry, different in almost every way. Different physically, different in the way she approached life, different in her job and upbringing. There was nothing posh about Sherry, nor did she pretend there was. She was simply a very smart, beautiful woman who'd used her brains to get ahead. While Tess was . . . well, Tess was a smart woman too, who'd come from a different world to him. He hadn't understood the rules of her world, the rules that said it was perfectly all right for her to break his heart.

'You're miles away,' said Sherry, turning back from her neighbour to talk to him. 'Tell me what's going on in that clever head of yours. Have you some fabulous plan to take over the world? Should I know about it? Would that be insider trading?' She leaned back in her chair, fingers wrapped lazily around the stem of her wine glass. She didn't drink much, he noticed. She was one of those women who looked around and watched carefully, smiling as if she was happy to be in this place at this time.

'No,' he lied. 'I was thinking how nice it was to be here with friends and how nice it was to meet you.'

Sherry Petrovsky didn't do anything as gauche as blush; she'd learned not to do that sort of thing years ago. But there was an undeniable glow to her cheeks as she smiled back at him. Cashel Reilly was gorgeous. Even more gorgeous than his photos. She was glad she'd come, even though in the beginning she'd resisted Rhona's efforts to persuade her.

'I don't have time to date guys who are emotionally stunted or who've been destroyed in the past, Rhona,' Sherry said with mild irritation. She knew Rhona from college, a million years ago when they were both art students, before Sherry had realized that art was so not her and had switched cleverly into economics.

'I didn't say he was emotionally stunted,' Rhona said. They were sitting in J. Sheekey's fish restaurant on a girls' night out with the old college crowd. Sherry liked going out with the gang. It was fun. She couldn't help the thrill she felt, the fact that she was the most successful of them all when it came to business.

Of course, she hadn't been quite so successful in those other female markers – family, husband, all that sort of stuff. But she had what she wanted – for now, anyway.

'All I said,' Rhona explained, already quite tipsy on champagne, 'was that there's this woman from his past, his first love – I know, such a cliché – but he's never quite got over her. She shaped him, she was part of his life when he was growing up. It's the classic poor-boy-made-good stuff, and

321

some of them have a chip on their shoulder – not that I'm saying Cashel has a chip on his shoulder, because he doesn't. He's very proud of where he came from, the fact that his mother cleaned houses. But you see, he fell in love with the girl whose house his mother cleaned, only for some reason she dumped him or betrayed him. I'm not sure exactly what happened because he would never talk about it, but it was obvious that it was niggling away at him. You know how guys like that can be: they can't stand for there to be any unfinished business, any battle they haven't won. So it's always there somewhere in the back of his mind, biting away at him.'

'And that was why you got divorced?' Sherry asked, feeling less and less interested in Cashel Reilly, even though his picture had caught her eye in the financial pages many times.

'No, we got divorced because we were different. Looking for different stuff really. You know me,' Rhona grinned, 'I like to have fun. Cashel is more of a work-horse. Right up your street, Sherry.'

'So he's not secretly pining after this woman from the past then?' Sherry said. 'I mean, he's had other girlfriends, yes?'

'Oh, loads of them,' Rhona explained. 'Loads before he met me and after we divorced. Every party we've invited him to, he brings a different girl. For a while, he was going for those young model girl types and I said, "Cashel, stop! You do need someone you can talk to." Eventually the message got through. No, he's had loads of girlfriends. Loads of relationships since then, but I think he's definitely over the one from the past and I think you are just his sort of girl.'

'Why are you trying to fix up your ex-husband, though?' said Sherry.

Rhona shrugged. 'It seems weird, I know. Most of my friends hate their ex-husbands, but Cashel was always so generous. The divorce settlement was fabulous. Then I met Rico, and now I'm happy. I never stopped *liking* Cashel; we weren't suited, that's all. I suppose you could say it's karma:

I feel I'm doing something good for the universe by doing something good for Cashel, helping him heal his wounds from the past.'

Sherry laughed at this. 'You are so funny, Rhona,' she said. 'You're adorable.'

Rhona beamed and waggled a finger on her right hand on which sat a beautiful cabochon diamond. 'I know,' she said. 'Rico thinks so too. Isn't this lovely? It was our third anniversary last week – our *third*. I said to him, "Isn't that tin or cotton or something?" And he said, "No, honey, for you it's gotta be diamonds!"'

Sherry thought of all this as she looked at Cashel Reilly. He really was the whole package. Tall, lean, muscular, none of that belly fat that some businessmen got from endless airplane journeys knocking back whiskies to help them relax, and endless rich dinners in fancy restaurants. Cashel was lean and sexy. She liked the dark hair flecked with grey and the dark eyes that were smiling at her now. She could imagine the fierce passion in them. Yes, she liked him very much, thank you.

Chapter Twenty-One

*M*ara loved Christmas morning, loved the crisp coolness, the sense of celebration. She lay in her bed and listened to the sounds of the cottage, the sounds she'd got used to. It was a windy morning and cold, even indoors she could feel the coldness, and yet she was snug in her bed in the little bedroom with its pretty blue floral wallpaper. In a jug by her bed was a posy of Christmas roses; Danae had put them there the night before, along with some sprigs of holly. There were a few with the berries on.

'I love them with the berries,' Mara had said wistfully.

'I do too,' said Danae, 'but the birds need them more than we do.'

'Oh, of course,' said Mara, realizing she'd been thoughtless. Feeding the birds was not something she'd ever done before, but here with Danae, making special bird cake from old cooking fat, seeds and nuts was part of everyday living. Danae cared for every creature who came near her, from her beloved hens to her darling Lady and every robin in between. She'd come back from her walks with Lady and tell Mara about the wildlife she'd seen. So much so that Mara started getting up extra early to go with her and experience for herself the scent of wet grass in the morning, admire the beauty of the ivy clustering over the old Abbey, touch the gnarled boughs of the old willows and magnolia trees in the grounds of Avalon House and stare down at the beauty that was Avalon Bay.

'It really is amazing here,' she'd said to Danae as they stood watching the sunrise together one morning.

'I know,' Danae agreed, 'it's peaceful and beautiful. This high up, I feel as if we're almost a part of nature and yet close to people too.'

There had been a time when Mara had wondered whether part of the charm of this beautiful house high above Avalon was its distance from people. But Danae had changed of late, and today, Christmas, was proof of that. There was so much to be done today!

Every bit as excited as she used to be when she was a child waiting for Santa Claus, Mara bounded out of bed, ran into the shower room and turned the heater on. The central heating was timed to come on early, but probably not yet and Mara was anxious to get up and have her shower, dress in her Christmas best and then serve Danae tea in bed and watch her open her present.

Mara was particularly excited about the present. She'd spent so long wondering what to get for Danae, who was probably the least material person she knew. It had been Rafe who'd come up with the idea.

'There's a guy I know, lives about fifty miles from here, and he makes animal sculptures out of wood. They're works of art,' he said, 'really beautiful and each one's unique. What about something like that?'

'Oh, what a wonderful idea,' Mara had exclaimed and kissed him. He was very easy to kiss, was Rafe. She was never careful with him, not the way she had been with Jack. With Jack she'd never acted without first trying to gauge what was the right thing to do, whether he was in the mood to be kissed or touched, or if he'd shrug off her embrace, irritated by it. With Rafe, she could spontaneously throw her arms around him and hug him and he'd hug right back, delighted. It wasn't that he was a less complex character than Jack – far from it. Rafe Berlin was very complex, but he was straightforward and honest in his love for her.

They'd driven down together in Rafe's truck to see the wood sculpture.

'I'm not taking you on the back of a bike yet,' he said. 'I don't think you're ready for it.'

'What do you mean? I love excitement, I love thrills,' Mara had said crossly.

'Yeah, well, I need to be sure,' said Rafe, 'because you're too precious for me to risk you on the back of a bike until I'm certain.'

So far they'd only been on short journeys around the village with Rafe going at what seemed like ten miles an hour.

'You all right, you all right?' he kept yelling over his shoulder.

'I'm fine,' Mara had screamed through the visor of her helmet. 'I'm not some little old lady, you know.'

'Oh, I know,' he'd growled, his voice lower.

Tom, the sculptor, had turned out to be a tall, intense man in his sixties with a shock of white hair and brown skin from many hours spent outdoors. When it was sunny, he preferred to move his lathe and tools to the yard at the back of his studio and work in the open air.

'It's only right to take the wood outside,' he said gravely.

He used a variety of woods: ash, willow, blackthorn, and beautiful driftwood he found on the beaches. He was a silent man, yet calming to be around. He reminded Mara of her aunt. Danae had a similar quiet serenity about her nowadays.

There was a carving of a wolf on a rock and Mara knew instantly that was the one.

'My aunt would love that,' she said. 'Her dog, Lady, is very wolf-like. I don't know what breed she is, but she looks exactly like this. Danae loves nature, she goes for long walks in the woods where she lives, and Lady is always by her side,' Mara went on. There was something about Tom that made her think he wouldn't let his pieces go to anyone.

'Tell her she can bring it back if it doesn't move her, doesn't touch her,' he said slowly. 'I hate to think of an animal I've made sitting in a place where it's not loved.'

'She'll love it,' Mara assured him. 'I guarantee, she'll love it.'

She ran her hands down the silky smooth body of the wolf, marvelling at the dexterity of the work that had breathed life into this magical creature. 'I think she'd love to see your studio, actually,' Mara added.

'Any time,' he'd said. 'Any time.'

Having finished her shower, Mara went down to the kitchen and let Lady out into the garden to do her business. Having stoked up the range with fresh wood, she boiled the kettle, made a strong coffee for herself and a tea for Danae. Then she turned the radio on and found a station playing soft Christmas music. The kitchen and the small living room looked so beautiful it brought a lump to her throat.

They'd spent ages putting up the decorations. Danae hadn't liked the idea of a Christmas tree: 'I hate plants that are killed for our amusement,' she'd said. 'No, I want a live one, then it can go into the garden when Christmas is over.' So their Christmas tree was a small one in a planter box. It stood in a corner of the living room, festooned with beautiful red and white decorations and tiny baubles that Mara had had great fun buying in Avalon. There was holly and ivy decorating the top of each window, candles everywhere.

And yet there was so much to be done. The food had to be prepared and the table laid so everything would be perfect when their guests started to arrive. Time to get Danae up.

Mara, holding the tea and coffee on a tray, knocked gently on Danae's door.

327

'I'm awake,' her aunt said. 'I heard you moving about and I was thinking I might stretch my creaking bones and come out and join you.'

'Well, you don't have to stretch your creaking bones yet awhile,' said Mara. 'I've brought you tea in bed.'

'Thank you,' Danae said, opening the door for her. 'I'm getting to love this tea in bed thing.'

'You deserve it. Now here's your present,' said Mara, picking it up from outside the bedroom door, bringing it in and placing it carefully on Danae's bed. 'Hold on a minute, I've got to nip downstairs and let Lady in.'

The dog bounded up the stairs and leapt on to Danae's bed and made herself comfortable. Danae ripped open the paper.

Mara looked on anxiously, hoped she'd like the wolf carving. She must. She stopped watching the ripping and instead concentrated on Danae's lovely face, its warmth and its gentleness. There had been nobody to bring her tea in bed until Mara came along – how terribly sad and what a waste, Mara thought. Danae should have someone in her life, someone she loved, who slept in this bed beside her and took care of her. Perhaps it wasn't too late. Perhaps she'd find someone who deserved her.

'Oh, it's beautiful,' Danae breathed, finally extricating the sculpture from its wrapping. Eyes wide, she ran her fingers over every inch of it, gently exploring. 'I love it. Thank you, Danae, thank you.' And Mara found herself thinking again that it had probably been years since anyone had brought her aunt a Christmas present in bed on Christmas morning.

Mr Dineen was the first guest to arrive. Mara opened the front door and he stared at her, blinking myopically behind thick glasses.

'You must be Mr Dineen,' said Mara warmly.

'Oh, yes, er, call me Denis,' he stammered. 'And you are . . . ?'

'Mara – Danae's niece. Please, come in, make yourself at home.'

She led him into the beautifully decorated room and took his coat from him. In return, he handed her a huge gift bag that appeared to be stuffed to the brim with goodies.

'I didn't know what to bring,' he said. 'I haven't, well, that is to say . . . Doris would have always taken care of the gift side of things and I didn't know what to bring or what your aunt would like because Mrs Rahill and I don't really—'

'Danae,' interrupted Mara. 'Do call her Danae.'

She sat him down in a comfortable chair and said, 'You are so kind, Denis, you've brought a veritable feast.'

There was a bottle of wine that even Mara, who knew little about fine wine, recognized as being something murderously expensive. There were handmade chocolates, French cheese crackers and a big scented candle.

'For the centre of the table, I thought,' said Denis nervously. 'But I see you don't need that, it all looks so beautiful.'

And it was. Danae had turned the large dining table into something resembling a bower of nature with garlands of ivy and holly, tiny sprigs of dried lavender and her Christmas roses in a selection of decorative bowls around the table.

'A candle is exactly what we need to put in the middle,' Mara said gravely. 'Now, what can I get you to drink? Do you drink? Would you like to start with a cup of tea? Some water, some wine?'

'Oh, tea would be lovely,' Denis said.

Next up were Father Liam and Father Olumbuko.

Father Liam looked slightly frenzied from having to do two Masses, one in the church in Avalon and another in the parish fifteen miles up the road. But Father Olumbuko, who had taken midnight Mass and another Mass that morning in a different parish, was a picture of serenity.

'I brought this,' he said, handing Mara a big bowl covered in tinfoil. 'It's a vegetable dish cooked the way my mother

329

used to. It's okra, my favourite vegetable,' he said. 'I thought it would be nice to bring a bit of home with me.'

'That's wonderful,' said Mara admiringly.

'I was going to bring wine,' fussed Father Liam, 'but I didn't know if I should. I don't think Danae drinks, does she?'

'No,' said Mara, 'she does not.'

'Oh good,' said Father Liam, as happy as if he'd scored a try in the rugby World Cup. He produced a carrier bag. 'Elderberry cordial, my own, two bottles.'

'Fabulous!' said Mara, taking the two slightly cloudy and very dodgy-looking bottles out of the bag. *Last year's elderberry cordial*, she thought, and put them away. 'You are absolute angels.'

'Is there anything I can do?' said Father Olumbuko.

'Not at all, Father, you go and sit down.'

'Please, call me Edgar,' he said to Mara. 'I like to help in the kitchen.'

Father Liam had already beetled off and was sitting down beside Denis.

At that moment Danae came in from settling the hens. The wind had decided it was a day for frenzied gales, so she'd locked her darlings in their henhouse, after scattering some special feed for Christmas Day in their indoor feeder.

'Edgar, Father Liam, Denis, how wonderful to see you all,' she said, and she hugged them all. 'What a lovely day we're going to have!' And the marvellous thing was, she absolutely believed that. She'd never thrown a Christmas party before, but today was going to be glorious. With Mara by her side, she could do anything.

'Edgar was offering to help in the kitchen,' said Mara.

'Oh, Edgar, there's nothing like a man's touch in the kitchen,' said Danae. 'Come on in here, let's get you fitted up with an apron and see what you can do.'

Belle dropped in for a very quick Christmas drink. She was wearing her Christmas hotel-owner uniform of a black velvet

330

skirt suit with a fur trim around the collar and a vast diamond spider brooch on one bosom.

'I'm trying to figure out if those two things are real,' Danae whispered to her. 'The fur and the brooch.'

'The fur,' said Belle, 'is fake. But the diamonds are real.'

'Oh my!' said Danae, laughing.

'Yes,' said Belle, 'darling Harold was very generous.'

She hugged Danae and Mara, and shook hands with the other guests.

'How are things down in the hotel?' asked Father Liam, who was terrified of Belle and desperately trying not to show it. She was so very capable and looked at him as if she could run Avalon parish and all the outlying parishes with no bother at all. For this very reason, Father Liam often thought it a pity that women weren't admitted into the priesthood. Someone like Belle could do it all with one hand tied behind her back, whereas Father Liam had to rely rather too much on his beta-blocker tablets.

'Oh, you know, down at the hotel it's the usual,' said Belle, sitting down, 'wild chaos and total panic. It's better for me to leave them for a while, otherwise I'd end up killing the staff. A tea would be lovely, Mara darling. I'd better not have a drink until later – I have to keep my wits about me. As I was saying, Father Liam, it's all going swimmingly, really. We're fully booked and they'll be moving on to lunch soon – if Chef gets over his panic attack – and I really have to be back in time for that. Then it's on to the games. Mind you, after last year's charades, I'm not sure I'm into games. There was mutiny when *The Unbearable Lightness of Being* came up twice.'

'We're going to be having games here later,' said Danae. 'Tess Power is coming up with her children, and you have to have games when there's children.'

'Well,' said Mara, 'I don't know if you can officially describe Zach Power as a child, given that he's seventeen. Besides, I'm putting Zach in charge of the music.'

'Ooh well, I'll have to come up for that,' said Belle delight-edly. 'It all gets a bit mad in the hotel in the evening. People can get quite sozzled and start sobbing about their problems. And for some reason they come to me looking for help. I think I'll take a break from it this year and come up here instead – then I can tell you all *my* problems!' She beamed at Father Liam and Denis, who both looked horrified at the prospect.

Danae stifled a grin. Belle really was one of a kind.

When Tess arrived, Mara and Danae insisted she sit down right away and not do a thing in the kitchen. Tess looked pale and tired, as if she hadn't been sleeping. The bones were a little too obvious in her beautiful face. Her mother-in-law, Helen, was nearly as pale; she sat down on the couch and dithered about what to drink, before saying that a small gin and tonic would be nice, if they had such a thing.

'Make it a big one,' whispered Belle. 'She looks a bit shell-shocked by the recent turn of events. A nice whack of gin will help her forget it all. Not that drink is the answer to all evils, but Helen's not the sort to turn to the bottle. I've known her for years. She's more of a one-sherry-a-week type – and believe me, working in the hotel trade, I know the difference.'

Mara instructed Zach to put on some cheery Christmas tunes, and with Denis's help she began to open up the Monopoly board on the coffee table. Kitty looked sad as she saw it being set up.

'It won't be the same,' she said. 'Daddy's with Claire and we're not going to see him until this evening.'

'But he came over this morning, didn't he?' said Mara cheerfully, knowing the plans that had been laid painstakingly the week before.

'He did, but he didn't bring Claire with him. Do you think Claire doesn't like us?' Kitty said.

Zach took her hand: 'Now then, Kittykins, we've talked

332

about it before. Claire needs her mum and dad this Christmas, like Mum told you. But next year, think of the fun we'll have with the baby.'

'Babies love Christmas,' agreed Mara. 'You'll have to get the baby a Santa suit.'

'I suggested a reindeer suit,' said Tess, thrilled that other people were joining in. She'd been having this discussion with Kitty all day and was beginning to despair.

'What about Silkie,' said Mara, gesturing to the fire where Silkie was stretched out luxuriously, nose to nose with Lady. 'She needs a reindeer suit too! In fact, I want one as well!'

'Me too,' said Father Edgar.

Kitty looked at him with narrowed eyes. 'Priests have to wear special clothes,' she said. 'They can't wear reindeer costumes.'

'I promise you,' Father Edgar said with his lovely smile, 'I shall have antlers this time next year!'

Suddenly, Kitty giggled. 'I'd love to dress Silkie up. And Lady.'

'Bet you Edgar won't dress up next year, though,' said Mara.

'Bet you he will,' said Zach.

'He won't.'

'He will!' shrieked Kitty.

Everyone joined in, even Father Liam and Denis, and soon the mood was as light as a feather.

Zach put on music Kitty liked and set up an impromptu disco, Mara produced balloons and a balloon-bouncing competition was begun, hampered slightly by the holly sprigs' propensity to burst all balloons. Silkie quite liked having a tinsel collar, a reindeer outfit not having been located.

Even Helen perked up a little at this, although Danae suspected the gin might have played its part.

When everyone was worn out, Danae planted a gentle kiss on Kitty's forehead: 'Why don't you teach lovely Father Edgar how to play Monopoly? I don't think he knows how, but I bet if you and him gang up on everyone else, you'll win.'

'Yes,' said Edgar gravely, 'I have no idea how to play. This game was not in my house when I was a child.'

'Oh, it's very easy, really,' said Kitty. 'Kneel down on the floor here – it's best to kneel down. Now, I always like being the boot, because that's the best thing. And Zach is always the racing car and Dad . . .'

'Could I have another drink?' said Helen.

'Of course you may,' said Danae, 'but listen, Helen, this is a very relaxed household, so whenever you feel like one, head on into the kitchen and help yourself. Is that all right?'

'But I wouldn't want to impose,' said Helen tremulously.

'You wouldn't be imposing at all,' said Danae. 'You're among friends here.'

When Rafe came up later he found a heated game of Monopoly going on. Bing Crosby was singing 'White Christmas' and the smell of amazing food scented the whole house. 'I've just had Christmas lunch,' he said, 'but I think I could stay for this too.'

'You're welcome to,' said Danae, who'd come to be very fond of Rafe on his visits to the cottage. He was such a kind man, she felt, and he was so good to Mara.

Mara led him off into her bedroom to give him his present. 'We're supposed to be doing presents after dinner, but you mightn't be staying.'

'I might well be staying,' he said, and shut the door.

'Everyone will think we've come in here for more than exchanging gifts,' Mara said.

'We'll be quick then,' said Rafe, taking her face in his hands and kissing her slowly, languorously.

'Wow!' Mara said, when they both came up for air. 'That could be my Christmas present. I don't need anything else.'

'Well, it isn't,' he said, and he produced something wrapped in tissue paper. It turned out to be a dolphin carved by the man who'd carved Danae's beautiful she-wolf.

'You see, you're a dolphin,' he said. 'I like to imagine what sort of animal everyone is, and you're a dolphin. Beautiful, intelligent, wild, free, affectionate, something people love to look at.'

Mara didn't know why, but her eyes filled with tears. There was something so beautiful about being described as a dolphin. 'Is that really how you see me?' she said.

'Oh, I see you as so much more, but in animal form, yes, you're a dolphin. You know, they're my favourite creatures,' he said. And when they kissed this time, they were a lot slower coming up for air.

'My present seems very boring in comparison with yours,' Mara said. It was an old motorbike manual she'd tracked down on the Internet. But when she handed it to him, she watched his face break into a delighted grin.

'I can't believe you found this! I've been trying for years to get hold of a copy – they're like gold dust.'

'Ah yes, well, some of us are better on computers than others,' Mara teased. 'Come on, we better go back out to the others.'

Nobody wanted to leave the table after dinner, they were all having so much fun, talking, laughing, pulling crackers, saying they were too full even to move.

'We should go for a walk, you know,' Danae said.

'I don't think I could,' said Rafe. 'I've had two Christmas dinners. I don't think I'll be able to walk until next week.'

'This has been amazing,' said Tess, tears welling in her eyes as she looked gratefully at Danae and Mara. 'Thank you, thank you.'

'No,' said Danae, 'thank you. I think this has been my best Christmas in a very, very long time.'

Chapter Twenty-Two

Cashel had flown back from Courchevel with a smile on his face and a feeling that maybe life wasn't so bad after all. Sherry had given him her number and he'd promised to call her and take her out to dinner next time he was in London. She'd held her card in her hand for ages before giving it to him.

'Don't mess with me,' she said, as coolly as she said everything. 'I'm not into wasting time, so if you're not planning on ringing me, Cashel, I won't give you the card. Let's cut out the "will he/won't he" bit in the middle, right?'

'Is this how you do business?' Cashel said, impressed.

'Yes, this is precisely how I do business,' she said crisply, 'and it works. I don't bullshit other people and I don't expect them to bullshit me.'

'Point taken,' Cashel said. 'I promise you, I'm not one of those men who doesn't keep his word.'

She handed him the card and he took it without their fingers even touching. It had been a long time since he'd felt attracted to somebody and it felt good, normal. Maybe he was getting over this misery that had been affecting his head for so long. The darkness that had settled when his mother had died. Perhaps Sherry might come over to Ireland for a weekend and he could show her Avalon House. That'd be fun he thought, he'd be proud to show it to her. To show her the town and say: 'This is where I came from, one of the smallest cottages, right at the bottom of the hill.'

'And now you're buying the big house,' he could imagine her saying, a certain admiration in her voice.

Sitting on the plane, flying back to Dublin, he felt a surge of embarrassment at this thought. It was so predictable, wasn't it? The local boy who makes good, then wants to come back and buy up the town.

Maybe he'd been crazy, maybe what he'd felt for Tess Power all those years ago had affected his brain. Perhaps he should stick the house back on the market and forget about it. Forget about the plans and the builder and the architect and his mad new Avalon assistant, Mara, although she made him smile. He could offer her a job in his empire, she'd fit in anywhere. She said she'd wanted to move to London, but he could offer her a place in New York perhaps. She'd like that. Get both of them away from Avalon and the past.

The Avalon Hotel was full. 'Sorry,' said Belle when he called. 'I rang your assistant in London to check if it was all right to rent the suite for one night because we were having a big party, and he said you'd be in London, so it was fine. It's the New Year's Eve celebrations. I can get you back in your normal suite on New Year's Day? Three o'clock? Two o'clock if you're lucky!'

'That'll be fine,' he said. 'I'll stay with my brother. Remind me to fire that assistant.'

'Don't be so mean,' said Belle firmly. 'Poor fella thought you were going to be in London. He's not psychic!'

Cashel felt wrong-footed from the first. He didn't like New Year's Eve. It was the emotional equivalent of end-of-year-accounting: when you worked out what had gone right and what had gone wrong. Sobering, horrible and not a good time to be alone.

He phoned Charlotte and asked to stay. Riach, Charlotte and the children were planning to go to a fireworks display down on the quay.

'Come on over and we'll all go.'

'OK,' said Cashel, 'that sounds good. Maybe we'll grab some dinner first.'

'I was going to cook,' said Charlotte.

'You're always cooking,' Cashel said kindly to his sister-in-law. 'Have a break, let me treat you.'

The fireworks were amazing, thirty solid minutes of unbelievable spectacle against the backdrop of a clear night sky. The children had loved it. He'd put little Martina up on his shoulders because at four she was the smallest and couldn't see. She was a little angel of a child, with dark hair, green eyes and the most loving nature. If children chose their parents, he was glad this little angel had chosen Charlotte and Riach, because they adored her. 'Now,' he said, 'isn't that wonderful?'

'Yes,' she said in her soft voice. 'It's like fairyland.'

Yes, he thought, it is like fairyland. He held on to his little niece even more tightly to make sure she never fell off.

The next morning he was up early, not sure what to do with himself. He'd sent a Happy New Year text to Sherry and had one back, as well as a mad one full of exclamation marks from Mara. The children were up, so he fixed them breakfast thinking that Charlotte and Riach could have a bit of a lie on for once. Eddie, his eight-year-old nephew, wanted to play on the Wii but Martina wanted to watch *Dora the Explorer*. A fierce battle ensued with Cashel only barely able to referee it.

'God,' he said when Riach came into the sitting room to see what all the noise was about, 'I thought that industrial negotiations were tough.'

'There's nothing tougher than negotiating with a four-year-old. Trust me,' said Riach, and went on with the wisdom of

Solomon to allot half an hour to *Dora the Explorer* and then half an hour to the Wii before suggesting everyone get up and out and have a good walk in the beautiful, fresh air.

'Good plan,' said Cashel. 'I think I'll head up to the house, see how things are coming along.'

'We could all go?'

'No,' said Cashel, 'it's not really safe for the children. They'll probably want to go inside, and Lord knows what state it's in. No, let's wait 'til it's had a bit of work done and it's totally safe, then the kids can come up. I'm going to take a quick walk around by myself, to see what's going on.' To see, he thought privately, if it was worth holding on to: if it held the same fascination for him as it had before.

He'd go to his mother's grave and talk to her too. It would be like making up for lost time, for the years when he couldn't tell her everything.

He probably never had told her everything, he thought sadly. What son ever did? There were always a few secrets, things you were ashamed of or things you couldn't tell your mother. Things like how hurt he'd been by Tess Power, how she'd delivered a body blow from which he'd never quite recovered. Even though he'd not told his mother the details, she'd spoken to him about it often enough.

'Don't let your pride stand in the way,' she'd said to him at the start, in the time he was away travelling, when he would call home from a payphone on a crackly line every month or so. Tess was alone, her father had died, and she'd had to sell the house, his mother said.

And then his mother had stopped saying that and stopped mentioning Tess at all, and Cashel hadn't asked, too proud to lower his guard. It wasn't until he arrived back in Avalon eighteen months later, Tess's image still engraved on his heart, that he found out why. Riach was the one who told him.

'She's married now – nice fella, carpenter, you'd like him,' he said.

Riach was never one for beating about the bush.

'I'd like him, would I?' said Cashel drily to his brother. 'Yeah, sure, love him already.'

'Well, you had your chance,' said Riach.

'No I didn't,' said Cashel. 'She made that very clear by what she did.'

'God, but you've turned into a hard man, Cashel Reilly,' said Riach. 'I wouldn't like you for an enemy.'

And Cashel had felt bad then. But when he'd found out that Tess was pregnant, that was the final blow. He'd never forgiven her for breaking his heart. Her actions showed that clearly he was the only one who'd really believed in their love.

As he drove through the town square, Cashel was astonished to find that the café was open and busy. The woman who owned it was very chatty and charming, and it was hard to resist the fabulous pastries that sat invitingly on the counter.

Brian was less scared of Cashel than he used to be. Until recently, Cashel wouldn't have noticed, but he was beginning to pay more attention to the effect he had on people around him. It was that minx Mara, he thought wryly. She had a way of speaking to him like an equal, reminding him he was an ordinary man after all. Being Master of the Universe was all very well, but when you came back to your home town, the place you'd run around as a grubby schoolboy – then you came back to what you'd been all along.

'Grand morning, isn't it?' he said to Brian behind the counter.

'Er yes, lovely, lovely. No rain forecast or anything,' stammered Brian.

'Tell me, Brian,' said Cashel, 'have I ever said a cross word to you in all the time I've been coming in here?'

'No, Mr Reilly,' said Brian.

'And you can call me Cashel.'

'Fine, Mr Reilly . . . er, Cashel.'

'Seriously, have I ever said a cross word? You seem terrified of me.'

Brian busied himself being a barista, giving himself time to think. Finally, he said, 'It's just, you know, you have that look.'

'What look?'

'The look of someone who's in charge and, and could buy up the whole town and everything,' Brian said fearfully.

'I'm not going to buy up the whole town,' said Cashel, exasperated. 'I've bought Avalon House, that's all. And if I'm going to live there, we are going to have to get to know each other better, Brian, so that when I come in here, you're not scared of me.'

Brian looked as if he couldn't quite believe this.

'Fine, Cashel,' he said, and put the Americano down on the counter. 'Would you like a pastry?' he added daringly. He'd never asked this before.

Cashel did not look like the sort of man who'd so much as glance at a sugary pastry, as if such beautified cake things would be beneath him. No, he looked like he might tear bricks apart with his bare hands and bite them in half like a Viking raider.

'Do you know what?' said Cashel, scrutinizing the selection. 'You've tempted me. I'll have that apple Danish over there.' He looked up at Brian. 'How come you have such nice cakes, today of all days.'

'The recession,' Brian said simply. 'People are willing to work all the hours to get their businesses going. These are made out the Dublin road by a Polish couple – they do amazing cakes.'

'I love entrepreneurs,' said Cashel, smiling.

'Me too,' said Brian.

His mother would be delighted. He was doing conversation – so there.

*　　*　　*

341

On New Year's Day, Zach and Kitty were going with their father to Dublin to visit an indoor funfair. As a family, they'd often done this, but this would be the first time they'd gone without Tess – and with Claire.

Even though she'd never really liked the funfair and hated watching Zach and Kevin on the terrifying roller coaster, today Tess wished with all her heart that she were going. Not necessarily with Kevin or Claire, but with Zach and Kitty. It felt wrong to start the new year by having her children go somewhere to enjoy themselves without her. There was a huge hole inside her at the thought that, from now on, they'd be enjoying things, seeing things, going places without her.

Separation was so hard. If only she'd known what an abyss lay ahead of her, she mightn't have suggested it. But then, she thought, this was a new year, there was no point looking back. She fixed herself her second cup of coffee of the day and looked at Silkie, who was lying in her bed in the kitchen, looking forlorn, big, dark eyes pools of misery.

'Will we go for a walk?' she said.

It was icy cold but still a beautiful day with the low winter sun bright in the sky. Cashel was around the left-hand side of the house, looking up at windows that were broken and thinking what a complete nightmare it was all going to be. Freddie the builder had explained that it took a long time to get proper windows made, in the original style, with double glazing.

'It's going to be difficult,' he said. 'It can be done, but it's slow and it'll cost you.'

'That's fine.' Cashel waved him away. 'Do up an estimate, I want to know the price of everything. No little add-ons afterwards, mind,' he said grimly.

'No, no, not at all,' said Freddie, chastened. 'I'd never do a thing like that.'

Suddenly, a dog sprinted round the back of the house, some

sort of miniature greyhound, a streak of fawn, with lolloping ears. The dog launched itself straight at Cashel in delight. Jumping and licking and desperate to be petted, barking crazily.

'Down, girl, down,' said Cashel. 'Calm down now.' He held the dog against him and petted its quivering flanks. 'You're a beauty, aren't you.'

'Silkie, where are you?' called a voice, and Cashel stiffened. He'd recognize that voice anywhere. He turned and saw her coming towards him: Tess Power.

'Oh, it's you,' she said and stopped a distance away. They hadn't spoken for nineteen years.

'Yes, it's me,' he said. 'I own this now.' Then he felt sorry for such a cheap shot.

'I know,' she said tautly, then she called the dog: 'Silkie, come on, we're leaving. I'm sorry, I never come here, I wanted to today for some reason, I don't know why.'

'You never come here?' Cashel said, intrigued.

'No,' she said. 'Why would I want to?'

He walked closer to her, Silkie dancing around him.

Tess glared at her dog, who was behaving so disloyally, cavorting with the enemy.

'Silkie, come here,' she hissed, but Silkie wouldn't obey, delighted to have found somebody new to play with.

'Silkie's lovely,' said Cashel. 'How old is she?'

'About six,' said Tess. 'At least, we think so. She's a rescue dog.'

'That's funny,' Cashel said, 'rescue dogs can sometimes be a bit scared of strangers.'

'She's not frightened at all, but you're right,' she said grudgingly, 'many rescue dogs are wary. How do you know that? You don't have dogs, surely? Not with all the travelling you do.'

'No,' he said, 'I don't have dogs any more. I did, though, Do you remember the little Jack Russell?'

'Pookie,' she said, and laughed.

'Yes, Pookie.'

And suddenly they both laughed, thinking of the adorable Jack Russell, named after the Irish word for ghost because his fur was snow white, apart from one fawn ear and one little diamond-shaped fawn patch on his hip. He'd been quite a character.

'He used to love it up here,' Tess said. 'Sometimes your mother would bring him up with her, and when you'd come home from school, you and Suki would run around playing hurling on the lawn? I wasn't allowed to play because I was too young, so I'd sit with Pookie and talk to him and tell him stories.'

'I remember,' Cashel said. 'You were such a quiet little thing and you'd sit there petting him. He loved you. I used to think I should give him to you, but then I'd look at him, curled up on my bed beside me, fast asleep, and I couldn't bear to do it. I'd have been heartbroken to part with him.'

'I never knew you'd even thought about it,' Tess said, stunned. 'I mean, dogs are great company,' she added, recovering. 'I'd be all on my own today if it wasn't for Silk—' She stopped herself. What was she doing? It was ludicrous, telling him something that personal.

'But why, why would you be on your own?' he said. 'You have two children, don't you?'

'Yes,' she said quietly, 'Zach and Kitty.'

'Where are they today?'

'They're with their father and his girlfriend. They've gone to the funfair in Dublin.' Tess knew her face must look bitter and twisted even as she said it.

'Right,' Cashel said. 'That must be difficult for you.'

'Yes,' said Tess, and she really thought she might cry.

This was all too surreal, standing outside her beloved old house, with the man she'd once loved, the man who'd turned his back on her. She wanted to break down and cry.

344

'I'd better go, Cashel. I'm sorry for trespassing, I won't do it again. I simply wanted to see the place one last time.'

She reached over and grabbed Silkie and clipped her lead on. Silkie wriggled, furious at being restrained when she wanted to bounce around and look for rabbits and be petted by the strange man.

'You don't need to go,' Cashel said gruffly. 'Please, stay. Come up any time, really. It was your home.'

'It's yours now,' said Tess as she marched down the avenue. 'Goodbye, Cashel. I wish you luck with it.'

In New York, Redmond Suarez sat at the very elegant New Year's Day lunch he'd been invited to and looked around the table, cataloguing his guests. Two facelifts for the soap actress over there, probably had the first one when she was thirty, the second at forty. That was the trick with young actresses, have your first facelift when you were very young so that the muscles hadn't had a chance to become weak. Nobody would ever notice the first facelift. Then, when you had the second one, you looked like you were ageing amazingly. Add in Botox, a bit of filler, perhaps some Sculptra to keep the plumpness in your cheeks, and you could stay looking like you were thirty until you were sixty. Although, by the time you got to sixty, people would have worked out you'd had the work done, no matter how many times you trotted out the *I have good genes, eat well, drink lots of water and exercise* schtick. Genes that good were pure science fiction.

Still, she looked pretty amazing, beautiful enough to have snagged the fifty-something-year-old billionaire on her right.

'Oh, darling you must sit beside me,' she'd said, completely ruining the hostess's table plan.

Clever girl, Redmond had thought approvingly; she'd obviously realized there were too many attractive women present to let her date out of her sight. Manhattan was a jungle when it came to holding on to single rich men.

345

There was a couple on the verge of divorce at the table. Redmond had heard all the details. The husband had been having an affair with the nanny. Really – such a cliché! They were a wealthy couple, not terribly famous, but sufficiently well known that if details of his fling were to become public it would prove a huge embarrassment both to them and to the stockholders of his publicly listed company. That was probably why they were here together today, Redmond figured: to quieten the rumours. But you didn't need to be a body language expert to sense the distance between them.

The hostess, Caroline, was one of Redmond's favourite people in the world. She loved all the gossip and scandal, although you'd never think it to meet her. She adored Redmond for what he could tell her. And she repaid him by inviting him to lunches like this one, with people who were quite startled to find themselves seated at a table with such a notorious biographer.

Redmond was charming to them all, telling them a few naughty titbits that would pique their interest. A few drinks later, and people were giggling and asking him for the latest gossip, wanting to know what was the story on the Richardson biography, was he really going to do it? The word on the street was that Senator Richardson's wife, Antoinette, was furious and determined to stop it at all costs.

'Really?' said Redmond, as if he hadn't already learned this from a reliable source. 'They're very interesting, these Richardsons.'

When he was being clever and opaque, his accent became even more pronounced. Redmond insisted he was descended from Portuguese nobility – born on the wrong side of the sheets, sadly. Having them think that he came from a wealthy aristocratic background made his life easier and smoothed his entrance into the great salons of New York. Very few people knew the truth: that Redmond had grown up in abject poverty in Puerto Rico. After years of hard work, he'd clawed his way out of the slums – and he intended to make sure that he

346

would never be poor again. And if that meant writing scandalous books that had the publishers' lawyers going grey in the face when they read them, well, that was fine with him.

'Yes,' he said, 'the Richardsons are very interesting.'

In truth, his latest project was proving tiresome. The research was taking for ever. There was no doubt that the Richardsons had clamped down on all the insiders, determined not to let anybody know anything about them. Of course, these rich people tended to overlook the staff, or to assume that their trusted family retainers would never breath a word of gossip. Ha!

Antoinette Richardson was notoriously mean with staff and there were plenty of ex-household and current members who were prepared to spill all – for a price, naturally. It was one of the servants who'd first tipped him off about Suki Power. She sounded interesting, and yet she seemed to have disappeared off the radar. Redmond needed to find her: that would speed things up no end, if he could only find out what she knew.

Why had she divorced Kyle Junior? That was something that had mystified a lot of people. Why leave one of the richest families in America – unless there was something horrendous going on? No, there was something there, and he was determined to find out what it was. He'd wasted the last couple of months tracking down Senior's myriad business dealings with the Pentagon, but with issues of national security involved, sources had been reluctant to talk. Pursuing the Suki Power angle would be much more likely to yield results.

Besides, his books sold on delicious gossip – scandal rather than scams. Suki Power could be the key. He made a mental note to talk to his chief researcher, Carmen, first thing tomorrow morning.

Mara lay in bed with Rafe in his house, which was on one side of the bike workshop. The house was a vision in wood and had a manly feel about it: in other words, as Mara explained to Rafe, he had no *stuff*.

'No vases, no knick-knacks, no stuff,' she said every time she went there.

'I have a king-size bed, though,' Rafe pointed out.

'There is that,' murmured Mara.

They'd spent the evening in bed, watching a movie on the big screen mounted on the wall opposite the bed, and now Mara was feeling pleasantly sleepy. From the side of the bed where her handbag was came the ping that signalled a text message on her mobile phone. Lazily, she reached down and picked the phone up.

Hey, Mara, how are you? Was thinking of you. Hope you're well. Think of you a lot. Happy New Year, love Jack.

She almost dropped the phone in fright. What the heck was Jack texting her for?

'Who was that from?' said Rafe, climbing back into bed and nuzzling her neck.

Mara tossed the phone to the floor. 'An old friend,' she fibbed. 'People do send lots of messages at New Year's, don't they?'

'Yeah, they do,' said Rafe. He moved towards her mouth. 'So many more interesting things they could be doing,' he murmured before kissing her.

Chapter Twenty-Three

Danae had never liked January. It was a dark month. A month where people who had been clinging on to life for Christmas finally gave up their desperate effort and let go. It was a month of many funerals and many cards of sympathy sent through the post. She hated to hear the news that some sweet pensioner she'd grown friendly with had died. She was also conscious of an other-world darkness to the month, before the lightening of spring that was February.

However, having Mara around certainly brightened the place up. It was hard to feel sad around her. She was as full of life and as wildly energetic as her namesake Mara the hen. Even more so, now that she was so in love with darling Rafe. The inner light that lit Mara up burned even more fiercely these days.

Meanwhile, the fluffy Mara was finally laying eggs. She'd laid three since Christmas: lovely brown speckled ones that Danae collected with pleasure. She loved it when the former battery hens began to lay again. Some of them never did – too traumatized. But Mara was clearly delighted with herself, and squawked loudly when Danae went to collect the eggs, as if to say 'Look! Look *what I did. I can do it. I am Hen, hear me squawk!'*

Mara and the feathered Mara were the bright sparks in the month of January, but even so there were many mornings when Danae felt her age as she woke up to the greyness of the sky and the sense that the sun would never shine down upon Avalon again.

She had a sense of foreboding too, a feeling that all was not well in the world, so it shouldn't have been a surprise when the letter arrived as she got ready to open up the post office that morning. As postmistress, she saw many letters first, and as soon as her eyes caught sight of this one, she knew it meant trouble. It was a letter sent to her as next of kin, arranging a meeting with an oncology consultant about Antonio. There was a number to ring and the letter seemed to imply that the nursing home would already have been in touch, that she would already know. But she knew nothing.

Danae phoned the consultant's office to confirm the appointment, not asking for any information and not expecting any. Such details would never be given out over the phone. She knew she had to ring the nursing home. Perhaps it was not a mistake that they hadn't told her that Antonio was ill. With any other patient, the information would have been relayed instantly in a phone call. But Antonio, he was different. Danae was different, and people who mattered in the home knew it.

They would not have wanted her upset over Christmas. They knew the history of how Antonio Rahill came to be lying in a nursing home bed with a catastrophic brain injury. They knew that his mother, Rosa, used to phone to make sure Danae would not be present when she visited. Not that this mattered any more; Rosa was long dead and nobody else visited Antonio Rahill, except his brothers at Christmas for an hour, perhaps.

Thanks to Mara and her magic, this had been the first Christmas that Danae hadn't spent tormented by the guilt of knowing that Antonio would never be able to participate in the seasonal celebration. Her niece had that amazing gift of making people come together, making them enjoy themselves. And that's what she'd done for Danae: she'd given Danae the gift of friendship, allowed her to make friends. Allowed her to open herself up to the community of Avalon, something she hadn't done in all the years she'd lived there.

And now Danae was being punished. Punished for casting aside all thought of her husband for a few days and enjoying a life that Antonio would never have.

The phone in Refuge House rang and rang and rang until finally it was picked up and a voice Danae knew well answered.

'Hello, Aggie,' said Danae. 'How are you?'

'Danae,' said the woman with the soft Cork accent that meant Danae would always recognize her voice on the phone, 'I know what you're phoning about. I'm sorry it wasn't handled well. The doctor's office phoned us after you'd phoned them and they said they were sorry. They'd thought you'd know, and we explained—'

'It's all right,' said Danae interrupting. 'I had to know sometime.'

'Of course you did,' said Aggie. 'But you didn't have to find out in such a blunt fashion. The director was going to discuss it with you on your next visit.'

'Is he in today?' Danae asked.

'He will be later.'

'Listen, I'll start driving now. I'll be with you by noon.'

'You don't have to come today,' said Aggie.

'No,' Danae said firmly, 'I'm coming.' It would mean having to close the post office, but there was no way round it. At such short notice, she wouldn't be able to arrange for someone to come in and cover in her absence. 'I'll shut up shop right away and see you later.'

Danae walked home quickly.

Lady, tired from her usual early-morning walk was surprised to see her mistress back unexpectedly. There was no sign of

Mara. She'd been up late with Rafe; Danae had heard them laughing and giggling at some old movie.

'It's the first *Airplane* one,' Mara had said. 'Please say you'll come and watch it with us, Danae.'

'No,' Danae had said, smiling, and she'd gone to bed with Lady.

Danae knew she could wake Mara and ask her to come with her to the nursing home, but she needed to do this alone. It was clearly the end, and she owed it to Antonio to face it.

In the nursing home, Danae went as usual to her husband's dorm, but there was no sign of him.

Steve, one of the nurses, appeared at her side.

'He was coughing and making noise in the night,' he said to Danae. 'We moved him to a private room. Come this way.'

Steve walked out of the dorm and further up the corridor to one of the rooms that Danae had always mentally assigned 'the dying rooms'. It was here that patients were moved when it was time for them to die. So it was true then: Antonio was dying.

Taking a deep breath, she walked into the room. All his things were there. The picture of the Virgin Mary his mother had brought at the very beginning. Rosa had insisted she didn't want ever to set eyes on Danae again, and in the early years, there had been one or two difficult incidents when a member of staff had intercepted Danae as she made her way to Antonio's dormitory, warning her that his mother was with him, and leading her off to somewhere she could sit and wait until Rosa was gone.

Now Rosa was dead, and Antonio's brothers were busy running their various empires: the food shops, the betting shops. It didn't look as though anyone had been to see him this Christmas. There were no other gifts except for the big box of chocolates she'd brought. Antonio's sweet tooth. There could never be enough chocolates in the world for him, and because he walked, walked round and round downstairs, he burned it off.

But this time, the big box of chocolates that she would have expected to be long gone was lying on the sideboard, barely touched.

'He's sleeping a lot now,' Steve said. 'It's the medication.'

'What happened exactly?' she said.

'He had a fall on Christmas Day, Danae, and we took him to hospital.'

'Why didn't you phone me?' she said.

Steve put a hand on her arm.

'The director made a decision not to tell you. I know, in any other case, we would have called, but, Danae, you've been through so much. The director insisted. It was when the hospital X-rayed him that they realised this wasn't a simple break. There was more to it. I don't know how they caught it, really, but someone was obviously on the ball that day. They kept him overnight to be on the safe side. A chest X-ray showed the tumours in his lungs. He needs full scans to establish where the primary site is, but it looks like he has secondaries in his lungs and it's spread to his bones.'

Danae had to hold herself up by grabbing the door.

'He's on a lot of pain medication,' said Steve. 'It's really all they can give him. Even without scans, they're pretty sure from his blood tests that it's all gone too far. It's only a matter of time now. We're doing everything we can to keep him comfortable, but we really need to move him to the hospice. The director will discuss it with you. I'll leave you alone now. Tell me if you want anything. A cup of tea after your long drive?'

'That would be lovely, Steve,' Danae said automatically, although she didn't think she could bring herself to drink anything; the liquid would feel like sand in her mouth.

The end was finally near.

*   *   *

Suki stretched at her desk, a stretch of satisfaction. The book was coming together. It wasn't exactly what she'd promised her agent, Melissa, or indeed the people at Box House Publishing. It was better. Instead of finding new ground to look at, Suki had come up with a brilliant idea. She would revisit the issues she'd raised in *Women and Their Wars* and pose the question: *What has changed?* There were so many areas in which no progress whatsoever had been made, and yet few people were battling any more. Feminism was a dirty word. Young female singers who should have been role models were portrayed as nothing more than sex objects. Despite everything, women didn't get paid as much as men. They did all the housework and caring for the children, even if they had an outside job. There was no such thing as having it all. Women's lives were like hamster wheels, endlessly turning. That was what she was writing about.

'Hey, you finished there?' said a voice at the door, and she turned to see Mick lounging against the door jamb, dressed in jeans and a T-shirt he'd been wearing for at least two days. His feet were bare, his toenails dirty, and suddenly she was sick of the sight of him. Sick of having someone living off her, parasitically. It would have been one thing if he couldn't find a job, but Mick refused even to look.

'I can't take no civilian gig, Suki,' he'd said a week before, when she'd brought it up for about the third time, 'I'm a musician, I can't sell out and become an ordinary joe, you know that.'

Today, finally, looking at him, knowing full well that even though she'd been working upstairs all day, it wouldn't have occurred to him to make an effort by cooking dinner, or tidying the house, or taking care of the laundry – hell, she was pretty sure he didn't even know how the washing machine worked. He hadn't showered, he hadn't shaved: he didn't care, basically. And she was fed up living with a man who not only didn't care about himself but, by proxy, didn't care

354

about her. If he gave a damn about their relationship, he wouldn't be living off her, he'd be looking for a job. And if he couldn't find a job, then he'd be taking care of her, looking after the house, finding cheaper ways to eat instead of ordering a takeout every night. He wouldn't be whining about his music when she was sitting up in her study, doing her job – which was pretty much the only thing standing between them and total bankruptcy.

'Mick,' she said, fixing him with a stare, 'I've been thinking. You're right: you are a musician and you shouldn't have to take any old civilian job.'

'What?' he looked at her, confused.

'The argument we had last week, when you said you couldn't possibly get a civilian job – well, you're right. If you don't want to live that way, you're entitled – it's your life, no one else's. But you know what . . . ?'

She saved the document she was working on, clicked the computer to shut down and got to her feet so she was facing him. Suddenly the strength that she thought had been drained from her began to return; she could feel it surging through her body. 'Mick, it's over between you and me. You clearly don't respect me, or you wouldn't be living off me like this. And I don't think I respect you any more either. It's time we broke up.'

'What do you mean, babe, break up? Things are good, and the band will get gigs soon . . .'

'No, the band won't get gigs. Bands are a dime a dozen out there, Mick, and you know it. If you haven't made it by now, you're never going to make it. You're clinging to a hopeless dream.'

'Yeah, you're saying that with all the knowledge of someone who screwed around with the lead singer of TradeWind, huh? That's where you get your inside information on the music industry,' he snarled.

'You don't have to resort to cheap shots,' said Suki. 'It's

been good, now it's over. OK? Why don't you get your stuff and move out. You were never really supposed to move in, but you have.'

He stared at her but she didn't feel any fear; Mick wouldn't try anything, she knew that. She'd hit him where it hurt most and he was going to go.

'I'm sorry it hasn't worked out,' she added, 'I really am. But we've got to face facts: you and I want different things.'

'Well, don't think you're gonna get anyone to replace me, baby,' he snapped at her. 'Look at you – you're not some hot rock chick any more, not with those wrinkles. Jethro wouldn't look twice at you now.'

Suki swallowed the insult. He couldn't hurt her. She was getting older. She knew that and she was writing about it in the book. Women and age. Ageing into invisibility, and why that was wrong. She'd spent so long teasing out the arguments in the book that she wasn't overwhelmed by Mick's spite.

'As I said, Mick,' she replied calmly, 'let's try and do this like grown-ups. We want different things out of life, so let's split up, that's all.'

He slammed her office door shut and she could hear him moving about in their bedroom, swearing. She recognized the sounds of cupboards being wrenched open, then the sound of him stomping downstairs, dragging a bag behind him. There wasn't much of his stuff in the house anyway.

'I'll be back later with a van to pick up my chair,' he roared up the stairs.

She didn't hear the door slam and she waited, breathing heavily now, feeling the anxiety hit her. She was not going to have a panic attack; Mick's leaving was a good thing in her life, there was no reason to get upset.

It took at least ten minutes before his car started up and then she heard him drive off down the street. Only when she heard that and knew he was gone for good, did she come out of her office and head downstairs. The front door was wide open and there in the living room, looking closely at one of the framed photos of her, Tess and Zach, was a strange woman. Tall, blonde, young, New York slim, wearing a neat black suit like she worked for the government, with a white shirt, low heels and a briefcase.

'Who the hell are you and what are you doing in my house?' Suki said.

'Oh hello,' said the woman, giving Suki the benefit of a syrupy smile and great dental work, 'how lovely to meet you. I'm Carmen LeMonte – I work with Redmond Suarez and we so want to talk to you. You've probably heard that Redmond is writing a book about the Richardsons and I'm sure you must want to tell your side of the story . . .'

Suki realized that in the outstretched hand was a small digital tape recorder, and it was obviously rolling because there was a little red light glowing.

'Talk about what?' said Suki. This she wasn't prepared for. This was her every nightmare rolled into one.

'Y'know, talk about your life with the Richardsons – I'm sure it must have been really challenging.' The woman smiled sympathetically. 'We'd like you to share your insights into their life, share some details about what really went on – readers would love to know. And why did you leave the family? Redmond Suarez thinks you might have a secret, 'cos there's got to be something there. And you might need the money, huh?' The woman's gaze took in the cottage, the open cupboard doors and scattered belongings Mick had left in his wake.

Suki didn't know what to say. Panic-stricken, she could only bluster, 'I don't know what you're talking about.'

'Oh, now come on, Suki, I think you do,' said the woman, still in that same wheedling tone. Suki was suddenly reminded of movie portrayals of hard-hearted tabloid reporters on the trail of a story, and how far they'd stoop to get it.

'Put down my photograph,' said Suki.

357

'And this is your sister, I guess, and her son? They live in Avalon, your home town. Would they be able to fill us in on anything?'

The young blonde woman moved closer, holding the small digital recorder out in front of her.

'We were wondering why you sort of disappeared out of the Richardson family. Is it true that Antoinette hounded you out?'

The way the woman hissed '*disappeared*' reminded Suki of a cobra about to strike. Desperate to get rid of her, she grabbed the photo and tossed it on the sofa, then took the woman by the shoulders, spun her round and pushed her out the door before she even had time to register what was happening.

'Get out of here,' she said. 'You are trespassing – next time I see you on my property, I'm calling the cops. And if you think you are going to get any salacious rumours out of me, you are very much mistaken. Leave me alone!' And she slammed the door in the woman's face.

Heart racing, tears brimming in her eyes, she leaned against the door, all strength deserting her. The fear, oh my God, the fear, came back.

She rang Tess's mobile, something she never did. It had to be at least eleven o'clock in Avalon, but she didn't care. Tess answered after about five rings, sounding tired. 'What is it?' she said.

'It's me,' said Suki. 'Oh, Tess, you've no idea. One of the researchers for that Suarez guy turned up, I found her in the house because I'd just thrown Mick out and he must have let her in and—'

'Slow down,' said Tess.

'I threw Mick out and when he was going, this woman must have been at the door – she's a researcher for the biographer who wants to write a book about the Richardsons. And they know something happened!'

'What do you mean, they know?' said Tess.

'They know,' hissed Suki. 'I'm finished. Nobody will want to publish my book by the time Redmond Suarez is finished with me – I'll look like the whore Antoinette called me.'

'How could they find out?' asked Tess, shocked.

Suki lost it. All the anxiety she'd been holding in came rushing out and, searching for a target, found one in Tess.

'People like Suarez can find out anything they want!' shrieked Suki. 'First example, Antoinette has never paid the staff a decent salary and she treats them like dirt, lest they figure out she's not as blue-blooded as she likes to pretend. All Suarez needs is to find one maid or housekeeper who'll talk, and the whole house of cards comes tumbling down. The people who worked in the Massachusetts house would know everything.'

Suki recalled the times she'd seen Antoinette use the bell beside the fire to summon a servant to perform some task so servile and pointless that it wasn't worth the effort of walking to the bell. Another log on the fire – when she was standing beside the log basket; some more ice for the Senator's drink – when the ice bucket was sitting (giving off less frost than Antoinette, admittedly) on a low table to his left. He'd have been able to reach it without moving from his seat.

But that wasn't the point for Antoinette. The family had servants, and by all that was holy, they were going to use them.

Suki had tried to make peace with the staff in her own way: smiling excessively, learning everyone's names and ostentatiously using them, but it was no good. As Kyle Junior once said in a rare moment of awareness: 'You're on the other side of the divide, Suki. The staff won't let you forget it, even if you do your best to.'

Any one of the many people routinely humiliated by Antoinette Richardson could have sold information to Suarez and his researchers.

'This will destroy me,' Suki went on.

359

Three thousand miles apart, the two Power sisters let out a breath at exactly the same time.

'I wish I could help,' Tess said.

'I know,' said Suki.

Tess sat up late in the kitchen, worrying about Suki. Zach was upstairs, studying or listening to music, and Kitty was asleep. She was alone at the kitchen table with nothing but the Something Old account books and a glass of red wine.

This had been her plan for the evening, but Suki's frantic phone call had upset her so much that she could barely concentrate on anything.

Poor Suki. She hadn't been exaggerating: if this nasty biographer twisted the story the wrong way, Suki's name would be mud. If only Tess could do something. But she couldn't. Money and power were the only things that could hold off people like that, and the Powers had neither.

She herself was broke. The business was on the verge of bankruptcy, nothing could save it now. Her only option was to sell her remaining stock to other antique shops or go to one of the big auction houses and let them offload it; either way, it would probably mean selling at way below what the stuff was worth. And you never quite knew what was going to happen at an auction house, it was like betting on a horse. Who knew which horse would win, which horse would lose?

Tess drank her wine and tried to concentrate. She couldn't help Suki, but she had to work out how to make enough money to keep herself, Zach and Kitty going. The problem was that the anxiety over her situation was so overwhelming it had paralysed her mind; try as she might, she couldn't think what she was going to do next. The only plus was, she seemed to have reached the point where she no longer cared that Kevin wasn't there to hug her and tell her it would be all right, to give her the fake assurances that they'd get through it.

She had finally realized that, in letting him go, she had

made the right decision. At the time of the separation, she hadn't really been sure. For months afterwards, she'd wavered, wondering whether they should get back together. When Claire had come into his life she'd felt anger at having been replaced so quickly. But that's all it had been: anger at being replaced. It wasn't the realization that she *did* love him desperately. It was more a feeling of incomprehension that her love didn't matter and another woman's love would do.

At least whatever she had to face now, she'd face on her own, with darling Zach and Kitty. They wouldn't suffer, she'd make sure of that. There was no telling what sort of job she'd get, but that didn't matter. She didn't care what she did; she'd be a cleaner, she'd take in ironing, anything – although nobody wanted cleaners or people taking in ironing any more. Nobody could afford it. There had to be something she could do to make sure they stayed in their home. There were a few things she'd hung on to from Avalon House that she could sell. Precious things, like the portrait of her mother, a beautiful oil by a minor artist who'd been popular in the 1960s, but it would be worth something now. Her mother had been so beautiful. Plus, there was a story to it. A beautiful woman cut down in her prime, killed in a car accident. The story might add to its saleability.

She'd bring it to Adams to get it valued. And there were a few pieces of her mother's jewellery too. Sadly, jewellery, albeit jewellery with precious stones, made very little. So many people were trying to sell off jewellery these days. The market was flooded with diamonds and rubies and emeralds. It was sad, seeing them in the shops. Gifts, given in love, sold out of desperation.

But Tess didn't care, the sentiment behind her jewellery and her mother's picture was immaterial now. What mattered was taking care of Zach and Kitty.

Blissfully unaware that their mother's business was disintegrating, Zach and Kitty were both blossoming. Zach was totally in love with Pixie Martin; the pair of them were now inseparable. Plus, Kitty loved having her around. Loved the sense of finally having a big sister to play with. And Pixie was endlessly kind to her. Helping dress dolls and playing Sylvanian Families at length, and listening to Kitty explain how she was going to be a big sister to whatever baby Claire had. 'So you'll have to teach me how I have to do it,' Kitty would say self-importantly to Pixie. Despite her pain, Tess smiled. As long as her children were happy, they'd muddle through. As long as they had each other, she would keep going no matter what.

Chapter Twenty-Four

Danae wasn't sure how she felt about accompanying Antonio to the hospice. She had always assumed that the nursing home would care for him right until the end, but the director had explained to her that they couldn't do that in Antonio's case. The cancer had metastasized into his bones, making it incredibly painful, and Refuge House was not equipped to provide the kind of pain management he would need. 'We simply don't have the staff,' he said. 'It's too difficult. I know you'd prefer him to be here, but . . .'

'No,' said Danae. 'I understand, totally. We want him to go as painlessly as possible.' It seemed like the last gift she could give her husband.

They'd been so lucky that a bed had become free.

'This is the right place for your husband in his final days,' the lady from the hospice had said to her when she phoned during her lunchbreak. 'We'll see you tomorrow. He's going into a lovely room overlooking the garden.'

It was that last little detail that had made Danae want to cry. How wonderful these people were, how caring, in their love of the dying, their gentleness, their kindness. She'd sobbed on the phone. And the lady, who was clearly used to it, told her it would be all right. 'You don't think you'll get through it, but you will,' she'd said. 'With your husband's brain injury, you've clearly gone through so much over these years. You must miss him terribly.'

Danae had felt like a charlatan, because she didn't miss him at all.

And then she'd hung up the phone and shut the post office and ventured out to buy herself some more teabags. A short journey, maybe one hundred yards, and she'd slipped on the ice and fallen down. She knew immediately that she'd done something unutterably painful to her ankle.

The doctor, summoned out of his surgery, took one look at it, bound it up and said, 'I'm afraid it's hospital for you, my dear. You need to get that X-rayed.'

Mara had immediately whisked Danae off to the local hospital, where she'd been told she had a fractured ankle bone that would need to be strapped up for at least six weeks.

'No weight on it,' the orthopaedic A&E doctor said, looking at the X-rays again. 'Absolutely no weight on it. This is a tricky little fracture.'

At this point, Danae had been given a shot of painkillers so she wasn't feeling any pain, but the anxiety in her head was destroying her.

'What's wrong, Danae?' said Mara. 'What are you not telling me?'

'I didn't want to drag you into all this, Mara,' said Danae, beginning to cry. 'But I need your help . . .'

They were on the road early the next morning, hens fed, Lady left outside because she'd have gone mad locked inside the house. Mara had spent ages settling Danae, pushing the car seat back and arranging cushions for her back, more cushions for her ankle to rest on, and blankets in case she got cold.

'Now,' said Mara finally, popping a CD in the car stereo, 'it's too exhausting for you to talk, so we'll listen to music on the way up and only talk if you want to. We've lots of time, so we can take it slow, stop for a coffee and a bite of brunch on the way, then we'll go to the nursing home and take it from there.'

'Thank you,' Danae said weakly.

They stopped at a small pub on the outskirts of Dublin, the sort of place that catered for passing trade and could feed you at any time of day. Mara ordered soup and a sandwich for each of them, even though Danae barely picked at hers.

'Come on, you need to eat,' said Mara, conscious how their roles had been entirely reversed.

'I can't,' said Danae. 'I'm sorry.' She drank her coffee though and nibbled a bit at the tiny biscuit that accompanied the coffee.

'Afterwards we're going to have something proper to eat,' Mara insisted.

Mara admired the nursing home gardens when they got there.

'It's lovely,' she said appreciatively, 'but this place must cost a fortune. Does it? Have you been paying for it all by yourself?'

'Yes,' said Danae.

'Wow,' said Mara, resolving not to ask any more questions because she could see it was upsetting for Danae. She wished she could get her hands on this vengeful family who'd been too mean to stump up any cash for Antonio's care, leaving it to his poor battered wife to pay for everything.

Inside, it was clear that everyone knew Danae, but they'd never seen her come with anyone else before. They were fascinated by Mara and delighted to be introduced to her, delighted that for once Danae would have some support.

'Your aunt's an amazing woman,' every second person said to her. 'Incredible. Every month she's here and she always brings him something – clothes, sweets, chocolates. He has an awful sweet tooth.'

'She is an amazing woman,' agreed Mara proudly.

'We have all his stuff ready,' one of the nurses said. 'We're going to miss him, you know, it's so sad when someone leaves us.'

Quite a few of the staff were crying and Danae somehow managed to gather the strength to say: 'You've been so good to him over the years, please, he needs to be in the hospice now. We know you can't possibly look after him here, not right now, not for the end.'

'It's all right,' one of the nurses whispered to Danae, 'they've been trained in palliative care and understand the need to transfer patients like Antonio.'

'Right,' nodded Mara.

The man who was wheeled out in front of her looked ancient, far older than her aunt. Yet he had a shock of shiny dark hair with streaks of grey running through it and the most amazing rich, mahogany eyes. But there was no light in the eyes, no awareness, no recognition. His features were slightly distorted. His mouth sank a little to one side.

She thought of Danae's monthly pilgrimages to the man who'd beaten her for years, and vowed that she would make this as easy as she possibly could for her sake.

'Hello, Antonio,' she said, patting him on the shoulder. 'Now, Danae,' she said, putting her arm around her aunt, because it looked as if Danae might collapse on to the floor, her face was drained white. Between the shock and the pain of her ankle, collapse was just round the corner. 'Come on.' She put an arm around Danae to help her. 'Let's go. Are we going in the ambulance or in the car?' she enquired.

'You won't both be able to go in the ambulance,' said one of the ambulance men.

'Fine,' said Mara, 'then Danae and I will follow in my car.'

She was making an executive decision on this: there was no way that Danae was leaving her side today. She could sense that some strange masochism would have made Danae opt to travel in the ambulance, watching her husband's lifeless eyes all the time. No, that was not happening. She firmly and gently steered Danae over to the car, going slowly so as not to hurt Danae's ankle.

'I should go in with him,' Danae began to say, as Mara began the process of sorting out cushions for her ankle and a plethora of blankets to lay across her legs.

'No,' said Mara gently, 'you're coming with me. You should be in a wheelchair yourself with that ankle, you poor darling. It's your turn to be taken care of now, Danae.' She turned the radio to a news station so there would be constant chatter in the background as they drove to the hospice. Every once in a while, Mara would remark on a news story: 'Gosh, that's very interesting isn't it?' she'd say, but Danae could only stare blankly out the window.

The hospice was a beautiful building with lovely grounds for people to walk in. The ambulance had arrived before them and by the time they got there, Antonio had already been installed in his room. A woman with a gentle face and kind eyes led them to an office to complete the final bits of paperwork. 'You've done most of it, Mrs Rahill, already,' said the woman. Danae still seemed stuck in her trance, and Mara and the woman exchanged worried glances.

When Danae left the room, Mara looked at the woman and said, 'Are most people like this?'

'Yes,' said the woman, 'unfortunately. But we will do our best to love and to care for your uncle.'

He was in a room painted sunflower yellow. It reminded Mara of the sun on a beautiful summer's day. It was both cosy and yet suitable as a hospital room. When Danae saw him there, already hooked up to various machines and with a drip already inserted to feed him the morphine he needed, she started to cry. Mara made one more executive decision: 'Danae why don't you kiss Antonio goodbye now? Then we can come back in a couple of days and see him. We need to get you home, put that ankle up like the doctor ordered.'

367

Danae stared at her, 'But, I . . . I should stay.'

'No,' said Mara firmly, 'you shouldn't stay. You should kiss him goodbye, for now,' she added quickly. 'It's time we went home. We can come back tomorrow, if you want. In the meantime, they have your phone number if they need us.'

They'd driven a few miles and were on the motorway when Danae said to pull over quickly, she felt sick.

At the edge of the motorway, she threw up until there was nothing left inside her.

It was almost over now, but the pain was huge.

Back in Avalon, Mara made some calls. Belle needed to know so she could comfort Danae. Hell, give her half a chance and Belle would probably drive to Dublin and stick a pickaxe in Antonio's chest to help him on his way.

She needed to phone her parents too. Danae needed all the support she could get.

Morris cried when she told him. Mara was shocked. She didn't think she'd ever heard her father cry.

'It's been so many years,' he sobbed. 'I hate what he's done to her.'

Having been upstairs to check on Danae, who appeared to be sleeping, Mara slumped, exhausted, at the kitchen table. The emotion of the day had drained her totally; not her own, but her aunt's shock, her father's sadness. She was about to phone Rafe and tell him all about the day when there was a knock on the door.

Hauling herself to her feet, Mara went over and opened it. There, clad in his uniform of designer jeans, expensive jacket and open-neck shirt, stood Jack.

'Hey, babe,' he said, moving forward and taking her in his arms.

Beside her, Lady started to growl.

'Jack!' she said, stepping back in utter astonishment.

'Whoa, will that dog attack?' he asked.

Mara patted Lady affectionately.

'She might,' she said.

'Mara, I miss you. I made a stupid mistake,' he began, and moved close again. This time, Lady moved forward, hackles raised.

'OK, you need to call the dog off,' said Jack, clearly rattled. 'Will she bite?'

'I don't know,' said Mara cheerfully. 'I've never seen her bite anyone, but there's always a first time.' She stopped patting the dog and fixed him with a glare. 'What are you here for, Jack?'

'To see you. Isn't that obvious?'

For a moment, suave Jack was gone to be replaced by vaguely annoyed Jack. It was clear that being kept on the doorstep by a growling dog hadn't been part of his master plan.

'I thought you'd be pleased to see me,' he added plaintively.

'You thought wrong. For a start, I prefer my friends to phone before they come round. And secondly – oh yes, you're not my friend any more, are you?'

'Look, honey—'

He moved forward, but a warning growl from Lady made him move back.

'Don't "honey" me,' said Mara.

'*Mara.* Sorry. I was in the neighbourhood and I thought I'd drop by.'

'In the neighbourhood?' she asked with interest. 'Since when is Avalon in your neighbourhood?'

'OK, you got me.' He smiled in a way she'd once have thought irresistible.

Strangely, she was having no difficulty resisting him tonight.

It was chilly standing outside, but she didn't want to invite him in. She was dealing with a genuine tragedy here and his visit couldn't have come at a worse time.

'Seriously,' she said, 'I'm busy, Jack. What do you want?

Have you got legal papers hidden somewhere? Are the lawyers begging you to get me to sign them?'

He looked embarrassed. 'Sorry about that, honey.'

'Stop with the "honey",' she hissed. 'I am not your honey. I have a name, use it. And if you want to talk, you may phone me. Not,' she added, 'that I'm likely to pick up. We are not friends and next time you're in my neighbourhood, don't feel free to drop in.'

'I only want to talk,' he said.

At that moment, Mara thought about all the things going on in her new life: about Danae, and all she was going through right now, and about Rafe, whom she wanted to talk to because he'd understand how hard today had been. He had the kindness to care about Danae, and he loved Mara enough to want to help her through this.

Suddenly, she smiled. Rafe loved her. She was sure of it. Properly sure. Not sure in the way she'd been with Jack, because there had been no surety there.

Deep down, she'd known all along that Jack's affection was a fickle thing. She'd danced around the issue, trying to be whatever he wanted her to be. She'd have tried to be a Ferrari, if only she'd known that's what he wanted. And that kind of love wasn't love at all.

Rafe loved her for herself, crazy clothes and all.

'Jack, is there any other reason you're here?' she asked.

'Well, to see you and to . . .' He paused, lost for words. Usually he liked to have his answers prepared in advance, but it had never occurred to him that she'd question his motives. 'I thought you'd be pleased to see me.'

Mara wrapped the cardigan she was wearing tighter around her.

'I've a lot going on, Jack, so now's not a good time.'

'But—'

'And I'm in love with someone else,' she added, 'so goodbye,' she said firmly.

370

If she never saw Jack again, she wouldn't care.

With the door shut, she knelt down and hugged Lady closely.

'Thank you, girl,' she said. 'You're a darling. I think you need a chewy treat to say thanks for your protection. And what's more . . .' she went to the cupboard where Danae kept the dog food and treats '. . . I am going to phone Rafe and tell him I love him. Good idea?'

Lady's beautiful face seemed to be smiling up at her.

'I knew you'd think so.' Mara smiled.

When the phone call came, Danae wasn't surprised.

It was the hospice.

'He's had a bad night and we think perhaps you should come up.'

'Of course,' said Danae, as if she was a wife like any other, wanting to be with her beloved husband in his last few hours on earth. She hung up and called Mara at work.

'Mara, it's Antonio. He's dying.'

'It's fine,' said Mara calmly. 'Everything's going to be fine. This day had to come. Leave everything to me.'

While Danae got her things, Mara made some high-speed phone calls.

First, she phoned Cashel to say she couldn't work.

'Someone close to Danae is dying and I have to drive her to the hospice. I'm really sorry, but it's important, otherwise I wouldn't—'

'Not a problem,' said Cashel. 'Go, do whatever you have to do.'

Next, she rang Rafe to tell him where she'd be.

'Tell me if you need anything – anything at all,' he said. 'Love you, and love to Danae too.'

Then she phoned Belle, followed by her parents. Her last call was to Cici in Galway.

Ever since she'd told Cici about Rafe, she'd been demanding

to see him: 'He sounds dreamy,' said Cici. 'I have nothing to report on the man front. I think I'm going to give up on it, become a nun. There must be another way . . . Maybe I should emigrate! What country is it where there are far more men than women? China? China, that's where I'll go.'

'No, Cici, don't go to China. Come and see me instead. If you spend a weekend with me and Danae, you'll get to meet Rafe. And you never know who else you might meet – Avalon's that kind of place. There's certain crazy magic in the air.'

And so they'd arranged that Cici would come to Avalon that weekend.

'We may have to change it to next weekend, sorry,' Mara told her friend on the phone.

'That's OK. You take care, you hear? Just don't let any of the gorgeous men leave town till I get there,' Cici said.

As they set off for Dublin, Danae was silent. There was a knot of tightness about her chest.

'I know I'm not going to see him alive again,' she said. 'I don't know how, but I know it.'

'Don't be silly,' said Mara. 'We'll get there in time.'

But she wondered if it wouldn't be better if Danae was right. Surely being there with him when he died would only bring her more pain.

They'd only gone a quarter of the way when Danae's phone rang again. She and Mara looked at each other; they both knew what the news would be.

'I'm so sorry to have to tell you this, Mrs Rahill, but your husband passed away fifteen minutes ago. It was very peaceful. Very peaceful.'

'Oh God,' said Danae, and the grief and guilt engulfed her again.

'Are you on the way to see him?'

Mara swiftly pulled over to the side of the road and took the phone from her aunt.

'Hello,' she said, 'this is Mara, Danae's niece – we met the other day. My aunt is actually incredibly upset right now. I think it would be better for her if we went home and came back to see him at the funeral. I don't think she's able for this. I'm afraid it might send her over the edge.'

'No.'

Danae was shaking her head, but Mara held firm:

'That's the best thing,' she said, then to the person at the other end of the phone: 'I'll call back in a little while to discuss funeral arrangements. I really think that's the best thing. I simply do not want to distress my aunt even more.' She took a risk. 'My uncle has been very ill for the past eighteen years. It's put a terrible strain on my aunt. I think we'd better wait for the funeral.' She hung up.

'No! Why did you do that?' cried Danae. 'I have to go and see him.'

Mara put down the phone and took both of her aunt's hands in hers.

'No, Danae,' she said, looking into her eyes, 'I really don't think you need to do this to yourself. Do you?'

In her heart, Mara felt certain that if Danae saw Antonio's body it would only serve to remind her that she was the one who had put him in a nursing home. Knowing Danae, she wouldn't stop to think about all the pain he'd caused her.

Finally, Danae nodded. 'You're right, Mara,' she said slowly. 'How come you're so wise?' she said wryly.

'You're teaching me,' Mara said, and hugged her.

They turned around and drove back to Avalon, where Danae went slowly out with Lady into the garden. She sat heavily on the wooden seat near the henhouse and grieved with her beloved Lady by her side. Mara took to the phone again and phoned her parents.

'We need to organize the funeral and tell Antonio's relatives. Not that there's been any sign of them at the hospice, even though we made sure they were informed. Can you handle some of that, Dad?'

'Of course,' said Morris, 'count on me.'

Then Mara was sitting at the table, wondering how to compose a suitable death notice for the newspapers. *Deeply beloved by his dear wife* somehow didn't quite work.

She rang home again: 'Dad,' she said, 'you'd be better at this than me. Will you take care of the funeral stuff and I'll try to mind Danae?'

Two days later, the first part of the funeral of Danae's husband took place. She wanted to go to the funeral home where his body lay resting before it was brought to the church in the evening. The following day, his funeral Mass would be followed by his burial.

'What should we do, Dad?' said Mara to her father. He, Elsie, Stephen, Rafe and Belle all stood there, dressed in black like soldiers guarding Danae.

'We've got to let her say goodbye to him, if that's what she wants.'

Belle stepped in. 'We'll all go with her for moral support,' she said firmly.

So it was that Danae was being supported by her brother on one side and her niece on the other when she walked into the viewing room in the undertaker's, where Antonio lay in an open coffin. It was strange, Danae thought, that he looked different now. Peaceful in death and like the man he had once been. The man who knew how to smile and laugh. It was as if the brain injury he'd suffered and the many nights of violent rage that had transformed his face into an ugly mask, had been wiped clean after his death.

His hands were folded in prayer, mother-of-pearl rosary beads around them. She knew his mother Rosa had given the beads to him when he was in the nursing home. Maybe Rosa would be waiting in Heaven, or whatever was out there, for her son. Danae hoped he'd tell her what had really happened that night. Tell her that he'd tried to kill Danae, so Rosa would know the truth, finally.

And those hands – they looked so peaceful, but how often had they punched her and hit her and been wrapped around her throat, threatening to end her life?

Tears streamed down Danae's face and Mara's too. Mara was crying not for the man in the coffin but for her aunt and the pain she'd put herself through for so many years. Living a life of penitence for killing a man who'd tried to kill her.

They drove slowly behind the funeral car to the church and walked behind the coffin. There weren't many people in the church.

'Brothers, sisters-in-law, an uncle,' whispered Elsie to Mara as they made their way slowly up the church's centre aisle behind Danae and Morris.

'They didn't visit him when he was in the nursing home,' whispered Mara. 'Just let them say one word to Danae and I swear I will kill them.' She meant it, too. If they'd heard the story of how Antonio had tried to murder her beloved aunt, they'd think differently. And she would tell them the whole ugly story, sparing no details, if any of them dared to upset Danae. She'd been through enough.

'Mara, you're in a church, you can't speak like that,' hissed her mother.

'Don't worry, Mara,' said Stephen, who was behind them. 'I'll help you kill them.'

'Count me in on that too,' muttered Rafe darkly.

They sank into a pew at the front and listened as the priest talked about a man he'd never known.

In funerals, all men were equal: the good and the bad. When it was time for the small service to end, Antonio's family filed out without once looking in Danae's direction.

*　　*　　*

375

Danae spent the night in Furlong Hill. Despite everyone making a fuss over her and trying to bring her out of herself, it was as if a light had been turned off inside her. She had reverted to the silent, old Danae again. She sat like a ghost, her face drained of colour, her eyes hollow.

'Do you think if I got her a Valium or something from Mrs MacLiammoir across the road, it'd help her?' whispered Elsie to Mara.

'To be honest, Mum,' said Mara, 'I don't think anything's going to help her.'

'But if she took a drink or something to calm herself?'

'Most of the time when he hit her he was drunk,' Mara explained. 'Danae doesn't drink. Not any more.'

The following morning, the funeral Mass was at ten. Mara steeled herself for another encounter with Antonio's family. She knew that Danae could feel the waves of hatred coming off them, and she wished they had brought Lady with them. Her aunt always drew such strength and comfort from Lady's presence, from running her hands through that beautiful, silvery grey fur.

There were more words about Antonio, prayers from his brothers, and a harpist playing. Then finally, it was over. At the cemetery, the priest said some prayers and it was time for the chief mourner to throw some earth on to the coffin. Danae hesitated; she wasn't the chief mourner. She turned and looked towards Antonio's older brother, Tomas. But it wasn't him who returned her gaze, it was his wife, Adriana.

'You do it, Danae,' she said loudly, and she smiled encouragingly, a flash of warmth amidst all the cold.

The entire Danae faction beamed at Adriana. Taking a handful of dirt, Danae threw it. In the silence, the earth was loud upon the hard wood. Nobody spoke. When everyone began to move away, Adriana grabbed Tomas by the hand and led him over to Danae.

Danae's people stood around her like sentinels.

'We don't know each other very well,' Adriana said, while Tomas stared at his shoes, 'but I've come to say something they should have said to you many years ago. The whole family knew what Antonio was.'

Danae began to shake and Adriana put her arms around her.

'I am so sorry, Danae, for all you've suffered. We all knew what he was like. Rosa was the only one who wouldn't admit it. She wouldn't let them admit it when she was alive.'

'But she's dead now,' said Danae. 'Dead a long time. They could have come to me . . .' She was too overcome with emotion to finish the sentence. All these years of living in pain, thinking everyone believed it had all been her fault.

'They're too proud,' Adriana said. 'But they are sorry. I don't think the others will ever be able to say it, but they are truly sorry for what he did to you. You did the right thing, as far as I'm concerned. But Tomas—'

Adriana prodded her husband and finally he looked up at Danae. His eyes, so dark like Antonio's, were wet with tears.

'I know what he did to you, Danae,' said Tomas. 'We heard about the babies you lost. I am so sorry. Mama wouldn't let any of us speak to you. And after she died – well, what was the point?'

'But I knew there was a point,' Adriana said angrily, glaring at her husband. 'The nursing home told me how you came every month, how you paid, how you tried to care for the man who killed your *bambinos*.'

Danae broke down. *Her bambinos.* She'd tried not to think of the babies she'd lost. Thinking of what she'd done to Antonio had kept her mind away from the most painful place of all. Her little babies, two of them.

In the psychiatric hospital, she'd blocked it out. She would not think about him, her mind couldn't deal with it. So she'd closed it all up, as if the pain could be locked behind a series of doors in her mind so that it would never re-emerge. Until now.

'I am so sorry, *cara*,' whispered Adriana, holding her close. 'I would have killed him myself if he had done to me what he did to you. I told Rosa that too, if it's any comfort to you. She was a stupid woman, so sure her boys were angels. She refused to see the anger in Antonio. You are the one who suffered. For that, all I can say is that we are sorry, me and Tomas. And the others too, although they have not the guts to come and say it themselves.'

They stood there together while the rest of the mourners left, until there was only Danae's party and Adriana and her husband at the graveside.

The grave-diggers began to fill in the grave. This was merely another job for them, another coffin to be hidden beneath the earth, part of their everyday life.

Then the rain began to fall, softly at first, and then a deluge. Held by Adriana, Danae didn't care about the rain. As she stood there, Danae felt her whole being relax. It was like Benediction and absolution for a terrible sin she'd been carrying around in her heart for so long.

'Thank you,' she said, 'you don't know what this means to me.'

'I am sorry it has taken so long,' Adriana said gently. 'I must go now, sorry.'

She pulled away, leaving her gloved hand in Danae's for as long as possible.

'I am sorry too,' said Tomas awkwardly.

'Come on, love, you'll catch your death,' said Morris.

He and Mara helped support Danae on her crutches as they made it back to the funeral car.

'She said they knew, they always knew,' Danae kept saying, 'and only Rosa wouldn't believe it because she was his mother and what mother could think that of her son and she said she was sorry for my bambinos . . .'

'Now you know,' said Morris. 'You did the only thing you could. The right thing. He stole your babies, he deserved more than he got. You're the one who's been serving a life sentence, Danae. But that has to stop.'

Danae leaned against him.

'Thank you, thank you,' she said.

Mara, watching her aunt anxiously, saw a softening in her face the likes of which she'd never seen in Danae before. Perhaps it would be all right.

Chapter Twenty-Five

*C*ashel got two surprising phone calls early in January. The first left him entirely astonished but after it, he phoned his lawyers and had a long, serious talk with them.

'Report back to me tomorrow,' he said.

The second call was from Sherry.

'Hello, stranger,' she said.

'Hello, Sherry,' he said, feeling guilty. Damn it, despite his occasional flirty texts to and fro, he hadn't called her and he'd said he would.

'I'm breaking a lot of rules for you,' said Sherry coolly down the phone.

'Yes,' said Cashel, unable to think of anything else to say. It was so unlike him to be gobsmacked, but he was. He'd meant to phone after the holiday in Courchevel, had planned to and yet somehow, every time he got to Avalon he forgot to do it. He kept driving past Tess's antique shop, Something Old, wondering if he should go in and talk to her again. It had been such a brief encounter at Avalon House on New Year's Day. And it had made him think that there was unfinished business and he needed to know what had happened, he needed to find out. For the first time in nineteen years, he needed to know what the other side of the story was.

'I told you I didn't ring men,' Sherry went on, 'I wait for them to ring me, and you said we'd do none of that "will I ring you/won't I ring you" stuff. And now, you haven't rung me.'

'Sherry, I'm sorry,' Cashel said recollecting himself. 'I meant to phone and I didn't. I've been so busy since I got back here.'

'Oh, and *I'm* not busy,' Sherry said. 'You know, I wish you'd been honest with me from the start.'

'I was being honest at the time,' Cashel said, 'and I'm sorry for not phoning you, because I did mean to. I apologize. Let's have dinner next time I'm in London—' he broke off. There was a silence. 'Look, I really like you, but there's someone in Avalon, the town I'm in at the moment where I'm restoring that old house, there's somebody here from the past and . . .'

He couldn't believe he was being so honest; this didn't sound like him at all. Normally he'd have taken her out a few times, seen what unfolded, said: *Sorry, wrong time, wrong place, see you some time*. But he felt he needed to explain, partly to her, partly to himself.

'There was a woman I was involved with twenty years ago and now that I'm back here, I need to see her again, and it would be unfair of me to be seeing you at the same time.'

'Right,' said Sherry. 'I see. Rhona told me all about that. Well, good luck.' And he could tell from the tone of her voice that she didn't see at all.

Cashel pressed end on his phone. That had hurt. He felt like a heel, and he didn't treat people like that.

He was heading for his car, having decided to drive down to Avalon and get a cappuccino from Lorena's, anything to get his head out of the space it was currently in, when he heard a commotion from the house.

'Cashel, Cashel,' roared a voice, and he turned to see Freddie rushing towards him as fast as a man could rush when he was encumbered with a large beer belly and a pair of hobnailed boots. 'Cashel, you're not going to believe what we've found, you've got to come.'

'What now?' demanded Cashel.

'In the basement, it's a hidden room, we're trying to break through.'

The basement was a danger zone, full of special beams, steel girders supporting the old ceiling for fear it would collapse on top of them. It was a major job, Freddie had said, and for once, Cashel hadn't contradicted him. Now Freddie and Cashel hurried through, wearing their hard hats. A group of men stood clustered around one end of the wine cellar. There had been no valuable bottles of wine left, nothing but cobwebs, dark corners, a smell of damp and spiders the size of your hand – or so the men had told Cashel.

'We're nearly through, boss,' said one of the men, working with a crowbar.

'It was hidden behind this brick wall,' Freddie explained. 'We were demolishing the wall to knock through to the wine cellar when we found it.'

Cashel peered past him to a cobweb-strewn door, double locked, and in front of that, a rusty iron gate like the one to the wine cellar, also locked. There seemed to be no way to get in except to rip the iron gate off the wall and then somehow gouge out the wooden door.

'Whatever's in there must be worth something,' Freddie remarked. 'They were sure keen on keeping it hidden. I've heard about old houses with these treasure rooms, but this is the first one I've actually seen. You'd have thought they'd have opened it up before the house was sold. Unless they didn't know it existed. Did you ever hear of a locked room when you were here, Cashel?' He'd stopped calling Cashel 'Mr Reilly' a long time ago, and Cashel didn't mind. It was clear that Freddie was now entirely up to date on the gossip

382

about Cashel's mother having worked for the Powers, and his relationship with Tess Power. In a place like Avalon, few things remained secret for long. There were always old folk around with long memories, who were eager to talk once the correct amount of Guinness was put up on the counter in front of them.

'No, I never heard anything about a locked room,' said Cashel. 'What would you keep in somewhere like that?'

'Lord, I don't know,' said Freddie. 'With rich people, it's anybody's guess. Some of these families hid away the mad relatives they didn't want anyone to see – like your sister,' he roared, turning to one of the other men, and suddenly the crew were all laughing.

'Your sister?' said Cashel, looking at the one man in the crowd who wasn't joining in the laughter. 'I'm sorry to hear that. Does she have a . . .' he tried to find the correct word, '. . . problem?'

'Oh Lord, my sister is a problem,' said the other man, his face splitting in a wide grin. 'I've never met a more temperamental woman in my life. She has her husband's heart scalded.'

Again, roars of laughter.

'I have the use of my ears, you know,' said another man, obviously the temperamental woman's husband. 'It's the decorating benders that are the worst. Now, the whole house has to be repapered. I only finished putting the bloody stuff up just before Christmas, and already she doesn't like it. She's gone off mushroom stripes, apparently . . .'

Cashel grinned and turned his attention to the men with crowbars, who'd now succeeded in wrenching the big steel gate off. Two more men moved in to start on the wooden door.

'It could be mummies,' said one man. 'King Tut's treasure.'

'They found that, you gobshite,' said someone else.

The old, decaying door was no match for the modern tools and finally, with a giant clang, it hit the floor. Torches were produced and Freddie handed one to Cashel.

'Do you want to go in first, seeing as it's your house? Or will I lead the way in case there's some mad dinosaur in there that's been locked up for hundreds of years and is very hungry?'

Cashel laughed: 'No, Freddie, I think I'll go in first, but you can follow close behind in case the dinosaur needs dessert.'

Cashel walked in carefully. First, there was a low hallway and he had to bend down. He winced at the sensation of cobwebs and all sorts of things going through his hair – he wasn't that keen on spiders – but now was not the time for fear. Then the hallway opened up into a bigger room that was at least thirty foot square. Cashel shone the torch around. There was nothing there.

'Hate to tell you, lads,' he roared out, 'but someone else has cleaned out the treasure room.'

'Ah, for feck's sake,' said a voice. 'I thought we'd get some of the salvage money. Isn't that how it works?'

'That's at sea,' said another voice.

'Ten per cent of nothing is nothing,' said Freddie, shining his torch around in case Cashel had missed anything.

Cashel was turning to leave when Freddie's torch beam caught a little indentation in the wall on one side. He shone his own torch at it. There was a small space, made by removing an old brick, and when he looked inside properly, he found an old leather box jammed in there. It took a minute or two to unwedge it, but it came free in the end.

'What have you got?' said Freddie.

'Don't know,' said Cashel. He put his torch in his pocket. 'Shine yours here, Freddie.'

The box was so old that the locking device fell apart when Cashel tried to open it. Inside was a necklace, covered in dust and mould, but it had clearly once been some sort of shiny choker.

'Diamonds?' said Freddie hopefully.

'Hard to tell,' said Cashel doubtfully. 'It might be glass. I think everything that wasn't nailed down was sold years ago.'

Well, it's your glass now,' said Freddie. 'Back out, lads – we've work to be getting on with.'

'It's not mine,' said Cashel. 'It's the property of the Powers, whatever it is.'

'Are you sure?' said Freddie.

'Oh, I'm sure,' said Cashel. 'This has obviously been in their family for hundreds of years, so well hidden they didn't even know anything about it. No, this belongs to them.'

'Fat lot of good that'll be to Tess Power if it's not worth tuppence,' said Freddie. 'Work, lads, come on.'

'Mara'll know how to check it,' Cashel said. 'Let's get her here. Then I think it's time I went to see Tess Power.'

Suki felt Avalon wrap itself round her like a fur-lined cloak from the moment she stepped off the bus. The people behind her were pushing to get off, so she had no time to experimentally *feel* what it was like to be home. She was just there. Home. Properly home, after so many years away.

Once, she might have minded people seeing her getting off the bus instead of arriving in a chauffeur-driven car – which was the way she had done it once, years ago. Gone were the Jethro years, when a bus trip or even a taxi were deemed too ordinary for the likes of her. She was a bus person now, no doubt about it. Funds demanded it.

The driver got off and wrenched open the luggage compartment in the side of the bus and everyone surged forward to grab their luggage. Suki had two bags, giant ones which had been classified as overweight baggage.

There was no such thing as overweight when you travelled on a private jet with TradeWind. Nor was it a problem when the publishers were picking up the tab. But there was nobody but Suki to pick up the tab now, and she'd had to pay the airline money she could ill afford for her speedy, uncoordinated packing.

January in Avalon could be freezing or mild, so she'd packed for all eventualities.

The driver offered to heft her bags on to the pavement. He was young, Eastern European from his accent, with pale skin and dark hair, very polite to everyone. He'd called her ma'am when she got on the bus. Probably thought she was as old as his granny – a thought which no longer horrified her.

'Thank you,' she said, and surveyed the town.

Avalon had changed in the years since she'd been gone. Her visits could have been counted on the fingers of one hand, and the last time had been what, well over four years ago? During her time with Jethro, at any rate; back in the crazy days.

It was prettier than she'd remembered, and more up to date. The cars weren't the wrecked old sedans of her youth, and the place looked polished, more modern, despite what was clearly a deliberate attempt to emphasize its heritage. The hotel was a case in point: in her youth, it had been a rambling place where farmers went on market day to fill themselves with giant plates of beef, spuds and turnips. Now, its beautiful old brickwork had been restored, arched stone windows recreated the sense of a Reformation monastery, and it had been renamed The Avalon Hotel and Spa instead of Lawlor's Hotel, Fine Food & Drink.

The town square was now pedestrianized and glossy SUVs that wouldn't have looked out of place in Hyannis Port were neatly parked in designated spaces. There was even a Maserati, sleek and grey like a waiting shark.

'Taxi?' said someone.

Mara had found a seat by the window of Lorena's Café and was sipping her hot chocolate and enjoying a forbidden piece of red velvet cake, when she spotted the glamorous blonde woman standing at the bus stop. Even though Avalon was a tourist town frequented by visitors from all over the

386

globe, the woman with the long mocha sheepskin coat thrown nonchalantly over her shoulders stood out. Her streaky platinum hair matched creamy retro sunglasses, even though nobody but people accompanied by guide dogs needed sunglasses in Avalon in January. Mara watched, transfixed, as the glossy blonde woman reached into a tan shoulder bag and removed cigarettes and a lighter. When she lit up it was like seeing Faye Dunaway in the original *Thomas Crown Affair* roll into town. Mara felt like a fourteen-year-old with her first girl crush. If she wasn't totally in love with Rafe, gorgeous Rafe, she'd follow this woman like a schoolgirl.

And then the woman turned so her profile was visible and Mara knew exactly who this glamorous outsider was: Tess's sister. This was the famous Suki.

Mara did an unheard of thing – she left some of her cake and the last of her chocolate, and raced out into the square. Here was excitement come to town.

'Hello, you might think I'm a bit mad, but you look like you could be a friend of mine's sister. She described you to me when I was working with her. Tess Power? Am I right? Are you her sister – Suki?'

Suki turned to face a very pretty, short girl dressed like a 1950s soda fountain waitress, with red hair cascading all over the scarlet coat she was struggling into. 'You don't need a taxi, I'll help you bring your bags over to Tess. She's in the shop. I'm Mara, by the way.'

'Hello, Mara,' smiled Suki. 'Everything in this town has improved since I've been away. We had nothing as gorgeous as you around. Except for me!'

Tess was stocktaking. She had so much stock it was unbelievable. As she looked at each item, she found herself remembering where she'd bought it, how much she'd paid. It was the jewellery that really got to her: beautiful pieces that weren't necessarily worth very much in terms of gold or jewels, but that must have meant so much to the owner. Lovely things that had been sent to country auctions for some much-needed hard cash. She picked up a bronze bracelet with a piece of amber set with a tiny prehistoric insect trapped inside; probably some 1920s lady's bracelet worn for amusement. There were quite a few exotic things, imported from all over the world, from another time, when the ruling classes had empires. All sorts of interesting carvings from India and the Far East, and a number of small tables inlaid with various woods.

Tess had always tried to get the stories of the things she sold in the shop. She was fascinated by the history of pieces: where they'd been, where they'd come from, what they meant. Most of the time, she was able to find out quite a lot of detail. She wrote it all down in her notebook and then transcribed it on to the luggage label she tied on each item along with the price. She left these labels on the items as she counted up the stock and organized it into categories. She was in the front room of the shop while Zach was helping in the back room. Every so often he'd shout, 'Ma, this thing – I don't know what to do with it.'

'What is it?' she'd call. A lot of the stock in the back room was stuff she hadn't got round to labelling or else items she had labelled that hadn't sold.

'Well, I'm not entirely sure what it is. It looks like some sort of sword.' A swishing noise accompanied this, making it clear that Zach was having a play with the sword.

'That's a samurai sword, darling,' she said. 'Well, a copy, at least. It's very sharp, so be careful. If it was a real samurai sword it would be worth thousands, but unfortunately it's a nineteenth-century – late nineteenth-century at that – copy, from when chinoiserie was all the rage.'

'OK,' he said. 'So which pile is that to go into?'

'You know, it's a lovely piece, I just hadn't got round to putting it in the front of the shop. Bring it out to me with the stuff that we could get a good price for at the auction house. And then maybe we'll stop for a cup of tea and a digestive biscuit,' she said.

It was painful, going through her beloved shop like this. At least having Zach there kept her from dissolving into floods of tears. She wouldn't cry in front of him. No, she'd said to Zach that this was a new beginning; the shop was taking up too much time and it was too difficult. She was going to try and get a more settled job where she'd be there more for him and Kitty. Especially seeing as later this year, when he moved into the sixth year, he would be starting to prepare for his state exams.

'But you love the shop, Mum,' Zach had said sadly.

'I do, but we have to be realistic, darling. It's hard to run a shop like Something Old in the modern world,' Tess had said, keeping her voice bright but altering her story somewhat because she realized he didn't quite believe her.

'I'd kill for some biscuits,' said Zach now.

'OK, you put on the kettle, I'll finish up here, and then we'll have a sit down,' said Tess.

At that moment there was a frantic knocking on the door of the shop. Tess had locked it and put the closed sign on the front. After all, it wasn't as if anyone was coming in to buy stuff any more, and it made it easier and safer just to have the door shut.

'Tess, it's me, Mara,' said a voice, and Tess smiled. Mara had that effect on people. She brought light into every room she entered.

'Coming,' said Tess, and she swung open the door. Then her hands flew to her mouth in astonishment. For there, standing beside Mara, was Suki, looking impossibly glamorous and in danger of bursting into tears at the same time.

'Oh, Tess,' said Suki, throwing out her arms and wrapping them around her sister. 'Oh, Tess, I need you, I need you.'

*   *   *

389

Zach quite liked being alone in the shop. His mother had whisked Suki off home and he'd volunteered to stay and do a bit more stocktaking to give them some time alone together.

'Only thing is, I'm not exactly sure what to do, Mum,' he'd said.

'Keep doing what you're doing,' said his mother. 'You're great, it'll be fine.' And then she was gone.

It was sort of cool being seventeen; people trusted you, you knew stuff. When he was fourteen, he used to think he knew everything. How dumb was that? Now, now he knew everything. Pixie often said so.

'You're only saying that,' he'd say with a laugh, but he liked it all the same.

He made himself his cup of tea and gave a couple of biscuits to Silkie, who was sitting with him, begging, slavering for a nibble of a digestive.

'You'll get fat,' said Zach, as Silkie gobbled down two biscuits. 'Nah, you probably won't, you were born skinny,' Zach decided, petting the dog.

Dogs were great, you could tell them things and they never told anyone else. Like when Mum and Dad had split up, Zach would bring Silkie into his room and lie on the bed and hug her and listen to music and tell Silkie that he'd known Mum and Dad weren't happy for a long time. That he'd been really scared something like this was going to happen and now it had, and all of a sudden the future was this big unknown. Parents never seemed to understand how frightening the unknown was for their kids. *They* knew what they were doing, they'd made the choices, but what about you? You didn't get to make any choices even though you were a part of it.

And yet it had sort of worked out, in some strange way. Mum seemed happy without Dad, and Dad was really happy with Claire. Who knew? Grown-ups were crazy. Once they hit thirty, it was all downhill and their minds started to go.

390

There was another knock on the door, a very firm one this time.

'We're closed,' Zach shouted.

'I'm looking for Tess Power,' came a deep voice through the door.

'She's not here,' Zach said.

'Please, may I come in?'

Zach gave Silkie the last of his biscuit, wiped the crumbs off his mouth, got to his feet and ambled over to the door. He unlocked it and pulled it open to see a very tall, well-built man with dark hair and amazing dark eyes staring down at him. Zach was pretty tall himself, the tallest in his class, but this guy, who was, like, old obviously, had a couple of inches on him.

'She's not here,' Zach said in a more respectful tone, because this man looked like the sort of person that you had to be respectful to.

For a moment the man just stared at him. Then finally he spoke: 'You must be Zach.'

'Yeah,' said Zach slowly.

'I'm Cashel Reilly. I was friends with your mother a long time ago.'

'Oh, OK,' said Zach. 'My aunt Suki turned up, so Mum's gone home with her. She's not going to be back today.'

'Suki's come home?'

Mr Reilly sounded very surprised at that.

'Yeah,' said Zach. 'You look a bit familiar. Do I know you?'

'I bought Avalon House so I've been around a lot lately.'

'Ah,' said Zach in a much less friendly tone. 'It used to belong to my family a long time ago.'

'I know,' said Cashel evenly.

'My mum doesn't talk about it, she never goes there. But I've been there, loads of times with my friends,' Zach said, as if daring the man to tell him he'd been trespassing. 'When something's in your family a long time, it's supposed to be part

391

of you, you know that? So I didn't think there was a problem with me going up there with my friends or my girlfriend.'

'No,' said Cashel, 'there was no problem with you doing that.'

He stared at the boy in fascination. Tess's son was a tall, strong young guy, with a warm face, eyes like his mother's, the dark hair of his grandfather and a firm chin that Cashel couldn't identify. He was polite, charming and had clearly inherited all his mother's good manners.

'Avalon House will always be open to you, Zach,' he said. 'I promise. It is your birthright.'

'Thanks,' said Zach. 'You should tell Mum that, because, like, she must want to go up sometimes. Dad – my parents are separated now – Dad says it means a lot to her but it hurts, and that's why she doesn't go there.'

'They've spilt up, your mum and dad?' Cashel said carefully.

'Yeah, it's sort of complicated,' Zach said.

'Oh?' said Cashel, in a way that invited more disclosure.

'My dad's got a new girlfriend and she's pregnant.'

'That must be hard,' Cashel said.

'No, not really, it's going to be fine, Mum says it's going to be fine.'

Cashel nodded. 'That sounds like your mum,' he said, 'practical.'

'Yeah, she is kind of practical, and she seems to be taking it OK really. Pixie – that's my girlfriend – Pixie said that if I went off and had a baby with someone else, well, she'd be pretty mad at me. But Mum, she seems fine about it.'

'Listen,' said Cashel, 'I do need to see your mum. Could you give me your exact address, because I don't know it?'

'Sure,' said Zach. 'Bet you she'll be delighted to see you.'

'I hope so,' said Cashel. 'Suki will be pleased to see me, that's for sure.'

*   *   *

Suki was no sooner through the front door than she dumped her bags on the floor and said to her sister, 'Where do you keep the drink in this house?'

'Er, in the kitchen,' said Tess.

'Fine.' Suki marched into the kitchen, opened cupboards and stumbled upon the bottles that were rarely touched. She poured herself a giant glass of Scotch. 'Do you have any ice?' she said.

'No,' sighed Tess, 'this is not a bar.'

'Oh, stop, Tess, please. I love you, and I'm sorry, but I'm stressed. I've flown over. I had to get the bus. It's been awful. I can't tell you how anxious I am.'

'I know, my love,' said Tess, and she put her arms around her sister.

Suki laid her head against Tess's shoulder and felt the peace envelop her. It felt good to be home, she'd been running away for so long.

When they parted, Suki opened the fridge, looking for some sort of mixer to take the hit away from the Scotch. Orange juice, that'd do. She only poured a little in because there wasn't much room left in the glass. 'I'm sorry, I know you disapprove, but I don't do drugs any more, I have the occasional drink, that's all.'

'I'm not your mother,' Tess said.

'I know, I know. That's part of the problem, isn't it?' said Suki, sinking down into a kitchen chair and suddenly looking her age. 'Maybe if we'd had a mother, things would have been different. We would have known about being women, understood it. It wouldn't have all gone wrong with you and Cashel. It wouldn't have all gone wrong with me and bloody Kyle Richardson Senior. I might have understood how to handle myself without putting myself on a plate for men.'

'Yeah, I know,' said Tess, sitting down at the table beside her and taking Suki's hand in hers. She knew all about Kyle Senior and what he'd done. It was definitely his fault, he'd taken advantage of her darling sister, although Suki had always blamed herself, thinking she had handled it all wrong.

If I hadn't had so much to drink, if I hadn't been so convinced I could wrap him round my finger . . . she'd say.

'Looking at Zach and Kitty, I can see how children need both parents, if at all possible,' Tess said. 'They need so much guidance. Dad was brilliant and he did his best, but he was only one half of the puzzle.'

At that moment, Tess heard the front door opening. 'Oh God,' she said to Suki, 'it's Lydia, my child minder. She picks Kitty up from school, brings her home, gives her a snack and looks after her until I get off work.'

'Coo-ee, I thought I saw you come in!' Kitty ran into the kitchen at high speed. 'Mum . . . Oh, Aunt Suki!' she said. Tess thought it was a miracle Kitty recognized Suki, because she'd only been four or five years old the last time she visited. But Kitty had always been fascinated by her glamorous aunt and used to look at her pictures endlessly: holding them up to the mirror, trying to adopt the same poses Suki did in the photos.

'Look at you, you little darling,' said Suki, hauling her on to her lap for a good cuddle. 'You have grown. You're a young lady!'

'I know,' said Kitty, flicking her ponytail in delight.

'Hello, everyone,' said Lydia, hovering in the doorway of the kitchen, dying to be invited in and introduced.

'Lydia,' said Tess, 'this is my sister, Suki.'

'It's lovely to meet you,' said Lydia, coming forward.

Lydia was a wonderful childminder, but sadly an inveterate gossip. Knowing that news of her sister's arrival would be all around the village within the hour, Tess was anxious to send her on her way:

'Thank you so much, Lydia,' she said. 'I won't need you to stay today. I came home early because Suki arrived unexpectedly.'

'A flying visit?' Lydia enquired, determined to get as much information as possible before she had to leave.

Luckily, Suki had the whole situation sized up. 'Yes,' she said getting to her feet and subtly steering Lydia out of the room, 'a flying visit, I don't have much time. It's been so wonderful to meet you. It would be lovely to chat but I want to make the most of every precious moment with my darling nephew and niece.'

And before she knew it, Lydia was at the front door, she was stepping outside and bang, the door was shut behind her. What an interesting lady, she thought as she marched down the path, determined to spread the news.

Back in the kitchen, Tess was fixing a snack for her daughter. She tried to signal that they wouldn't be able to talk now that Kitty was there.

'Big ears. Big ears,' she mouthed at Suki.

Suki nodded, then opened her beautiful leather handbag and took out a make-up case.

'Do you know,' she said to Kitty, 'I have some lovely stuff in here. Look at this.' She opened her Bobbi Brown lip palette, a darling thing she'd treated herself to recently, with every lip colour one could possibly need inside.

'Oooh,' said Kitty delightedly.

'You should try some of them,' said Suki. 'After your snack, maybe you could sit there at the table and have a go. I have some sparkly eyeshadows too. Your mum and I are going to run into the living room to have a chat.'

'Stroke of genius!' Tess grinned at her sister.

'Well, I didn't think she had much experience of make-up,' Suki grinned. 'Although, I have to take that back – you've certainly improved your look since the last time I was here.'

'Oh, well, I guess I have,' said Tess, reaching up and rubbing her hair self-consciously. Vivienne had very pointedly given her a hairdressing voucher for Christmas and Mara had given her a cosmetics bag containing eyeshadow, mascara and lipstick. She'd started wearing these products and found that putting on make-up was one of those skills that you never quite forget. She used to love make-up years ago, trying on Suki's while she was out. During her marriage, she'd forgotten that. Forgotten the whole concept of making yourself beautiful in front of the mirror in the morning. It had been lost, the way so many things had been lost.

'That short cut really suits you. And I like the blonde streaks, very good. They really bring out the natural blonde in your own hair,' pronounced Suki. 'Who does it? Not Eileen, I'm pretty sure of that.'

'No,' laughed Tess, 'there's a fabulous new salon in town. But I doubt I'll ever be able to go again, there's no way I can afford it. I'm having to close the business, Suki. We're officially broke.'

'No!' said Suki. 'That is not going to happen, honey. Look, my book is nearly finished and when I get my delivery money from the publishers, you can have some of it. You've got to keep it going. You love that shop.'

Tess shook her head. 'I've realized that keeping the shop was some sort of crazy link to home, buying the sort of things that were in Avalon House when we were growing up. It was reminding me of the past. Do you know who's bought the house?'

'Who?' said Suki, but she didn't look at Tess as she spoke. 'Cashel.'

'Oh, right.' Suki drained the rest of her Scotch. 'I'm sorry, Tess. I don't think I ever said how sorry I was. It's partly my fault that it ended with him, and he was a great guy.'

'It wasn't your fault,' Tess said. 'It was his fault, and a bit my fault, and the fault of us all being young and stupid. Let's not talk about that,' said Tess. 'It's water under the bridge. Let's talk about these biography people: they're not really that bad, are they?'

'You've no idea,' said Suki. 'They're like hounds on the trail and they're convinced that I'm hiding a secret, which of course I am. They're going to turn up here, I know it.'

'So? We'll tell them we're not talking to them, that's all.'

'You don't understand, Tess,' Suki said sadly. 'These people won't give up. The only thing that could possibly stop them is an injunction, bigshot lawyers and the money to back up the threat. I hoped that the Richardsons would help, let the biographer know I had their full protection, but they made it pretty clear that they simply expect me to maintain the family line of silence. No, far as they're concerned, I'm on my own. So Suarez can write what he wants about me – and he'll certainly put in stuff about me coming from the once-great Power family, so you'll be dragged into it too. I'm sorry.'

The doorbell rang. 'For God's sake,' said Suki, exasperated, 'what is this, Grand Central station?'

'I don't know who that can be,' said Tess. 'I'm not expecting anybody. Whoever it is, they can go away.'

She got up, went to the front door, opened it and stood stock still. Standing there, looking faintly uneasy but maintaining his customary glower, was Cashel.

'Can I come in?' he said.

'This isn't a good time,' said Tess.

She was totally thrown. She didn't know what to say. Seeing him again was upsetting. Or maybe it wasn't upsetting, maybe it was something else. She hadn't been able to stop thinking about him since she'd met him on New Year's Day at the house, which was ridiculous, she knew.

'I know Suki's here,' said Cashel. 'I went into the shop. I talked to Zach.'

Tess's face softened at the mention of her son, and Cashel thought again how beautiful she was. She looked different from the last time he'd seen her: more polished or something. But lovely, like the beautiful girl he'd loved.

'He's great, isn't he?' said Tess. 'If you'd stayed around, you could have got to meet him sooner.'

Suki appeared behind her.

'Cashel. Great,' she said. 'Perfect timing.'

Tess looked at Suki in alarm. What on earth was she talking about?

'I need someone else who drinks Scotch,' continued Suki. 'It's very bad to drink on your own.'

'I don't think you should have any more,' said Tess. If Cashel turning up on the doorstep was her idea of perfect timing, Suki must have had several drinks on the way over.

'Oh stop! Bring the bottle into the living room, Tess, and another glass for Cashel.'

In the kitchen, Kitty was experimenting wildly. Thanks to the cosmetics in Suki's bag, her look was part Burlesque dancer, part Tinkerbell explosion.

'Don't I look lovely, Mum?' she said.

Tess kissed her on her forehead. 'You look beautiful, darling,' she said.

When she went back into the living room with a pot of coffee and another glass and the bottle of Scotch, in case Cashel decided he did want a drink, he and Suki were talking away as if it hadn't been years since they'd met. They were discussing lawyers and private detectives, it seemed. Bewildering. Tess poured coffee for everyone.

Suki took a coffee and then grabbed the Scotch bottle too, pouring herself a healthy measure. 'That's my last one,' she said, 'but it's been a stressful day, folks.'

Tess took a deep breath. Having Cashel in her house was making her heart beat erratically, and she had her big sister thrown into the mix too.

'I've got some news,' said Cashel.

The two women looked at him.

'Good or bad?' said Suki. 'Because good has been in short supply around here lately.'

398

'This is good news,' said Cashel, but he had eyes only for Tess.

Strangely she found she couldn't stop looking at him either. It had all been too rushed, too upsetting when they'd met on New Year's Day. Now she could see the greying temples, could see the dark eyes with crow's feet, the dark shadow on his jaw and the strong face of a man, but still with traces of the boy he'd once been. 'What's the news?' she said.

'A couple of hours ago, the builders found a secret room in the basement of the house.'

'What?' said Tess. This was all too startling.

'It was well hidden,' said Cashel. 'It was down in the wine cellar. We only came across it when we demolished a wall and revealed an old door. Unfortunately, the room was empty. Apart from this.'

He held up the dirty, tarnished necklace.

'I have no idea what it is,' said Cashel, 'but it belongs to both of you. When your father sold the house, he sold it with an explicit list of contents. I've seen that list. And then, when the place was sold to me, it was only the house. The property that belonged to the Power family continues to legally belong to the Power family. It's yours.'

'It looks like junk to me,' said Suki.

'That's what I thought,' said Cashel, 'but I reckoned Tess would know. Either way, you should have it. It must have belonged to one of your ancestors.'

'Are you sure?' said Suki, looking at the necklace with more interest. 'Because you're the owner – essentially, possession is nine points of the law or something.'

'No,' said Cashel, his eyes firmly on Tess. 'It's yours. It could be something.'

'I doubt it,' said Tess, but she took it from him anyway. 'I'll have it valued. I know a wonderful diamond man, but I'm sure Suki's right and it's yours.'

She stared hard at him.

'I'm sure it's not,' he replied.

'You pair,' groaned Suki. 'Are you ever going to make up?'

'Suki, you really should stay away from Scotch,' said Tess coldly, sitting up. 'It clearly does not agree with you. Makes you a little crazy.'

'Scotch doesn't make me crazy,' said Suki, 'I am crazy. Hey, we should get Zach. We did rather leave him there in the shop.'

Redmond Suarez's hottest researcher, Carmen, booked herself into the Avalon Hotel and Spa. It wasn't such a bad town, kinda cute really, she thought. Lincoln, one of the very junior researchers, had been here for ages looking through old parish history records and had drawn a blank. There was interesting stuff on the Powers and how they'd once been rich, but no scandal. If there was any, Carmen would find it.

Redmond wouldn't like it here. He only liked cities. Anything rural made him nervous; reminded him too much of his roots. Carmen grinned as she let herself into her room. She knew that Redmond wasn't really Portuguese nobility, but hey, everyone had their little secrets, she thought with a grin, even her employer. There were plenty of secrets in Avalon, she was certain of that.

Redmond had done some amazing digging on the Richardsons. His job had been made easier by the fact that there were plenty of people who hated Antoinette Richardson – *hated* her. People who'd been snubbed by her, staff who'd been underpaid by her: the list was endless. It was going to be his best book yet.

With so much good material already, she didn't know why Redmond was so keen on getting this particular angle to the story. Sure, Suki Power was interesting in her own right and Carmen would have chewed off her leg without anaesthetic to find out what had gone on during the years Suki lived with Jethro from TradeWind, but there was no point. Anyone who printed rumours involving Jethro got sued; the guy was a multimillionaire, incredibly well connected, and he had libel lawyers on standby 24/7. Redmond wouldn't like that. Didn't matter if they struck gold, any stories involving Jethro would have to stay out of the book. And the Jethro years aside, there didn't seem to be anything else to uncover about Suki. Sure, there had been talk about a few tempestuous years with Kyle Junior and Suki barely talking to each other, but nothing to back it up. Nothing but a little gossip.

Sometimes a little gossip made for the most amazing chapter in a book, she'd learned that from Redmond. But her instinct told her that wasn't the case here. Yes, Suki Power had thrown her out of her house, but she hadn't looked frightened. If anything, she'd looked contemptuous. It wasn't the first time Carmen had come across that look, and she hated it. One day she'd get away from Redmond and she'd be free to write her own books – and they wouldn't be smutty biographies either. Smut paid the rent, more than paid the rent, but she wanted to write something else, maybe a lucrative gig like Suki had: something noble, she decided. Something her mother would be proud of, instead of saying: 'Why, Carmen, why do you write this stuff? Is this what you went to college for?'

In the meantime, she had an assignment to complete.

Tess Power owned an antique shop called Something Old. That was where Carmen was going. She'd changed out of her travel clothes into her interviewing clothes, which were always formal, and thrown a heavy coat on top. It was cold out here. Armed with her digital tape recorder, notebook and a capacious bag in case she found anything incriminating that she could appropriate, Carmen headed off to find Something Old.

None of the cab drivers wanted to take her. 'It's only up the hill love, about five minutes' walk, wouldn't be worth the fare to drive you up there.'

'I thought cab drivers were supposed to take you wherever

you wanted to go whenever you wanted to go,' yelled Carmen in fury.

'Ha, maybe in New York, love, but not here,' said one guy, and rolled his window up with a snap.

She trudged up the hill and then she saw it, pretty sign in scroll lettering and hanging on an iron bar: *Something Old*. Cute, olde worlde.

There was a little hallway inside the street door and to one side there was some sort of dress shop; older women's stuff, nothing cool, Carmen decided from her brief look in, nothing fashionable whatsoever. On the other side was the antique shop. The door was shut ... no, on closer inspection, she realized it was ajar. She was standing in the hallway, listening for voices, when a dog began to growl. Damn dogs, they always figured out when you were snooping around.

'Hey, anyone at home,' she said, knocking on the door and then letting herself in. She only hoped that the dog wasn't going to savage her.

There were four people in the room: a teenage boy; a tall, very good-looking guy – late forties, and rich – that was for sure, Carmen could spot rich ones a mile away – and then a woman with blonde hair cut in a fashionable, short style. She was tall, stunning-looking. Definitely Suki's sister, but different, sort of finer, more elegant. And there was Suki herself, looking glamorous and self-assured. Damn.

'Hi,' said Carmen, in her best syrupy voice, 'I'm Carmen LeMonte, I work for Redmond Suarez and I'm looking for Tess Power – I assume that's you,' she said, pointing her finger at Tess, completely ignoring Suki. 'I'm trying to find out if the information I've got is true.' The digital recorder in her pocket was on. It was set to tape anything within radius of her pocket and was very, very sensitive.

'And what exactly is this information you have?' said the man, and he looked menacing now. Yes, definitely menacing.

Beside the woman was the other source of Carmen's

402

problem: some lean houndy thing, and it was snarling at her, teeth bared. Looking at her with nearly as much naked dislike was Suki.

'That's the bitch who doorstepped me back home looking for information!' she hissed.

Speed was of the essence, Carmen decided. You really only got one chance to ask these incredibly tough questions, and when everyone was so hostile, you might as well go in with it straight away. Suki wasn't going to give anything away – Carmen had to try to shock some information out of the sister.

'We understand that Suki Power Richardson had a facade of a marriage with Kyle Junior – but the word is that she was very close to his father, Kyle Senior, and that Antoinette Richardson ran her out of the family as a result. We know she came to stay here afterwards.'

It was a wild allegation, but often it was a case of the wilder the better when it came to rooting out a few decent facts. Anxious to defend themselves against the allegation, innocent people had a tendency to get flustered and divulge a lot more of the truth than they otherwise would have in an effort to point out how you'd got it all wrong.

Tess was rooted to the spot. She had a hand on Silkie's collar because for the first time in her entire life, the gentle little whippet looked as if she might actually pounce on someone.

Cashel moved forward until he was right up close to the woman.

'I know you're taping us,' he said. 'One moment.' He found his mobile phone and clicked on its recording mechanism.

'OK, so now we're all taping. My name is Cashel Reilly and my company is C. Reilly Enterprises Worldwide.'

'Oh,' Carmen said, feeling a little shiver of doubt. She liked to be the only one in the room taping the conversation: it upped the stakes considerably when anyone else taped too.

403

'My lawyers in New York, Steinberg & Retzen, are in the process of taking out an injunction against Mr Suarez or his agents harassing any member of the Power family.'

Carmen winced. Steinberg & Retzen were dangerous – more than dangerous. They had built a fearsome reputation for securing record-breaking damages in libel and defamation cases. And they always, always won.

'So I suggest you abandon this particular line of enquiry or else it could prove very expensive indeed for your employer. I'm sure Redmond Suarez won't want to risk ending up back in Puerto Rico without a dollar to his name.'

Carmen was used to looking impassive: it was part of her job. Redmond had drilled it into her that she had to learn to hide her emotions, but not this time. She knew she'd gone white. She managed a shrug.

'Of course, I understand. Sometimes, leads turn out to be false. People make up stuff. Sorry for bothering you all.' She picked up her bag and with a brittle smile she was gone.

'Oh my God,' said Tess, and sat down on a packing box. She was shaking. 'I can't believe that happened.'

'You were brilliant,' said Zach. 'I haven't a clue what was going on, but it looked good.'

'Thank you,' said Cashel, making sure the door was firmly shut. He was watching Carmen hurrying down the street, talking on her mobile. Redmond Suarez was not going to enjoy that phone call one bit.

'How did you know to say those things about the biographer?' Tess said.

'Suki phoned me and asked for help. The Richardsons had hung her out to dry, so I got my lawyers on to it.'

Silkie was whining and Zach excused himself to walk her back home.

'C'mon,' said Suki, putting an arm round Zach, 'I'll come too. This store is cold, Tess, you need some heating in it.'

Then it was just the two of them. Cashel was looking at

Tess. She was reeling from all the revelations, not least that Suki had reached out to Cashel.

But suddenly she was aware that she was standing alone with Cashel Reilly, who'd been in her mind so much lately. Would it be worth saying all the things she should have said years ago?

She glanced at him and his face was stony.

No, she thought. The time for talking had passed a long time ago.

'Thank you, Cashel,' she said stiffly. 'And about this—' She held up the necklace. 'I can have it checked out, but I'm sure it's yours.'

'No,' he said. 'The contents of the house that were sold all those years ago were listed. This wasn't on the list, it's definitely yours.'

He was waiting for something, anything from her, but she was deliberately not looking at him any more.

It was as clear in her mind as if it had happened yesterday, not nineteen years before. It had been when Suki was home from America, filled with angst and anxiety over what had happened. 'They're a nightmare, those people, a bloody nightmare,' Suki had raged, striding up and down the old house's library, creating a breeze as she went.

Even now, Tess felt sorry that she hadn't truly appreciated what Suki was going through. Instead she'd felt angry that all Suki could think about was herself and not about their father, who lay upstairs in bed – a cold bedroom, at that – wheezing. He should be in hospital, she was convinced of it. Pneumonia couldn't be properly treated at home, but he insisted he was fine.

'You can take the stiff upper lip thing too far, Dad,' Tess had said. 'Please let me bring you to hospital.'

Nothing, however, could persuade him to budge. He insisted on staying in his own bed.

And now Suki was there, almost screaming the house down, talking about that bitch Antoinette but refusing to tell Tess why.

Suki's eyes had blazed with fury. 'I don't understand women like that; they're prepared to put up with anything, as long as they stay Mrs So-and-So. The dignity of being the wife. Well, I'm not going to stay and be Kyle Junior's wife any more, there's no dignity in that. It's all over.'

'Suki, if I knew what you were talking about, I could help, but right now, my priority is Dad. I know you're upset about Antoinette, I know she drives you mad, but have you any idea how sick Dad is? And we're so broke the house is going to have to go. The bank won't give us any more time.'

'Oh for God's sake, sell the bloody thing,' Suki had snapped, irritated. 'I need some support here.'

'And so do I,' Tess had shouted back at her.

'Fine, I'll go down to the village, see if there's anyone there who's ready to listen to my story,' Suki snarled and marched out, slamming the door behind her.

Tess was never entirely sure what had been said between Suki and Cashel that evening. Suki had called around to his mother's first, knowing he was home, thinking he might take her for a drink. And somehow, Suki's story of how Tess wouldn't support her and was instead only wrapped up with life here in Avalon, had fed a fire in Cashel, always a passionate creature, and he'd come to the house to give her an ultimatum. He had saved enough for plane tickets for them both, for their big adventure.

'There's no life for us here, Tess. We're young, let's get away from this town and start a new life,' he'd pleaded.

London was where it was at. London was where people like Cashel could make money. She'd promised to come with him. He loved Tess. He wanted to marry her, but she needed to choose.

'Cashel, I can't go yet,' Tess had said. 'Let's wait another couple of months, till Dad's better and maybe the bank will change their minds. Please, a few months, that's all.'

'You keep saying that,' he'd answered angrily. 'Is this a game to you, Tess? Are you stringing me along?'

Unlike Suki, with her white-hot heat, Tess never lost her temper: she was too like her father for that.

But that night, she lost it: 'Don't you dare accuse me of being that sort of girl!' she'd hissed.

'You need to choose between me and bloody Avalon and your father,' he'd shouted over his shoulder as he stormed out.

Early the next morning, Cashel had come up to the house again. Tess was exhausted. Her father had been coughing much of the night and she'd been terrified, so terrified that she'd stayed up in the chair in his bedroom, blankets wrapped around her. Drifting in and out of sleep. Hearing that frightening noise in his chest. Recalling the doctor's words:

'I don't know if there's much more I can do, Tess. He needs to go to hospital. You're going to have to override him, if you can.'

When morning came, his breathing seemed easier, as if the medicine was finally kicking in. She had gone down to the kitchen, in two minds about whether to ring an ambulance to take him into hospital.

And Cashel had been there in the doorway, his bag packed. He was going back to London now, he said, and then on to New York – alone, if she wouldn't come with him. He stood there in the kitchen as she boiled water on the stove, white-faced and shaking with exhaustion.

'I need to talk to you,' Cashel had said, standing there. Not even sitting down. Tess wanted him to put his arms around her. She wanted to rest her head against his shoulder and feel him comforting her. He was wearing her favourite jumper. The beautiful Aran sweater his mother had knitted for him. How many times had she lain against it on dates, when they'd been to the cinema, out to dinner, or even those nights when he'd taken it off and they'd lain in each other's arms and made love.

She needed him to say he was sorry for all the things he'd said before, that he knew it wasn't fair to expect her to choose right now, with her father terribly ill. On top of that Suki was driving her mad, so wrapped up in her own concerns she was totally oblivious to how close they were to losing the roof over their heads.

'I need you to decide, Tess,' said Cashel, his voice a throaty growl. And Tess had turned from the stove and looked at him. 'I'm going to go and this is your last chance. I want to see the world. I want to make something of myself.'

'But you don't have to go yet. I don't have to decide now, Cashel. My father is sick.' Tess put her hand up to her forehead. Her head ached from the sleepless night. She was so tired. A cup of coffee might bring her back to herself.

'No, you *do* have to decide,' Cashel said. 'Have you been messing with me all along? You're a Power, you've got Avalon House – you've always had that, while I have nothing. My mother cleaned your house, cooked your dinners. Years ago, I wouldn't have been allowed inside this house, I wouldn't have been allowed to touch you.

'Now I need you to choose me. Don't you understand?'

'But, Cashel,' Tess said wearily, 'all that stuff means nothing to me. I love you. I love who you are. You know I don't think that I'm different or special because I'm a Power and my family own the big house – I've never thought that.'

'Then, come away with me. Come away with me now.'

She had stared at him in exasperation, had run her hands through her hair. 'You don't understand, I can't come now, Dad is ill, the bank is threatening him, we have to work out if we need to sell the house. Give me some time . . .'

'Oh, I understand all right,' Cashel said. 'Suki and I were

talking about it last night. This house, your father, they're the only things you care about. There will never be a right time for you to leave. I've been asking you to come away with me for the past year now.'

'Suki's stirring things,' Tess said angrily. 'She's annoyed because I didn't want to listen to her tale of woe about those damn Richardsons.'

'She's right this time,' Cashel said, 'you don't care about anyone else except you and your father and this bloody house. Are you coming or not?'

Tess's temper, rarely roused, flared up and she pulled herself up to her full height.

'If you think you can make me abandon my father or my principles just because you lay down an ultimatum, then you don't understand me at all, Cashel Reilly.' Her voice was icy.

His face darkened, he looked at her in a way he'd never looked at her before. 'It's clear that you don't understand me very well, either, Tess Power.' He almost spat out the words. 'That was your chance. You obviously don't love me enough. I'll always be the Cottage Row boy to you, that's it, isn't it?'

'If that's what you want to believe of me, then carry on,' said Tess, trying not to cry. 'That's not who I am and you should know it. Clearly you don't.'

'Goodbye, Tess.' And he had turned on his heel and left.

She stood in the kitchen, staring after him while the kettle on the stove began to hiss, telling her it was boiled, the lid clattering loudly. He didn't understand her at all: she loved him with all her heart. If Cashel was so ambitious and hell-bent on success that he couldn't let her stay with her father for a few months, then he wasn't the man for her. Despite the love and the passion and the wildness they'd experienced together, the fierce intensity of his touch, how he made her feel . . . Despite all that, he didn't understand her at all.

And then the tears came. She had waited in the kitchen for

him to come back to her, to tell her he knew that she loved him and that he'd wait. But when he didn't come back, she knew he never would. Cashel Reilly had never changed his mind in his life.

Later that day, finding Tess in floods of tears, Suki had felt guilty.

'Oh, go on, follow him to London, you idiot,' she'd said, trying to assuage some of her guilt.

Tess shook her head. 'It's too late. He's gone and I won't run after him. Either he comes back or it's over.'

'Oh shit,' said Suki, sitting down and putting her head in her hands. 'I've messed up on two continents.'

Tess looked up finally. 'What do you mean?' she asked, her voice dangerously low.

'I was angry with you for not listening to me yesterday,' Suki admitted. 'I may have stoked Cashel's fire a bit when it came to how annoyed he was with you for not leaving Avalon.'

'How?'

'It's not my fault,' Suki said. 'I said he ought to give you an ultimatum. My road or the high-road.' She laughed bitterly. 'Something along the lines of what Kyle Senior explained to me when it turned out his bitch of a wife knew about us. Except in his case, it was Antoinette's road or the high road.'

'You said what?' Tess wasn't sure what part of the news was more shocking – Suki blithely admitting that she'd had a hand in wrecking Tess's relationship with Cashel, or the fact that Suki had been having some sort of sexual liaison with her father-in-law.

'If only you'd listened yesterday, none of this would have happened,' Suki muttered defensively.

Suki always thought that the reason Antoinette didn't like her was because Kyle Senior did.

'You're the prettiest little daughter-in-law I've ever seen,' he used to say, every time he set eyes on Suki. Taking in the curvaceous figure, liking the raw sexuality that emanated from his son's Irish wife.

'I'm the only daughter-in-law you have,' Suki would reply cheekily, and he liked that even more. Few people were ever cheeky to Kyle Senior, but it was acceptable in a sexy-looking girl.

Kyle Junior never stood up to his father. No matter what Suki said, it seemed nothing could persuade him that they were perfectly entitled to spend their money the way they wanted to.

'If we want a house in New Mexico, we should have a house in New Mexico,' she said. 'It's your money. It's not as if it's in trust, waiting until you hit thirty-five or something.'

'I've told you before: Dad controls everything. We do something he doesn't like, he cuts off the money. Don't you get it? Then we'll both have to go out and get jobs. Not so much fun redecorating the beautiful house in New Mexico if you don't have a dime to your name, huh, Suki!'

'Oh, Kyle,' she'd said, disgusted with him. 'You are so weak.'

He'd stormed out of their house that night and hadn't come back until the following afternoon. She thought perhaps he'd been with another woman, there was a scent of perfume on him, but maybe he'd been in a bar or something. That hurt, because she loved him, she didn't want him to go to other women. Not the way Kyle Senior did.

Antoinette had to be the only woman in America who didn't know her husband had a mistress. But then, on the subject of mistresses, Antoinette probably worked on the same theory as Queen Victoria did about lesbians: she refused to countenance such a thing, therefore it didn't exist.

If Antoinette decided not to believe in the existence of a mistress, there could be no mistress.

'Did you sleep with another woman?' Suki demanded.

411

Kyle looked up at her, his eyes bloodshot from a night of drinking too much bourbon. 'So what if I did?' he said. 'I'd prefer to sleep with another woman than sleep in the same bed as a wife who tells me I'm weak.'

That was it as far as Suki was concerned; she'd had it with this family, totally had it. She didn't want to stay with a man who was gutless and would sleep with other women. She would not become another Antoinette, betrayed and pretending not to know.

And then she had an idea: if Kyle couldn't manage his father, she would. She'd show him exactly how to deal with Kyle Senior, and then maybe they could get on with their life – provided he swore never to cheat on her again.

She took time figuring out what to wear; something elegant but sexy at the same time. She phoned Kyle Senior on his private line in the Senate and got him immediately.

'Senior,' she said. He loved them all calling him Senior. 'I need to see you, if you can squeeze me in. It's about me and Kyle and . . . well, a few important things. Maybe you can help?' She left the word help dangling in such a way that no man could resist it.

'Sure thing, baby doll. How about you meet me at my club tonight?'

He gave her the address. She was there at eight o'clock. He was having a pre-dinner drink. 'Care to join me, pretty lady?' he said.

'Why sure,' said Suki, playing along. If this was what it took to handle Senior, she could do it.

He could sure pack away a lot of alcohol, she thought, as the evening progressed. There were two bottles of wine gone and several after-dinner liqueurs by the time they left the restaurant. Suki, who was well able to take a drink, could feel herself getting very wobbly.

Senior had deliberately kept off the subject of his son. Every time she brought it up, he said, 'Nah, we'll talk about that

412

later. Let's have a little bit of fun, you and me. Tell me about yourself.'

It was flattering, and when they got into the vast limo he used to be driven around in, he said to the chauffeur: 'Gotta get this little lady home.'

Suki felt both pleased and happy. He'd do exactly what she wanted, she knew it. Kyle simply had no clue how to handle his father. All you had to do was butter him up, which she'd been doing all night, then ask him for a teeny-weeny house in Taos, which she planned to do now. How could he refuse?

In the car she did her best: 'You see, Senior, Kyle thinks that he can't spend so much as a quarter without going to you.'

'Right. Let's not spoil the mood,' Senior said. 'George,' he commanded the driver, 'screen.' Suddenly the screen came up between the driver and the back of the limo.

Suki felt a faint flicker of alarm. From a compartment, Senior produced a bottle of brandy. 'Very special stuff,' he said, getting out two beautiful Cognac glasses. 'Wouldn't like to tell you what this costs for a snifter, but it's the business, honey.'

She didn't like the taste, but it would have been rude to say no. The next thing she knew, Senior's arm was around her shoulders. He'd finished his brandy, his glass was nowhere to be seen and his hands were sliding up between her thighs.

'Senior, this wasn't . . .'

'Come on, little Suki, I know you've wanted me from the moment you saw me, and if you want to get what you want from me, this is part of the deal. Otherwise, of course, I could always tell Junior that you came on to me – but that's gonna look pretty bad, isn't it?' He leaned in and now he was kissing her.

He was big and strong and Suki wasn't sure what to do. 'Relax, honey, you're gonna enjoy this,' he said. And she thought, as he began pushing up the black crepe dress she'd

413

worn, that this was all her own fault. How could she not have seen this coming? Nobody would believe she hadn't wanted this, and if she protested . . .

When he was done, Senior leaned over and kissed her on the cheek.

'Oh, honey, you're real sweet,' he said. 'Like a nice ripe peach. Go ahead and buy your little house in New Mexico, I kinda like Taos. Hey, I might come and visit you some time, y'know, when Junior's away on business. He needs to be away on business some more, don't you think?'

'Yes,' breathed Suki, fighting back tears.

She felt dirty and stupid and like she'd brought it all on herself. The limo dropped her home and there was no sign of Kyle Junior's car.

'See you soon, little lady,' said her father-in-law, escorting her to her front door and giving her an avuncular kiss on the doorstep. After all, who knew who might be watching. But nobody had been watching in the back of the limo.

'Goodbye,' she said, and ran in and threw herself under the shower fully dressed, as if she could wash away the taint of having been touched by him. She didn't know what to do, who to tell.

If only she could forget about this for ever.

But that wasn't to be.

'My mother for you,' said Kyle the next morning. He stood over Suki as she lay in one of the guest bedrooms, still feeling half drunk from the night before.

'Your mother?'

She put the phone to her ear.

'If you think that sleeping with my husband was a clever thing to do, then you are sorely mistaken, you little bitch!' The venom in Antoinette's voice made Suki recoil. For a moment she was speechless.

'It wasn't like that!' said Suki. 'If he's told you, he's only told you half of it. He forced himself on me . . .'

414

'That's what little bitches like you always say,' her mother-in-law hissed. 'He told me nothing. But I've had people following you. How interesting that's proved to be. At least I know what you really are: a whore. You are divorcing my son and leaving my family right now. I never want to see you again. Kyle Junior knows nothing of this, and you won't tell him. Pack your bags and my lawyers will be in touch. And,' Antoinette's voice was snake-like now, 'if you *ever* speak about this, I will personally destroy you. Do you understand?'

The phone slammed down and Suki was left shaking, holding on to the receiver.

The shaking worsened, she couldn't stop. She pulled the covers over her head and lay there, sobbing and wanting to die.

And then she realized there was only one thing to do: run home to Avalon and Tess. She'd be safe there.

Spring

Chapter Twenty-Six

Spring brought a warm breeze and mildness to Avalon. Tulips and daffodils filled people's gardens with colour. The magnolia trees in Danae's garden had pink sticky buds reaching out towards the sun, and the ancient oak she'd been so scared of losing came back to life again, like a wise old man giving his wisdom to the earth for another year after the sleep of winter.

One beautiful, sunny March morning, Danae walked Lady high above Avalon, in the grounds of the old ruined abbey with the small stone graves that she used to find so tragic. As Lady bounded along, Danae realized that she had merely been projecting her own personal tragedy on to everything around her. She didn't know the stories of the people buried here, whether they were famine victims, whether they had lived long, happy lives. She simply didn't know. Nobody did.

Her own life had convinced her that their circumstances must have been sad, because sadness was all she'd known. Now joyfully, she felt free of that sadness.

She thought of all those years ago, sitting on the fire-escape step of the shelter and being told that it would be all right. Only it hadn't been all right at all, because later that same day Antonio had found her. He had almost succeeded in killing part of her soul that day, but now it was well again. The shrivelled heart was beating again, ready to open, ready to welcome happiness in.

Avalon seemed changed, now that she looked at it with a different eye.

The people in the town were her friends. When she walked down the main street people said, 'Hello, Danae, how are you?'

She was no longer Mrs Rahill, the kind but distant lady behind the plexi-glass in the post office; she was Danae, a woman they liked, a woman they would talk to, a woman they would invite into their home for coffee or dinner or to attend one of their parties.

And it was all thanks to Mara, and her refusal to let Danae shut herself away from the world.

Lady began running off towards Avalon House. It was very much a building site now, Danae thought, as she began to walk around it. Lady was forever dancing in and out of the scaffolding, but after having been called back so many times she now understood that she had to keep away from the house itself.

The landscaping was taking shape. There were two wonderful young men doing it all and Danae had spent many hours, at Cashel's behest, talking to them about the kind of plants that really thrived up here. She knew so much about gardening on the hill at the end of Willow Street, where the sea breeze blew in.

Even the house itself seemed changed. Before, it had been lonely. That wasn't the case any more. There was joy coming from every brick, as though the old house was exuding contentment at being loved again.

But what made Danae happiest of all was the love she could see between Rafe and Mara. They were so close, so happy. There was laughter and joking every time they were together, along with mutual respect and true tenderness. Mara had chosen wisely.

'It's thanks to you, Danae,' Mara said one evening as the two of them sat in front of the fire, Lady at their feet. 'If I hadn't come to Avalon, I'd never have met Rafe. I'd have gone off to New York or London or somewhere, convinced that all men were pigs, nobody was to be trusted and thinking that it was all my fault for not having changed myself enough to be lovable. When actually all I needed was someone who would love me the way I am.'

'And I've you to thank,' said Danae, 'for letting me out of the prison I'd made for myself. Without you, I'd have faced Antonio's death alone and probably would have watched the funeral from a distance, so Adriana couldn't have come to me and said what she did.'

'Danae, you let yourself out,' said Mara firmly.

Danae thought about that as she walked around the back of the house, where a little Victorian knot garden was being constructed by the two landscape gardeners.

'Isn't it coming along nicely, Danae?' one of the gardeners called her. They loved her to look at their work, approve of it and tell them how well they were doing.

'Absolutely fabulous! Boys, I don't know how you do it so quickly,' she said, and they both beamed with delight at her. 'You'll have to come in for a cup of tea later, when you're finished. You must be frozen.'

'That'd be great,' they said.

Danae walked on. Adriana's graveside gift had been huge, lifting the burden of guilt Danae had carried for so long, but Mara had also given her a precious gift – the gift of letting people in, of understanding that friends mattered. People mattered. Community mattered. And she mattered to other people. She'd never seen that before.

It hadn't been easy, taking the plunge. She'd spent so long avoiding anything that might involve socializing with strangers, terrified that they might start asking questions, wanting to know more about her, that the prospect of going out and meeting people seemed completely overwhelming at first.

If it hadn't been for Mara, she never would have signed up for the course at the community centre. Even though she'd been drawn to the idea from the moment she spotted the notice decorated with swirling Celtic symbols in the window of the convenience shop. A six-week course on Celtic and pre-Celtic Ireland, with lectures by noted historians on Irish myths and legends, as well as the saints and gods and goddesses who had played a part in shaping Ireland's culture. She'd always been fascinated with the old Irish myths in school and once thought it might have been interesting to study them in college, but there had been no college for Danae and dreams of studying history had been put away. On the spur of the moment, she'd written down the phone number for the course.

'What do you think?' she'd said to Mara later that day as they shared a coffee in Lorena's Café. 'It might be a complete waste of money, I mean . . . I don't know.'

'You're not going to find out unless you try,' said Mara. 'Give it a go.'

Danae had laughed. That was Mara all over: give it a go. She'd give anything a go.

'But I'm not like you,' she protested. 'I can't drift into something and make friends instantly. I mean, I like the idea of studying this, but . . .'

'But what?' said Mara. 'What's the worst that can happen? You're going to sit in a room with lots of like-minded people and listen to somebody talk. You don't have to ask any questions afterwards. There's no rule about asking questions. You don't have to say anything if you don't want to. Take the odd note, look interested – that's all there is to it. Simply go along. Just be.'

Just be, thought Danae. What sort of *being* did that mean? For years, she'd been afraid of being. For so many years she'd been afraid of Antonio and his rages, afraid to move, afraid to breathe the wrong way in case she'd upset him. And then for eighteen long years in Avalon, unable to shake off the habit of fear, she'd carried on being afraid to move, hardly able to believe that she had a new life.

Now, she was part of a community, with friends and a life and warmth from whatever divinity was up there. She was failing them by not living a life.

'You're right,' she told Mara. 'I'll book it tomorrow.' And she did.

The course had proved to be fascinating, sparking off something in Danae that she hadn't known existed. The first session, she hadn't opened her mouth, nodding shyly at the other course participants: a mixture of men and women, some of them people she recognized from the post office, others she didn't. But by the second week, when they moved on to the story of Brigid, she was full of energy, full of excitement, asking questions, writing things down. Engaged in it. Part of the whole thing. By the time the tea break came, she was sitting with a group of women, chatting wildly, telling them she hadn't done any night-time study ever, that this was her first time.

'Oh, me too,' said another woman. 'I was terribly nervous. I was afraid to say anything.'

And Danae had laughed and said, 'Snap!'

'Weren't we daft!' said the woman, whose name was Sally. 'I mean, what were we afraid of?'

'Appearing stupid,' said another woman, Norah.

'I was thinking I might sign up for the next course as well,' revealed Sally. 'It's all about family genealogy. They teach you how to do the research, go back and discover your roots. You could do it as a job. Lots of people are tracing their ancestors these days.'

'That might be interesting,' Danae said. Ancestors had never been something she'd given much thought to. Her family, the past, had been too painful to want to dwell on it. But there were lots of other family members she knew nothing about:

grandparents, great-grandparents and beyond. Who knew where they'd come from, where they'd lived, what they'd done?

'I think I'd like to do that,' she said to Sally.

Browsing the board, she'd seen one other notice that got her attention. It was an appeal for volunteers to rattle collection boxes for the local women's shelter:

... Domestic abuse can affect anyone. Doesn't matter how much money they have, where they live, what their job is. It cuts across all ages, socio-economic groups and races. We need help raising funds. Our government subsidy has been cut. If you want to help, please call ...

Danae had ripped off one of the tiny bits of paper at the bottom with the phone number. She'd kept it in her pocket for days, feeling it sometimes, wondering if she had the strength to ring. She thought back to the shelter and Mary, the woman who'd helped her. Mary in the red dress, who'd been so kind. Mary had been beaten by her husband too. So badly that she'd almost died, and yet she'd turned around and given back to women like herself. Danae wasn't sure if she had the strength to do it now. But one day she would, one day in the future. She'd learned so much, it was only right to give a little something back.

Kitty's class in school were making Valentine cards. There was much giggling whenever Kitty's classmate, Julia, came around to play, much muttering about big red hearts and crepe paper and what they were going to say.

'They're supposed to be secret, you know. You don't write who it's from,' Tess overheard them saying and then they shut up and giggled frantically when she came back into the kitchen.

'I didn't hear anything,' said Tess, 'not a thing.'

'Mum,' said Kitty, 'do you think Zach will get lots of

Valentine's cards, because all the girls really like him even though he's going out with Pixie?'

'I'd say Pixie will carve their hearts out with a spoon if they do,' said Suki, who was cooking dinner.

Tess glared at her.

'Sorry,' said Suki. 'I forget sometimes . . .'

'How do you carve someone's heart out with a spoon?' asked Kitty, interested.

'I was joking!' said Suki. 'I meant carve the way you carve a name on a tree with something, perhaps a spoon . . . ?'

'Nice save,' said Tess, grinning.

It was definitely interesting, having Suki around.

Suki adored spending time with Zach: the two of them had always shared a special closeness. And she loved to babysit Kitty, encouraging Tess to 'go out and date people!'

'I don't want to date people,' Tess told her.

'Well, go out anyhow,' Suki said. 'I'll be heading back to the States for my book tour soon enough. Take advantage of free home-grown babysitting while you still have it.'

Suki's book was brilliant, Tess thought – and so did everyone in Box House Publishing. The reception had blown Suki away – and Melissa, who was honest enough to admit it. Somehow, through all the tough months, Suki had written some of her best prose, and she'd managed to strike a topical note that captured everyone's interest.

They'd already lined up a twenty-city tour for Suki, and all the major chat shows wanted to book her.

Suki was jogging every day to get in shape.

'Television adds pounds,' she said. 'I need to get my waist back – I can't be seen on TV without a waist!'

'Hey,' said Tess, '*hello*! Haven't you recently written a book about how it should be OK for a woman to age in a womanly manner and not in the manner of a fifteen-year-old model?'

'Yes,' Suki said. 'I have. It's hard to break the habit of a lifetime, though.'

'You look beautiful, Sis,' said Tess, smiling at her sister with love.

Suki smiled. 'And so do you, honey.'

The best news of all had been the spate of deals with foreign publishers, which had meant that she'd been able to lend Tess the money to keep Something Old going.

'You've always been there for me,' Suki said. 'It's nice to be able to do something for you for a change.'

'My sister got five Valentine's cards last year. She's thirteen,' said Julia thoughtfully. 'I hope when I'm thirteen I get six, so I can beat her because she was boasting and I didn't get any ... well, except for that one from my mum and dad, and that doesn't count.'

'My dad always gives Mum one,' said Kitty, 'and he gives me one too. I like that. It must be horrible to get none.'

'Oh, I think we'll all survive if we don't get Valentine's cards,' Tess said, smiling. 'Now girls, have you done your homework?'

'Nearly everything, Tess,' said Julia. 'Except sums. I hate sums.'

'Me too,' said Kitty, anxious not to be left out. If hating sums was where it was at, she was going to hate sums too.

'Girls, you're both fabulous at sums! Honestly, you're so clever,' Tess said, automatically going into the 'tell children how wonderful they are and then they'll like schoolwork' mantra.

Eventually the girls settled down to do their sums while Tess checked the rest of their homework, her mind half on the subject of Valentine's cards. Back when they were at school, Suki used to get scores of them. Some would be stuffed into her school bag when she wasn't looking. Or left in her desk in her form room. She'd been so blithely uninterested in them, whereas Tess, who'd never got any except from her father – one he'd signed – would have loved to get Valentine's cards.

'Suki's seven years older, so she's bound to get more cards than you,' Anna Reilly had explained to her. 'Don't worry, pet. When it's your turn, you'll be getting tons of them. You're going to be beautiful. You *are* beautiful.'

'Thanks, Anna,' said Tess, although she didn't really believe her. Suki, with her full cheekbones, her pillowy lips and that slanted way she had of looking at people, was beautiful. Men flocked to her. Men and boys. Tess didn't have that. She knew. Even at twelve, she knew.

After dinner, Suki tidied up and Tess drove Julia home. The two little girls sat in the back of the car and chatted nineteen to the dozen, as if they had to stretch out these last few minutes of being together. 'Thanks for having her,' Julia's mother said when they dropped her off. 'Was she good?' she added, ruffling Julia's short, dark hair.

'She was fabulous, as usual,' said Tess. 'They've both done their homework – you need to sign her homework notebook – and they ate their dinner too, although not much of the cauliflower.'

'Bleuch,' said Julia.

'Bleuch,' agreed Kitty.

'No, cauliflower doesn't go down too well here, either,' said Julia's mum.

'Can I stay up a bit late and watch telly, Mum?' wheedled Kitty as they drove home through the town.

'No,' said Tess, 'you know you're always tired after you've had someone over to play. And it's only Thursday night. Tomorrow is a school day, after all.'

'Oh, Mum.'

It was at that moment that Kitty and Tess spotted them: Kevin and Claire, walking across the pedestrian crossing holding hands. Claire was visibly pregnant now, her belly swollen to a melon-sized bump. The rest of her looked exactly the same: long slender legs encased in her skinny jeans and flat Ugg boots. Her pretty cardigan-type thing swinging out

427

behind her. Why were young people never cold? Tess wondered for a moment. For the drive to Julia's house, she'd put on her anorak. She hated the cold. But then Claire had the extra central heating of a baby inside her.

'Look, Mum, look, Mum! Can we stop, can we stop?' said Kitty delightedly. 'Aw, beep the horn or something.' They were three cars back from the crossing and it had started to flash orange, meaning that the cars could pass. Kevin and Claire were on the other side of the road.

'No, darling,' said Tess hurriedly, 'we can't stop really and we don't have time and plus . . .' She searched her mind desperately, 'you are going to be seeing Dad and Claire on Saturday so we'll give them a beep of the horn and a wave and we'll keep going.'

'No. I want to stop,' said Kitty mutinously.

'Darling, we don't have time. I'll beep and you wave.'

She gave the lightest beep of the horn, hoping that neither Kevin nor Claire would look round. And yet they did, caught sight of the car and waved energetically, Claire beaming the happy smile of someone who was utterly content. Tess smiled and waved back, feeling like the biggest hypocrite in the world. She took a right turn up a road she wouldn't normally go. It was probably a longer route to their house, but she didn't care. She just needed to get out of the town square quickly. Halfway up the road was the McMillan card shop, an orgy of red in advance of Valentine's Day.

'Oh, look at the shop, Mum,' said Kitty delightedly. 'Can I get a card for Claire? She'd love it.'

'It's closed. It's quarter past six,' Tess said.

'Can we go tomorrow? Please, please? I'll use my pocket money.'

'Of course, darling,' she said. 'If you want to, we'll go in tomorrow.'

Tess could remember when Kitty wanted to give her Valentine's cards. When making Tess a big 'I Love You Mummy' Valentine's card had been the biggest thrill. Now she wanted to buy one, with her own pocket money, for Claire. Tess swallowed back the pain, the loneliness, the sadness. Cashel came unbidden into her mind. Why did she keep thinking of him? Suki was driving her mad, saying that he was around the town, staying in the hotel a lot and very involved in the house.

'Stop meddling, Suki,' begged Tess. 'I don't want any pain in my life any more.'

'It's not like you to give up,' Suki had said naughtily.

Tess had sent the necklace Cashel had brought off to be valued and her diamond expert had been cautiously optimistic.

'These days you can never tell till the auction, but I think you could be on to a winner here, Tess. This could be real money.'

And the money would be hers and Suki's. After her insistence that she didn't want his charity, Cashel had sent over the documents to prove that only listed items were sold with the house the first time round, and the necklace most definitely wasn't on the list.

An injection of cash would be nice. More than nice.

Right now, all she wanted from life was to have her kids happy, to know Suki was doing well, and to be able to run her business. She didn't need anything or anyone else, thank you very much.

Chapter Twenty-Seven

Cashel sat in his office, the temporary one on the square in Avalon. His chair – not the wildly expensive one Mara had teased him about wanting – was pushed back and his feet were up on the desk, long legs crossed at the ankle. From this position he could see out over the square, watch the goings on in Avalon. It was nearly lunchtime and he could see Rafe riding down Castle Street, coming on to the square on a beautiful bike. He came nearly every day to take Mara to lunch.

Cashel liked him. Rafe had an easy way about him, a laid-back charm that said he took life very seriously indeed but had his priorities worked out. He was good to Mara too. Cashel had asked. He felt a strong fatherly feeling for her, which was utterly bewildering since he was nobody's father.

Rafe hadn't tried to get him to order one of Berlin Bikes' custom-made machines, another good point in his favour. Cashel disliked people who, upon learning of his wealth, tried to get him to spend a little of it in their shop. No, Rafe was one of the good guys, and he and Mara were clearly besotted with each other.

From her office next door, he could hear Nina Simone. She was on a Nina Simone bender this week. Last week, it had been Lady Gaga, but not too loud.

430

Lord knows what the music was like when he wasn't here, which was most of the time. He'd been coming to Avalon less and less recently, business taking him all over the world. And yet there was always the pull back here. He felt sad that he hadn't come back as much when his mother was alive. And now she was gone, what was it that was keeping him here?

Riach, Charlotte and the children could come to him anywhere in the world.

There was merely Avalon House, a beautiful house that was never going to be his home because he'd no one to share it with. Which was what it all came down to at the end of the day: having someone to share your life.

He could see Belle emerging from the beautiful oak doors of the hotel, clad in her usual finery. Today it was a purple velvet ensemble with a vast, twinkling brooch on one lapel. She felt like an old friend now, he'd been staying there so long. He kept his suite permanently booked now. 'Suits me,' Belle had said, smiling at him, 'we all know you're loaded, darling, you won't miss it.'

Cashel had laughed. 'And you, a hotel owner, daring to say that to a customer?' he'd teased.

Belle had eyed him up shrewdly. 'I'd say, Cashel Reilly, that you're the sort of man who hates people standing on ceremony with you and kowtowing because you have a lot of money in the bank or wherever it is that smart people keep their money these days. I don't like those sort of kowtowing people myself. As you've long since figured out, I call a spade a spade. I'm delighted you're staying in the hotel and that you're paying for the suite whether you're there or not. It's good for the bank balance, and these days we all need a helping hand. And of course it doesn't hurt things that you're so gorgeous and rich either.'

She twinkled her eyes at him.

'Some of the business people we have staying come in,

431

notice you and I can *see* their minds whirring, thinking that if the likes of Cashel Reilly are staying here, this must be the right spot to stay in. Which is also very good for the bank balance.' She beamed at him.

Cashel had beamed back. 'If I was the marrying sort, I'd put a ring on your finger, Belle,' he said.

'Don't be ridiculous, Cashel,' she said. 'Sure, you're far too old for me. I'm a cougar, don't you know?' And this time, she roared with laughter, seeing the surprised look on his face.

Kitty-corner to the hotel was Lorena's Café, and it was getting busy, Cashel could see. He imagined Brian behind the counter, doing his best to chat to the customers. Brian was quite relaxed in Cashel's presence now. Not one hundred per cent relaxed, and he probably never would be, but they could have a bit of mild chat about the weather. The usual stuff.

'Not a bad day out there,' Brian might say.

'No, very nice,' said Cashel, who hated talking about the weather or small talk of any kind. Yet in Avalon, he was inclined to go along with it. Particularly because he knew that if he said one cross word to Brian *ever*, it would frighten the hell out of the poor boy and Cashel felt that wouldn't be fair. Brian was a nice lad.

Thinking of the café made Cashel hungry. A sandwich, he thought; a nice sandwich on rye bread with one of Brian's Americanos. Yes, that'd be the business. He made his way out into the foyer to find Mara there, along with Rafe, who was taking off his motorbike helmet.

'Cashel, how's it going?' said Rafe. 'I thought you'd be up at the house because of the accident. A wall fell in,' he said, 'and Tess—'

'Tess,' said Cashel. *Tess had been at the house and she was hurt.* Fear gripped his heart. Fear so cold and black that he didn't think he could breathe. 'Oh my God, I've got to get up there now. Now.'

'No, Cashel, wait,' Rafe was yelling after him. 'I was only saying—'

But Cashel was gone, down the stairs, vaulting them at high speed, out on to the street. He had his keys in his pocket but there was no point taking the car, he'd run it faster. He began to sprint. It was cool for an April day, he was in his shirt and trousers, but he didn't feel the cold. He ran like a man possessed, across the square and up the street. In two minutes, Church Street where Tess had her shop would join up with Willow Street and then he could sprint up the hill.

Tess – he couldn't bear anything to have happened to her. And what was she doing at the house? Maybe she'd gone in looking at it when she knew he wasn't there.

He ran faster. He was on Willow Street now. Everything was a blur. People were looking at him as if he was crazy, but he didn't care. It was a steep hill, but he didn't care. He ran, unthinking, unaware almost of his breath, his heart pumping. He was nearly there. And suddenly, out of nowhere he could see a figure appearing, walking a dog. It was Tess. He'd know that long-legged, elegant walk anywhere. Tess with that stupid dog of hers. Cashel ran up and the dog threw herself on him in complete joy, muddy paws all over his shirt, and he didn't care.

'Tess – you're OK!' he said, grabbing her.

Tess pulled away from him, startled. 'Of course, I'm OK,' she said. 'Why wouldn't I be?'

'I was in the office, Rafe came in and said the wall had fallen, then he said your name and at that, I rushed off, half-cocked,' Cashel said, panting from his run. 'All I could think was that you were buried underneath.'

'You thought I was hurt?' she said quietly.

He nodded as if speech was now beyond him.

'I think a wall came down,' she said. 'I'd taken Silkie for a walk up there – I sometimes do that,' she said, as if admitting something shameful. 'Just to see. Because I love the house. You know that.'

'I know,' he said, 'I know.'

'Nobody was hurt, but it's a bit of a mess. Freddie is going completely mad. He's trying to work out who to kill first and they're all running scared of him.'

Cashel laughed weakly, all he could manage, a laugh more of relief than humour.

'Rafe had come to pick up some papers from the architect for Mara, and I was talking to him, that's all. I said that if he was talking to Mara, he was to explain that nobody was hurt.'

Cashel took her hands now, one hand clutching Silkie's lead. The dog was sitting between them, looking up curiously from one to the other.

'You haven't had a dog for years, I bet,' she said.

'Yeah,' said Cashel. 'There are lots of things I haven't had for years ... fun, love, happiness.' He didn't know what it was: the after-effects of the shock, relief at finding her unhurt, or finally being alone with her.

This was his chance to tell her everything, to be honest.

'I bought the house out of vengefulness, spite, some childish emotion. I'm sorry. I felt so hurt when my mother died, and then I saw you at the funeral. It all turned into this huge rage, rage at my mother dying and you hurting me in the past.'

'But you never let me explain, not at the time, not after,' Tess protested. 'Suki got you all riled up because she was angry at me. I'd never have hurt you, Cashel. We simply had different priorities at the time. You were so headstrong, so determined to get out of Avalon and make something of yourself. I knew you thought you had to *be somebody* to marry me – because of Avalon House and my background – and you didn't.'

He stared down at her.

'That was what hurt most,' she said. 'That you could accuse

434

me of that when you should have known better. I loved you with all my heart, but I had to do my duty and take care of my father, especially when he was so ill and needed me. When you couldn't understand, when it was clear you really didn't know me . . .' She looked at him sadly. 'Well, I decided you weren't the man I'd thought you were. I told myself that if you truly loved me, Cashel, you'd wait for me. Instead you abandoned me.' Her voice trembled a little, even now. 'I waited, you know. I kept waiting for you, but you never came.'

There, she'd said it: all the pain she'd kept inside for so long.

'I was stupid,' Cashel said, 'stupid and headstrong. My mother always told me so. She knew you were the right woman for me.'

'I'm sorry she's gone, Cashel,' Tess said, squeezing his hands.

'But you *didn't* wait for me,' he came back, his face a picture of misery. 'I know I was a fool, but I thought when I returned, you'd be waiting here for me, that you'd be in love with me despite everything . . .' he tailed off, aware how he sounded.

'I waited over a year for you, Cashel Reilly. A year. A year when my world collapsed. You left, Suki went away again, I only had a few months with Dad before he died, and then I was all alone. I had to sell the house. I had to do it all myself. Kevin was kind to me.'

She stopped. She didn't want to justify herself.

Suddenly she was aware of what a curious tableau they must be presenting: her and Cashel standing, holding hands at the top of Willow Street. Him sweating in a dirty shirt from Silkie's paws and the dog sitting in between them, totally happy.

'I should go,' Tess said. 'I brought Silkie out for a quick lunchtime walk and the shop is closed, I need to get back,' she said.

'No,' said Cashel, 'hear me out for one minute.'

435

She stopped because she didn't really want to go, but this was all too much. She looked up into that face she'd thought of so many times, the face she'd dreamed of. The only man who'd truly broken her heart.

'I am so sorry,' he said slowly. 'I was so childish, convinced that it had to be leave with me or nothing. I can't believe you had to do all that on your own.'

He remembered his mother trying to tell him about Tess, but he'd refused to listen. He didn't want to know.

'I'm a different man now. A man who understands what he lost and who mourns for it. Do you think we could try again, Tess, please?'

Tess looked at him. She could see the truth in his eyes. He meant this. 'I can't be hurt again, Cashel. You hurt me so much all those years ago and after what I've gone through with Kevin . . .' her voice tailed off. 'That's been horrendous. So I can't be hurt again. Plus I have Zach and Kitty to think about. It's different now,' she said fiercely. 'My children have to come first, do you understand that?'

'I understand that,' he said. 'But, please, can we try again knowing all those things, knowing that the children come first, knowing that I'm never going to hurt you again?'

And she nodded, slowly. Cashel watched the smile take over her face and then he kissed her.

Down in Avalon, Mara and Rafe walked hand-in-hand down the street, Mara chattering and Rafe silently listening, a smile on his face. He loved this town, loved the craziness of it, the way Belle waved to them from the other side of the street, shrewd eyes taking everything in. He loved mad Joe McCreddin with his baler-twine belt, stomping down to his car, a battered pick-up truck, talking to himself as he went. He loved the smell coming out of Lorena's, where coffee mingled with the scent of the red velvet cake Mara loved.

He and Mara had been talking about the man who'd made

the beautiful carved wooden animal sculptures. Mara had had that glint in her eye, that dangerous glint.

'I think Danae ought to meet him,' she said, thoughtfully. 'He's a very calming person, zen-like. Loves animals, nature. He'd be good for Danae.'

'Cici's right – you are an awful meddler,' Rafe said, smiling down at her with love.

'I'm only saying . . . they could be friends. He looks like the sort of man who doesn't get out much. They could go for walks on the beach. I think we'll have to bring her to see him some day, on the pretext of buying something else. She loves her she-wolf.'

'I love my she-wolf,' Rafe said, holding her tightly as they walked. 'Now, important matters. It's lunch. Soup and sandwiches? Or just sandwiches, so we can leave room for a bit of cake?'

Mara's wonderful eyes twinkled up at him.

'Let's leave room for cake, definitely,' she said. 'A bit of cake makes everything better.'

Acknowledgements

I haven't written acknowledgements for years – it's so hard. I live in mortal fear of hurting someone by leaving them out and my memory is so bad, this is inevitable. I am the woman who went to New Zealand, met a *dear* friend of my brother's who came to a reading, meant to email him about it, promised her I would, then totally forgot until nine months later he said he'd got a Christmas card from her talking about how lovely it had been . . . oh, the *guilt*.

The people who know me and love me understand. But other people might be offended and I hate that. So acknowledgements equal nightmare and that's why these are so long.

To my family, my husband John and our beautiful, wise and kind sons Dylan and Murray. We are blessed. To Dinky, Licky and Scamp who give me such pleasure as they sit around me – or on me – being adoring, lovable and a never-ending source of joy. To Mum, who works so tirelessly for charity with good humour and her customary love; to my big brother, Francis, who is kind, funny and loving, not to mention a genius; to my darling sister Lucy, who does so much for other people and who is an earth angel with a light that shines from her. To Dave, such a gentle, kind brother-in-law; to Anne, who works so hard and has raised such wonderful girls; to my nieces Laura, Naomi and Emer – I am SO proud to be your aunt. To Robert, a gentleman. To the animals: Dexter and Jasper. To Margaret, definitely a sister in another life. To Maggie. To Sarah Conroy – what did I ever do till I met you? Thanks to Ted and to Joana.

To Emma, soul sister who always has my back and I have yours, darling. To Fiona, another soul sister. To Marian, another sister – I love you. To darling Judy, for everything. To the angels on earth who are Patricia Scanlan; Aisling Carroll; Martina Garner; Aidan Storey; Kelly Callaghan (there's a Rudi & Madison shop in this book); Maureen Hassett; Beccy Cameron; Suzy McMullen; Kate Thompson; Terry Prone; Alyson Stanley; Lola Simpson; Sheila O'Flanagan; Alex Barclay and Mary Canavan for the journey.

Enormous thanks – there isn't enough room on the page to list how good he is – to Jonathan Lloyd: a kinder, more debonair man never existed. He has a heart of gold. To everyone at Curtis Brown – to Lucia, Willow, Melissa, Felicity, Sheila, Jonny, *everyone* in CB. Thanks to my HarperCollins family, starting with the Irish branch, so first thanks to the wonderful Moira Reilly and Tony Purdue. In London, a mammoth thanks to Lynne Drew, Kate Elton, Rachel Hore, Anne O'Brien, Belinda Budge, Vicky Barnsley, Liz Dawson, Thalia Suzuma, Damon Greeney, Oli Malcolm, Lucy Upton, Louise Swannell, to Alice Moore for the fabulous new covers.

In HarperCollins Australia, a huge thanks to Christine Farmer who is a legend; to Karen-Maree Griffiths, an angel; Michael Moynahan; to Shona Martin, and everyone else on the team who work so hard on my behalf. In HC New Zealand thanks to Tony Fisk, Sandra Noakes, Lise Taylor and everyone who works so hard on my behalf there; thanks to the lovely people at HC Canada, especially David Kent, Leo McDonald, and gorgeous Charidy Johnston and Cory Beatty for the loveliest tour and for introducing me to Twitter! Thanks to lovely Deborah Schneider in New York and to Carolyn Reidy and all at Simon and Schuster US. Thanks to Louise Paige and Ailsa MacAllister. Thanks to my UNICEF Ireland family, especially Julianne Savage, and thanks to former UNICEF ladies, Thora Mackey and Grace Kelly for continuing friendship.

Thanks to the wonderful publishers around the world who bring my books everywhere. I appreciate it so much! A toast to you all. Slainte.

To all my Saturday morning yoga girls who face the word with laughter, strength and love. To Eva Berg, AnneMarie Casey O'Connor, Eleanor Stoney, Ella Griffin, Sinead Moriarty, AnneMarie Scanlon, LisaMarie Redmond, to artists extraordinaire Carole Shubotham, Fiona Rahill and Kimberley Rogers. To the twin mommy federation of Barbara Stack and Susan Zaidan; to Thelma O Reilly for minding my princesses; to the friends who are always there: Barbara Durkan,

Bernie Murphy, Mary Begley, Claire O'Donovan, Dara Byrne, Felicity Carney, Pauline Moroney, Patte O Reilly, Trish Morrissey, Louise Stanley, and anyone I've forgotten. To Jim Hatton, Claire Darmody, Stevie Holly and Janet Barnes: to the Santina's crew Santina, Andrew, Martha, Paula, Margaret, Annette, and anyone I've left out. To John O'Brien, owner of Enniskerry's glorious antique shop, Aladdin's Cave, who gave me advice and marvellous stories.

To all of you, the wonderful people who read my books and do me the honour of telling me what they mean to you. I love to talk to you, to meet you, to know again that we share so much and that together, human beings can do so much. So please write to me, be it via www. cathykelly.com, my Facebook page or Twitter @cathykellybooks.

Finally, to all the women in the world who have lived with abuse or are living with abuse – help exists. There are people who will welcome you with kindness. You are not worthless. You are special, wonderful, deserving of respect. To everyone else, we can help by donating money to our local women's shelters and we can help women and children in danger in the developing world by donating to UNICEF.

Love and thanks,
Cathy